MW01136091

Paulie Maki

Misadventures of an Alcoholic Engineer

Gail Wickstrom

PAULIE MAKI
MISADVENTURES OF AN ALCOHOLIC ENGINEER

iUniverse books may be ordered through booksellers or by contacting:

iUniverse
1663 Liberty Drive
Bloomington, IN 47403
www.iuniverse.com
844-349-9409

ISBN: 978-1-6632-2893-2 (sc)
ISBN: 978-1-6632-2892-5 (e)

Library of Congress Control Number: 2021921495

Print information available on the last page.

iUniverse rev. date: 11/02/2021

DEDICATION

Paulie Maki is dedicated to the memory of my beloved wife Linda, my Abby, who passed away after our forty-six years of a most happy marriage. Without her patience, objectivity and insightful recommendations *Paulie Maki* would not exist.

My sister, Mary Penzien, is acknowledged for her patience in undertaking a thorough review of *Paulie Maki.*

To Gus and Connie Shakalis appreciation is extended for their thoughtful appraisal of my novel and for providing helpful critiques.

CONTENTS

INTRODUCTION

How many people know an engineer who's a big drunkard? Does anyone know of a college boy engineer who becomes a hopeless alcoholic? Most engineers, at least the ones who work in offices, lead stable lives. They prosper in their work, have interesting hobbies and raise families.

Not Paulie Maki. He is raised by loving parents, is reasonably smart and has lasting friendships. He is expected to go far in life. He has a healthy normal childhood growing up in a small town with fun-loving friends—friends as good as they get. Meet Rotten Mugga, Football, Hicks and Magooch. It's almost inconceivable how an advantaged young man such as Maki could go astray.

Maki's progression into alcoholism is gradual. What begins as a pastime of having a few brews with his chums degenerates into wholesale binges. What kind of clay is Maki made of? To better understand this man, one is not only exposed to Maki's drunken excesses but also to his oft-productive periods of sobriety.

One would think that after an extended period of abstinence he would have his problem licked. Instead, he repeatedly forfeits success for failure and the cycle is seemingly endless. An engagement to be married is broken. Paulie Maki is fired from promising positions as an aerospace engineer. He is no stranger to jails.

There is a murder. Saddled with guilt, he believes for long that without his presence at a drunken spree the murder might not have happened. His life spirals downward and he winds up on skid row. Is there any hope for Maki who's become totally addicted to alcohol?

Much of the narrative is based on the author's real-life experiences. All the characters are fictional.

A bright future is possible for anyone battling an addiction to alcohol. At the very least alcoholics and non-alcoholics alike may find *Paulie Maki* an entertaining read.

CHAPTER 1

The Heights Bunch

"Saatana perkele," a man's guttural voice boomed from somewhere off the roadside. This famous Finnish cussword translates as "Satan the devil."

"Perkele," the voice boomed out again. The short version of the curse is pronounced "**pĕd**-gĕ-lĕh."

"Saatana auttaa minua," or "Satan help me," the voice bellowed angrily.

Three young boys from Heights had just rounded a bend on Red Jacket Road in time to witness a startling sight. The loud cussing prevailed above sounds they heard of splashing water.

The unholy imprecations came from Willard Janke, the town drunkard. He'd taken a tumble into Karhu's Ditch from a narrow path running alongside Red Jacket Road. Willard had spent his day hitting some bars in Calumet, and staggering back to Heights, he stumbled and fell. Karhu's Ditch, a small stream routed through a culvert crossing the road, drains a big stagnant swamp near Red Jacket Shaft, a small community between Heights and Calumet.

Thoroughly soused, Willard belly-flopped like a frog into a waist-deep, weed-infested pool of murky water at the outlet end of the culvert. After floundering about for a long minute he managed to emerge to safety. He ignored the trio of boys. "Perkele," he bellowed once more as he staggered homeward, his drenched clothing draped with long strings of green, slimy algae.

On a hot summer afternoon, the boys were on their way from Heights to the nearest party store in Calumet to buy some ice cream when they witnessed the sight. It had happened before, more than once. "Willard's going to drown himself one of these days," one of the lads said as the trio continued to the store.

"I'll never be a drunkard like old Willard," a second boy vowed. His chums, Aldo and Hicks, did not reply.

Willard Janke, a bachelor, lived in a shack near the big bulrush swamp in Heights. He was found frozen to death in a snowdrift not far from his shack the following winter.

“Here comes Football and Rotten Mugga,” Hicks cried out.

The gang scattered in all directions but it was too late for Hicks. Rotten Mugga zeroed in on him and grabbed him before he even got fifty feet away. Football quickly came to her aid, not that she needed any, and after swiftly pinning him to the ground she set her hefty weight squarely atop his spindly chest. Hicks began to whine.

“Please stop, Mugga,” he wailed as she began to hike up her skirt. “I won’t call you Rotten Mugga anymore.”

While families were still struggling to pay bills and young men were being sent off to battlefields in the post-depression days of the early 1940s, certain of the nation’s youth were plagued with afflictions of a different sort. In Centennial Heights, my small hometown in the Keweenawland, a pair of tomboys terrorized our neighborhood gang. One of the girls we called “Football” and the other “Rotten Mugga.” A year or two older than the dozen seven and eight-year-old boys in our “Heights Bunch,” not only did these girls regard themselves as full-fledged gang members but they acted as its ringleaders. Football and Rotten Mugga were the only girl members of our gang.

Everyone calls our town “Heights” for short. Each peer group in town formed gangs and each called itself the Heights Bunch. Out-of-towners collectively applied the name to every group. Despite the hardship we endured from Football and Rotten Mugga, we of course considered our Heights Bunch the best of all.

The Keweenawland or simply the Keweenaw sits atop Michigan’s Upper Peninsula. We’re popularly called Yoopers by those from the Lower Peninsula, especially after completion of the Mackinaw Bridge connecting the Upper and Lower Peninsula (U.P. and L.P.) of Michigan. “Yooper” obviously derives from “U.P.” We got the best of it, however. The down-staters below the bridge got to be called trolls. Remember big Billy Goat Gruff?

This curved finger of land poking into Lake Superior is peopled with hardy copper miners, farmers, fishermen, stone masons and lumberjacks of widely disparate backgrounds. The Keweenaw is a melting pot. Many of these people at the time of the Great Depression were first or second-generation settlers from Finland, Ireland, Cornwall England and various Croatian countries. Number-wise, the Finnish settlers eventually became the predominant ethnic group in the Keweenaw. In this potpourri of ethnic groups, inclusive of men, women and children, one knew exactly where he stood and he often had to fight to assert his position. Both Football and Rotten Mugga were admirably endowed with traits needed to hold sway above their inferior gang members.

Football, a hefty rotund lass for her age, earned her moniker not only because of her imposing physical attributes but also because of her skills at the game. She did most of the blocking whenever she orchestrated a sandlot scrimmage with her closest friend, Rotten Mugga. Some claimed she even looked like a football. Others insisted she earned the name because of the way she bounced around when delivering one solid block after another. Easy to spot coming to play, a rich cluster of blond, naturally curly hair gracing her head shone like a globe in the sunlight. Her showing up never boded well for the gang members.

A leathery young woman, lean, strapping and as tough as a well-done porterhouse, Rotten Mugga ran for most of the touchdowns. As far as the gang members were concerned the nickname "Rotten Mugga" suited her well. "She's got a mug like those Nazis in the comic books," a gang member said. Comic books depicting German soldiers as mean looking villains were very popular with the youth during the war. Crew-cut flaxen hair and greenish uniforms, these big ugly louts were scary. Her grim, unflinching visage studded with warts made matters even worse for us. The nickname stuck to Abby, her real name. Abby Tulppo in her baptismal record. Adults viewed her in a different light. "Abby's a tomboy now but she'll get over it," one of the neighborhood ladies said. "It might take Shirley a bit longer."

Shirley Binoniemi, aka Football, acquired her Christian name through popular means as did many other baby girls in the 1930s. "Doesn't she look like Shirley Temple," her mother beseeched friends of her two-year-old daughter. Her resemblance to the young star ended with the curly hair. Even though plump she wasn't too bad looking. "Puppy fat," my dad said.

When these young ladies took offense, swift retribution could be expected. Pouncing on their victim, one assisted in flattening him while the other sat flush on his face. To enhance their face-sitting sport they took turns. We somehow managed to breathe.

Football's magnificent pet collie and constant companion, Tipsy, participated in the humiliations. Tipsy would race around, and barking full blast, would grab at the culprit's trousers and try to yank them off. The townspeople knew what was happening whenever they heard Tipsy carrying on.

Hicks hadn't offended the young ladies any more than the rest of us had with his name calling; he merely had the bad luck to get caught.

"Your bloomers left a rotten taste in my mouth," he whined after the ordeal. "Just wait 'til I tell my dad."

"Go ahead and tell him. You'll probably get a spanking for being such a crybaby," Football said.

People bathed much less frequently in the 1940s than they do today although many are loath to admit this. This would have dire consequences for the young lads of our Heights Bunch. Back then it meant a Saturday evening bath for most—a once-a-week ritual. Some of the more fastidious took a bi-weekly sauna—a midweek sauna on Wednesday and a more customary steam on Saturday evening. Men and women, boys and girls; it made no difference. Ripe by the end of the week, residue accumulated in the underwear due to the inferior quality of the toilet tissue used. For many it meant orange wrappers or pages from an old Montgomery Ward catalogue applied in an outhouse, the prevalent toilet facility—few Heights residents at the time enjoyed the luxury of indoor plumbing. Grandpa Maki called the residues "nicotine stains." Hicks had good reason to whine.

To their credit Football and Rotten Mugga dressed well. Most of the time they wore home-sewn dresses fabricated from one-hundred-pound flour sacks. In the depression days and early 1940s many families bought flour in bulk quantities; not only were families fed but the emptied sacks meant yards of cloth. Nothing went to waste. "Pillsbury's Best" read one of Football's skirts, appropriately advertising her broad rear end. Rotten Mugga could occasionally be seen sporting a dress similarly reading "Gold Medal," which loosely spanned her narrow bony butt. Folds in the fabric hung down apologetically like Grandma Maki's drapes sagging over a big bay window in her parlor. But unlike the apologetic fabric, Rotten Mugga never apologized; she had no sympathy to spare. A hiked skirt ensured full benefit to her victim as she descended to settle her buttocks.

The only time we got any peace from Football and Rotten Mugga occurred during Sunday school at the Emmaus Hall. That's where many families in Centennial Heights attended evening church services and sent their kids to Sunday school. The girls acted prim and proper while in church, and judging by their good behavior, no one could have ever surmised their mischief on the sandlot. Me and my chums were quite safe in Sunday school.

My name is Paul Maki. I'm the only child of my parents, Oscar and Elsa Maki. Most of my friends call me Paulie but I've got a nickname or two like everyone else in the gang. I'll get to that later. "Maki" is a Finnish name translating as "Hill." About half of our gang are Finns, as we call them. "What's your nationality?" we first asked of a new kid in town. Nobody said, "I'm an American." Mostly they identified with countries of their European extraction. If he said "I'm an Italian," he probably got a punch on the nose to start with. In the early 1940s when the United States and its allies were fighting Mussolini and Hitler, the raging conflict inflamed many of us to view with suspicion, however unwarranted, one's origin and sympathies.

Most of our grandparents or parents came to the states from various European countries. We called the kids from families of Cornish miners "Cousin Jacks." They were always bragging they were the first ones to come here about a hundred years ago. So? Many of our grandparents came here from Finland around 1900 they tell me. Maybe a little earlier. That's enough of a "long time ago" for me.

Shortly after they were married in the late 1800s, Grandpa and Grandma Maki emigrated from Finland to America. They'd come from a place in central Finland called Pudasjarvi. Grandma and Grandpa both claimed the Keweenaw reminded them very much of Pudasjarvi in terms of climate and landscape and that's why they chose to settle there.

So far all my buddies in the gang had their faces sat on by these trouble-loving girls except me. I bragged about being a fast runner and always escaped these harpies, un-sat upon and a clean face to show for it. Sometimes I got to see a slower kid get caught and it made me glad to see the rascal "getting the dingleberry pie," even if he didn't have one coming. Like poor Hicks. Just so long as it wasn't me.

But my luck ran out.

Standing in a fenced alley I nonchalantly observed Football coming toward me taking a shortcut to her home. Fenced on each side for its entire length with few breaks, I hadn't paid attention to this detail, an oversight that would cost me ruinously. I wanted to tease her. Halfway down the alley I hollered, "Hey you fat Football, aren't you going to try and catch me? Or are you getting too slow, Shirley Temple?"

"The 'hey' is in the barn with the cows and the horses," she replied over her shoulder. "Haven't you learned anything at all in school?"

I continued to follow her when near the end of the alley she suddenly turned about to face me, not more than twenty feet away.

"OK, Abby, let's see how fast he can run now."

What should I do? There stood the formidable Football guarding the exit to freedom. A quick glance to my rear revealed Rotten Mugga barreling down upon me. My prospects of an escape diminished. Either way I chose to run my chances to elude capture did not look promising, and no doubt I'd be seized if I attempted to jump over a rather high fence. Matters had become grim, my capture imminent.

I ran full speed ahead toward the exit. A swift dodge of Football and I would be free. At the last moment I veered sharply to her left attempting to gallop through a space between her and the fence.

All of Football's blocking skills came into play, her timing perfect. Just as I thought I'd made it she delivered a tremendous block knocking me off balance into the arms of that fearsome basilisk, Rotten Mugga, who'd arrived on the spot well-timed.

I vainly struggled to free myself. We were taught never to strike a girl; we could only resist. They took turns. After Football hiked her Pillsbury's Best skirt and served her ample pie I got the Gold Medal treatment for dessert.

"Well, Pieru Kouret," Football sneered, "Little boys have got to learn to be nice to good girls. Isn't that true, Abby." They still had a firm hold on me. I did not say anything which would encourage more pies. I wisely kept my mouth shut altogether.

For a moment Rotten Mugga remained silent. She looked at me curiously, not too unkindly.

"Shirley, I don't think we'll have any more problems with Pieru Kouret," she finally said.

There were only one or two more sittings after that. But how wrong she was about the distant future.

I responded to Pieru Kouret, a name almost everyone deemed appropriate for me then. "Pieru Kouret" literally translates from the Finnish as "Fart Peeling." It's pronounced "Beedoo Goodet," with the accent on the first syllable of each word, which is always the case with spoken Finnish. This loosely translates as "Fartblossom." When cornflakes first made their appearance on the shelves in the early 1900s immigrant Finns who settled in the Keweenawland regarded the cereal as a joke. Accustomed to "puuroa," which is a thick lumpy porridge, they laughingly derided the insubstantial flakes as "peelings of a fart," not to be identified with the stink coming from a mature blast, mind you, but only its mere essence. It's a wonder my buddies didn't call me Fartblossom; I guess Pieru Kouret suited everyone well enough. Maybe I dodged a bullet there except for Hicks Huhta who felt impelled to call me "Fartblossom" as occasion demanded, but just directly to me with no one else around. For some reason he kept the moniker concealed from our fellow gang members. Most likely he feared I'd somehow arrange another face sitting for him; I was not above doing this if necessary, which Hicks maybe suspected. By the time I'd become twelve years old almost everyone quit calling me Pieru Kouret as it may have been too difficult to say, except for those fluent in the old country language, where it rolled from tongues.

Hicks Huhta and an Italian kid by the name of Aldo Vella were my closest friends. Aldo had earned the reputation as being the oldest and wisest member of our Heights Bunch except for the girls, and maybe Hicks, a Finn like me. Nobody called him Phillip, his real name. Each new day held promise of adventure for the three of us who'd become inseparable chums. We'd found no shortage of outdoor activity. There were woods nearby in which to build tree houses and shacks. Big Rock in Tamarack Junior was an excellent off-the-path site for hatching conspiracies. And if anyone wanted to hide out and create mischiefs a dense thicket we called Cedar Bush provided cover. A couple of creeks a mile from home afforded great fishing for speckies. A forty-foot-high circular water tower located at the highest point in town posed a challenge for a climb. Actually quite safe, a ringed frame enclosure protected the ladder up to a gently sloped roof, although one had to be very careful once he got to the top. This activity came to a permanent stop when one of the kids, clutching a steel ring, froze in panic near the top of the tower and had to be rescued, after which the tower remained off limits.

The bulrush swamp near the bottom of Crooked Hill or Jefferson

Street and a pond everyone called "Roundy Pond" invited searches for bullfrogs or muskrats. A small lake known as "Big Dam" situated beyond Roundy Pond discouraged adventure there owing to intervening thickets thriving in a rank, marshy swamp. Some of the older guys told us there were four-foot-long grass snakes and snapping turtles near the pond although we never saw any snakes even close to that length or any snapping turtles at all. We called garter snakes grass snakes and the biggest ones we ever caught were only about thirty inches long.

Our summer vacation neared its end and the time had come to even the score with Football and Rotten Mugga. We had to act fast before school began if these girls were to get a comeuppance. All the gang members had had face sittings. Aldo, the streetwise Italian kid, got his too.

"They ruined my looks," he told us in describing his sitting. "If it hadn't been for what they did to me I'd be a lot more handsome than I am right now."

They were not derelict in their performance. Football roosted comfortably for a full minute, her fat bum flush on his face, before being relieved by Rotten Mugga, who without hesitation aptly took her turn.

"You've got to respect these girls," he said, biding time until something could be done. To avoid further humiliation he thereafter addressed them both by their proper names.

All the girls I know hate snakes. Football and Rotten Mugga were no exceptions.

Aldo, Hicks and I captured seven respectable snakes at Roundy Pond, the best place to look for them, one afternoon where we found them sunning lethargically near the edge of the pond. Football and Rotten Mugga were to be the recipients of the snakes, which we contained inside a cardboard box.

"We better make sure they don't hear them slithering around," Aldo said. Just to make sure this didn't happen we put them in small sack and stuffed the intervening space in the box with old newspapers and rags. This method of acoustical isolation worked well.

We presented the box to the girls.

"Here's a present for you," Hicks told them. "We found some nice hazelnuts and picked some ripe blackberries. They are delicious. You can share them with others if you like. We hope you enjoy them."

"Oh, thank you, Hicks, how nice of you to think of us. We'll never sit on your face again," Rotten Mugga promised before we walked to a safe distance where we could see what happened when they opened the box and its sack full of surprise.

Our scheme worked perfectly. Before we dashed off, their piercing screams resounded as music to our ears when the snakes came slithering out of the bag. By the time they recovered their wits we were gone.

Nothing happened! We expected reprisal, swift and severe. But nothing happened at all. Football and Rotten Mugga merely scolded us and told us what nasty boys we were. They also made sure word got out around town of what we had done. But something didn't seem right—tattletaling to anyone willing to lend them an ear seemed out of character for these no-nonsense tomboys. Troublemakers they were to be sure but snitches never. Or maybe they were growing out of their tomboy-hood as the neighborhood lady had suggested and were becoming proper young ladies. We'd expected some more face sittings, perhaps meted out in double measure, but the girls pretended we didn't even exist.

Only a scolding and some tattletaling? While we still were savoring the joy of our victory we'd quite forgotten about the scolding. But niggling doubts crept into our minds about the tattletaling. Maybe they'd been hatching surprises of their own.

School started again in early September. Aldo, Hicks and I were now third graders in Miss Kentala's classroom in the Centennial School. People are always getting our town and Centennial mixed up. Centennial Heights and Centennial are two separate towns. We walked a short mile down Crooked Hill to the Centennial School each day. We didn't mind this too much then as we didn't know any better. Bus transportation for the students would come later.

The old Centennial School evokes warm memories. The students and teachers arrived early each day. For fifteen minutes everyone horsed around outside on the playground before we settled in for study. Playing "foot hockey" or maybe shooting some hoops gave the boys a chance to unwind. The girls usually skipped rope or played hopscotch. The teachers were always present to see that nothing got too wild. At times we participated in a maypole dance, a novel sight for both locals and tourists to see. Performed mostly during an afternoon recess in the spring, the students at times clamored for the dance just to avoid the classroom. The school board unwittingly enhanced the quaintness of the maypole dance by imposing a rather strict dress code on their unsophisticated pupils. Third and fourth grade sons of copper miners, farmers and fishermen incongruously seen wearing short pants or knickerbockers solemnly paraded in and out around the pole, weaving the streamers in intricate patterns. In greater numbers, girls always wearing long dresses, capered about with them and somehow managed to keep the streamers from getting tangled. Performing elaborately, round and round the pole everyone danced, some going clockwise and others counterclockwise. The maypole dance later fell into disfavor in the USA owing to May Day observances in communist countries.

At the time the third, fourth and fifth grades were taught in the same room by Miss Kentala, a formidable portly woman. Dividing time equally between the classes educating the sons and daughters of copper miners, farmers, lumberjacks and fisherman living together in a polyglot community posed a particular challenge for her, mainly because immigrant or second-generation parents and their children accustomed to speaking Finnish or Italian in their homes were still struggling to speak English, a task especially daunting for the Finns. The primary cause for their difficulty is the absence of articles in the Finnish language. There were other impediments as well. Many words in English sounding the same but having different meanings conduced only to intensify learning difficulties. Even dissimilar sounding words caused confusion.

"But Dr. Roche, I ain't got any balls," fifteen-year-old Impi Juntunen, a farm girl, replied when questioned by her family doctor concerning a bout of constipation. He'd asked her, "Impi, how long has it been since your bowels moved?"

Mischiefs abounded. Miss Kentala had her hands full. The janitor claimed she kept as busy as a beetle on a dung heap. Not only language difficulties—a kid might be expected to jump out the classroom window if he got too bored. This happened often if Miss Kentala for some reason had to leave the room. There were spitball fights and a girl lucky if she didn't have her pigtails pulled by an unruly boy. The desks were of a hardwood construction supported by a grid-work of cast iron. A space existing between the folding seat and the backrest made it convenient for an urchin to poke a girl seated in front of him with his old-fashioned dip pen. If the pigtails were long enough, the girl suffered the misfortune of having tip ends dipped into an inkwell, especially if she were a blond.

Matters would get even worse for Miss Kentala.

After a summer of rustic idling, Aldo, Hicks and I still gloated over the tremendous victory we'd scored on Football and Rotten Mugga who were one year ahead of us. We exchanged winks as the pair aloofly passed us in the hallway. Aldo chortled in an inimitable fashion, gleefully within their earshot, and as they walked by he cupped a hand over his mouth, pretending to whisper suggestively to Hicks and me some choice gossip he'd heard about them. Large white teeth flashing from a broad smirking vulpine mouth considerably enhanced the effect.

Then disaster struck.

With classroom activity underway shortly after the nine o'clock bell signaled startup, a piercing shriek interrupted the whisperings and the exchange of notes among the young scholars. It came from Miss Kentala who jumped up from her seat at her desk as spryly as any acrobat. Could she be having a seizure or maybe a fit?

The students gasped. At least initially. For wrapped around Miss Kentala's right ankle a handsome grass snake, at least three feet long progressed up her leg, its bright yellow stripes glowing in the early morning sunlight admitted through large classroom windows. No one had ever before witnessed Miss Kentala as lively. She pranced helplessly as the sickening serpent slowly undulated toward an uncertain destination, and in her fright did not realize she'd hiked her dress exposing a big, baggy pair of pink bloomers.

The snake had buddies. Two lesser reptiles slithered across the floor in the general direction of the transfixed students. Pandemonium erupted. Most of the students left their desks and scurried for the safety of the cloakroom. After gathering their wits some of the boys began to find the proceedings hilarious. Most, however, remained in a stage of fright. Football and Rotten Mugga appeared to take matters in stride after at first acting surprised like everyone else.

"What in the dickens is going on in here?" a gruff voice demanded. It came from Jan Beeha, the janitor, who'd barged in to check the commotion. He swiftly perceived his responsibility—after a few clumsy attempts, Beeha removed the reluctant reptile that had progressed its way up Miss Kentala's ample thigh. Getting a firm grip just behind the snake's head, Beeha freed the serpent from her fat leg by exerting a slow, gentle pull on the snugly-fitting coils. He tossed the unwilling creature out an open window where it slithered away. Two brave students grabbed the other offenders and likewise heaved them out the window.

With a semblance of calm restored, a distraught Miss Kentala dismissed the class until the following day.

Jan Beeha remained behind to investigate. He discovered incriminating evidence: Three lunch buckets belonging to Paulie Maki, Hicks Huhta and Aldo Vella were found cleverly hidden beneath Miss Kentala's desk. Obviously the lunch buckets had concealed the snakes. Ample room in the buckets existed for the snakes to occupy beside the lunches. Most of the students carried their lunches in large metal buckets used by copper miners deep in the underground shafts. Box-shaped on the bottom and secured by a large domed hinged lid fastened down with two clamps, Jan Beeha found the clamps loosened. The three buckets were wedged partially open with sticks, enabling the imprisoned snakes to slither out. Whoever put them under Miss Kentala's desk must have hoped the reptiles would not crawl out too soon. The scheme worked perfectly for the culprits. How the offenders got the snake-laden lunch buckets into the classroom without being discovered remains a mystery.

The trio in vain vociferously proclaimed innocence of the act. Innocence even showed on their faces. But their protests were unavailing. Justice, except perhaps in a cosmic sense, miscarried and Aldo, Hicks and Paulie Maki got the blame.

The accused stood humbly before the class the next morning, Aldo and Paulie in their knickerbockers and Hicks in his short pants. After stern admonitions from Miss Kentala about bad behavior she administered swift punishment. A strap made from a short but hefty length of a flattened fire hose served for this purpose.

"Boys, do you have anything to say for yourselves?" she sternly asked while testing the strap for suppleness. Using a well-practiced wrist action, she slapped it on her desktop. Loud thuds caused a deadly silence in the classroom.

Knowing what lie in store Hicks started bawling. "I didn't do it," he lamely whined.

It did him no good. Miss Kentala had no sympathy for any wrong doer who acted like a baby. Hicks therefore got his spanking first. As a precaution Miss Kentala held his wrist while wielding the strap on an outstretched hand. She soundly spanked each hand five times.

His bawling increased substantially in volume. Despite the

grimness of these circumstances both Aldo and I began to laugh. Poor Hicks. Miss Kentala did not appreciate this. She doubled up the spankings on us and made both of us stay after school for an extra half hour each day for the rest of the week. "I must try harder to be a good person," she made us write on the blackboard, over and over after which we erased and washed the slates.

"We've been had," Aldo said. Although we couldn't prove it, we suspected treachery on the part of Football and Rotten Mugga. Rotten Mugga cupped her mouth toward Football and began chuckling as we later approached them.

Score a major victory for Rotten Mugga and Football.

Things got better for our Heights Bunch. Football and Rotten Mugga began to ignore us. They didn't play in the sandlot scrimmages as often as they did a year ago, which we did not mind in the least. Yet we kind of missed them even if they caused us a lot of trouble at times. Calling them by their right names, however, stayed out of the question. We still had too much pride for that. Besides they could still be scary.

How could Football and Rotten Mugga, the terrorists of the sandlot, have changed so drastically? Both girls were becoming more serious. We found this troubling. The girls became occupied in pursuits other than playing sandlot football and terrorizing boys. The neighbor lady had to be right; the girls were outgrowing their tomboy-hood. Not only that, they did not appear to be as physically formidable as we'd previously perceived them to be. The gang members had caught up with them in size except for the cricket-sized Hicks. It reached a point where Football and Rotten Mugga would hardly even talk to us. Face sittings were rare. Although they both seemed to be progressing out of their tomboy-hood the girls were not the type who liked to play with dolls, skip rope or maybe play hopscotch. They had no interest skipping rope while chanting "Bobby Shafto Went to Sea." Such activity did not bring them any fun.

Football wanted to be a nurse when she grew up. Despite the uncompromisingly stern way she treated the gang members, she loved young children. As she grew older she could always be counted on as a reliable baby sitter or someone to help look after an ailing elderly person. She liked animals as well. Dogs, cats, chipmunks and squirrels were her friends, besides Tipsy who seldom left her side. She fed the stray dogs and cats with whatever scraps and leftovers she could find and the wild critters from an abundant stash of wild hazelnuts she hoarded each autumn. People claimed Football to be a good-hearted young woman although we didn't appreciate this as mischievous youngsters. In fairness to ourselves how could we.

Rotten Mugga did a lot of reading, much of it serious stuff, even when she went about sitting on boy's faces. I remember one occasion when she gave a book report on the Civil War.

The students in the classroom listened enthralled when Rotten Mugga gave her report, mostly concerning military engagements fought during the conflict. From the battles at Manassas, the Peninsular campaign, Fredericksburg, Chancellorsville, Gettysburg, the bloody campaigns of eighteen sixty-four, clear up through Lee's surrender at Appomattox, one couldn't hear a pin drop in the room as she spoke. There were poignant moments when she spoke of Lincoln's Emancipation Proclamation and his Gettysburg Address. Heavy stuff for a kid her age able to hold her listeners spellbound the way she did for a half hour. Some of her students said they saw tears welling in Miss Kentala's eyes as she sat listening to her precocious charge.

"How can anyone be so smart," Hicks said when school let out. "Listening to Rotten Mugga is like hearing a grownup give a speech. She's almost as good as a grownup. Maybe even just as good."

Happily for us the face sittings eventually petered out altogether. Football and Rotten Mugga no longer played sandlot football with us. They'd both become quieter and more reserved. Both girls seemed content with more reading and caretaking.

Aldo and Hicks remained my closest friends.

Of the three of us, Aldo Vella, a product of New York City, had the most interesting boyhood. Involved in the insurance business, his father had relatives in the Copper Country as our area in the Keweenaw is commonly called, and after many visits, decided to open an office in Houghton, the principal city in the region. Armando Vella purchased a comfortable home in our town before leaving New York. He opted to live close to woods, open fields and small streams. But Armando claimed the unique charm and friendliness of our citizens mainly influenced his decision to live in Heights. His wife, Celeste, agreed. Mr. Vella could have situated closer to his job in Houghton, fifteen miles away from Heights.

The youngest in the Vella family, Aldo had two older brothers and an older sister. Accepted as a "wise guy" in Heights, the fun-loving and generous Aldo always stood ready to participate in creative mischief. But like Football he had a soft spot for animals. Once while Hicks and I were engaged in tying cans to a dog's tail with long lengths of string he ordered us to stop. "We just don't do that," he told us. But other well-established mischiefs such as displacing outhouses from their moorings on Halloween were within his limits. He fit in well with the Heights Bunch and he added a welcome new dimension to our provincial small-town habits and our views on life.

"You guys need to get some street smarts," he told us shortly after being initiated into our gang. Aldo claimed he acquired his "street smarts" from fast-city-life lessons learned on playgrounds, in corner candy stores and on neighboring streets. Kids had to learn fast to be accepted by their peers. Those able to keep up were "cool cats." Kids slow in learning the ways of the city neighborhoods were "squares." Aldo considered himself a cool cat.

He had large mischievous eyes which darted about with "you'll never guess what I know about you" glances which put Hicks and me into stitches of laughter. He had a superb knack for making one feel uncomfortable, especially if one were an adolescent stranger, and could often make his victim feel as though he knew his innermost secrets and shortcomings. Sometimes his efforts backfired.

He tried his act on Willie Juntunen whom he considered a square. An easygoing and likable brother of the constipated Impi, Willie, a large, stolid taciturn boy a year younger than Aldo, resembled a broad open-faced bumpkin. A head topped with almost pure white hair enhanced the image. Those of Finnish extraction referred him as a true "Piimä Pää" or "buttermilk head." As a square, Willie thus became a natural target for Aldo's merciless teasing. Whenever Willie happened along, Aldo would nudge another gang member and pull off his whisper act, sometimes chortling almost inaudibly or clucking like a hen in his hand cupped-over-mouth-toward-listener pose. But much to his annoyance Willie remained imperturbable to his badgering.

The needling went on for some time before matters came to a head. Willie continued to ignore Aldo and merely regarded him as nuisance he had to live with. This caused Aldo to push matters further. He had to teach Willie a lesson. One day as Willie approached a gang meeting spot along a narrow path Aldo lie in wait hiding behind a tree. Just as Willie came alongside he stuck out a foot, tripping him. Aldo then started to whistle nonchalantly and looked up at the sky as though nothing happened.

This time Aldo could not be ignored. Willie bounced up from the turf and with an inspiration grabbed Aldo and tossed him to the ground like a sack of bran. Aldo did not fight back. He really didn't want to fight in the first place even though he might have acquitted himself well, being almost a year older than Willie. And neither would he hold a grudge. "Willie's got cajones," Aldo said. Cajones? Its meaning remained hidden from us for years. Maybe that's just what it took for Willie to win Aldo's respect. And in short time Aldo inveigled Willie into becoming a close confidant. "Listen kid, if you ever need a couple nickels or even a quarter, just come to see old Magooch and he'll take good care of you."

From what Aldo told us, "Magooch" is a title of respect conferred upon one having authority. "Something like a boss or a goombah for Italian guys," he claimed. Aldo had conferred the title on himself without approval or recognition from an official source, remote or otherwise. Aldo and Willie got along well after the tripping incident.

The street-smart Magooch brought refreshing new insights to our provincial Heights Bunch. This New York City wise guy had a lot of people flummoxed until they got to know him better.

Hicks, the youngest member of the gang, and regarded by many as a bright young boy, possessed a scientific bent. Curious, almost certain, he wondered whether the distressing stink caused by bodily passed gas would ripen into an even more profound state of putridity after having undergone hermetic encapsulation. He would find out. He farted into a mason jar and capped it as expeditiously as circumstances permitted. Opening the bottle a week later, it wasn't the outcome he'd hoped for—the odor had appreciably diminished rather than intensified. Too much gas had escaped initially, and when he whiffed the jar, he found the effluvium to be barely perceptible of stink.

After this fiasco an undefeated Hicks topped off his already pregnant bowels with liberal helpings of pork & beans and hard-boiled eggs. He'd decided on a new tack; he proceeded to fart into a balloon. After several failed attempts, and before he ran out of gas, he managed to inflate the balloon to an extent it resembled a flaccid pouch. A two-handed operation, Hicks boasted he'd perfected an airtight seal.

He'd let go and captured a good one, a dirty mean "legää," which is a moist and extremely potent fart—a real stinkeroo. To minimize loss of his prized essence he deftly twisted the neck of the balloon, and after tying it off, allowed the entrapped gas to mature for a week before evaluating the results of his experiment. He then prudently lanced the pliant receptacle rather than struggle with a tough knot. Bringing his nose close to the faint, barely audible hissing sound of release, he inhaled deeply. He got a good whiff.

Hicks hailed his experiment a success. He claimed the odor worsened under encapsulation. Others scoffed. "You probably crapped into that balloon and got your nose too close," his dad told him.

Poor Hicks. He could always be counted on to participate in some monkey business, however unwittingly, when an opportunity arose. At an earlier six years of age, he hadn't acquired street smarts.

"Now Hicks, listen to what I'm going to tell you," said Reggie, one of the older guys in town and a member of the next oldest Heights Bunch. "It's very important. We're going to have some fun and you're the guy I need to help me."

"OK, Reggie, I'm listening. I'm always ready for fun."

"You never know what you're going to see under a woman's skirt. People say there's some kind of bird hiding up there and now we're going to find out."

"Are you sure? My mom never told me anything like that."

"She must be keeping it a secret from you, Hicks. Now make sure you pay close attention to what I say. There's one coming now. See, she's only a half block away and she hasn't spotted us yet."

Faye Entdorff, our Sunday school teacher and an attractive buxom girl in her late teens slowly approached, as though abstracted in deep thought.

"Yup, Faye's our neighbor. She's not walking very fast."

"That's good. Now let's go behind these bushes where she won't see us. Here's what I want you to do as soon as she walks by us," Reggie replied, handing Hicks a small mirror. "When you get a chance, sneak up right behind her. You're still small and chances are you won't be spotted. Then what you must do is lift up her skirt and see what's under it in the mirror. Afterwards you can tell me what kind of bird she's hiding."

What a stroke of luck. After she passed the hiding place, Faye stopped no more than ten feet away, distracted by something. Reggie and Hicks failed to notice the object of her attention as they were too busy doing important work.

Hicks crept up behind her undetected. Faye had not resumed her walk. He crouched down with his mirror. The plan proceeded perfectly and the decisive moment neared. He stealthily hiked up her dress and looked in the mirror. He got a good look. Faye remained oblivious. Only when Hicks lifted her skirt higher to more closely examine her nether regions were the proceedings aborted.

"Shame on you, Hicks. You are a very nice boy but what you did was bad. You must tell me who put you up to this," she said after arresting him.

Hicks spilt the beans. The word spread rapidly through Heights.

Reggie got the "black licorice" as family members called their father's thick black belt. His father unsparingly wielded it on his butt. He further made him stack a load of firewood for the Entdorffs.

Sunday school following Hicks's exploit saw full attendance at the Emmaus Hall. The topic for the pupils during this particular morning was "Lessons Learned from Bad Behavior."

"What have we learned about bad behavior?" Miss Entdorff asked her class after delivering a short lecture.

"My bad behavior not only hurts others but hurts me as well," Rotten Mugga ventured.

Another girl volunteered, "Jesus wants me to be a sunbeam and I want to shine for him. Then I won't be a bad girl and do as many naughty things."

"Now Hicks, what lesson have you learned from bad behavior?" Miss Entdorff asked, smiling sweetly.

"I didn't see any bird but I'm pretty sure I saw a nest. I could see it through your underwear," he replied in pure innocence.

From the mouths of babes shall come words of wisdom. The old hall erupted in laughter.

The gang splintered. At least six families left Centennial Heights for Detroit and other cities where jobs were plentiful during World War II and the postwar days. Some of the kids left behind found less time for play. Willie Juntunen kept busy on his family's farm a short distance outside of town. Two other members of our Heights Bunch were fast becoming fisherman by helping their fathers who fished commercially for herring and lake trout in the icy waters of Lake Superior. A sad day occurred when Shirley, her parents and Tipsy left for Portland, Oregon, where the family would begin a new life after the war ended. Everyone wept at a going away party given them at the Emmaus Hall. Shirley would realize a childhood ambition by becoming a registered nurse. Of our Heights Bunch only Aldo and Hicks remained. And of course, Abby. Our gang had splintered.

I started to read a lot. Hicks and Aldo called me a book worm. Enamored of sagas and legendary tales of heroism, Homer's Iliad became a great favorite. Alexander, Hannibal and Julius Caesar were among the great generals of antiquity captivating my interest. Particularly Hannibal for his great battles won against the Romans in Italy. Later I would delve into philosophy and history. "I'll become a great scholar," I mused, "and never be like old Willard Janke. How could anyone turn out to be like him?"

Then there were the facts of life. We did not require classroom instruction to comprehend these facts. Just be in the right place at the right time, be observant and talk to the right people.

Summer vacations spent at the Maki family cottage at Five Mile Point on the north shore of Lake Superior signaled long weeks of fun activity from dawn to dusk. With extra room, available guests often included my chums, Aldo and Hicks. Weekend stays were all too short when no uncles were available to pinch hit for my dad during the week. After my dad had worked as a lumberjack for more than five years, he kept busy distributing foodstuffs, mostly canned goods and flour, for a large wholesaler in Hancock.

Lake Superior is cold, oft-times frigid, but we swam nonetheless since we always kept the sauna heated. After an icy dunk we'd scamper to the sauna to warm up before venturing another dip. Absent of my friends, I keenly anticipated trolling for lake trout with my dad and my Uncle Flash, an affable carefree bachelor. Uncle Flash loved to brag to his nieces and nephews of his dazzling skills as a hockey player. "The fastest man on ice," he'd boast. Whether true or not it had earned him his nickname.

There came the inevitable daily expedition to the blueberry patch with our Grandma Maki during prime picking. With hawk-like scrutiny Grandma monitored her homely brood of five grandchildren, a number that would increase substantially with time. To discourage us from filling bellies with berries instead of pails she gave each of us a stick of chewing gum. Even with such meager incentive, the prospect of Grandma's scrumptious blueberry pies kept us going strong. She'd preserve the surplus for a long, cold winter.

Grandma Maki's philosophy, having evolved from struggling through too many lean years during the depression, necessitated picking every berry in the patch. If one of her urchins began to skip about looking for only the choicest berries, leaving those less desired for others to glean, Grandma quickly reproved the laggard for his dereliction.

Grandma had two modes of disciplining the laggard. At first offense she'd gently tug on an earlobe and merely point at what he'd missed. The second time around, without lenience, she'd administer a series of sharp raps upon the skull of the offender with thin hard knuckles, and with a grating voice would exclaim "Katso, Katso," which from Finnish means "Look, Look." Grandma sounded like an impatient hen cackling over her brood.

On one such outing I felt the familiar raps against my head and heard the all too familiar "Katso, Katso." I was indeed looking, but not at a clump of berries. For there on a branch of a pine tree, as though sprung for a singular purpose, hung a gorilla-sized pair of bloomers just off the two-rut road where we were busy picking.

Uncle Flash happened to be with us but he paid no particular attention to the discovery. He nonchalantly whistled a nondescript tune.

"How did those bloomers get there, Grandma?" I asked, this time doing the pointing while remaining impervious to the woodpecker-like blows hammering upon my benumbed skull.

At first she gave me a look which seemed to say "How can a twelve-year-old grandson of mine be such an imbecile?" But she composed herself and said, "Pieru Kouret, perhaps people camped here. A woman must have forgotten them after doing her laundry and hanging them out to dry."

Grandma's answer made perfect sense to me at first blush but bothersome doubts began to surface. Whoever washed the bloomers did a poor job. Nicotine stains were still plainly visible, blemishing the seat of the fabric. The truth about those bloomers would soon be revealed.

In early youth I'd become an accomplished eavesdropper on adult conversation but only after some initial failure.

"What we're talking about is not for young ears," Grandma Maki told me on one occasion. I'd been loitering, feigning nonchalance in what she and several friends were discussing at the dining room table.

I found their discussion riveting, a source of fascination, far more interesting than anything I'd heard in Sunday school or church or even what my friends had to say. My gossipy ears pricked up. It had something to do with young girls without husbands having babies; I'd always thought people had to be married before babies came along.

"Pieru Kouret, if you want to listen you'll have to get under the table," Grandma said after noticing my idling.

Curiosity trumped pride. Unabashed, I crawled under the table to listen some more. Disappointed, frustrated, Grandma and her friends continued their discussion in Finnish. My parents spoke only English.

My eavesdropping skills improved. A short time after the incident in the blueberry patch Uncle Flash invited two friends to the camp where they'd lit a bonfire on the beach. I sat around with them toasting hot dogs and marshmallows. Uncle Flash and his buddies enjoyed a few beers, looking ahead to fishing trip planned for the next day.

"Pieru Kouret, don't you think it's getting late? Maybe you'd better run up and get a good night's sleep. Remember we've got to get up real early tomorrow," Uncle Flash said. "We've got to be on the lake at sunrise."

But their conversation happened to be far too interesting for me to go to sleep just then, fishing trip or not. Instead of going to the camp I sidled off and concealed myself in some bushes a short distance from their conversation. There I crouched in the shadows.

The men were talking about the bloomers Grandma and I had seen on the pine tree. One of the guys got a lot of questions from his companions.

His tongue lubricated by four beers, "Perch" needed little encouragement to divulge the details of his foray into the woods with a companion to his chums. I sat in the shadows listening, captivated in a heart-beating silence.

Perch had picked up a woman called Fatso by almost everyone at the High Steps Tavern in Calumet and drove her on the seldom-used two-rut road to a stand of pine trees in Grandma's blueberry patch. According to Perch, she weighed at least two hundred fifty pounds. Fatso, a jolly likable woman, sometimes pinch hit as a barmaid at the Tavern.

What happened in the blueberry patch between Perch and Fatso boggled the head of the innocent Pieru Kouret. (No longer Paulie Maki, I'd become Pieru Kouret—entirely—nothing more than a peeling of a fart, its merest essence.) Though thoroughly fascinated Pieru Kouret failed to apprehend the substance of what Perch related to his companions. Perch had divested Fatso of her drawers and strung them on the pine tree after they finished their business and before they left the stand for Calumet. The memory, the image of those voluminous, baggy bloomers strung to the branch of a pine tree best stuck in his head At least he could identify with the bloomers, his recollections of them still fresh after Grandma's skull-rapping. Uncle Flash and his buddy said something about "claiming the bloomers," whatever that meant. The guys had some loud laughs and enjoyed some more beer. Perch's buddy said claiming Fatso's drawers earned him a well-deserved prize for his accomplishment in the berry patch. Pieru Kouret's head spun, muddled with confusion, before he sneaked away from the shadows to his room in the camp.

He remembered the skidmarks. It took but a brief reflection on the matter to cast into disrepute Grandma's whopper about the campers and the woman washing her bloomers, vindicating his skepticism.

Too much left unresolved, too much had happened in the blueberry patch. This required a discussion with Aldo and Hicks. I briefed Aldo on my concerns.

"You've come to the right man," Aldo said, smiling unctuously. A man? Indeed a man. For a thin, pencil-like moustache already beginning to appear on his thirteen-year-old lip would eventually complement a head of dark, naturally wavy hair he always kept well-groomed. "Old goombah Magooch is going to give you an education," he continued, "but for what I'm going to tell you, we need some privacy."

Aldo, Hicks and I repaired to a ramshackle shack constructed by some of the older guys used mainly for exchanging cock-and-bull stories and smoking cigarette butts picked from the roadside. Occasionally they were lucky enough to enjoy a full pack. We found the shack empty. None of the big guys were present.

Aldo listened patronizingly as I fully divulged the tale I'd heard at the bonfire.

"Let's go over this carefully. I've got a reputation to preserve and I've got to be professional about this," he said. "We're not going to use any bad language.

"What Perch did to Fatso is called "fottuto." That's the Italian word for what they did. You guys got to remember Italian is the language of lovers."

"Do you mean to say Perch and Fatso are in love?" I asked.

"Sometimes people fall in love after fottuto but mostly it happens before," Aldo said. "Then they go their separate ways."

As youngsters we'd heard a lot of bragging from older guys about what they knew about the facts of life, but nothing they said came even close to what we were getting from Aldo. Aldo gave us pure gold.

Hicks, the scholar, kept busy taking notes.

"How do you spell fottuto?" he asked.

I remembered Grandma's discussion with her friends concerning unmarried girls having babies. Since they talked in Finnish I did not get a satisfactory answer.

"How can this happen, Magooch? Aren't people supposed to be married before they can have any babies?"

"Most of the time that's true," he instructed, equal to the task, "but here's what happens. Now you guys listen close.

"A man puts his wee-wee in a lady's birdie and pees some magic stuff in there."

"A birdie!" Hicks exclaimed. "Reggie was right."

"In about three weeks the lady has a baby. That's how long it takes for it to grow in its mama's belly," he added authoritatively. "It doesn't matter if they're married or not."

Smiling some more, Aldo mimicked a mother cradling her baby in her arms.

"Does that mean Fatso is going to have a baby?" Hicks asked.

"We'll have to wait and see. It doesn't always work."

"What's this magic stuff?" I asked. "This has got to be humbug," I thought.

"We've had enough instruction for one day. We can talk about this later."

One had to look really close to see the moustache. More telling, his voice still hadn't changed.

What Hicks heard from Aldo made a profound impression—he did some research. During a subsequent Sunday service at the Emmaus Hall, the minister asked whether anyone had a special prayer request.

"I have a heavy burden on my heart," Hicks implored humbly, "we must pray for fornicators."

"Yes, we must pray for them," the ministered murmured after a momentary study of Hicks's deadpanned features. "We must pray for everyone."

CHAPTER 2

Moose Lake Bible Camp

Manly and tough. That's what I had to be. I sat stiffly erect and stoically managed to feign indifference to the other passengers in the car. We were on our way to bible camp. Except for a trip to Chicago as a six-year-old I'd never been more than fifty miles from Centennial Heights. Now as a thirteen-year-old, my parents were sending me to the Moose Lake Bible Camp more than two hundred fifty miles from home. Some of the kids in the Heights Bunch had never been more than ten miles from home. I could thumb my nose at them when I got back.

The Moose Lake Bible Camp, located fifty miles west of Duluth, Minnesota, was the destination for small groups coming from Marquette, Michigan, Ely, Minnesota, and from some place called Bloomer. Bloomer is in Wisconsin. Most of the kids came from Duluth and its close neighbor, Cloquet. The groups represented members of a loose affiliation of churches sharing a common set of beliefs and a common faith. Except for Duluth and Cloquet, no more than a half dozen kids from each place would be joining the camp for a two week stay.

Three adults and one other child besides myself on their way to the bible camp. Henry Bylkas, our pastor and one of the few in town who owned a car drove us along with his wife, Sylvia, and Gladys Bloomdahl. Gladys's copper miner husband coached sandlot baseball and our hockey team, the Centennial Heights Junior Huskies. That other child was Rotten Mugga.

Ugh. Two hundred fifty miles to go and two hundred fifty miles to ride alongside Rotten Mugga, seated between me and Gladys Bloomdahl in the back. No other way could this work out unless I sat in front with Pastor Bylkas and Sylvia. I strove to keep my mind on other matters.

A woman hater like me riding with a girl? Yep, a woman hater—that's the way it had to be. For during the past year I'd vowed to have nothing to do with girls. Like I said a guy like me had to be manly and tough. Girls would have no part in my life and that applied to

Rotten Mugga. Guys my age who liked girls were "girl sucks." No brownnosing around girls for me. But despite my misgivings, and even grudgingly glad, I reconciled Rotten Mugga's presence alongside me as we travelled through the thinly populated countryside.

Rotten Mugga, however, didn't mind my presence. She sat dignified and ladylike, freshly scrubbed and neatly dressed, conversing mostly with Gladys about her plans in life. Her warts, I'd noticed, were beginning to disappear. They'd become a minor distraction. While not ignoring me completely she made no overt effort to engage me in conversation. I continued to sit stiffly, looking straight ahead. Even the lush rolling hills populated with fir trees and hardwood in Ontonagon County, which matched the verdant scenery in the Keweenaw, failed to attract my attention. The adults' attempt to engage me in their conversation resulted in a few curt replies.

"Maybe I'll be trapper or a lumberjack," I mumbled.

After we stopped in Ewen for a quick lunch I relaxed and began to enjoy the ride as we drove westward toward Superior, Wisconsin. I selfishly hogged the window seat for the entire trip, not once offering to trade places with Mugga. Oh well, tough luck for her. And I couldn't very well risk a sharp rebuke from the adults by calling her Rotten Mugga. So I settled for Mugga. I kept it at that for the entire trip and nobody got too nosy about it. Everyone else called her Abby.

Talk about a big river. I'd never seen a river so large as the mighty St. Louis River, even bigger than our own Sturgeon River just outside of Chassell, only twenty miles from Heights. We'd driven through Wisconsin and crossed into Minnesota. After crossing the river, we spent the night in Duluth where we were bedded down at the home of the Jacobsons', a kindly couple belonging to the Duluth congregation. The next morning we completed our journey to the Moose Lake Bible Camp.

What greeted our eyes at the camp site were four large tents, one substantially larger than the other three. A wooden building serving as the camp kitchen, a small open-air canteen for purchasing candy bars and soda pop, also of wood construction, and two outdoor johns; what more could we ask for?

Morning instruction and evening services would be observed in the large tent, which served as the camp center. It used to be an old circus tent in Superior. A piano had been brought in, set on a platform near the front. The smaller tents served as sleeping quarters, one tent for the boys, another for the girls and yet another partitioned tent for the staff members. During afternoons and after the evening service the canteen opened for Milky Way candy bars or "Oh-So-Grape" pop, a now defunct favorite.

The thirty or so of us in the boys' tent each slept on a cot furnished with a straw tick mattress, literally fabricated from a bag stuffed with straw and sewn at several seams along its length. The girls fared no better. Neither did the adults. There were perhaps sixty kids altogether, roughly half boys and half girls. One blanket for each camper sufficed for the warm Minnesota summer nights—when we laid over in Duluth the mid-July daytime temperature swelled above ninety degrees and it did not cool off much during the evening or throughout the night.

Once the lanterns were snuffed out in the tents we long reminisced about day's events before dozing off into the nothingness of youthful sleep.

"He died, He died," a sepulchral voice intoned during timely intervals in the darkness, repeated over and over. Whispered exchanges between the motley agglomeration of boys, ranging in age from nine through fourteen, became subdued.

"Who is this wise guy," I wondered before falling asleep. The last words I heard were, "He died, He died."

The voice, tinged with mockery, belonged to Rolfe Ellefson, a cynical guy my age from Cloquet. Tall for his age, gangly and flaxen-haired, a lantern jaw thrust prominently from a bony face. At times he could be sarcastic and abrasive but I discovered him to be full of mischief and fun. Most of the kids avoided him until they found out he wasn't such a bad guy.

As I said I'd become somewhat of a book worm. I went through a stage of priggishly accosting anyone—without glasses and pimples—with abstruse tidbits of historical knowledge I'd acquired. "Tell me everything you can about Zoroaster and his ideas," I pedantically challenged Rolfe the next morning. I had to find out what this guy knew. When I asked kids what they knew of Zoroaster or of a matter equally arcane most of them considered me nuts. To my astonishment and chagrin, Rolfe proceeded to tell me everything about him and then some, being somewhat of a pedant himself. But he had more street smarts. After some subsequent verbal sparring, we not only became reconciled to each other's presence but became friends—I'd discovered a kindred spirit. It wasn't merely from claiming erudition or pretenses thereof, however, through which we established a common bond as I would discover. And except for Rotten Mugga, Rolfe Ellefson impressed me as being the smartest kid I'd ever met if you got right down to it.

The adults were called either Brother or Sister. "Keep an eye on those two," Brother Hoekstra, the minister from the Duluth congregation and headmaster of the camp, advised Brother Rigo, a retired policeman from Superior. Brother Hoekstra had his eyes set on Rolfe Ellefson and me, after wisely consulting with our respective pastors the first day of camp. He made it his business to know who the potential troublemakers were. A short but sturdy man, easygoing and well-liked by the kids, Brother Rigo acted as the official policeman of the Moose Lake Bible Camp.

"I will not tolerate disobedience in the camp. Offenders will be punished severely," Brother Hoekstra had admonished during the first morning bible study.

We kept Brother Rigo busy.

Most of our pranks were harmless such as sending Bobby Olson, the youngest boy in camp, on a goose chase to find some striped red and white paint with which to paint our daredevles, our favorite spoons we used when casting for northern pike. Bobby searched for at least fifteen minutes, quitting his hunt after asking Brother Rigo if he knew anything about the paint. "H'm," Brother Rigo murmured thoughtfully after Bobby told him who'd sent him on his search.

"Call me 'kiss lips'," Bobby said. Before the lights went out, Kay, Brother Hoekstra's eighteen-year-old daughter, made it her business to provide comfort to any homesick camper. Bobby always looked ahead to his evening kiss from Kay.

Rolfe and his mosquitos. As we sat listening to an evening service, hordes of mosquitoes kept us company in the balmy long-summer-daylight ambiance of the big open-sided tent, while their high frequency buzz competed with the refrains of hymn-singers. This evening an absorbed Brother Rigo sat in front of us listening to a riveting sermon. Rolfe sat behind him preoccupied in other matters. Overcome by temptation, Rolfe took a straw and deftly tickled him on his neck. Brother Rigo responded with a resounding slap at the "mosquito." After an appropriate delay, another "mosquito" landed on his neck with the same response. This went on a half dozen times leaving Brother Rigo none the wiser.

We embellished Brother Hoekstra's admonition. "Offenders will be punished severely, sufficiently, effectively, efficiently, justly, well-judged and the burden of punishment will be heavily laden upon them," Rolfe and I would utter jocosely in Brother Rigo's presence. He would merely smile patronizingly at us.

Brother Rigo finally got an opportunity to demonstrate his savvy as policeman. A quarter mile from the camp site resided the inviting Nordic Resort, just past a narrowed region where Moose Lake necked down. From a map Moose Lake appeared as two lakes, the necked region causing it to look like the lobes of a person's lungs.

We were explicitly warned by our elders to avoid going there. But temptation is strong. The resort boasted an offshore platform with a ten-foot-high diving board. One afternoon while most of the kids went fishing or swimming, Rolfe, myself and two others sneaked off to the resort. What a blast we had, sporting about, diving from the tall board and enjoying uninterrupted fun for over an hour.

Brother Rigo's keen bloodhound intuition, acquired from years of walking a beat in Superior, had not deserted him. He discovered our absence after doing a head count of the swimmers and those about to go fishing in a big scow. How could he know the miscreants had to be at the Nordic Resort? We failed to observe his presence as he watched us perform some spectacular dives.

"Severely and sufficiently did you say," he said after rounding us up. "And how about justly and well-judged," he added.

That meant KP. Lots of it. And perhaps an unvoiced vindication for Rolfe's "mosquitos".

Brother Rigo made sure we washed and scrubbed the dishes, silverware and pots and pans scrupulously. We four offenders spent the entire next day doing KP duty at the crude Moose Lake kitchen. Breakfast, lunch and dinner, all by ourselves. Plenty of soap and hot water facilitated our task despite the crudeness of the facility, which consisted of a couple of large sinks and a wood-burning a stove. The water supply consisted of three large barrels kept replenished from a nearby spring. Brother Rigo related cases of food poisoning resulting from tainted utensils while he served in the army. Our dishes, pots and pans and silverware emerged sparkling clean.

It wasn't just hymns we heard in the big tent. Axel Gustafsson, or "Widdle Weenie Wen Ben" as we called him, already at twelve years of age had gained recognition as an accomplished pianist and a decent vocalist. Unknown to stage fright this chubby rascal from the Duluth congregation performed with aplomb whether giving a formal recital or hamming it up before friends.

"*Widdle weenie wen ben, widdle weenie wen ben,*" he'd babble from his high chair during his infancy, sometimes pointing at a Gustafsson household visitor. A connection to something tangible could not be proven but at least Axel won himself an enduring nickname. When morning bible studies ended he'd willingly play and sing for us at the camp piano. Although his ditties were harmless, he performed with the abandon of an entertainer in a bordello, and at timely moments, he'd roll his eyes and purse his lips while bumping and grinding his pudgy buttocks on the sturdy bench. Certainly not what Brother Hoekstra had in mind, but much to his credit, he did not stop Widdle Weenie Wen Ben from entertaining us. "We are not prudes," he said. The lyrics of our favorite song went like this:

Mother sent me to the store, she told me not to stay,
I fell in love with a pretty little girl and just couldn't get away
First she gave me peaches and then she gave me pears,
Then she gave me fifteen cents and kissed me on the ears,
Whooo!
Boy when I got home that night was mother ever sore,
She spanked me on the hinder and sent me to my door.

Included in Widdle Weenie's audience were Sister Bloomdahl and Sister Bylkas standing off to the side attempting to remain inconspicuous.

Mugga had a great time. She got along well with her fellow campers. She became known as "that nice girl from Michigan." Mugga was one of the older girls in camp, a year older than me going on fourteen. Looked up to by the other girls, not only for her quiet unassuming manners but also for being an interesting person, she made friends easily.

Wait a minute, what did I say? A year older than me? Perhaps that's what I mentioned when we played football, thereby justifying my inferiority at the sandlot competitions and the subsequent chastisement

I got as being caused by a one-year age difference. Actually she's only six months older.

Growing up in a small town is not by any means a unique experience but her description of an upbringing in a small polyglot town in Yooperland produced howls of delight from her new friends. Mugga did not mention the face-despoiling incidents inflicted by herself and Football, nor did she once mention me in an unflattering light. She had plenty of ammunition to fire without having to expose the foibles of our Heights Bunch. Her stories of kids jumping out of the classroom windows or tales of exploits of town characters drew their rapt attention. Most of all, her audience delighted in hearing her story of Skipper Jack, a maritime sailor on one of the Great Lakes ore carriers.

Some called him Nature Boy. He adhered to a unique regimen for preserving his health during the winter off-season. Skipper Jack ran down Crooked Hill to a natural spring in Cedar Bush while hollering at the top of his lungs all the way to the spring. Skipper claimed the hollering cleared his lungs. He'd refresh himself with the spring water he claimed possessed vital minerals not found on tap. Each morning at eight o'clock the townsfolk could hear Nature Boy yelling loudly while pounding his way down the hill. Some late risers claimed they didn't have to set an alarm. Every day he whizzed by, almost in flight.

"Here comes Skipper Jack," I said to Hicks and Aldo. Sure enough, the black-bearded Nature Boy came flying down the hill.

"Go get 'em Skipper," we shouted as he passed us. He increased his pace and yelled even louder.

"Eee Yoooooh! Eee Yoooooh! Eee Yoooooh!"

"He sounds like a donkey braying," Hicks said.

No one ever complained about the quaint spectacle; rather, we looked ahead to see Skipper Jack zooming by us and hear him bellowing his way toward the spring. Other than practicing his health regimen Nature Boy ranked as being pretty much 'normal' like the rest of us.

Enhancing her story to her listeners Mugga imitated the sounds Skipper Jack made with an unrestrained gusto. Brother Rigo rushed to the scene fearing mayhem. He asked for a repeat performance once he understood her attempt to impersonate a real-life character.

"Paulie Maki doesn't say too much," one of the girls noted to Mugga. "At least not to you." Indeed, our exchanges were of a perfunctory nature. While neither overtly friendly nor unfriendly toward her at camp, I made no attempt to avoid her whether during the morning and evening services or at leisure time.

The campers liked her, all except one. Marie Loonsfoot detested Mugga. The reason for her dislike did not become apparent to anyone except me.

Slender, pretty, with shoulder length dark hair, Marie Loonsfoot lived on an Indian reservation not far from Marquette. She proudly proclaimed her heritage as being a full-blooded Ojibwa Indian. The Ojibwa tribe for centuries has been and still is the predominant Native American tribe in Michigan's Upper Peninsula.

Everyone looked ahead to the afternoon swim at the "Berquist Beach," located at a close-by campsite belonging to a family of the Duluth congregation. Swim races and games of water tag were among the favorite activities at which we sported in the tepid summer waters of Moose Lake. Horseback dunking competitions never grew tiresome wherein "riders" astride the shoulders of their "horses" contested to unseat rival aqua-equestrians. Some swimmers demonstrated their crawl stroke, exaggerating text-book arm movements in hopes of being envied. Widdle Weenie Wen Ben could always be seen splashing happily in the shallows and heard barking like a seal.

C'mon, Weenie, let's hear it again," we'd holler.

"Orkk! Orkk! Orkk!" he'd respond.

Temptation too great to resist, she caught me unaware. During an afternoon dip at the Berquist, Mugga, an excellent underwater swimmer, popped up before me like a cork and began to splash water in my face as I tentatively waded further out.

"I'll get you used to this," she laughed, having noticed my goose bumps in getting acclimated to the cooler offshore water.

"Oh no you won't," I said, grabbing her and giving her a dunking. We laughed and playfully splashed and grabbed at each other some more, oblivious to the other swimmers.

Marie Loonsfoot stood on the beach watching these proceedings. She decided to join the fun. She waded in stealthily and suddenly pushed the unsuspecting Mugga aside. She began some face splashing and horse play of her own when it came to an abrupt halt: Mugga seized the unfortunate Loonsfoot in her face-sitting grip. Marie vainly struggled to free herself—it would be full body immersion for Marie—holding her nose, Mugga baptized her three times before retiring.

I had some idea concerning the tension building between Marie and Mugga, naïve as I might have been at the time of the ways of women.

Marie had been eyeing me, giving me sweet smiles. And every time my pal Rolfe and I took a stroll, Marie and one of her girlfriends tailed behind us. She didn't look too bad either, but as I said, there'd be no fooling around or brownnosing with her from a professed woman hater like me.

She finally spoke to me. "What's your name?" she asked when Rolfe and I stopped to examine some gopher holes.

I had to sound tough.

"Maki," I replied with my most disdainful frown. I did not ask hers and we continued our stroll, leaving Marie and her friend behind wondering what kind of a strange person she had to deal with.

All she got for her trouble was a thorough dunking from Mugga. She sought revenge and I would be the victim. She'd had enough of Rotten Mugga and wisely chose to avoid further conflict with her.

"So I'm a sissy," I heard Donald Boltz's voice say. I looked about to see to whom he addressed his remark. He'd addressed his remark to me.

I didn't like the guy whom I considered to be a humorless drudge. He reciprocated dislike. A sturdy farm lad of my age from Bloomer, Wisconsin, bronzed from working in the field long hours each day, Donald Boltz regarded me and Rolfe as a couple of smart alecs. Particularly me.

I'd given him the Zoroaster routine. He could not believe his ears as I gratuitously explained to him, according to some historians, Zoroaster, an ancient theologian, lived roughly 1000 years BC in the land of Medea-Persia. "Who is this prig of misery," he had to be thinking.

"Two primary forces," I expounded, "characterize man's intrinsic makeup: Ahura Mazda, a benevolent entity representing the good inherent in man, while Ahriman, a demonic being, identifies with man's proclivity to commit acts of evil at times." I had this one well-rehearsed.

"What's Ahura Mazda got to do with farmers' growing corn in

Wisconsin," he replied tersely. Harrows, plows and tractors kept him busy. Boltz and another farm boy everyone called "Smelly" would argue the better qualities of a John Deere versus a Farmall.

Can you imagine that? No sense of humor at all, a real square. Now he stood in my face no more than a foot away.

"Well what is it, bud, did you call me a sissy or not? Just what is it you've been telling Loonsfoot."

I never detested anyone so much as I did then.

"Come to think of it I did," although in fact I hadn't told Marie Loonsfoot anything of the sort. "Furthermore anybody from a town called Bloomer has got to be a big sissy."

A crowd had gathered. I noticed Mugga and Marie among the spectators. No way out of this, I had to save face and I had to act fast to preserve my reputation. Manly and tough it had to be.

I let go with a straight right. My punch landed dead center on his fireplug torso. He barely moved.

Then in no time I found myself flat on my back with the hefty farm lad from Bloomer, Wisconsin, planted squarely on my chest. He had my wrists pinned. I could not budge.

What a humiliation. An impassive Mugga looked on. What would she tell my friends back home?

I struggled vainly to free myself. My frustration mounted as I looked up into Donald Boltz's stern gaze. No hope for sympathy there. I began to weep, not bawl or cry, in self-pity. Tears of misery streamed copiously from my defeated eyes. Only then did he release me.

I've always had a problem with mucous whenever I wept. I sat up to catch Marie Loonsfoot looking at me just as immense boogers flared from both my nostrils, only to vanish back inside with a noisy inhalation. Marie smirked triumphantly.

"Marie, you're too good for that bum," Donald Boltz said as they walked off together.

"Here, use this," Mugga said, handing me a clean handkerchief. My humiliation complete, I'd at least discovered the reason for the farm lad's dislike of me.

"Pay no attention to Boltz," Rolfe said. "He's a gorp and he's kidding himself if he thinks he has a chance with Marie. She likes you for what it's worth."

"A gorp? What's a gorp?"

"That's a guy who farts in the bathtub and bites at the bubbles."

I felt better after that.

We were leaving the Moose Lake Bible Camp after fourteen days; two weeks of new friendship and discovery had passed too swiftly. Brother Hoekstra led a brief but spirited prayer session before we left.

I'd made some good friends, especially Rolfe, and only two enemies. Mugga made many friends and only one enemy. Yet before parting ways the farm lad from Bloomer, Wisconsin came over to see me. We both shuffled about awkwardly, neither of us speaking. I studied the swampers on his feet, which are rubber-bottomed boots worn by farmers when mucking their stalls. The swampers appeared to have been well-used. Obviously there were cattle and perhaps some pigs on the farm.

Manly and tough? What a joke. I didn't stand a chance against this guy. He had at least fifteen pounds on me and it wasn't blubber. Why did I drag Zoroaster into this business in the first place? I felt a loser's ambivalent remorse for having started the fight and then getting whipped. How could I have been so unintelligent? A straight answer might have avoided the trouble altogether whether the accusations were false or not. Then we'd see what would happen after that. But now I ate crow. Breaking the awkward silence while still looking at his swampers I humbly apologized for causing the trouble, grateful for his magnanimity.

"I just got lucky and I'm sorry it happened too," he replied after we shook hands. "I hope you can make it to camp again next summer."

Even Marie Loonsfoot came over shyly to say goodbye to Mugga and me. She would leave camp with the Marquette contingent. She gave each of us a big hug before scampering off.

Although we'd have a long distance to travel Pastor Bylkas accepted an evening dinner invitation from the Jacobsons where we'd laid over on our way to Moose Lake. But he did so only after talking it over with his wife and Gladys Bloomdahl. Mugga and I were not indisposed for a such a trip even if it meant arriving home late. We had no worries—travelling at night would be a new adventure. Pastor Bylkas phoned our parents who gave him their OK.

Time disappeared after hours of animated conversation. Well into the evening we departed our generous hosts.

Gladys, Mugga and I dozed off almost at once. When I awoke somewhere in Wisconsin Gladys and Mugga were still sound asleep.

I at first resisted a temptation to jostle Mugga for her head lay nestled on my shoulder. But I let her sleep. I studied her closely in the partial moonlight, the dim glow briefly enhanced by headlights of occasional westbound traffic.

I'd never seen her like this before. I looked at her for a long while. Her lips were slightly parted, her breathing regular and silent, and her features peacefully composed in slumber. "She looks like an angel," I told myself. I'd only seen her before as Rotten Mugga. I could not believe how attractive she was.

I felt protective. I carefully slipped an arm about her shoulder hoping she would not awaken. She did not stir. I fell back into a deep sleep.

This time Mugga awoke first. We were well into Yooperland but we still had some way to go when I finally stirred. I shook off my grogginess, enough to realize she'd been looking intently at me.

"You sure got some good shuteye, Paulie," Pastor Bylkas said as he drove on in the darkness.

"And he snores like an old buzz-saw," Gladys added.

"You can say that again," Sylvia said.

Mugga said nothing. I hoped she hadn't examined my Adam's apple too closely, which I've been told, always protrudes like a knob whenever I snore with my head back and mouth wide open. That must have been why she'd looked at me the way she did. The Adam's apple would eventually progress to an XTRA-Large size.

But it got even worse for me.

"You had some wild dreams, boy. Talk about talking in your sleep," Pastor Bylkas continued. "You were muttering something about grandma's drapes hanging loosely down in the parlor. Sure didn't make any sense to me."

It didn't make any sense to me either. No wonder Mugga had been watching me. Good thing the darkness prevented anyone from seeing me reddening with embarrassment. Feigning sleep, I pretended to ignore further conversation. The conversation quieted down. Sylvia and Gladys soon dozed off.

She'd made no effort to remove my arm, still around her shoulder. I faced her and returned her intent gaze Her steadfast expression could not have been caused by my loud snoring or the mutterings about grandma's drapes. Rather she regarded me as though she'd only seen me for the first time. She'd looked at me the same way a long time ago, but only with a brief glimpse, right after she and Football took turns sitting on my face. I held her gaze.

"Who is this girl?" I asked myself. I'd known her my entire life and never once did we have a personal conversation. I couldn't remember when we had a close talk, if only to discuss a hockey game, a book, or even to relate to her some choice gossip I'd heard. At most I'd hollered "Hey Mugga, are you going to play football with us today," or some other thing like that. The brief interlude at the lake where we playfully splashed about together came about as close as we ever got to experiencing rapport. And then Marie Loonsfoot had to barge in and ruin the moment.

I'd discovered a diamond. The cobwebs in my dusty head seemed to vanish at once. Me a woman hater? How could I have been such a foolish man. We sat transfixed for long minutes, entranced in a newly discovered joy, and newly born to an existence in a wondrous world of delight and expectation. We did not smile. Nor did I kiss her.

I wanted to talk to her. Nothing came to mind but I found the right word at last. I removed my arm from her shoulder and held her hand.

"Abby," I said quietly. She held my hand warmly.

The moonlight ride back from camp would remain our secret. Neither of us ever mentioned to anyone the significant looks we'd exchanged and our hand holding nearly all the way home. Only at daybreak did we release our warm clasp. And I don't think the Bylkases and Gladys Bloomdahl were aware of our infatuation. If they were, they said nothing at all. Besides they were once young themselves.

CHAPTER 3

Growing Pains

"C'mon, Hicks, grow up," I said.

It did not take long for the gang to see things had changed between Abby and me when we got back from camp. Abby and I both pretended nothing had changed. For one thing I no longer called her Rotten Mugga. I played it safe and instead referred to her as just plain Mugga. For another, I pretended to ignore her when my pals were around and studiously avoided conversation with her.

When together we found conversation easy. Abby and I would spin fanciful yarns of our futures. Her plans were more realistic than my own.

"I'm going to be a teacher," Abby said. "I only hope I can teach as well as Miss Kentala."

"When I graduate from high school that'll probably be it for me. I'll probably work as a lumberjack. Working in the bush is all a man can ask for."

Not averse to hard work, I didn't mind shoveling out deep snowdrifts and the heaps plowed across driveways during long winter months seeing upwards of two hundred inches of snow, sometimes reaching three hundred inches. After a January storm, snowdrifts topping garages required clearing driveways of ten-foot heaps of snow after the plow made its rounds.

She never once revealed to anyone the ignominious drubbing I'd been dealt by the hands of the farm lad, nor did she ever intimate to me she'd divulge the details if I somehow failed to please her.

"I like you just the way you are," she said holding both my hands when I brought it up.

Our unnatural quiet in each other's presence soon became obvious to the gang. Aldo first noticed. Once he realized our studied aloofness, he displayed his vast rack of teeth in an approving smile while clucking like a hen.

"It's about time, boy. It's called "amore." It lights up the whole world and makes a man feel ten feet tall." Aldo himself had not yet experienced amore.

Hicks's opinion of the whole affair was less favorable.

"What happened at that bible camp? Did you and Rotten Mugga fall in love? It looks like you're becoming a real girl suck."

The lame admonition to Hicks to grow up failed. A good little Sunday school boy exhorting the neighborhood bully to be nice could have done better. Hicks hooted raucously and teased me some more.

Actually I did not mind the teasing and made no further attempt to reprove Hicks and the others. For I wallowed in a dream world, happily in love with Abby. "Puppy love" my dad called it. "You'll get over it soon enough," he told me, although I hadn't even mentioned anything to him. The mawkish, moonstruck expression on my face told him everything.

Abby handled her teasing well. She laughed at her gossipy friends when discussing the subject of her boyfriend. She decided to settle matter with her friends, leaving nothing to rumor. Her birthday party would be the occasion for straightening everyone out.

After the sandwiches and cake she served the ice cream herself. My substantially larger serving did not escape notice by anyone. No one protested but rather nudges and winks were exchanged. Aldo cleared his throat audibly.

This breach of decorum by her daughter did not evade Abby's mother.

"Shame on you, Abby. You must learn to be fair to everyone," her mother said while doling out extra portions of ice cream to the rest of the kids as Abby reached over to help herself to some of mine.

"Paulie and Abby, Paulie and Abby," the kids chimed in chorus.

I glowed inwardly. I smiled inanely, certain my chums were envious of me, pleased to be the center of attention along with Abby.

"Paulie, you look just like a happy Halloween pumpkin. Grab a black cape, a couple of cornstalks and put on some straw trousers and you'll be ready to go out on a date," Hicks said.

A month after the party my dream world crashed. The Tulppos were moving to downstate Flint, where Abby's father accepted a job in an automobile plant. His experience as a capable machinist in the Calumet and Hecla Mining Company repair shop provided an excellent fit for his new well-paying job. As with Shirley, another joyous but tearful festivity at the Emmaus Hall took place. Abby and I both cried at the evening's end but it didn't bother either of us. Other kids wept as well.

"Paulie's my dearest friend and I'm going to miss him very much," Abby lamented to her parents before they left.

"You'll be facing many new challenges and finding new friends in Flint. You must keep your mind on your studies," Abby's mother gently advised her. "I'm sure Paulie will do the same."

The next morning the Tulppos left for Flint with their only child. Before they drove away Abby and I hugged each other for a long moment. Kissing her for the first time ever, I planted a loud baby smack on her cheek. She returned my kiss but hers didn't make any noise. Previously, our intimacy did not extend beyond an occasional holding of hands.

We exchanged a series of letters following a brief, homesick note from Abby after the Tulppos got situated in Flint. My letters, at least initially, were windy and hyper-inflated. My vocabulary for too long limited to playground chat, I had to impress her. I strove to become a man of big words, the bigger the better. I'd gleaned some good ones from the sagas and from Zoroaster. And I'd heard some downstate college boy at the ice rink shack giving his hometown buddies a big snow job about "the psychoanalysis."

"A libidinous fixation can be sublimated toward a loftier aim. Too many elect to dwell in a primordial swamp of self-inhibiting fantasy," he told his chums, after which he attempted to elaborate on these profundities in layman's terms while I listened intently. He said something about "unfulfilled sexual desires."

I was duly impressed.

Groping tirelessly to find the right words I spent countless hours penning my first letter: "From the rollicking escapades we shared as children, from a mutually happy adolescence to a kindred bonding of our souls, to an ultimate realization we might together aspire unto the unfathomable joy which corporeal being has to offer, at the end of the day I remain confident we will once again amble side by side in the sunshine, nevermore to part," I'd gushed.

Abby's letters were cheerful but her steady-minded missives were not what I'd hoped for. She always wished me well. Although very glad to hear from her how well the girls' volleyball team on which she played performed, I'd expected more. Lacking were soaring passages of reciprocation of the love I'd so grandly expressed to her. Maybe she thought I was too young, being six months younger than her. "Puppy love" my dad had called it—it had to be more than that—phooey on him.

I brooded over this while I continued to write to her in a lofty vein. I did not bring up the subject of our age difference. My pride prevented me from doing that. Anyway she most likely would have mentioned this before. Steady-mindedness, that's all I got from her. Yet wasn't steadiness of course in life what Abby had always been about? Always even-tempered and cheerful despite her mischievous proclivities as a younger girl but never once a scatterbrain? She'd always been quietly studious and intelligent.

It took time for this realization to sink in, and with time, my letters became more prosaic and our exchanges dwindled until after three years, our correspondence stopped altogether. I tried without avail to forget her; that would have been impossible.

From this experience, I gathered a new strength. I resolved I'd never allow any infatuation, however involved and consuming of my emotional faculties, to ultimately dominate my life. This would serve me well, regardless of how I'd otherwise progress. There would be setbacks.

Done with the Centennial School, I opted for an engineering curriculum at the Calumet High School rather than history or literature, where my first interests resided. Michigan Tech, a first-rate engineering college only fifteen miles from home, pragmatically dictated this choice. Hicks also opted for an engineering curriculum with emphasis on chemistry and physics. He intended to pursue a degree in chemistry at Michigan Tech following high school graduation. Aldo chose a course in academics. Our high school years went by smoothly with some notable highlights.

The three of us had nearly completed our junior year of high school. Just one year to go. And Abby had just completed high school in Flint, having graduated as valedictorian of a sizable class of some one hundred seventy students. She planned to major in philosophy at a downstate university.

High school sports? Forget it. We kept busy on the sandlots with our improvised football teams. During the winter the three of us played for the Centennial Heights Junior Huskies coached by Jake Bloomdahl, Gladys Bloomdahl's husband. We weren't bad either, taking two championships in a league composed of teams from six neighboring towns.

Aldo, Hicks and I instead enrolled in the high school ROTC program. Two of our instructors were World War II vets, one of whom had fought in the Battle of the Bulge while another had seen action in the Pacific at New Guinea and Tarawa.

These guys didn't care two cents about spit and polish or whether your neckties were knotted properly. Outfitted in olive drab uniforms we made for a sorry spectacle as we stood in formation wearing our piss-cutter private-first-class hats and our baggy trousers. Only during the annual ROTC parade everyone had to be spic-and-span.

"Maki, did you shine your shoes?" Piggy, one of our instructors, asked me as we stood in formation. Tall in persona but not in height, the five-feet four-inch Sgt. Engstrom had seen action in the Bulge. He'd been affectionately dubbed "Piggy" by cadets in the program,

"Yes sir," I replied.

"Maki shined his shoes with the cover on the can. He looks like he just took a walk through the chicken coop," Sergeant Engstrom announced loudly to the entire troupe.

I didn't receive any demerits. Sergeant Engstrom mainly cared whether we learned how to shoot straight. We got in a lot of practice firing twenty-two caliber target rifles at the Calumet Armory where we became decent marksmen. Hicks became a member of the ROTC rifle team that fared well in national competition. The team placed third in one of the matches and within the top ten in several others.

Then there were the M1 thirty-caliber rifles, the standard weapon of the US soldier in WWII, which we carried in marching formation and in close order drill. We learned to disassemble and reassemble these pieces until we could almost do it with our eyes closed. Close order drill honed to perfection required long hours of practice under our watchful instructors.

"You peckerwoods learn to shoot straight, march properly and take orders and you'll be alright," Piggy admonished. "There's no need for pomp and circumstance now. We've had enough crap from the Nazi's in Hitler's parades. And one more thing, no brownnosing."

In the three companies comprising the Calumet High School ROTC were a handful of one-ringers, a two-ringer and even a three-ringer. According to Hicks, a one-ringer tried to get his schnozzle up Piggy's grommet only once. Regular guys who avoided toadying couldn't stomach brownnosers.

"You can count the brown rings on his nose," Hicks said of a toady.

Two-ringers were insufferable and three-ringers ostracized. Piggy detested these apple polishers as much as we did.

Every spring the ROTC participated in a Memorial Day parade just before the school year ended. The three of us decided to skip the parade. We would be spectators instead.

Down the road the Calumet High School ROTC came, marching out the armory up Red Jacket Road to Fifth Street in Calumet. We stood in front of the Parkside Restaurant jeering as the platoons gravely marched by to the resounding beat of a big bass drum, with horns blowing and the smaller parade drums rattling in a frenzied accompaniment. The resounding beat of the drums and blare of the trumpets augmented a bully scene, which made the unrecognized caught up in the loud, harmonious din feel important and heroic. I almost wished I'd joined the march.

"Look at those brownnosers," we hollered as a couple of the toadies aloofly marched by us.

Our dues had to be paid. We'd completely overlooked the fact that Piggy and the other instructors had taken muster before the parade began. Our names along with two others were found absent. The other two had legitimate excuses for their absence. And much to their credit the toadies did not squeal on us. We were singled out and ordered to get into uniform the very next morning. This time our uniforms were pressed, ties properly knotted, shoes spit-shined, our large brass belt buckles polished to a high degree of luster and our piss-cutter hats cocked at the correct angle.

We would have a parade of our own following the exact same route, at least to start with. This time there were no rolling drums to stir up lofty sentiments, only Piggy calling cadence. Bystanders watched and smiled as we marched on the sidewalk in single file up Fifth Street during the morning rush hour. We heard hoots and hollers from some. Reaching Pine Street at its terminal end our tiny squad turned right for a lengthy trek to Calumet Avenue. Our parade route formed a big loop. After another right flank maneuver at Calumet Avenue, we marched past the best homes in town where executives of the Calumet and Hecla Mining Company resided. A final right turn onto Red Jacket Road took us back to the armory where we got started, two short blocks away for a total of two miles, twice the distance of the original march.

We hoofed to the large rink arena in the armory where we'd assembled. Floorboards covered the rink used for roller skating in the summer and fall months, and once removed, spectators enjoyed ice hockey and public skating during the winter months.

With Piggy in charge we weren't done yet. "Duck-walking" from an awkward squat position followed three sets of pushups with ten pushups per set. We stooped down, and holding our ankles, proceeded to waddle across the one-hundred-foot-wide rink. It didn't take long to run out of steam; duck-walking is a tough one. The duck-walking would have been it, but once again, as in the case of the snakes incident in Miss Kentala's classroom, Aldo and I exploded in laughter. After waddling for perhaps a dozen paces Hicks began to quack loudly. He sounded like a real duck. Piggy did not mind this and appeared to be impressed. I looked over at Hicks and it seemed the noise only came from the corners of his mouth. He'd stretched his lips widely causing creases near each corner to appear when he quacked. Laughing so hard, Aldo and I couldn't complete our duck-walk. We had to quit. Hicks successfully continued to waddle and quack to the other side of the rink.

That meant extra exercise for Aldo and me. Having sized both of us up strength-wise, Piggy determined we were perfect horses for his one hundred-thirty-pound frame. Both Aldo and I were strong. Although not as large as Aldo, I'd acquired physically fitness, my strength having derived from shoveling a lot of snow and chopping many cords of firewood. Piggy would take turns at riding both of us the length of the rink, nearly two hundred feet. Hicks stood at the finish line holding a watch.

Aldo went first. I joined Hicks at the finish line to get a better view. Little five-feet four-inch Piggy jumped on his back, got his arms around Aldo's neck and his short legs secured in his grasp. Down the rink the thoroughbred Aldo galloped. He made it look easy and even picked up his pace coming down the home stretch. He even looked like a blue-ribbon winner as he approached the finish line while smiling his patented broad grin and displaying his vast rack of large, white horsey teeth.

I thought my knees would buckle but I managed a spirited burst of energy. At the halfway mark, I increased my speed as I ran toward the finish line. I made it in good time.

Hicks kept time of both runs. Aldo beat me by one second.

"OK, boys," Piggy said when we were done. "Good job. But next year make sure you make the parade or what you did today will be like toddlers playing in the sandbox," he reminded, after which he regarded us as though nothing had happened. We were given a clean slate.

"Get those stinking uniforms cleaned up and I'll see you at the next drill," he simply told us.

"Hey, Ma Maki, how would you like to dance with me?" This came from Hicks. Once again we were occupied in an escapade, this one posing more serious risk than a backfired scheme involving snakes or missing an ROTC parade. Proceedings began in late August, shortly before the start of our senior year. A mild, pleasant breeze wafting during a warm sunny summer afternoon created perfect conditions for a party. The party, however, would be held indoors. No ice cream or soda pop would be served at this one.

As teenagers neither Hicks nor I had rarely, if ever, had sampled an alcoholic beverage. At a very early age I'd had some beer on but one occasion. Hicks had never consumed a single beer or glass of wine. Aldo enjoyed the luxury of having a small glass of wine with the Vella evening meal, his small libation approved of and even encouraged by both his parents.

We'd come into possession of a large bottle of wine. "Dago Red" is a dry but mellow home-vintnered red wine, which Mr. Vella prided himself in making. Every fall he put up a new batch. He had his merlot and zinfandel grapes shipped by a friend in Chicago who'd carefully selected the choicest grapes from an open-air market on Halsted Street. Each year he produced at least twenty gallons of highly praised wine, which he generously shared with friends.

We procured the wine without difficulty. The three of us were pitching horseshoes in the backyard of the Vella home, a favorite spot for friendly neighborhood competition. Mr. Vella had not taken shortcuts: the posts were boxed in at regulation distance and he'd even ordered special clay to lay the pits—a clay widely used in professional tournaments. Most of all, the imbibing adults looked ahead to a glass or two of his excellent Dago Red, which he offered up with cheese and nutritious bread baked by Mrs. Vella.

Aldo's parents and his sister had gone shopping and had been invited afterward to a dinner by friends in Houghton. They'd be gone for several hours.

"What's this Dago Red stuff I hear the dads and grandpas talk about?" Hicks asked. "They say it's as good a wine as they've ever tasted."

"My dad knows his wine," Aldo replied. "He nurses it like a baby and makes sure his barrels and bottles are sterilized before he starts—you'll never see any scum at the bottom of the bottle you'll see in an amateur's homemade wine."

We were getting an education.

"My dad racks his wine, which means siphoning it from one barrel to another after it's fermented until it's perfectly clear of lees. That's the scum. No sugar or water added to his wine either, just natural fermentation. Sometimes I help my dad crush the grapes."

"I wonder what it tastes like," I asked. "Your dad's friends say it's the best ever."

"Well maybe when you're older you can come over and we'll try some. My dad won't object so long as it's OK with your parents."

Temptation had got the best of me. "How about trying some right now?"

"I'm all for that," Hicks said.

"No, we'd better not," Aldo said. "It wouldn't be a smart thing to do."

Neither Hicks nor I could understand why our worldly-wise friend was being such a square. We'd listened to a lecture and now we were ready to sample the wine.

"Come on, Magooch," Hicks prodded, "One little taste isn't going to hurt anyone."

"Yeah, just one little taste," I added.

"All right, one sample is what you guys are going to get and that's it," Aldo said reluctantly. "Let's go down to the basement."

Aldo uncorked what had to be at least a five-liter jug of wine which he claimed had been aging for nearly two years. He poured some into cups and handed them to us. He poured some for himself.

"OK, boys, bottoms up."

I'd never tasted anything so vile in my life but I bravely didn't spit any out; I'd anticipated ambrosial nectar. I grimaced as I forced the dry astringent liquid down my unwilling gullet.

Hicks didn't mind it all. "This stuff is pretty good. You shouldn't be making faces, Paulie. How about some more, Magooch? Just one more half cup."

His resolve weakened, Aldo obliged us. This time I didn't chug it down all at once. I didn't mind the dryness at all. My taste buds burst in a glory of complex, exotic flavors as I swirled some wine about in my mouth before swallowing it. Shortly after I began to experience a most pleasant glow, as did Aldo and Hicks.

Aldo faced a dilemma. Believing his father would not notice the slight dilution, he'd intended to replace the small volume lost by the first sampling with water. Now after a third sample almost a quart of the wine had vanished. Water would not do the trick. Only one obstacle blocked our path to more enjoyment: casting caution to the winds, one jug of wine would not be missed.

"OK boys, were going to have a party," he announced. "And were going to do it right. You guys wait right here while I go upstairs."

He came back with a large shopping bag containing a plump wheel of premium Camembert cheese and a fresh loaf of bread his mother had recently baked.

"There's plenty of room for the wine in the bag. What do you say we party at the shack near Big Rock?" Aldo suggested.

"That would be a great place but suppose some of the big guys show up. I don't think we should share anything we've got with anyone else. This should only be our feast." Hicks replied, evincing a foolproof logic. Aldo and I became of the same accord.

"I know just the spot. The old barn behind our house is hardly ever used and we can sneak in through the back door without anyone seeing us. No one will even know we're there," I said.

Mainly used for stowing a few miscellaneous items, the barn had previously housed teams of horses. The uncluttered floor space contained several folding chairs and a picnic table, a perfect setup for our party. At one end an assortment of weights, dumbbells and barbells, which my dad used after he quit his job as a lumberjack, lay safely out of the way—he followed a strict regimen of physical conditioning that included snowshoeing and long hikes. My dad had a new garage built for his 1936 Dodge.

The festivities began. Safely ensconced in the barn and seated around the table, we imbibed the wine, munched the bread and put away liberal scads of the Camembert cheese, which we washed down with more wine.

"Let's light them up, guys," Aldo said. He produced three fine Cuban cigars he'd filched from his father's cache. They were Cohiba robustos. Three Hoyo de Monterey coronas lie in reserve. No problems getting the Cubans; the trade embargo on Cuba wouldn't kick in until several years later.

We found the cigars most agreeable. Not being strangers to tobacco, we'd chewed plug tobacco and smoked drug store cigars at the shack at Big Rock. Sometimes we lit up a few in a Cedar Bush thicket.

The spree continued well into the afternoon. The contents of the jug had diminished appreciably. Our inhibitions having vanished completely we were feeling great.

I then became maudlin. "I miss Abby so much," I lamented to Aldo and Hicks. "What if she's found someone else?" I began to sing: *"Wondering, wondering, if you're wondering too,"* I wailed the lyrics of a current hillbilly hit in a loud quavering voice.

"Paulie, you and Abby ought to get married," Hicks kept saying.

"I'm going to give you guys some Ezio Pinza, some real high-classed opera," Aldo announced, which he proceeded to do. He didn't sound that bad either.

Taking stage on the center of the floor, his arms outspread imploringly and his head tilted back, he sang an aria in Italian from *La Traviata* in a pleasing tenor voice. His mustache had become more noticeable.

The noise we created had increased by decibels. We did not hear my dad drive up after returning home from work. Neither did we notice him looking in through a window at the proceedings in his barn. He did not come in at once but instead went into the house.

"Our son is carousing in the barn with his buddies. We'd better go take a look," he told my mother. "Listen to that singing."

"It sounds pretty good," my mom replied. Aldo had just hit a soaring passage.

Hicks staggered about on the floor. Wearing a lopsided grin, he held a lighted Hoyo, his jaw slack. A purplish spittle oozed from the corners of his mouth. That's when he invited my mother to dance.

From where I slouched in my chair I held up the nearly exhausted jug. Less than a pint of the wine remained. "What's up dad, how about a drink," I said.

Only Aldo apprehended the gravity of the situation. Bent over, his head cradled between both hands, he repeatedly muttered "Mea culpa, mea culpa."

I began to feel woozy. I arose from my stoop, and seized with a fit of nausea, violently heaved up half-digested chunks of bread and cheese propelled by a bilious torrent of wine. I puked squarely on my mother's shoes.

There would be no dancing.

After a fitful night of nausea and weird dreams I awoke the next morning with a splitting headache. I'd discovered a hangover. Other than enduring the hangover nothing happened. My parents acted as though nothing had happened until they asked me into the living room a day later. Their mood somber, I dreaded the worst.

"Sit down, Paul," my dad said. I shuffled uncomfortably on the couch.

"I was young once myself and did some things I regretted later," he began. "Stuff like stealing a neighbor's apples and then lying about it after I got caught. And I got some hell for it. I didn't think anyone saw me but it seems like there's a bird watching in every bush. In this case a nosy neighbor lady across the street kept herself busy just waiting for kids to cause trouble. I even had some home brews one time but didn't get caught at that. I only got a wicked hangover like you.

"I don't think I have to remind you of what you and your friends did. You took what didn't belong to you. At least you didn't have a car to drive around town drunk. That would have been dangerous and stupid."

My mom interjected, "You've got a bright future ahead of you, Paul, and we're here to support you in any way we can. We only want the best for you."

"Now here's what we're going to do," my dad continued, "I've talked things over with the Vellas and Al and Irene Huhta as well. Mr. Vella has refused payment from us for the wine and the cheese, not to mention the bread and the cigars. Those were Cuban cigars, Habanas, no slouch grocery store pack-of-six cigars you can buy for two bits. But we're going to make things right with him anyway. And that's where you come in. I can't speak for Hicks but Mr. Huhta told me Hicks will fit right in.

"That means work. The Vellas have had a problem with a leaky drain pipe for some time that's starting to stink. It's getting clogged up and needs replacing. It's buried four feet underground and runs for thirty feet from their house before it meets the main. You're going to do the digging. And Al Huhta assured me Hicks will be helping you."

Aldo and Hicks had both received lectures from their parents in a same vein. And after matters were sorted out we three culprits were found equally guilty even though Hicks and I instigated the affair. "That's it, Paulie. If you've got anything to say we can talk about it later."

Magooch did not fare well. He'd received no leniency from his father. "You're going to start digging before Paulie and Hicks come and to make up for it you can work a bit longer after they've gone home."

Our senior year in high school had just begun. We cleared the drain pipe within a week working an hour or two after school let out and nearly a full shift on Saturday. The entire thirty feet. The seepages and the foul odor increased as we dug. Progress slowed when we hit the pipe. There we had to fill buckets to muck out the soupy putrefied soil, which we carted off to a landfill near the bulrush swamp. A large two-wheel cart served this purpose.

"If you don't mind limburger cheese you won't mind the stink," Aldo said as we approached pay dirt. Despite the demands of our task an air of jocularity prevailed.

"Paulie, it looks like you finally found your niche in life. How does it go, 'A weak mind but a strong back'," Hicks jested, "or maybe it's the other way around."

"Who put dat pipe dere? Huhta put dat pipe dere," I responded. If said properly this bit of nonsense rolled nicely off the tongue, almost alliteratively. Hicks had been mercilessly teased with this waggery as had many others with his surname. When addressed to him he'd stomp the earth in frustration. He never quite got used to hearing it. And now we were talking about a real pipe.

"You're making my English blood boil. A weak mind but a strong back," he reiterated to me. Hicks's grandparents on both sides of his family had emigrated from Finland as had my own.

"Huhta put dat pipe dere," I repeated.

"Look, you English bum, keep that shovel working."

Mr. Vella came out to check on our progress.

"We're having a great time, papa. I never thought digging a ditch could be so much fun," Aldo quipped.

"That's good, sonny boy, I might find some more for you to dig once you're done here."

Filling the trench after replacing the drain pipe and the putrefied soil took little time. Back to school, during our senior year we found plenty of time in addition to our studies to play sandlot football during the fall and play hockey, ski and snowshoe throughout the winter months. The arrival of spring meant fishing the small creeks behind Heights and playing softball after the snow melted and the grounds dried.

Graduation day from the Calumet High School finally arrived. Hicks graduated as valedictorian of our class of one hundred and thirty-eight students. I finished third from the top and Aldo found himself well within the top quarter of the class. Our futures could not have shone brighter.

But the hangover would not be the last.

CHAPTER 4

Fulfillment

"Go ahead, Paulie, this summer is yours. It may be the last one you have before you get caught up in the rat race," my father encouraged. "That's a luxury I never had."

I needed no further encouragement. Aldo and Hicks were both afforded the same self-indulgence by their parents. Neither had to beg. Why go to work at some crummy job? Let's have some fun. We'd be going to college in the fall.

Following graduation the three of us did nothing but fool around for two weeks. With so much free time, I could handle only so much fishing the creeks or hanging out at the shack near Big Rock. Aldo and Hicks were likewise becoming bored.

Getting on everyone's nerves, my parents sent me to my Uncle George Koskinen's farm for strawberry picking. George owned a small summer cottage, fully wired and plumbed, on one of his forties where I could stay free of charge. He said it would be OK to bring Aldo and Hicks along as he needed extra help. They needed little convincing

The prime strawberry season in the Keweenaw lasts for about three weeks, starting near the last week of June, sometimes a little earlier. That's when pickers are in the greatest demand by the growers. High school kids take full advantage of this opportunity to earn a few extra bucks.

Uncle George, a strawberry grower in Keweenaw Bay and my mom's older brother, owned an eighty-acre plot and two forty-acre plots. That's a lot of acreage for growing strawberries. Almost half of the plots were ready for harvesting while the rest were sown with yearling plants to augment or supplant the next summer's yield. Some of the acreage remained fallow.

Most pickers had their own transportation and drove to his fields from nearby farming communities or neighboring towns. Early each day my uncle drove those lacking transportation to the fields in his pickup truck. We also had transportation of our own. Aldo's parents bought him a 1938 Ford, still in good running condition, as a graduation gift for which they payed only ninety dollars. The tires had a lot of mileage left and the engine didn't burn much oil. Keweenaw Bay is about forty miles from our homes in Centennial Heights. The eighty-mile round-trip drive every day would have been impractical so staying at Uncle George's cottage saved us and the car wear and tear. This also meant a lot of free time.

Picking started at sunrise and finished in the early afternoon, which is the premium time for harvesting. Spoilage had to be avoided. Berries just coming into their early ripening stage are the most salable and are even quite palatable when eaten right away. They get tastier yet after sitting out for a day or two.

We had a place to stay free of charge, got six cents for every quart of berries we picked and had Aldo's car to get around. We only had to buy our own grub. Even on an average day in the field picking eighty quarts of super delicious Robinson or Jersey Belle strawberries, solid red throughout and sweet, was not an unachievable goal for a steady picker. We cultivated yearling sets in the afternoon. Getting up at five-thirty in the morning gave us enough time for breakfast before the picking began. Once started, we picked straight through until one o'clock. After a quick lunch we hoed the new plants for a couple hours. During evenings we played softball and swam in the frigid waters of Lake Superior in the shallows of Keweenaw Bay or fished for speckled trout, or "brookies" as we call them, in the nearby Kelsey Creek.

We made new acquaintances. Just ahead of Hicks in the next row a teenage girl, bent over and intense on her business, gathered berries in earnest. Hicks found her shapely butt a perfect a target—he let fly with a large over-ripe Jersey Belle. His bull's-eye hit splattered on the left cheek of her buttocks, leaving a juicy red splotch on her white shorts. A strawberry war ensued. Aldo, Hicks and I ganged up on the victim and several of her girlfriends. The battle lasted until Uncle George came along and ended the fun. Some claimed he had at least a foot-long face from hairline to chin. An otherwise kindly and soft-spoken man, Uncle George would indicate displeasure when needed by making his long face even longer, just by dropping his jaw an inch. He lowered his chin.

Friendships with the girls ensued, especially between Hicks and the girl he'd beaned on her gluteus maximus. Rita St. Cloud, known to her friends as "Bugsy," was an intense, strikingly beautiful young woman. Most of her friends were from L'Anse and Baraga, towns a few short miles away from Uncle George's farm. Like Marie Loonsfoot, a lot of them including Rita herself claimed Native American ancestry.

Bugsy and her friends loved to play softball—the Zeba Bearwalkers on whose team they played won their league's championship by defeating the Pelkie Cows in a thrilling eight-inning overtime contest the previous summer. Other teams in the league included the Elo Sowbellies and the North End Bouncers. The Bouncers were sponsored by a neighborhood tavern in Calumet noted for its convivial atmosphere and for its generosity in supporting worthy youth causes. The Cows and the Sowbellies teams comprised sturdy farm girls living in the Sturgeon River Valley.

Among the strawberry pickers were members of the Pelkie and Elo teams.

"The Cows? The Sowbellies? Why did you pick such unflattering names?" I asked one of the Cows.

"We didn't. We didn't like the names, at least at first. But that's the way it had to be our smart managers said. We could have called ourselves something cute like the "Pelkie Pixies" but I don't think we'd be the draw we are today."

"I don't understand. What girl wants to be called a cow or a sowbelly?"

"The attendance got bigger at our games just because of our names and so did the money coming in. Our fans got to love the names and our opponents find it very easy to "moo" us. 'Hey, Cows, give us some milk.' The Sowbellies or "oinkers" from Elo hear it a lot worse than we do at their road games. And you can guess what our mascots are. You can see them at our home games."

"So you can take the ribbing. How about the money coming in?"

"We were able to double the ticket price from a quarter to fifty cents. More people coming to watch us means more colorful uniforms and we get to look ahead for a milkshake."

"More colorful uniforms or a milkshake for being called a cow?"

"Believe it or not our increased exposure has helped to land scholarships for some of the girls. That works OK for us."

With picking done and our afternoon chores completed, we drove to a field in Baraga to play softball. The Keweenaw summer evenings are long with daylight lasting almost to ten PM. A goodly number of pickers representing members of the Cows, Sowbellies and the

Bearwalkers, and other friends we made on the strawberry fields, showed up to play ball. Some non-picker guys from L'Anse and Baraga were also present, and altogether there were easily enough players for two softball teams. To minimize partiality sides were chosen by "grabbing the bat." First one of the elected captains tossed a vertically held bat to his opponent, obliged to make a single-handed grab near its downward-facing business end. Passing the bat back and forth, grip over grip, the one with the "better grab" got first pick of the players. This meant a full-hand grip closest to the top of the handle, which left no room for his opponent to make another complete grip. Seldom did he three of us get to play on the same team. A refreshing swim in Keweenaw Bay usually followed the competitions.

Romance appeared to be in the offing for Hicks and Bugsy. Hicks found less time for Aldo and me during the evenings when he devoted his attention to Bugsy. The couple made no attempt to conceal their affection for each other, whether on the softball field or at the beach in Keweenaw Bay. When it came to work, however, both were serious and took little notice of each other's presence. Long-faced Uncle George would not have stood for such nonsense anyway when picking or hoeing plants had to be done.

We got invited to a dance in Zeba by our new friends. Most attendees were teenagers of Native American extraction. We got some frosty looks from strangers as we entered the large dance hall, but misgivings soon vanished when our fellow pickers and some of the guys told of friendships made at the strawberry farm and on the softball diamond.

Our new friends made Aldo an honorary chief, naming him "Chief Laughing Whitefish." Outfitted in ceremonial garb featuring a magnificent, fully-feathered head dress, he inspired an image of a real chief despite his youth. Hicks and I were honored as braves and festooned with head bands to which several large eagle feathers were attached. I became Brave Grunting Bear and Hicks, Brave Stinking Badger

A ceremonial dance initiated the proceedings. We would dance barefoot. Before we started the girls painted our toenails bright red with fingernail polish. Chief Laughing Whitefish got special treatment. His large toenails were first painted white and then accentuated with thin red stripes in the shape of arrows. Round and round the floor we tramped, whooping and grunting as we progressed in a large circle. By appointment of our hosts, Chief Laughing Whitefish led the long string of dancers while Braves Stinking Badger and Grunting Bear took up the rear position.

After this ritual dance everyone settled into slow dancing to the music of schmaltzy songs of the early 1950s. Aldo fit in well, just as he must have growing up with his candy store chums in New York. His big, white horsey teeth were on full display and his lips formed a crafty smile as he skimmed across the floor with one of the Bearwalker girls. Hicks and I both lacked dancing experience and it took all we had to fake the maneuvers. We tried to mimic Aldo but without much success, and had a hard time mastering the two-step.

Hicks shuffled with his partner Bugsy from side to side, shifting his weight from one foot to the other. She remained his only partner throughout the entire evening. When other guys tried to cut in, she promptly refused them. It may have been Hicks's inept dancing that encouraged them to try to cut in in the first place. Bugsy didn't mind his lack of prowess and she appeared happy.

Hicks and Bugsy remained on the dance floor when the refrains of a slow number ended. They stood in a close embrace, still shuffling from side to side absorbed in conversation. They kept right on going the same way until the music started again.

"I couldn't get off the floor just then so we continued to dance without the music. Let me just say I was compromised," he replied when I later asked him what they were doing out there. "We had to stay close."

I did not press the issue any further.

The season neared its end, the picking almost completed and the cultivation of the yearling sets done.

"Here are the keys," Aldo said handing them to Hicks. "You and Bugsy deserve an evening to yourselves."

"Are you sure? How about you and Paulie?"

"Don't worry about us. Go out and have some fun.

"They're not a bad looking couple," Aldo said after Hicks drove off.

They indeed made a good-looking pair with Bugsy's noble features and intense expression providing a winsome contrast to Hicks's plain but strong and rather flat pug-nosed face.

"How about you, Chief Laughing Whitefish?" I asked.

"There's plenty of time for romance. I'm going to spread myself thin and give all the girls a break."

Brave Stinking Badger returned late. Aldo and I were fast asleep when he got back at three o'clock in the morning. Not wasting any time at breakfast we of course had to pry into his adventure. Although Hicks had less than three hours of sleep he appeared refreshed.

"You're looking at a man in love," he smugly said. "And I'm fully confident Rita's in love with me."

"So now it's Rita. What happened to Bugsy?" I pried. Aldo pursed his lips and affixed Hicks in a serious gaze. "Don't hold anything back from me, chum," his expression implied. We both expected him to divulge the details of his outing with Bugsy.

"Why don't you henceforth refer to me as Phillip, or better yet, just plain Phil will do for you. Rita promises the worst for anyone calling me Hicks," he replied with a grin.

"Seven whole hours. Must have been quite some date," Aldo teased.

"I'd tell you more but you guys are already jealous enough," Hicks smugly concluded. "Some other time maybe."

The season ended. We were each one hundred dollars wealthier when we left a satisfied Uncle George and his strawberry farm. "Great work, guys, thanks a lot for the help," he said before we drove off.

Hicks claimed his bloomers in Keweenaw Bay. Claiming bloomers is a feat to which most young men in Heights and elsewhere aspire to this very day. This means a seduction. "Conquering bloomers," is how some guys put it. Such an event is more significant to the claimant than bagging a ten-point buck. The standard mode of operation for a guy in the early 1950s involved a drive around town in search of a young lady he perhaps knew willing to go for a ride and ultimately park on some remote spot. Methods have perhaps become more sophisticated since then. If successful in his endeavor, the young woman would be divested of her drawers. Her bloomers would then be knotted to a branch of a tree at the site of his triumph for his buddies to admire the next day. Perch's famed adventure with Fatso in the blueberry patch had become widely heralded amongst the young bucks in Heights, to which most aspired to emulate. Sometimes a pair of a mother's bloomers turned up missing if one failed in his quest, and if his fraud exposed, the braggart acquired a brand: "Junior Drawers" would stick for a long time. Definitely not a Junior Drawers, Hicks had proof positive of his achievement and did not find it necessary to boast. The old 1938 Ford came to be known as the "Impregnatorium."

"How's it going, pops," Aldo greeted him six weeks after the strawberry season ended. For Phillip Huhta's union with Rita St. Cloud would be blessed with a child.

Hicks received the news of his impending paternity on one of his frequent dates with Rita in L'Anse. He had no car of his own but Aldo let him use his. He made an arrangement with Hicks whereby he had only to keep the gas tank full and pay for any oil changes. At only twenty-three cents a gallon it worked well for both. Hicks offered to pay extra but Aldo generously turned him down.

"If the car ever needs some repair you can help me then," Aldo said.

When Rita presented him the news Hicks did not panic as many seventeen-year olds would have. He accepted the revelation with equanimity.

"Good," he said when Rita related her predicament.

Rita added, "It is yours and the first thing you ought to know is there never has been anyone else."

Neither Aldo nor I pressed him for details. We only wished him the best of luck as he'd promised Rita he'd marry her if she would have him. She readily agreed.

"I need not search further," Hicks ventured, "I've attained fulfillment."

Taken aback, silent, Major Maurice St. Cloud, the owner of a prospering trucking firm in L'Anse and an active member of a council promoting tribal affairs of the Ojibwa Reservation in Keweenaw Bay, sternly gazed at the short young man standing erectly before him. St. Cloud had attained the rank of an army major during World War II.

"Fulfillment," he bellowed. "Just exactly what is that supposed to mean. If it means what I think it means you've got a lot of explaining to do, buddy."

Hicks did not flinch. "I could not desire a more splendid creature than heaven has provided me. I'm going to make Rita happy. I want to marry her."

The major could not believe his ears. No one had ever spoken to him this way before. As a council member, he'd heard too many lame promises from young men in similar predicaments and had seen too many shotgun marriages go awry. Yet despite his strong misgivings he perceived a sincerity in the lad standing before him. Besides he secretly admired his bravado. Keeping his fingers crossed, he finally gave his consent and permitted his pregnant sixteen-year-old daughter to marry.

"What do you see in this kid?" Major St. Cloud asked his daughter. "He's got a face like a pancake and if wasn't for his pug nose you'd not be able to tell the difference."

"Daddy, you can't judge a book by its cover. Phillip is highly intelligent and he cares for me a lot."

Rita's finely chiseled, striking features contrasted starkly with Hicks's flat, homely face. Her shoulder-length black hair complemented her beauty; his unruly mud-colored thatch did little to enhance his appearance. As to height, Hicks stood an inch shorter. They shared one feature in common: the eyes. Rita's dark eyes were lustrous and intelligent of expression; Hicks's clear blue eyes were likewise intelligent.

Confusing matters concerning the nature of the wedding ceremony were harmoniously sorted out. The St. Clouds were devout Catholics while the Huhtas were Apostolic Lutherans. After some amicable give and take, both parties agreed a justice of the peace in L'Anse would officiate the nuptials.

The ceremony took place in the justice's private chambers. In attendance besides the couple's parents were Aldo, myself and several of Rita's Bearwalker friends.

"You've had fottuto of the very best kind," Aldo counseled the groom. "Amore before and amore after."

After the vows were exchanged the wedding party enjoyed a delicious whitefish dinner at the St. Clouds' residence. The newlyweds then repaired to Major St. Cloud's hunting camp in the Huron Mountains for a brief honeymoon.

Hicks in time would also make Major Maurice St. Cloud happy.

CHAPTER 5

Jealousy

We followed separate paths. Aldo enrolled as a history major at the Northern Michigan University in Marquette, Michigan. "Northern" as the university is commonly called is a liberal arts school. I'd been accepted and enrolled in a mechanical engineering curriculum at Michigan Tech, the engineering school in Houghton.

Hicks faced a major dilemma. He'd also enrolled at "da Tech" as Michigan Tech is known by the locals. He faced the practicality of his choice with college about to start, shortly after his hasty marriage and a brief honeymoon. Housing and living expenses in addition to the costs of tuition and books cast serious doubt whether he'd be able to initiate his studies as a chemistry major. More significantly, he would soon be a father.

His parents and Maurice St. Cloud resolved the issue of housing and college tuition. With their aid, the newlyweds set up housekeeping in Houghton in an on-campus apartment unit available for married students.

"Son, you've got to make what could have been a great wrong into a right," Mr. Huhta advised Hicks. "You can count on our support. Your mom and I are not going to see your talent go to waste."

Major St. Cloud offered no such assurance. "You better do this right or I'll have your hide," he promised his son-in-law.

Aldo, Hicks and I got together during the two-week Christmas break. An unpleasant surprise awaited me.

She did not come alone. Abby arrived with her parents for the Christmas holidays. This would be their first visit since the Tulppos left for Flint four years ago. I'd not communicated with Abby for over a year, prior to which our letters had become more prosaic and infrequent until our correspondence stopped altogether. Someone else came with them.

Lucas Wagonhoffer, a tall, handsome, sandy-haired and blue-eyed young man possessed of a splendid physique accompanied Abby and her parents. Abby had not mentioned him in any of her letters. A year older than Abby and presently in his junior year, they'd met at Michigan State.

Most of the Heights Bunch attended a social gathering for the Tulppos at the Emmaus Hall. "What a fine young couple," Sylvia Bylkas exclaimed as Abby and Lucas arrived at the hall with her parents.

"My, oh my, what a handsome young man," Gladys Bloomdahl clucked to one of her friends.

"Handsome indeed," I thought as I measured from a discrete distance his six-foot, two-inch son-of a soybean-grower frame. If I'd had the power I would have had this guy vanish into thin air.

I compared myself against Wagonhoffer, stacking my attributes against his like a bull moose sizing up his opponent during the rutting season. Although three inches shorter I was broader and more muscular. In terms of looks he had me beat by a long shot, as I compared my homely round face with his disgustingly handsome poster boy features. Wagonhoffer's neatly groomed, sandy hair made my unruly thatch look like a bundle of straw. My big Adam's apple sticking out didn't help either. I grimly realized the displeasure a troll might experience being compared to an Adonis.

Why did Abby bring this guy here? I should be the one to have exclusive rights to her company. I should be the one for her. The time had come to be manly and tough.

My hands are like large clams, not too long but wide at the palms. From the back, my fingers appear long but seem much shorter when seen from the palm side up. This is due to a pronounced almost duck-like webbing at the base of my fingers. My palms are broad and thick. And because of shoveling tons of snow and chopping many cords of firewood I developed a strong grip to be administered when meeting imposters like Lucas Wagonhoffer. Some of my friends called me "Bone Crusher." Others called me an asshole if I flaunted my talent.

"I'm glad to meet you," Wagonhoffer cordially greeted me. "Same here," I lamely replied. I could not resist applying the pressure to his big basketball mitt when we shook hands. He reciprocated and our handshake immediately developed into a contest of strength. Remaining steady, neither of us winced as we both applied one last squeeze before releasing our grip. No one, I thought, appeared to notice.

The more I listened the more I hated this guy.

"So I hear you've got a pilot's license," I heard Jake Bloomdahl say.

"Yes, I fly a crop duster from time to time to service my family's soybean fields. But mostly I dust corn fields for relatives in Iowa during the summer."

"I hear you play some basketball," Jake continued.

"We were Class B runners-up in the state basketball tournament in my senior year in high school."

"How about college?"

"I play guard for the varsity team at Michigan State. We haven't been doing too badly. Right now we're seven and two for the season."

On and on it went. Not only a talented jock but this guy was modest. No one heard any braggadocious talk one might expect from a Joe College guy who appeared to have everything going for him and who might easily get away with flaunting his exploits before a captive small-town audience. I resented him even more for this. Had he been a blowhole I could have found it easy to dismiss him; Abby most likely would not have brought such a guy with her in the first place. I struggled to keep a happy face.

After the handshake we made some small talk. I brooded inwardly but I had to be a nice guy; I went so far as to invite him to join Aldo, Hicks and me for some cross-country skiing the next day. He looked ahead to the outing: "Sounds great, I'll be ready," he said.

I casually moved about the company feigning interest in everyone's affairs. "Lucas sure is a nice guy," I dissembled. They all agreed. As the evening progressed, I had an even rougher time of it. I felt like a newcomer at a formal gathering obliged to force polite words from a throat that had become parched. No one seemed to take notice of my strained efforts except Aldo.

"You're trying too hard, Paulie. Relax. Let's get some fresh air."

Stepping outside into the ten-degree clear-night-freeze helped. "There's nothing you can do about this now, Paulie," Aldo advised. "I saw the handshake and you held your ground. His hand will be as sore as yours tomorrow."

My face muscles were already sore from smiling too much.

I returned to the hall. The adults occupied Abby in conversation and would not let her go. Without barging in, I'd had no chance to engage her except for a quick hello. I studied her closely as I moped about the hall.

While by no means a beauty queen, Abby had become a very comely young woman. Her beauty resided not so much on externals but more from an intelligence shining through on her features. She moved about the company with poise, almost grave of aspect, graced with wide-set intelligent blue eyes quick to light up as she mingled in the crowd. Her light brown hair styled modestly gracefully framed her intelligent face; her smile complemented her dimpled cheeks. There were only bare traces of the warts, I noticed, that we as young rapscallions dreaded so much and which now did not in any way detract from her appearance. I found Abby to be a very pleasing and an attractive young woman.

My mind took a bizarre tack. I put the blame on Lucas for causing this. The dream I had returning from bible camp years ago popped into my head. "Any more dreams about those drapes?" Gladys Bloomdahl used to kid me. The one where I muttered about grandma's drapes. Now I noticed no pronounced looseness in the outfit Abby wore as there had been when her homespun Gold Medal dress blossomed above my stricken features in preparation for my sitting. Maybe this is what caused me to become abstracted. She'd made no attempt to disguise a fine figure but she did not wear her clothes too snugly to accentuate a shapely posterior. No more looseness, everything nice and tidy, the mystery surrounding the dream finally solved. Perhaps I knew the answer all along and just wanted to forget the whole stupid business. Grandma's drapes? Abby's loose-fitting, billowing Gold Medal dress? Good grief.

Totally abstracted over the drapes I didn't even notice Abby's approach. She looked puzzled. Why wasn't I talking? Why didn't I notice her?

"You're looking great, Abby," I finally said, snapping out of my reverie.

She replied in kind.

"Lucas certainly seems to be a fine person," I lied.

"I met Lucas six months ago. He invited me out for a movie and we've been dating ever since."

I did not pry any further. We made small talk instead.

My strained voice did not go unnoticed by Abby. “Here, try one of these,” she said, handing me a box of Luden’s Concilia cough drops.

“Got some hoarseness, they asked me to sing Christmas carols with the group. I’m not used to singing,” I dissembled some more.

We’d got started discussing college life when Faye Entdorff preempted her company. Continuing a pretense of detachment from Abby’s presence, I went about making small talk to anyone obliged to listen.

I got some temporary relief.

Two of our oldest and the most distinguished men in our community were present. These old-timers were octogenarians. Each man considered himself to be the most important citizen in town. Niilo Kaipio, at eighty-two years of age and a Republican, still busily involved himself in an auto dealership in Calumet he’d passed on to his sons, and he made sure he presided at the forefront of a group of citizens deciding civic matters in Centennial Heights. Niilo also held a substantial interest in a lumber business in Calumet. His friendly nemesis, Football’s grandfather Jacob Binoniemi, at eighty-three and a Democrat, owned a public sauna patronized by many of the townsfolk. The two could often be seen in front of Riisumaki’s store on Second Street arguing politics while wagging fingers in each other’s face.

Niilo prided himself on his mastery of English.

“I tell you now liddle bit of da Finnish culture in dis town,” he said to Lucas after telling him what a fine young man he was. “Dere’s da high ‘lass Finn and da low ‘lass Finn. You can tell by my conservation what I are,” he said while bobbing his head repeatedly in self-affirmation. “An vee gonna put arr hedds togedder an pilt pord sidewalk here in Centennial Heights.”

“Tont pelieve effry ting dis man say,” Jacob Binoniemi interrupted, “but dis time he speaks troot ven he say you fine young man. An vile you are here, I want you come my sauna wit Paulie, Aldo and Hicks. Dey sometime pad poys but mostly fine young man.”

“Both these men are bullshitters,” an authoritative woman’s voice resounded. It belonged to Old Lady Mattila (**Mutt’**-ē-lə), as the Heights Bunch called her. Adults referred to her as Mrs. Mattila. An outspoken old widow, she lived just a few doors away from the Maki household on Second Street. A good family friend and a frequent visitor at our home, she and my mom reciprocated midweek coffee sessions for as long as I could remember.

Known for her mouthwatering home-baked apple pies, she maintained a small orchard of five apple trees in her back yard she prided herself in and which became a target of raids by our gang. This didn't seem to bother her too much; she rather looked ahead to our forays into the orchard each fall and would lie skulking in wait for us to come. On one occasion she had Hicks treed while the rest of us scampered off.

Hicks started bawling. He promised her to be a good boy and not steal any more apples. She did not inform his parents.

Imposing of visage, endowed with a strong jutting chin and high cheek bones, Old Lady Mattila possessed a sharp sense of humor. If one looked at her closely a merry twinkle in her eyes could always be seen. A stern grey-haired minister, a proud person, once lectured her on the virtue of humility:

"Pride goeth before a fall. One must strive to be humble in the sight of the Lord," he officiously admonished her in a deep monotone voice.

"Are you humble?" she asked, her eyes twinkling.

Flummoxed, the minister could only mumble words of self-abasement. The effect it had on him could not have been less devastating had one asked a stuck-up cheerleader if she were cute.

"But you are a fine young man," Old Lady Mattila told Lucas.

The skiing the next day went well. While still having a difficult time warming to Lucas Wagonhoffer's presence, I again managed to put on a happy face. Aldo, Hicks, Lucas and I set out at mid-morning. Abby would spend the day with Rita. We fastened our feet onto long homemade cross-country skis, our boots retained in single straps. Rubber rings cut from an inner tube fitted under the toes and looped over the straps to the back of our heels prevented slippage. Long cane poles completed the outfit. Every so often, a skier had to knock off ice patches from the skis, formed under the heels of his boots. Icy patches caused by friction of warm, mobile boots on the cold skis. Two feet of December snow on the ground made for excellent skiing conditions. By mid-February, an average snow depth of five feet is not an uncommon sight in the wintry Keweenaw.

We started at the stone battleship erected in the field across from the old Centennial Heights School, which closed in 1941, regrettably for students then obliged to walk to the Centennial School.

I let Aldo and Hicks do most of the talking. “A rock battleship?” Lucas asked. There it stood, embedded in the earth, a forty-foot-long ship unintentionally designed to last for at least one thousand years, armed with pipes for guns. The “guns” were great for lighting firecrackers on the Fourth of July. Some of the old-timers found the ship a great spot for puffing on cigars and doting on the good old days. They can still be seen sitting there on a balmy summer day.

“Built during the 1930s by the WPA during the depression. Kept otherwise jobless guys busy. They used mine rocks to build it. Built it with poor rock. Pure copper is crushed from the richer stuff at stamp mills and then smelted into ingots,” Hicks said.

We skied west to Big Rock and from there progressed on a northerly tack along the edge of a stand of hardwoods after which we picked up the county road back of Heights. Hicks kept Lucas, who showed a genuine interest in the Keweenaw, apprised of its history as we skied.

“Copper mining has been the staple of our economy in this area since the Civil War,” Hicks informed him. “Got started by the Cornish or “Cousin Jacks” as we call them.”

“I read somewhere that some of the mine shafts are a mile deep,” Lucas said.

“We’re probably skiing over an underground shaft as we speak,” Aldo added.

“Then there’s logging, commercial fishing and a lot of small farms,” Hicks continued. “They call this place a melting pot. Settlers came here from almost every country in Europe.”

We’d made our way to Hills Creek, which crossed the county road at Jack Raudio’s farm.

“If you make it back here next spring there’s some decent speckie fishing in this creek, either up or downstream from this bridge,” Hicks said. “About a half-mile downstream from here there’s Koljonen’s Pool. It’s really great for early morning fishing or an afternoon bare-assed dip.”

The exertion of breaking new trail and some upgrade climbs produced a therapeutic effect on us, especially me. Now we were just four guys out enjoying a salubrious activity. My reservations about Lucas diminished.

Good old Magooch. I marveled at his insight to human nature. The guy had empathy for the afflicted.

"How's your hand? Old Bone Crusher here has always got to test every new jock he meets," Aldo said, attempting to dispel any misgivings Lucas might be entertaining of me. "Maybe Aldo should become a diplomat," I thought.

"Really sore at first but it feels a lot better now," Lucas replied. "I thought I might have to miss a few basketball games when I got back."

"Probably no worse than mine is now," I said. "You've got a strong mitt."

We hit the "tee" at the end of the county road and took a right turn toward Bumbletown. After a second crossing of Hills Creek we skied for another half-mile zig-zag trek before turning back. We returned through the bush, taking turns breaking a new trail, rather than retracing our original course. A tough one, we slogged our way through numerous thickets of spruce and balsam on a mostly upgrade course. Easier skiing through groves of second growth hardwood trees interspersing the firs brought scant relief.

For bearing we kept Lake Superior, almost always visible to the north, at our back. Hicks had brought a compass along just in case. Our conversation ebbed as we huffed, puffed and sweated our way back to Heights. While scarcely more than five-mile trek, the demands of the skiing through the soft snow in dense, tortuous bush made for a complete workout. A hot sauna would bring much needed relief from our exertions.

While we were skiing, Rita and Abby spent the day at her in-laws'. Rita did not know what to expect, as she'd encountered judgmental people during her pregnancy, now in its fifth month. Her not yet seventeen-year-old body already showed prominently. Would Abby be as many others had been toward her, stiffly polite and formal while not openly disdainful? Equally circumspect, Abby had little idea of the girl Hicks had married. Did they marry only out of a sense of duty?

Rita's friends were openly accepting of her plight. She had, however, encountered coarse gibes and some open hostility, mostly from punks she'd passed on sidewalks while alone.

"You had your fun, get your buggy ready to push it," a young punk shouted at her.

"Go back to the reservation, squaw," another yelled.

She held her head high ignoring these boorish louts. Deeming her tormentors too unworthy of mention, she had not related these incidents to anyone, not even to Hicks, despite the unreserved love she got from him. Her in-laws, who'd become as second parents to her, provided additional strength. Still she felt a need to open to someone and get matters off her chest. Missing her Bearwalker friends, she needed some girl-to-girl talk.

Rita's reservations vanished. Abby, while not chatty, pitched in and helped with some household chores. Sensing a kindred spirit, Rita opened to her quiet friendliness without misgivings and related her experiences with Hicks at Keweenaw Bay. She spared no details how her relationship with Hicks afterward progressed.

"Everyone thought we made a big mistake. We are both very young and we hardly knew each other at the time. Yet I sensed strength of character in Phillip, someone I could trust. We got carried away but I truly love him," Rita said.

"And his friends are great," she continued, "they've been so supportive of Phillip and me."

"You can certainly count on them. I've known Paulie, Aldo and Phillip nearly all my life. I want to be your friend too," Abby said, won over by Rita's sincerity and her obvious love for Hicks.

She clasped the girl in her arms as she began to weep.

"You must think I'm a fool," Rita said when she composed herself. She found it unnecessary to bring up the punks.

"Not at all, Rita. You are doing the right thing now and please know I will help you in any way I can."

"Abby, I'd like to be your friend too."

They conversed on their upbringings and friendships. Rita laughed heartily at Abby's stories of the sandlot football games and the box of snakes the trio of boys had presented to her and Shirley. She mentioned their nicknames but not how they'd come about.

"They called Shirley 'Football' and me 'Rotten Mugga.' I'm going to let it go at that."

"Lucas has a rival." Rita said.

"Oh, who would it be?" Abby asked, reddening slightly.

"I thought at first Paulie had a headache at your reception."

"A headache? Why do you say that?"

"He wasn't saying anything at first and that's unusual for him. But he couldn't keep his eyes off you for the whole evening."

"I must have missed it but then again everyone kept me busy."

"Then he started talking a streak and joking with everyone there. I think he was just putting on a big front."

"It looks like the guys are coming back," Abby said in reply.

We took old Jacob Binoniemi up on his offer of a sauna when we got back from skiing. Erected as an outbuilding close to his home, Jacob patterned his sauna after a duplex with one side for the men and the other for women. There were no private facilities; the men bathed communally as did the women. The entrances and the changing and steam rooms were partitioned off by a common bulkhead. Leo Nippa sauna stoves in both units fueled by wood kept beds of rocks fenced above the fireboxes blazing hot. A dash of water from a dipper tossed on the rocks would instantly flash into steam.

All the facilities in the sauna were quite convenient for the bathers except for the plumbing, which consisted of a maze of pipes and valves. The spacious changing rooms and the saunas proper were kept scrupulously clean. Clean towels and washcloths were always available. But if one wanted moderately hot water, he simply could not turn a single valve for at least two other valves had to be either opened or shut in a proper sequence. Otherwise one stood the risk of being scorched. Jacob, refusing offers of help from those with more expertise, had designed the plumbing system himself. Proud of his complicated plumbing network, others were less impressed. Jacob's tortuous complex of pipes and valves earned him the nickname "Major Hoople" after the cartoon character famous for his bungling inventions.

Jacob monitored his business through a single open window in the partition between the men and women's changing rooms, a window privy only to himself. Old Jacob could plainly see the damsels on the other side *au naturel* as he collected ten-cent sauna fares from the women and sold them nickel soft drinks. He sometimes had to add wood to the stove on the ladies' side which meant he had to pass through their entrance and changing room in order to gain access.

"Now ladies, close your eyes," he'd say on his way through.

"Don't you be looking at my tiddies," women would often respond, not always demurely, even though Jacob saw them all the time from his side of the open window.

A crawl space above the changing rooms provided enough room for small boys to maneuver. Somehow Reggie and Willie Juntunen managed access to the space on a particularly busy Saturday evening. They peered unnoticed through a small vent in the ceiling on the women's side at the proceedings below.

"You can tell how big a lady's birdie is just by looking at her bush," Reggie whispered. "The more hair and the bigger the bush, the bigger her birdie is. It's not like men where you can see everything," he instructed Willie silently. "But it's a lot different with Tracy."

Tracy Hukkasaari, a huge manatee of a woman sat comfortably, her ample buttocks spread over the bench and her thatch concealed by a large apron of fat that spilled generously onto her thighs. Clearly room for doubt existed as to the size of her birdie.

"What do you think, Willie?" Reggie asked.

"Tracy must have big pussy, hair or no hair," Willie replied.

Willie's assertion had merit: Early in her marriage, Tracy gave birth to a jumbo twelve-pound baby boy.

"The delivery went well enough," her doctor told her, "but there were complications. I had to put in thirteen stitches."

"Thirteen stitches," Tracy replied, "a potato sack only takes seven."

The boys' edifying discourse continued uninterrupted. Undetected, both lads slunk off the premises to impart their newly acquired knowledge to the rapt ears of the Heights Bunch.

This would be Lucas' first experience of bathing in a well-heated sauna. He bravely endured blast after blast of searing steam caused by Matt Roces, a middle-aged Heights man and one of Jacob's regulars who handled the dipper. Aldo, Hicks and I sat in stoic silence hoping Matt would ease up even though we'd become inured to steam over the years. Roces had to put young-buck-newcomers to test. We'd tipped Lucas off beforehand Matt would try to flush him off the top bench back into the cool changing room with his busy dipper. We didn't tell him what to expect if Matt Roces failed to do this.

"Let's get rid of that city slicker scum," Matt said, grabbing a hose tapped into icy cold water, with which he proceeded to douse Lucas.

Caught off guard, the true Spartan Lucas did not flinch but only laughed good-naturedly.

Roces bought each of us a Copper City Bottling Works cream soda for being such good sports. "This guy almost made you look like a bunch of chumps," he told the three of us. He'd kept close notice of our increasing discomfort as he tossed more water on the rocks.

"That's one experience I'll never forget," Lucas said after we'd changed into fresh clothing.

The Tulppos were invited by Armando and Celeste Vella to a dinner at their home before they left town. Hicks, Rita, myself and our parents were among others invited.

Celeste Vella had outdone herself in preparing pans of lasagna layered with ricotta and sweet sausage, sausage expertly blended by Armando and seasoned to perfection. Schnapps followed the Dago Red served with the meal along with Italian pastries. Additionally, the strong of heart drank espresso; most of us preferred regular coffee.

Roxanna Vella, a dark-eyed, dark-haired beautiful young woman and a year older than Aldo helped to serve the food. She'd recently completed a secretarial course at the Suomi College in Hancock, a school which at the time, offered mostly business courses. Poised and well-mannered, Roxanna had won recognition as an accomplished "fancy skater", as figure skaters were sometimes called then. She'd won several local competitions as well as a few area competitions. Not a few young men courted her but none had won her heart.

Entertainment followed dinner. Singing and dancing ensued.

Roxanna Vella's talents transcended figure skating. The Vellas were devout Catholics. They worshiped at St. John's in Calumet where Roxanna led the choir and often rendered solos. My mother asked her to sing "Oh Holy Night." A stillness enveloped the gathering as she sang the lofty refrains in a limpid soprano voice—she performed with the poise of a six-year-old child or an opera diva. Both the men and women were visibly moved.

"You're doing great, son," Major St. Cloud said, slapping Hicks on a shoulder. "Rita can't say enough good things about you and how well you're doing at Tech. We're proud of you."

In addition to admirably discharging his duties as a husband, Hicks aced all his courses and made the dean's list.

The St. Clouds readily made friends with the Heights Bunch.

"How about giving us a dance," I asked the Major and his stately wife, Theresé. Rita had mentioned something about Ojibwa ceremonial dances.

They readily obliged. A space cleared in a large living room provided needed room where they gravely began to dance in measured steps. As they gradually picked up the pace the Major grunted occasionally, his features stoic and immobile, while Theresé matched his movements alongside him. As their pace quickened to an even faster rhythm Rita joined in, hip-hopping about her parents and raising her knees high. Brave Stinking Badger joined the act. Stomping behind Rita he raised the hem of her long dress. Held high, the billowing fabric resembled the proud tail of a matriarch hen strutting in the barnyard. Her pregnant belly enhanced the effect. Honorary Chief Laughing Whitefish joined the procession showing off the steps he'd learned at the dance in Zeba.

The highlight of the evening arrived for our dads. Armando broke out some fine imported cigars to be enjoyed with the espresso and the schnapps. Refreshed and invigorated the men repaired to his smoking room to enjoy a long sybaritic hour of pure pleasure. Softly-lit, well ventilated as not to offend non-smokers throughout the house, this bastion of civilization furnished with a comfortable sofa and armchairs set before a glowing fireplace provided an ambiance needed for complete relaxation.

While the men puffed on a Punch or a Hoyo, idly reminiscing on the year's events, everyone else went out of their way to entertain Abby, her mother and Lucas. Again, as at the Emmaus Hall, the guests present occupied Abby in conversation while I moseyed about feigning nonchalance. I kept my gears in neutral whether I needed to or not. Who cared? I made some college small talk with Lucas and anyone else willing to listen. Everyone had a good time except me. Faking nonchalance over Abby began to make me irritable but somehow I managed not to show it. I could hardly wait until this miserable evening ended.

A *faux pas* occurred, interrupting my dismal thoughts. Major St. Cloud thought he'd perceived an aura.

"Well, well, well," he said to Lucas and Roxanna who'd been engaged in a rather lengthy conversation. "What a fine young couple. And if I might be a bit nosy have you made any long-term plans?"

Flummoxed, Lucas hemmed and hawed but Roxanna, equal to the occasion, replied laughingly

"you've got the right man but the wrong woman. And she's a lucky woman."

Abby, mingling with guests, did not appear to be disconcerted. The Tulppos and the right man departed for Flint the next day.

The bogeyman of gloom returned. After the euphoria I'd felt during the ski outing, and my pretense at detachment from Abby throughout her stay, the bogeyman came back.

I tried my best to cast Lucas Wagonhoffer as a villain but failed to do so. After numerous mind twists I had to deem him a decent and unpretentious fellow. As much as I wanted to I could not put horns on a man of worthy avocations with a clear goal in life.

"I'm going into veterinary science," he'd told me during our conversation at the Emmaus Hall.

He seemed an almost ideal match for Abby. "This guy flies airplanes to dust crops," I fretted unhappily. "What do I do? I slog through fields on skies or snowshoes during the winter months. I know how to use an axe and a shovel."

Molehills became mountains. Frustrated, gloomy, I analyzed to death what had happened. Hadn't I overheard Major St. Cloud's remark to Roxanna and Lucas about long-range plans? "The right man but the wrong woman," she'd replied. In my muddled head the right woman for Lucas had to be Abby although I'd heard no mention made of long-range plans. If there were any plans the Heights Bunch would have been the first to know of them. Plans or no plans this realization provided meager consolation. My tortured analysis intensified. Didn't I hear Roxanna declare Abby a lucky woman to the Major? Due to an unerring intuition of Lucas Wagonhoffer's fine character perhaps? After all she'd hardly known him and had only talked to him less than a half hour. My frustration worsened. I felt petty and impotent. "Now I know how a jilted lover must feel," I lamented.

"What can I do to win Abby back?" I wondered. "Should I aspire to become a great poet? Should I learn to play a guitar and sing? Would I become a chivalrous Lochinvar and come careering to her, not out of the sunny west, but from the frigid northlands? Would I then play my guitar and sing to her, causing her to swoon? Or how about performing an impressive physical feat such as swimming from one end of the Portage Canal to the other, a swim distance of at least twenty-four miles? Would Lucas Wagonhoffer then realize he'd been bested by a superior rival and perhaps say, 'I take courage, Paul, I accede to you Abby, and I will now depart.'? 'She will be in most worthy hands,' he might say as he stood proud and erect, nobly acknowledging his defeat. 'Congratulations,' he might add, man to man, as he looked frankly at me with his sincere blue eyes while shaking hands in a warm manner before departing on his forlorn way. Humbled by this generous spirit, this giant of a man, I would reply with equal sincerity, 'Please come to visit us, Lucas; there will always be a place at our table for you and a room for you in our home'." A myriad of unsettling and puerile thoughts swept through my mind.

"Was I nuts?" Stymied with a sense of inadequacy, overwhelmed from a morbid preoccupation with a childhood infatuation, I believed Abby forever lost. But didn't I have matters sorted out before Abby came to visit? Should I then have any claim whatsoever on her affection? I questioned my own maturity for so stubbornly clinging to a fantasy having not the slightest basis in reality. Lucas Wagonhoffer had won the battle without even having the foggiest notion of the inclinations his rival.

After many protracted struggles I finally exorcised the bogeyman. I settled for student life. Except for ROTC, I buckled down into serious study at Michigan Tech. I'd earned a solid B average for my first quarter and was determined to do even better.

I never did learn to play a guitar.

CHAPTER 6

A Turn in the Road

"OK, Maki, get down and give me ten pushups," Cadet Colonel Tyler Locke bawled out. Just like high school ROTC I still had a hard time getting the cover off the can to polish my shoes. This fact did not go unnoticed by Tyler Locke. Shining shoes, properly knotting ties and burnishing brass buckles were tasks heartily disdained by many of the Keweenaw locals who'd enrolled in the program, particularly by me. My aversion to spit and polish had only gotten worse since my high school ROTC days and more often than not I left the cover on the can. Un-shined shoes, flannel shirts and baggy pants worn for many days in a row had always good enough for me.

I could always count on being gigged by Cadet Colonel Tyler Locke because of those shoes and therefore acquired a list of demerits, most of which were redeemed on the spot by doing pushups. There were academics as well. As the list grew longer Locke assigned additional studies as punishment, mainly on topics relating to military decorum.

I'd joined the Army ROTC on an impulse. During a coffee session at the Maki kitchen table a family friend persuaded me to join the program. I made what I regarded as a big mistake.

"Why be a grunt when you can be a second lieutenant," Lloyd Kocjan told me.

Lloyd Kocjan had just been discharged from the navy as a third-class petty officer having served in the Far East during the Korean conflict. I had no intention of enlisting in the ROTC program when I enrolled for my freshman year at Michigan Tech. But shortly before the fall quarter began Lloyd gave me a pitch on how much better I could serve the country as a second lieutenant rather than face an eventual draft as an enlisted man.

"Just having a college degree is no guarantee that you won't be drafted," he told me.

"I really have no intention of avoiding the draft, engineering degree or not. In fact, I've given no consideration about a hitch in the army. Besides I had enough ROTC in high school." I hadn't ever given a single thought about avoiding the draft.

My dad took sides with Lloyd and they ultimately convinced me to enroll in the ROTC despite the lukewarm enthusiasm I entertained for making such a commitment. After four years in the program I'd emerge as a second lieutenant in the U.S. Army, Lloyd informed me, after which a minimum of two years of active service would ensue. After being swayed to enroll, I reconciled myself to the decision I'd made, however half-heartedly. So it would be olive drab trousers and a piss-cutter hat for four more years.

Doing pushups for Cadet Colonel Tyler Locke on the grinder or drill area for not shining my shoes had become routine. I'd heard "give me ten pushups" more than once from him.

Tyler Locke slept, dreamt and breathed the military. Born and raised as an army brat he followed in the footsteps of his forebears who formed a long line of military men going back to pre-Civil War days. Narrowly missing an appointment to the West Point Military Academy, a major disappointment, he settled for the Michigan Tech ROTC.

As the most gung-ho cadet in the entire outfit, Locke rose rapidly through the ranks to become the top cadet in the ROTC program. Well versed in drill, marksmanship and military theory he also functioned as a consummate "spit and polish" man. Tall, spare, bony-faced and leathery of appearance, he inspired a stereotypic image of how a soldier should appear. Almost as good as General Douglas MacArthur in an "I shall return" pose. Locke would go far in the army following his graduation, rising to the rank of Lieutenant Colonel in fourteen short years.

Tyler Locke loved cold air. One could see his breath in the subzero air during brisk, frosty, clear winter mornings. He not only exhaled vast clouds of oxygen-depleted air, he snorted them out, producing huge puffs that hung frozen in the air resembling comic strip balloons minus scripts. On one particularly cold wintry morning, the solidly frozen bare ground provided an excellent turf for doing pushups. Perfect, because I'd conceived a plan aimed at getting even with this guy. In preparation I'd put on my most drab but comfortable "chicken coop" shoes.

"OK Maki, get down and give me ten," he barked. This had to be at least the sixth time I had to oblige him for this dereliction. But this time it would be different. Knowing he'd swallow the bait of noticing my conspicuously drab shoes I had a compact camera set for a snapshot, having guessed at the adjustments beforehand for what I hoped would turn out to be a good picture. Right after I completed the pushups an opportune moment arose. Tyler Locke stood close-by in the act of bawling out another lowly cadet because of an improperly knotted tie when I deftly reached the camera from my pocket. Taking quick aim, I got a shot of him just as he snorted a huge cloud of foggy vapor. Too busy giving the buck private an ass-chewing he didn't even notice me. If anyone else noticed what happened they didn't say a word.

The picture turned out perfectly. I'd captured him in profile. There Tyler Locke stood in ramrod posture scowling at the offending cadet. His huge foggy exhalation hanging in the frozen air billowed into clear focus. Had the photo been in color, the brisk ruddy flush glowing from his angry, bony face would have been captured as well. I had some extra prints developed by Patrick McKinstry, a photographer in Calumet, which I captioned "DEDICATION." I surreptitiously managed to post them at conspicuous spots inside the old ROTC building where they drew appreciable plaudit from long-suffering unfortunates in the lower echelons. There were several nods and winks.

Despite the pushups the first quarter in the program went well enough mostly due to the excellent training I'd received in the high school program under Sgt. Engstrom's auspices where we'd honed the basics of drill and marksmanship almost to perfection. Academics in the Michigan Tech U.S. Army ROTC were a different matter. Matters deteriorated rapidly in the second quarter; I failed miserably on most written tests. Unlike high school ROTC, a thorough grasp of academic topics counted a lot toward overall grades and a good standing in the program. We were being rigorously tested on our understanding of topics relating to U.S. military history and basic strategy.

"Maki, I'd like to speak to you privately. Please come to my office after this drill is over. It'll only take minute or two," Colonel Huntington told me where our company had just assembled on the large grinder in front of the ROTC building and the old Hubbell Hall early one wintry morning. I stood stiffly in formation, still wearing a piss-cutter private-first-class hat and an olive drab uniform not much different from the attire I'd donned during my high school days.

Colonel Huntington, the commander of the entire program, and as our high school instructors served, had likewise seen action in World War II. He'd advanced from the lowest levels to eventually become a full colonel. They called guys like Colonel Huntington who'd risen through the ranks of enlisted men to become commissioned officers "mustangs."

A fair but demanding man, Colonel Huntington required excellence from his cadets. During one of his lectures he'd postulated a scenario in which the Cold War Soviets launched a major attack eventuating in conflict on American soil. Our assignment for the coming week required a composition from each cadet describing how the U.S. Army would cope with this horrific threat. I looked ahead to this one; it only would take a little imagination.

I doubt a more bombastic, sophomoric theme on this subject had ever before been written, and I afterward vouchsafed it would take many generations for some green cadet to equal it in naiveté and pomposity.

I had a massive Soviet army somehow crossing the Bering Strait with relative ease. I had them coming with five million men and four thousand T34 tanks. The formidable logistical obstacles posed by the rugged Alaskan interior and the Canadian Rockies were likewise easily surmounted. Once firmly implanted on Canadian soil, the Soviet forces assembled for an all-out assault on the northern boundary of the United States after meeting but token resistance from the Canadian military. Once on U.S. soil, however, matters took a different course.

"Brave men and women would rise up in defense of their beloved land and would rout the aggressor to ignominious flight," I chirped.

"Hogwash," Colonel Huntington wrote on my essay in bold letters, otherwise bloodied with red ink. "This theme is sophomoric." He nonetheless gave me a "68", or a D-minus for my effort.

"Maki, you most likely know why you're here. You're dragging your feet and not living up to your potential. You don't strike me as being immature. I can even overlook the demerits you got on the grinder. Is there anything you'd like to say for yourself?" Colonel Huntington asked me.

"Only one thing, sir. I let myself be talked into joining the ROTC program against my better judgment." I went on to describe the discussion I'd had with Lloyd Kocjan and my dad at the kitchen table. "And I'm really not cut out for this spit and polish stuff."

"I'm really not too big on spit and polish either," he chuckled. "Whoever put up that DEDICATION poster made my day a little brighter. We need some levity from time to time. What we're really looking for is leadership qualities in men, men who can make the right decisions and inspire their troops in a combat situation."

"I thought the poster quite appropriate myself, sir." I did not notice any discerning looks from Colonel Huntington.

"I want you to succeed, Maki, and I believe you have the potential to make a good officer. Academically you're doing alright in your major studies. But let me give you a warning. If you don't make the grade in this program, there are two things which can happen to you: If you can't shape up and get with it, you'll find yourself drummed out of the corps. Should you decide to quit the program, well, you can expect an automatic hitch in the army. You can forget college for then."

"I'll do my best, sir," I replied.

"Good luck, son."

I watched another parade, again in the spring. In the parade a single elite unit from the Michigan Tech ROTC marched north up Hecla street in Laurium, passing me from where I stood in front of the Casino Tavern, located directly across the street from the municipal building housing the police and fire departments. Led by Tyler Locke, some thirty members attired in ROTC officer's garb puffed and snorted their way up the street. Epaulets and braids decorated shoulders while white leggings adorned trousers. All the members wore billed officer's hats except for Tyler Locke who sported a flamboyant, crested parade master's hat towering high above the rest. No piss-cutters for them. I did not boo or hiss as I'd previously done when watching the brownnosers in my high school marching unit. For the first time, I noticed the ruddy-faced Locke had a large, protuberant Adam's apple, almost the equal of my own. How did I ever miss this?

"Oollie-Iy-yI, Oollie-ay-yay," Tyler Locke would chant periodically.

"Hu-haw, Hu-hu-haw!" his well-starched unit huffed in response.

My britches were still too tight to participate in such ostentatious pomp. Questions about my involvement in the program ran through my mind. Would I become a military leader or would I simply remain a grunt? Most likely I'd be a grunt and the hell with being a second lieutenant. I did not need to wear epaulets or a billed officer's hat to shoot straight or to follow sensible orders. Stuff the hats, stuff the braids and epaulets and stuff the nonsense. My dad always said I had a contrary streak the size of Calumet Avenue. Tyler Locke once told me "Maki, you're being contumacious."

I heeded Colonel Huntington's admonitions, however, and my ROTC grades improved to an acceptable level. I also applied myself more assiduously in my major studies. By the end of the first year I'd earned a solid B average. But it didn't come easy; I spent much of my spare time studying. I made some new friends with "toots" as the locals commonly call Tech students. Our main break from our studies occurred on Friday evenings when we'd have a couple beers.

Beer agreed well. I found myself enjoying beer. After the debacle with the wine in my dad's barn I'd sworn to avoid any alcoholic beverage. My resolve weakened—what would it hurt to have a few brews with my friends? Hey, I belonged to a worthy group. Four or five of us would pile into a car and drive to some remote spot on a bush road to safely imbibe away from the law enforcement officers prowling the main roads. Although my toot chums and I were underage we had no difficulty getting a guy twenty-one or older to buy us a couple six-packs. Just enough for each of us to have maybe three or four brews.

We were indeed "squares" as Aldo put it. There were no girls along to share our refreshment. We spent most of our time having big discussions on the subjects we were taking, if one can imagine talking about topics in chemistry or difficult math problems. A guy from Allouez everyone called Diggy, a sophomore, and I had both taken German as an elective course. The rest of us were freshmen. Diggy and I would challenge each other on our prowess in learning German:

"Zu viele Umdrehungen in der Strasse," Diggy tested me as we drove to a secluded spot on a twisting old farm road in Woodland.

"Too many turns in the road," I smugly replied. *"Sind Sie schlau, oder bist du ein dummer grauen Esel?"* I challenged him in turn.

"What the heck are you guys carrying on about?" Louie, another one of our chums asked.

"Are you smart or are you a dumb ass is what Paulie said," Diggy instructed. "Or to be more exact, a stupid grey donkey."

"Entweder du bist ein Narr oder Ich bin einer," Diggy continued to jab at me.

"Either you are a fool or I am one," I answered without hesitation. "I'd say we both are," getting in a final lick.

Diggy, a math whiz, then got on to Maclaurin series expansions in a new attempt to snow us. None of us were able to keep up with him.

Max, another guy from a hamlet known as Florida Location, had a tough time with chemistry. Florida Location is a small adjunct of much larger Laurium, which is a well-known town in the Keweenaw.

"Magnesium," he kept saying repeatedly. "It's got a valence of two. How do those professors expect me to understand stuff you can't see?"

"You've got to study harder," Louie said.

Occasionally after we had a few brews we'd go looking for girls. We were almost always unsuccessful but not unexpectedly so as odds prevailed against us. Most of the time we'd have to settle for a hamburger at either the Bon Ton or the Cozy Garden in Laurium, both "hot spots" for the younger set.

A lot of competition took place for the women in town. It came from two main sources: In the first place, the guys at Michigan Tech outnumbered the girls by about twenty to one in the 1950s, and that's a quite conservative estimate. Even worse for us were the hundred or so Air Force guys stationed at the Keweenaw Radar Base, situated atop Mount Horace Greeley, the highest elevation in the Keweenaw. The "fly boys" definitely held sway over us when it came to the girls. For one thing they had more discretionary cash in their pockets, and insofar as many of the local girls were concerned, more élan. Stacking up the numbers the odds of finding girls were far from being in our favor. Wrestling with *Umdrehungen*, magnesium, Maclaurin series expansions and other arcane matters had to do for us now. The hell with the girls. We'd come to accept our lot as being humble drudges.

"C'mon, Paulie, put it down. Show these guys who's the real champ," a toot from Ahmeek hollered. I drained a twelve-ounce mug in one go, and following that, five more beers slid down my gullet just as easily as the first. We were celebrating a spring bash and had started a traditional chug-a-lug contest—bottoms up from start to finish.

I'd joined the Keweenaw Independents, an organization comprising Tech students local to the school in Houghton and Keweenaw counties. The Independents, at least initially, existed primarily for the purpose of having an occasional beer bash. Two official events were observed, one in the fall and another event in the spring before school got out for the summer, with lesser events occurring on the spot with no planning, mostly after some tough midterms.

My thirst had increased. Three or four beers on an outing increased to five or six bottles and even more as time passed. By the time the spring bash arrived I'd acquired a reputation with my buddies for being a beer drinker of considerable renown. Others were less impressed. I began to binge quite frequently and some of my chums called me a drunk. My binges, however, were limited to weekends.

During the spring bash I got sloppy drunk. The Independents rented a large hall in Hubbell for the event. We'd bought two fifteen-gallon kegs of Bosch beer, a product of a local brewery, more than enough for our two dozen members and perhaps a dozen guests. Our third, or spring quarter term, neared completion and only final exams remained before the summer break. We'd nearly succeeded in fulfilling course requirements and we deserved a celebration. Laggards who'd started Tech had been washed out of school by the end of the first quarter, and with the school year nearly done, the rest of us were succeeding academically.

The chug-a-lug contest began after we'd already worked well into the kegs and had some food. Most contestants admitted defeat after only two or three mugs of beer. Some of them became nauseous and didn't make it to the john. Then it got down to just me and a guy we called "Yuffo," a senior chemical engineering major and the reigning chug-a-lug champion of the Independents. I'd matched him beer for beer: two, three, four beers all went down in one go with little break time between the quaffs. Now we were on our fifth chug-a-lug: After putting down five mugs a queasy Yuffo finally had to be disqualified. He puked on the floor, ending the contest for him.

Declared the new chug-a-lug champion, I put down an extra mug for good measure. After leisurely imbibing a few more mugs, the foamy brew I'd slugged down without restraint got the best of me. Sick to my stomach and wobbly, I heaved up a vast fountain of beer and scads of partially digested hotdogs and potato salad.

Some of the more sober-minded Independents could be relied on for safely driving their drunken classmates home when the party ended. One of them was Eugene Seppala, an upper classman majoring in accounting. Although primarily an engineering school Michigan Tech offered courses in accounting.

"Let's get some fresh air, Paulie," he said after I cleaned up my slop. A mop and a bucket of fresh water were kept handy for the offenders. Still wobbly on my feet, Seppala carefully guided me out of the hall.

Seppala who'd imbibed in moderation tried to sober me up as I stumbled alongside him. Grim-faced but solicitous and looking straight ahead, Seppala walked me around the block at least four times in the brisk evening air.

"You've got too many brains to be fooling around like this," I remembered him telling me. "Everyone likes you. You don't have to be the drinking champ to prove yourself."

Years later, I found out Eugene Seppala had risen to the ranks of top management of a major oil conglomerate. A merited recompence for a good man.

"I've had enough college for now," Aldo told Hicks and me just after he'd finished his second semester at Northern. "I'll be enlisting in the navy. Not to make career of it like my older brother but only putting in a hitch until I decide what I really want to do."

"Are you sure?" Hicks asked. "You're not having problems with your studies."

Although doing quite well academically at Northern Michigan University, Aldo had grown restless. I offered him no encouragement to continue.

"I don't have a good handle on where I'm going with college. Maybe I'll have a better grasp on things once the four years in the navy is over with. One thing I know for sure is I've no interest in becoming a history or a literature instructor. Besides I'm still young and I've got to see some more of the world. A couple of my chums from New York I knew when we were kids are serving now and tell me they're having a good time. They're both on a ship operating in the Pacific."

Soon after he'd completed his first year at Northern, Aldo resided in boot camp at the Great Lakes Naval Training Center. Before he left, we gave him a party. On a warm mid-June Saturday evening eight of us guys chipped in to buy a chilled eight-gallon keg of beer. Luckily for us one of the guys had just turned twenty-one.

This time we even managed to talk two girls into joining our party. We would be partying at a clearing on the south side of Rice Lake, a place seldom occupied during evenings, and accessible only by a two-rut sandy track. A heavy rainfall would prohibit access through a near mile-long stretch of deep ruts, now dry. It hadn't rained for over a week.

Hicks who'd become a dedicated family man did not attend. Hicks and Rita were now the proud parents of eight-pound Alfred Maurice Huhta, born in April in the third quarter of our freshman year. Their life had eased. Vacating the apartment in Houghton the small family, at the behest of his parents, moved to live with them in Centennial Heights two months before the birth.

"I'm truly a happy man," Hicks exulted upon the arrival of his son. Having more time for study as the result of the eased living arrangement he buckled down even more and aced his freshman year, where grade-wise, he stood at the very top of his class. Several months after the birth, the couple rented a small house of their own in Centennial Heights.

"Let's get back to town. I've had enough to drink for one night," Diggy said. Others agreed with him, including Aldo.

This made no sense to me whatsoever. Here we were with almost a half a keg of beer—we'd drunk maybe five gallons at most. Here we were with a nice bonfire blazing and these slouches wanted to quit and go home to bed just when the fun should be accelerating. And for once we had a couple of girls with us, a novel experience. The girls, however, having listened to too much fuss about chemistry and differential equations had become very restless.

Louie and Max tried to make out. During their few previous encounters with girls they almost always failed to impress. This time Louie hoped knowledge would be the key to success—what better way to impress a girl than to wow her with a display of profound knowledge. Armed with his new weapon, he'd cornered one of them and for at least a half hour gratuitously explained to her the benefit of plating steel washers with chromium.

Aldo and I sat listening with disbelief.

"The washer must be made corrosion resistant to serve its function on bolted joints," Louie expatiated. "A bolted joint must have torque integrity. The washer keeps it tight."

"Good grief," she murmured when Louie finished his lengthy dissertation. Max, carrying on about chemistry problems, fared no better. Silent and exasperated, the girls couldn't wait to leave. They had no ear for hearing of college exploits or what these guys were going to do once they graduated. Besides hordes of mosquitoes swarmed the party.

Girls or no girls I was not about to abandon our costly keg of beer. I'd completely forgotten the advice Eugene Seppala had given me.

"I'm staying," I told everyone before they left. "You can pick me up tomorrow. I've got the bonfire to keep me warm and I'll have this beer and the mosquitoes for company."

"You're nuts," Diggy said. "The beer can wait. Get your butt in the car. You need to get some rest."

"After hearing this nonsense about bolted joints, washers and chemistry I won't be having any problems with that. Make sure someone comes to get me tomorrow."

This would be the first time I'd be doing some heavy drinking by myself. Aldo volunteered to stay but I convinced him I wanted to be alone. Besides he only had two days left before reporting to the Great Lakes Naval Training Center.

"I don't really want to see you doing this, old buddy, but it's your call. Take care. I'll come get you tomorrow."

"Take your time. I'm in no hurry to leave."

Not at all lonely once everyone left, euphoric in the peaceful surroundings and with no one else around within miles; I had the bush to myself. The zesty Bosch beer agreed well as I tapped mug after mug from the keg beside the bonfire. I'd obtained a sixteen-ounce copper mug for occasions such as this.

"Beer tastes the best if drunk from a copper mug," a copper miner once told me. "No question about that," I mused, as I sat before the fire studying the dense sparkling head and beads of condensation forming on the mug before taking a deep swig. The beer, of a bitter make, agreed well—not one of a green bitterness originating from a hurried fermentation—but a brew of a tangy sharpness, which significantly made the drink more potable. The only problem I noticed was that we'd failed to bring enough ice. We'd made a bath in a tub for keeping the keg cooled with tea-colored water drawn from the lake. The added ice had almost completely melted: Still the beer would stay cold and refreshing enough throughout the night.

I'd made sure to gather up an abundant supply of firewood beforehand. Having plenty of windfall pine, well-seasoned and dry, I kept a robust fire going, with hardwood to be added later for a slower burn.

All alone and at peace, I savored my achievements of the past year. I'd passed the third quarter finals without difficulty. My grades were solid and I'd even salvaged my grades in ROTC to the satisfaction of Colonel Huntington. "You're doing well, Maki," Colonel Huntington said to me just before the end of my freshman year. "You'll make a fine officer someday." My best friends, Aldo and Hicks, were succeeding and I'd made new friends as well. Prospects could not have looked better. "The beer drinking means nothing—I can handle it—I showed the guys who's the champ and my grades will be even better the next quarter," I thought. Out here in the bush in my lone reverie, I drank many more mugs of the sharp-tasting brew before I fell into a deep slumber.

The sun had well arisen by the time I awoke, and although a bit groggy, I otherwise did not feel too bad. A couple more beers took care of the cobwebs in my head after which I became hungry. The hot dogs and the potato salad we'd brought were all gone. Remnants lay wasting in the sand. Low-lying blueberry bushes thriving amidst a growth of fiddle ferns promised an abundant crop, but unfortunately for me, ripe berries were a month off from harvest. Luckily, I found a source of food: lots of freshwater clams flourishing in the sandy shallows of Rice Lake were available. As the waters warmed there would be annoying leeches as well but presently they were not of concern.

I waded in, and after gathering up a dozen clams, roasted them on the guttering embers. No need to keep the fire going as the day promised to be hot. Not only hot but muggy. The clams, although tough and very chewy, were quite tasty and more to be had if needed.

The mosquitoes didn't bother me too much but a swarm of black flies, or deer fly as they are also known by Yoopers, got to me. They're at their worst during the hot, muggy days of June. Allergic to the deer fly bite and totally unprepared for the numberless black swarm attacking from nearby marshes on this stifling morning, rapidly becoming oppressive for me, I had neither insect repellent nor protective screening of any sort.

The deer fly takes its time. Unable to swat all the pests as they landed, some got through to inflict an almost painless bite, and that's what it took to cause swelling. I subsequently discovered the swelling would occur on only one area of my body where I'd been bitten the most. In this instance my forehead had become hot, puffy and sensitive to touch. The swelling extended significantly to the area near my eyes.

I nonetheless continued working on the keg. The ice in the tub had long melted. Pine needles, leaves and debris from the smoldering fire floated on the tea-colored water. Draft beer does not hold up well without chilling and the tepid brew already started to taste skunky. This failed to stop me from drinking more of it. Beer, either fresh or skunky, should not be wasted. But the euphoria of the previous evening had vanished to be replaced with irritability and a growing sense of dejection as I baked in the hot sun. When Aldo arrived the swelling had increased to an extent my eyes were almost swollen shut. I could barely see as I moped in the mugginess, which became more oppressive with each passing hour.

"What in the hell happened to you," Aldo exclaimed. "You look like Frankenstein. All you need is a seam of stitches on your neck," he said trying to make light of the matter.

"Damn deer fly. Let's get out of here."

"When are you going to stop punishing yourself?" People were starting to talk.

I had no answer.

The swelling had subsided by the following day when Aldo left for Great Lakes. Aldo's parents, Roxanna, Hicks and I saw him off on a Greyhound bus from a stop in Laurium.

"Who will we come to for advice once you're gone?" I asked just before he boarded.

"You're on your own now, pal. Just remember who taught you the facts of life," he joshed, poking me in the ribs. "And just take it easy on the beer."

An unexpected visitor arrived in June a week after Aldo departed. He said he'd come to do some fishing. He came at the right time. The streams were in prime condition, not too high or too low after the spring runoff. Coming to Centennial Heights just to do some fishing? He'd come to see Roxanna Vella. This time I welcomed Lucas Wagonhoffer without a bone-crushing handshake.

"What had happened between him and Abby?" I wondered. I did not probe the matter. Presumably he had not been aware of my interest concerning her, nor did I have any reason to suspect Abby revealed to him our puppy love. What difference would it have made anyway? She'd told me our secret remained secret, and explaining a childhood infatuation to him would have been foolish. I felt embarrassed just thinking about this.

Lucas regarded me as just another guy in town, a strange character perhaps, bent on crushing strangers' hands. Although tempted to be nosy, I tactfully did not probe what his interests were with Roxanna. All I know is Lucas and Roxanna dated during the evenings. We didn't do too badly on the trout streams during the day and we took in another sauna at Jacob Binoniemi's. Matt Roces didn't bother to put him to test again. I finally put to bed my misgivings by accepting Lucas Wagonhoffer aa a straight-arrow guy. I only hoped he'd forgotten about Abby.

He left after three days. Roxanna saw him off.

"Riisto, it's going to fall the wrong way."

"Pound that wedge into the cut to tip the tree where you want it to fall," he replied.

"Take your time, boy. There's never any hurry in this business," he added.

I'd taken a job in the bush shortly after the keg party at Rice Lake. I became the rookie member of a small six-man crew cutting stands of pulpwood near Mud Lake. The other members were older lumberjacks experienced in the hardwoods, the pines and the pulpwood bush. We mostly cut spruce and balsam trees.

Conditions at Mud Lake were ideal for the rapid growth of spruce and balsam. Clear a forty-acre plot and within forty years a new stand would be available for harvesting. The terrain is low-lying and flat, and elevation-wise, is not too many feet above Lake Superior, and very much a wilderness area in the 1950s. Mud Lake is located a few short miles from Small Traverse Bay, a tiny settlement of cottages on Lake Superior. A high water table in the seldom-dry terrain spurred new growth of the water-sucking firs.

Word spread fast regarding the circumstances of Hicks's shotgun wedding—loose tongues had got the better of discretion. "I'll tell you something if you can keep it a secret," Aldo and I had both confided to some of the guys. "There goes the Impregnatorium," a young guy hollered from the sidewalk as I drove up Fifth Street. Aldo let me have the car for fifty bucks shortly before he left for boot camp. The old 1938 Ford, still in excellent running condition, provided the means of transportation for me and one of the old-timer 'jacks.

I picked up Riisto Salmi in Laurium at five-thirty every morning. We had to take advantage of the dawn and be ready to start cutting by sunrise. The earlier the start, the cooler the air, the better. Even in June temperatures not too far above the freezing point at early dawn could often be expected. During the oncoming hot muggy afternoons temperatures could rise into the eighties, slowing progress. We worked practically nonstop until early afternoon with maybe a coffee break and a light lunch at mid-morning—seven hours at most of practically nonstop work meant optimum productivity. Since June is the worst month for mosquitoes and deer fly, I kept an ample supply of insect repellent handy after the reaction I had to the bites at Rice Lake. The best repellent against the fly is pure diethyltoluamide, which everyone calls DEET.

All the guys in our six-man crew had power saws except for Riisto Salmi, the oldest man on our crew, and me. Everyone called him "Old Bones." He'd earned his nickname from a peculiar musical talent he possessed. When a Saturday night polka band rolled into the North Country Tavern in Calumet, Old Bones, off to the side, accompanied them free of charge. His instruments consisted of four rib bones hewn from a buck bagged during the deer hunting season he'd cut into lengths of roughly six inches. He held two bones in each hand between his fingers like a patron of a Chinese restaurant using chopsticks. But instead of picking up clumps of rice, he'd manipulate the bones with effortless facility to produce sharp, snappy sounds to accompany the band. His rhythm and timing were perfect; at the peak of a refrain, he'd roll both his hands above his head, his fingers and instruments visible only as a blur of motion as the rattling bones furnished an inspiring accompaniment to the peals of the accordion. Dancers would twirl about faster and stomp harder on the floor of the old North Country Tavern.

Seldom did anyone buy Old Bones a beer for his effort. "Let's hear those bones rattle again," some drunk at the bar would holler.

We both cut with a swede saw, which is nothing more than a blade restrained in tension in a bowed metal frame. We worked as partners, which worked out well for me. I took full advantage of his considerable expertise—in addition to his considerable logging skills, Old Bones had few peers when it came to sharpening the saw blades or an axe. Old Bones hewed through the soft firs as though he were slicing a birthday cake. His judgment in determining the direction of a tree's fall eliminated hang-ups altogether. I acquired a worthy education working in the woods with Riisto Salmi.

We worked a two-man crosscut saw for felling larger trees. My youthful strength came into play when it involved stacking the logs. We first peeled the bark from the logs with spuds after lopping off the branches. During the spring and early summer months, the firs suck up a lot of water from the soil and the bark becomes slick, slimy and easy to remove. Peeling bark thankfully is not a part of winter cutting in the Keweenaw.

Twelve cents a log or sticks as we called them, all piece work; one had to keep going to make a decent buck. This meant felling trees cleanly without hanging a cut on nearby trees; clearing a hung tree results in a costly delay and a substantial reduction in earnings. Under normal market circumstances a log had to be a certain size to count. A good tree would yield at least three nine-foot-long "sticks."

Twelve cents a stick, not bad money. Equipped with only our swede and crosscut saws, on a typical day we jointly cut one hundred and twenty sticks. Not nearly as good as the guys with the power saws but it still meant seven bucks a day for each of us, which meant plenty of money for beer.

Riisto drank away his earnings. No going home for him at midnight or even at two in the morning as expected by my chums of me when out having a few beers. There were no German lessons for him to learn or experiments to perform in the chemistry lab. A widower and a father of grown children, he owed no responsibilities to anyone. So long as he had a few bucks in his pocket his time belonged solely to himself. For Riisto, this meant beer until the money ran out. It made no difference to the boss if he missed a day or two of work—this is how Riisto operated during his many long years in the bush. The boss could always count on him to produce well while on the job. Anyway he had the power saws running, which ensured him most of his profits.

I joined in the fun. I'd at last discovered an ideal drinking companion. I had the transportation and we both chipped in for the refreshment. The Independents beer bash in Hubbell and the overnight stay at Rice Lake with the keg were nothing compared with the good times Riisto and I shared together. Some of our sprees lasted for two or three days. Money? Who cared about that? I pissed away the money I'd earned in the bush. Further, I'd arranged for a student loan to cover the cost of tuition and books for the forthcoming fall quarter at da Tech. What more could I ask for?

"Welcome, boys, welcome," Oiva Saarinen greeted us.

Riisto and I had just arrived at Oiva's farm, known all over town as the "Hell's Gate Ranch." We lugged in two cases of Bosch. A little after 2:00 AM, Oiva's sleepy boarders grumbled at first but the grumbling soon turned into murmurs of approval once they heard footsteps and the dull, clinking thuds of bottles. Forty-eight full bottles of beer rattling in their cases, a familiar sound to these old retirees at the Hell's Gate Ranch.

A sanctuary for his select friends once the joints in town closed, Oiva extended his welcome to others as long as his guests did not arrive empty-handed in the early hours and only if he knew who they were. Riisto and I as always came well supplied. Riisto and Oiva Saarinen were long-time friends. Roisterers were not welcomed.

Oiva's farm, located on a hill just outside of town, overlooked the Trap Rock Valley. He managed a herd of sixteen milking cows and a large flock of chickens. Oiva's farmhouse, barn and chicken coop imperiously viewed the arable farmland in the valley below. His boarders kept his large, modern barn tidy—the troughs running along two long rows of stalls were always mucked clean. The essences of sweet hay and fresh droppings combined to produce a soothing redolence in the warm barn. We carried the redolence to town.

On a Saturday afternoon we'd pile in Oiva's horse-drawn wagon, one of the last seen in town, and head to the Casino Tavern in Laurium for a few brews where his team, tethered in front of the tavern, could reliably be seen. Under the wary eye of the police directly across the street, his crew members were only obliged to shovel the horse apples deposited by Dodo and Old Henry before departure from a lengthy stay. A large leather bag served this purpose.

"Humble Huhta," one of the boarders at Hell's Gate Ranch, kept us entertained. A bachelor and Hicks's uncle, he'd managed his way through life as an itinerant worker. He'd quit sobriety for good at an early age, and after landing at the ranch, became Oiva's oldest boarder. He subsisted on a modest pension.

"C'mon, Humble, let's hear that song," one of the guys at the bar yelled.

There's a humble weeping willow, down in the meadow
I'm so humble and so lonesome I could cry
Will my honey be a-weepin', when I'm layin' in my coffin
I'm so humble and so lonesome I could die

Humble sang with a trembling voice, groaning loudly. He sounded as though his sonorous lament came from somewhere deep in his bowels. At timely intervals, he punctuated his mournful dirge with a high-pitched, falsetto whine. The guy at the bar bought him a beer.

If low on funds, Humble Huhta could always be counted on to cadge a few bucks. A World War I veteran, he'd sustained a minor leg injury of which he opportunely took advantage. Not a solitary imbiber, and as a long-time friend of his nephew, I'd become one of his favorite drinking partners.

"Oh, woe, oh, woe," he groaned as we entered the Cozy Garden together. His deeply furrowed face appeared to be etched with pain.

"Oh, no, not him again," Carmen Ulizzio grumbled.

"Carmen, that bum leg's got me again." He hobbled about and continued to groan. "Can you spare an old soldier a couple bucks 'til next Wednesday?"

On one of his earliest visits to the Cozy Garden, Humble related to Ulizzio, the proprietor, how he'd sustained his injury. A gruff but soft-hearted man, Carmen listened sympathetically as he related his combat experience at the St. Mihiel Salient where a bullet grazed his thigh. Huhta made the injury sound a lot worse. His drinks were on the house for a whole afternoon. "You've earned it, my friend, you've earned it," Ulizzio assured him.

He'd won a permanent customer as a result. Here again he showed up broke as he'd had several times since. Always dressed in his best outfit whenever he went to town, and despite the fact his time-worn dark suit showed signs of wear, he managed to look respectable. His trousers bagged loosely and the brim of his battered Stetson draped low over his forehead, adding to his "humbleness." He groaned some more and began to whine in his patented fashion.

"Just a couple bucks. Like I said, I'll pay you back next Wednesday."

Carmen Ulizzio caved in as always. He never got paid.

By the time school started in the fall I'd got into a big rut. Old Bones and I drank until we were broke before returning to the bush to make some more money. Rapidly wearing out my welcome at home I often slept in Oiva's barn, which featured a commodious hayloft. Somehow we managed to keep our boss happy, mainly because Riisto had been on good terms with him for many years. Otherwise, I would've undoubtedly been fired.

Good old Diggy. One dense, foggy night after some heavy drinking I lost my way in Heights when he gave me a ride home from Calumet.

He'd keep the keys to my own car, parked in town, until the next day when I would be sober enough to drive. He dropped me off near the old rock battleship where I could get some fresh air before I went inside. More importantly, I still had a couple inches left in a pint of Old Crow that needed to be finished. After polishing off the whiskey atop the boat, I stashed the empty bottle in a large curved pipe mounted on an amidships deck just forward of a larger pipe intended as the smoke stack. I didn't make it home. Instead I staggered down the street and spent a night passed out in Old Lady Mattila's back-door shed. I received a rude awakening the next morning.

"Paulie Maki, go home, you bum," she said shooing me off with a broom. To her credit she did not complain to my parents.

And the wicked hangovers. No longer merely a bout of nausea to fight off, which often followed an evening out with the fellows, I could always count on a night or two of sleeplessness as my nerves jangled following a three-day binge. Worse yet I started worrying what everyone thought of me. I'd never worry-warted or felt guilty about anything before. Maybe a bit guilty when mom caught me raiding the cherry chocolates as a six-year-old. What was happening?

The nights of sleeplessness increased as time passed and the drinking began to extract a higher toll on my weakening system. I would have gladly traded the raw nerves for puke had I that option. The apprehensions of what people were thinking got worse. Could it simply be paranoia? It got to the point where I couldn't look anyone in the face. I tried to make up for it by being humble and obsequious to everyone. "What's wrong with Maki," I overheard a toot say in the Memorial Union Building. Some guy I'd teamed up with once at the shuffleboard. "His phony nice guy act is giving me the creeps," he added. "What's he trying to prove? He's as stiff as a board."

To make up for the occasional negative remarks, I attempted to become even more humble and strove to become more presentable, despite the chafing discomfort caused by starched shirt collars and having to avoid wrinkling pressed trousers. There were no more days-worn flannel shirts and baggy pants. Sometimes I even shined my shoes.

My days as a student had become surreal. "What am I doing on this campus going about in a fog?" I wondered. In this nineteen fifties decade of conventionality everyone did what they were supposed to do and were expected to walk a straight line, which they did with little exception. "You've got all these clean-cut looking guys, cheerful and smiling complacently on their way to class, happy as larks. Lots of crew-cut stubby little guys still afflicted with pimples. One guy had hair sticking out of his pimples. Some of these "toots" are even wearing beanie caps with little windmills on the top," I observed. A few of them went around smoking pipes. Then there are the insufferable jocks parading around in their varsity jackets. "Shit. What in hell am I doing here?"

A complete lush not yet twenty years old, seldom heard of in the predictable '50s, did not fit into anything happening at this respectable engineering campus. And there were no more six-packs to be enjoyed on some bush road while discussing chemical reactions with my college cronies or trying to give them snow jobs in German with business as usual the next day. Me and Old Bones drank until we were weary and spent.

Except for Hicks my friends avoided me as much as they could. They acted friendly enough but had little desire to share my company, whether playing a game of shuffleboard at the Memorial Union Building or going to see a Huskies' football game. These guys were not prudes, but who knew whether I'd show up sober or sloppy drunk? My participation in outings with my college chums ended when I puked all over the side of Diggy's car as he drove Louie, Max and me to a football game. Soused when the guys picked me up, I'd had quite a few brews earlier. Further, I didn't quite get my head out of the window in time and splattered Max who sat on the front seat directly ahead of me. Even the Keweenaw Independents wanted nothing more to do with me, and no longer welcomed to participate in their festivities, was politely asked to quit the organization.

Even Old Bones turned a skeptical eye. At first he thought I had the willpower to not let the binges interfere with my aims but he finally put the brakes on our escapades when he saw I lacked the resolve to come to grips with life as a serious student.

"You're ruining your life. Get a handle boy, show some moxie. Listen, I didn't think you'd wind up like this. Cut out the crap right now and do what you set out to do. I can't help you with that."

Having someone else buy my beer did not pose a problem; I'd come up with fake IDs when I hung out at the Hell's Gate Ranch. The hangovers I'd endured caused me to look haggard and older, which made it easier to get served in the bars. I had bags under my eyes; my eyes were bleary and my expression blank.

"See the kid sitting at the end of the bar," I heard a guy say to his companion in the North Country Tavern, "I never saw a kid with bags under his eyes like he's got and his eyes are dead."

"A young guy like him should be jumping with joy," his companion replied.

My solitary sprees lasted longer and longer. Only the beer and the booze and the complacent mood the potables induced mattered. Beer subsequently failed to satisfy my needs so I began to hit the hard stuff whenever I could find someone to buy a pint of Imperial or Old Crow from the liquor store where my IDs were too suspect.

The hell with college and let college go to hell. Halfway through the fall quarter of my sophomore year I quit for good reason besides the drinking; I was failing, not just a little bit, but flunking miserably. "Let's see if chump Maki can answer this one," my math professor announced to the class when I finally showed up after missing three classes in a row. He'd posed an easy problem I totally flubbed. He did not call me "Mr. Maki" or just plain "Paul"; "chump" did it then for losers. No one cared two cents about the self-esteem of those deliberately bent on failing.

ROTC had become a complete disaster. By the time I dropped out I'd acquired failing grades on all my exams and so many demerits on the parade ground that I would have been drummed out of the Corps anyway. My preemptive move spared everyone the trouble of having to kick out a failed student who wasn't going anywhere.

A few things had to be cleaned up in the chemistry lab. A quantitative analysis experiment of a pinkish cast on which I'd spent hours working stood unfinished in its beaker. We were individually testing for a sulfate. I took one last look, and cementing my decision to leave school, I fatalistically poured the experiment down the drain.

Turning in my uniform and my piss-cutter hat at the ROTC building, I guardedly walked past Colonel Huntington's office to avoid eye contact. He'd not given me any more admonitions. He did not appear to notice me as I crept by. "A mature person did he say?" I wondered what thoughts ran through his head now.

There were no tears shed by anyone when I made my decision to quit. There were no commiserating professors urging me to stay on and come to grips with myself. On the contrary, they were glad to see me go, especially the new top cadets in the ROTC program. Tyler Locke, had he been present when I left, undoubtedly would have rejoiced. Having graduated the past spring as a second lieutenant and assigned duty in Germany, he would begin his rapid ascent in the army chain of command.

I had company when I quit. Two of us quit on the same day. My college buddy from Florida Location, "Magnesium Max" as we'd come to call him, quit alongside me. With Max it wasn't poor grades; like Aldo, Max simply wanted to move on.

Our parents had no problems with our quitting Michigan Tech. In my case I wasn't getting anywhere and my parents were fed up with my drunken sprees. "Pack your rags and head for boot camp," my dad finally told me after I'd made one too many false promises to cut out my drinking and get back to serious business. Max's dropping out of school didn't make one bit of difference with his father, a formally uneducated man. "Those kids didn't have any business beating their brains out at that college in the first place," he said.

Magnesium Max enlisted in the Air Force and later secured an enrollment into flight school after which he became a pilot in the US Air Force. I sat back contemplating an automatic hitch in the army.

Time passed tortuously slow. I did nothing except get drunk as my meager funds permitted, now nearly depleted. Days crept by as I contemplated alternatives to a hitch in the army. Despite Colonel Huntington's well-intentioned admonitions I couldn't help but have resentment toward letting that happen.

I stopped in occasionally to say hello to Hicks and Rita and to see baby Alfred Maurice Huhta. But not too often. I'd listened to a stern lecture during my last visit.

"Why do you drink so much?" Hicks asked me. "I don't understand this. You're such a normal guy, or at least you always were. Look how we grew up—few kids can claim a healthier, more carefree existence than you and I and Aldo had. You're the best friend I've got. You and Aldo and now he's gone and joined the Navy. Good for him. I might have done the same thing if I were in his shoes. But my future is cut out for me and if I must say so I'm enjoying life perfectly well with Rita and Alfred. But your quitting school to be a drunk—I just don't get it. Why can't you get your butt in gear and shape up?"

"There's no need to make me the center of attention. I happen to like the lifestyle I've taken up," I replied. "I think there's a lot more to life than having the nose stuck in a book. For what? Become an eight-to-five stiff in some office with fifty other guys and have some worried boss chewing your ass out? Doesn't make any sense to me at all. Might as well be in prison for nine hours a day. A long time ago I told Abby working as a lumberjack in the bush would be good enough for me. I still feel the same way."

"Cut out the crap, Paulie. Stop this nonsense. You've got enough brains to do things right when the time comes. Quitting and letting yourself go with this boozing you're just looking for an easy way out."

"Maybe not so easy—I've joined the navy."

I'd beat the army to the punch—there would be no boots for me. I'd most likely wind up swabbing decks on some ship.

Hicks appeared stunned at this revelation. "Maybe a few years in the service is what you need," he ventured lamely.

"Once I get the hitch finished maybe I'll make some long-range plans. But most likely I'll wind up working in the bush again just like I've done this summer. So for now it's the navy or otherwise it would have been a no-way-out hitch in the army for quitting ROTC. That's about it, Hicks. Besides I like getting drunk if you want to know the truth."

"You like to get drunk," he said, having fully recovered his wits. "Fartblossom, you're full of shit. You don't make any sense at all. I wish I knew what to say but there's got to be more to it than that. And you're not quite the same guy I grew up with and knew so well. You know what, pal, you've changed, and changed a lot."

"What do you mean I've changed? I don't cause anyone any trouble, my parents perhaps, but I'll be leaving them soon. And I try to be a nice guy."

"That's what I'm talking about—this nice guy, this humble stuff. You don't speak your mind anymore. And you're going overboard trying to be nice. There are times when you shouldn't be. Your words are too measured. Nobody knows where you stand on anything. Even your shoes are shiny. You've become distant, pal. I don't expect you to confide to me all your problems or whatever is causing your trouble but still you can unload on me any time. But the way you're going right now with this drinking, you're losing it fast. You're no longer spontaneous and it seems you're becoming afraid of people and withdrawn from those who love and know you the best. The Paulie Maki I used to know didn't fear anything or anyone."

"Thanks, Hicks. I'll keep in mind everything you've said. But I guess I don't see the changes in myself you apparently do."

He looked at me steadily, the expression in his clear blue eyes frank and solicitous. He brought his round, flat homely face close to my own. Major St. Cloud had described Hicks's face as a pancake to Rita. Not far off the mark. There were a lot of similarities in our features I noted. We were both "pugs", our short but wide noses turned up at the ends. With our broad skulls we were often referred to as "roundheads" as are many others of Finnish extraction. Phrenologists term this shape of skull as "brachycephalic."

"Just one last thing, Paulie. Pardon me if I'm a little bit nosy. It's not about Abby, by any chance? I guess everyone knows by now she and Lucas have gone their separate ways. And Lucas and Roxanna are hitting it off well. He didn't come here just to do some trout fishing."

"C'mon, Hicks, it's got nothing to do with Abby. Nothing more than puppy love as my dad called it. That happened a long time ago. Sure I liked her a lot and I still do. Remember we were just kids."

Hicks remained silent as though deep in thought. A long moment passed.

"We're done for good," I added flatly. "I'll be leaving for basic training at Great Lakes in a week."

"Good luck buddy. I'll be hoping you can straighten things out."

After listening to Alfred Maurice Huhta babbling contentedly in his crib I bade farewell to my good friends Hicks and Rita. I could already see Alfred's resemblance to his father.

I received a letter from Abby several weeks after Lucas Wagonhoffer's visit to Centennial Heights. Too personal a matter, I hadn't mentioned this to Hicks. I'd not expected to hear from her:

Dear Paul,

By now you may realize Lucas and I are no longer dating. Despite a happy relationship of one year, events transpired precluding one of a longer duration, if not permanence for us. I thought you should know this.

We parted company as friends and trustfully we shall remain friends. And in no way has my respect for Lucas as a person of strong character diminished. I have no doubt he will succeed well in life in his chosen field of veterinary science and will find happiness with Roxanna, as it appears his heart truly resides with her own. I could see an attraction developing between them at the Vella's Christmas party and began to understand even then, if you will pardon a cliché, "they were meant for each other." Even Major St. Cloud in so brief a setting could perceive their mutual affinity. And on our drive back to Flint after the holidays we were not quite comfortable with each other. We both realized our spontaneity had vanished, and our conversation had become restrained and stilted. His heart and mind dwelt elsewhere.

But I'm not a fatalistic person and at first held out hope for our relationship. We continued dating as though nothing were amiss. I'd even thought at first the affinity between Lucas and Roxanna would be of a fleeting concern; after all, on a sheer physical plane, one might expect two most attractive and vibrant people to be drawn toward each other. But as time passed, their affinity became quite obvious, and prevailed greater than any which Lucas and I had ever experienced.

Our parting of ways did not come as a shock but rather as a slow, dwindling erosion of our feelings toward each other. It was not without sadness, not without bitterness and even jealousy on my part when the final realization struck home that Lucas's affection for me had grown cold, and for Lucas, considerable pangs of guilt. But we ultimately understood our parting was the best for both of us for to continue in a farce would have become a total charade.

I am now devoting my energies to my studies and I'm happy to say I'm doing quite well. Majoring in philosophy and having acquired a minor in American History in less in two years, I'll be done with my undergraduate studies, and am already looking ahead to doing post-graduate work. Afterwards, perhaps, I'll pursue a career in teaching.

Well that's enough talk about me. Just one more thing—Lucas asked me to tell you he had a great time on the trout streams with you during his visit when he wasn't spending time with Roxanna. And to this day he has no idea of our adolescent infatuation for each other. Insofar as he's concerned, you're just another friend with whom I grew up.

Why am I telling you this? I suppose I could say as a loser in love I could simply forget the whole affair and move on to find someone else, and that "someone else" of course would be you. But I have too much pride to entertain any such fancy and I believe you would feel the same had you found yourself in my situation. I can state with certainty you have as much pride as I do and I respect you very much for it. Despite anything else, I know I can relate freely to you and that's what I'm doing now.

Paul, I will always think well of you and will hope the best for you in whatever you do.

Your friend always,
Abby

I did not reply to Abby. What could I tell her? "Hey, Abby, guess what? I've become a big drunk."

There were no going away parties for me before I left for the Great Lakes Naval Training Center. Everyone in Centennial Heights was glad to see me go. They did not like losers. I'd refused all offers of help. In addition to my parents, well-meaning people such as Pastor Henry Bylkas and Jake Bloomdahl tried to counsel me before I left. Nothing they told me mattered. Nothing Hicks said mattered. I would take my chances on a new path. Me a loser? Hell no.

I left the Keweenaw behind as quietly as possible on an early morning bus. There were no goodbyes to anyone except to my parents.

CHAPTER 7

Blue Water Moonshine

One liberty. One liberty for the entire twelve weeks. Most of the guys from Camp Downey went to see a movie or to a local roller skating rink in hopes of meeting girls. Some went out to get a milkshake after attending a church service. Carl "Boats" Finerty and I went to Chicago on our short one-day pass. We wound up on West Madison Street after hitting a bar in the Loop. I still had my fake ID's, and after we both switched into civilian clothes, we stashed our uniforms in a locker at the train station. At least I would not be questioned for my military identification when hitting the bars. A Sunday afternoon found us in a dive called the Foxhead Tavern close to where the major skid row section on West Madison began.

I had to take a first-hand look. I'd romanticized skid row—I developed a fascination for skid rows after reading tales of down-and-outers. A magazine featured a droll story of a Christmas spent with bums on skid row. A hospitable group of men feted the bums with all the food and liquor they could handle in one day. Thoroughly soused and maudlin, babbling how they'd left broken-hearted God-fearing mothers behind to become drunkards, many of the bums promised themselves to quit their dissolute way of life to begin life afresh. More fascinating were stories of respectable judges who'd ruined careers on the bench through alcoholism. This fit in perfectly with my view of skid row in which I expected to discover some romantic or even an enlightening element involving someone caught up in a down-and-out situation. I pulled for the underdog. I hoped the derelict judge would someday reform, and having obtained a superior wisdom from his debauchery, would return to the bench more eminent and resourceful than ever before. Sadly, in the stories I read, the judge once again fell from his bench and the well-fed, well-liquored bums retreated back to the gutter.

Perhaps I would meet such a romantic figure at the Foxhead Tavern, which hopefully would offer an authentic skid row environment. Lively discussions could be heard in the 1930s and '40s as to which was the true skid row in Chicago: a stretch of blocks on South State Street near the heralded Pacific Garden Mission where drunks would go for a free meal and to perhaps get saved, or a similar neighborhood on West Madison Street, minus any such notable mission. Visits to both locales some years later convinced me that West Madison Street, skid row-wise, easily won as the more authentic and superior down-and-out place to visit. Here the bums remained unrepentant and more reconciled to their lot in life. Drink until their money is spent, do some panhandling for more money, maybe put in a shift or two of unloading trucks through a temporary agency and then back to the bar stool. What more could one ask? The denizens on West Madison Street most likely boasted of a much lower recovery rate from alcoholism than the guys on South State Street.

A quasi-skid row establishment at best, the Foxhead Tavern on West Madison Street hosted a diverse element of patrons including working class citizens, in addition to some actual skid row habitués, and surprising, hillbillies. I didn't expect to see hillbillies in Chicago. Not a few forlorn customers straggled in from the surrounding down-and-out environs in hopes of cadging a drink or two. We found the ambiance quite agreeable and were close enough to a real skid row to capture some of its flavor.

Boats Finerty, an older guy from Kentucky, enlisted in the navy at the age of twenty-two. Our company commander, a first-class petty officer, designated him as the recruit boatswain's mate. Similarly, I was appointed as the gunner's mate. Our responsibilities were simple: for Finerty it meant designating personnel to keep our barracks clean or procuring whatever paraphernalia needed to augment our mode of dress for each new day. These were posted in the "plan for the day," and usually meant items such as leggings or special belts. As the company gunner's mate, I had to ensure the rifles we carried during drill, vintage thirty-caliber Springfield rifles, were duly accounted for at the day's end and properly stowed. We did not carry live ammunition.

There wasn't anything Boats Finerty wouldn't do to have a good time. Prior to enlisting he'd spent a year in Wyoming working as farmhand on a ranch not far from Rock Springs. Leaving cars behind Carl and a couple of his fellow ranch hands would often ride their horses to a bar fashioned in a wild-west motif on the outskirts of town, which featured a high swinging door entrance and a hitching post. On one occasion Boats did not bother to tether his horse, Old Billie. He instead on a daring bet rode him directly inside the tavern showcasing a country and western band.

Old Billie took center stage just as the band struck up one of their favorites with guitars twanging and fiddles screeching at full volume. Whether he appreciated their music or not, he began to neigh and stomp about. And before Finerty got him under control and guided him back outside, Old Billie managed to crush several tables and chairs and spill the contents of numerous bottles and glasses.

Repair costs drained the contents of Boats Finery's wallet. After he settled with the proprietor and made it good with disgruntled customers, he decided he'd had enough of the Wild West and returned to his home in Kentucky, shortly after which he enlisted in the navy.

So here we were on the outskirts of skid row seeking adventure on a wintry afternoon in Chicago after eight straight weeks without a drink. Quartered in a barracks at Camp Downey with seventy-five other enlistees, and completely dry, I felt great. Up at early dawn, breakfast, out on the grinder for drill by 8:00 AM with classroom instruction following, and then some gymnastics. After the evening meal, evenings all to ourselves in the barracks or at the gedunk for a candy bar or a soda pop. On a rotation basis we took turns putting in a four-hour midnight or an early morning watch. Being a routine man I accommodated well to a regimented life, knowing what to expect during each day. Sobered up, clear of mind, no longer did I have to go about trying to be a "nice guy." Whether I liked it or not shoes were kept shined.

It got to the point where I did not miss having a beer or a highball. "I'll never touch the stuff again," I promised myself. "When I get out of here and complete my enlistment I'll go back and finish what I started to do at Michigan Tech," I resolved. A resolve short-lived, making false promises to myself wasn't difficult with the booze safely out of reach. But the bars were waiting. Impatient, my anticipation of hitting a few of them grew as the time approached to go on liberty. We would take a train to Chicago from Great Lakes.

"Only one little drink. That's all I'm going to have," I told Boats Finerty when we got off the train in the Loop.

"It's your call, Maki. Are you sure you want to do this?" Finerty asked.

During the eight weeks I'd got to know Finerty I'd related to him the problems my excessive imbibing had caused me from my flunking out of school and being asked to leave home by my parents. "Pack your rags and head for boot camp," my dad had told me.

We'd intended to take in an afternoon Blackhawks' hockey game once we arrived in Chicago and then mosey about idly before going back to the barracks. In other words, no fun after the game—hanging around some drugstore soda fountain getting bored had no appeal for me.

"That one little drink isn't going to hurt anything. Besides we've got almost two hours to kill before the game starts. We've got plenty of time for a drink and still make it to the stadium. Let's get changed into our civvies."

The one little drink led to two, then three and more after that. We soon forgot about the hockey game. A few drinks were what I wanted in the first place. As I said having civilian clothes with us ensured I'd made the proper preparations to do some bar hopping without having to show a military ID. I'd thought of everything. No such problem for Boats Finerty, already of legal age.

"I hear the drinks are a lot cheaper out on West Madison," I told Boats. "We're going to go broke if we stay here in the Loop."

We hailed a cab and off we went. True, the beer and mixed drinks in the Foxhead Tavern cost only a third of what we'd paid downtown. But I did not meet a fallen judge or even a derelict justice of the peace. Had we ventured deeper into the heart of skid row this might have happened. But there would be no story to listen to this afternoon of how a good man allowed himself to be enslaved by alcohol. On the contrary, subsequent events promised fulfillment of a most basic sort, if not the edification which might have evolved from commiseration shown a fallen man relating his tale of woe.

"Hi guys, may we join you?" Marcy asked.

"Why sure ladies, be our quests," I replied. "Please sit down."

"Thank you," Patricia said as she and Marcy seated themselves at our table. "But right now let me warn you we're both a little low on cash."

"That's no problem at all," Boats said. "Bartender, serve the ladies what they'd like to drink and bring another round for my buddy and me."

"What are a couple of nice ladies like you doing in a low-class dump like this?" I asked, trying to sound like some tough in a Humphrey Bogart movie.

Patricia winced. "Who is this cornball," had to be her first impression. "What's this stuff about nice ladies," she said. "We're only looking to have some fun just like you guys."

Marcy and Patricia. A good thing the dim lights in the bar made them appear a lot younger and prettier than they actually were. Removed from the gloaming-like ambiance they looked somewhat careworn and had to be pushing forty. Nonetheless both appeared quite fit and reasonably attractive. "Just right," one might say under the circumstances.

I found their frankness refreshing. We hit it off well; these ladies only wanted to have some fun without any bother. Marcy and Patricia both came from "hillbilly country" as they described their home region in southern Illinois. The drinks kept flowing and the jukebox kept playing. We got up from our table only to shuffle about on a small space for dancing to some hillbilly music:

There's a ramshackle sh-haCk, in old Caroline
it's calling me ba-haCk, to that girl of mine
those two brown ey-hieS, I'm longing to see
for the girl of my dre-heeMS, she'll always be

"Sparkling Brown Eyes," we kept hearing that one all afternoon and evening while enjoying plenty of drinks with Marcy and Patricia. The more we drank the better they looked and the more intelligent they sounded. They both claimed to have been school teachers in southern Illinois and we'd no good reason to gainsay their claims in what would no doubt be a fleeting acquaintance. We didn't question why they came to Chicago and could only guess what their present occupations were. I'd filled Patricia in on our status minus any more Humphrey Bogart nonsense, after which matters improved significantly.

We'd established a semblance of bonding. We danced a two-step, our bodies close and slowly undulating—four square feet of floor space sufficed for our maneuvers. Now she sat near to me, rubbing my thighs. "I'm experiencing a powerful urge to procreate," I told her.

"So am I," she replied, "but that's going to cost money. Ten bucks for you, sailor boy."

"It looks like we'll have to leave the task of increasing the world's population to others," Patricia said after Boats and I tallied our dwindled resources. "Boys, it's been a fun evening. Thanks for showing us a good time."

"Just a minute, ladies," Boats interjected. "I need to talk with my buddy privately."

"Don't take too long," Marcy advised. "We're busy girls."

Off to one side, we took count of our remaining cash. Discounting the cab fare it would take to get us back to the train station we had exactly fourteen dollars and twenty-three cents left between the two of us. At least we'd purchased round-trip train tickets to get us back to Great Lakes.

Finerty had a suggestion.

"One of us should get laid. After the money we've splurged on these hookers it just isn't fair to go back empty-handed. What are we going to tell the guys in the barracks? We owe it to ourselves to do a little bragging.

"I've done some thinking. We've only got enough money for one jump," he continued. "We know Marcy and Patricia don't come cheap, at least for us. Ten bucks is a lot of money right now. While you were dancing with Patricia I did some negotiating with Marcy. 'Ten dollars, rock bottom price,' is what she said, just what Patricia told you.

"So here's the deal. What do you say we flip a coin to see who has the fun? And while that's being had, there're still a couple bucks for the loser to have a few beers. I'll flip the coin and you call. The evening's getting late so we've got to move fast."

I chose heads and lost.

"Come on honey, our place is just around the corner. Just you and me," Marcy told Boats as they rose to leave. "We shouldn't be gone long," she told Patricia and me as I ordered a fresh round of drinks for us.

"Tough luck, kid," Patricia said, "but I've got to make a living. I just wasn't cut out to be a schoolteacher in case you were wondering."

"Man, what a good jump," Boats Finerty bragged to the "old tars" once we got back to Camp Downey.

My two-week leave from basic training meant spending most of my time in the bars of Calumet and Laurium. My fake ID's were good enough to gain admission in most of the taverns. Having a big wad of money helped, which the bartenders knew. Throwing my cash around, word spread fast throughout, and for a week I bummed about town with a gaggle of hangers-on I'd accumulated in the taverns. The hundred fifty bucks of spare cash I had in my wallet went far enough to keep my entourage and the bartenders happy all the while. Most of the taverns in town still offered a shell of beer for a dime.

My new-found pals kept me entertained. One of them removed his upper plate and made Popeye faces. Another sang a creditable version of *Bill Grogan's Goat.* Another still sang *Sixteen Tons* in a mellifluous baritone in imitation of Tennessee Ernie Ford. One afternoon we imitated animals as we moseyed from bar to bar. A couple of the guys brayed like donkeys while others squealed like pigs or mooed like cattle. I joined them, honking like a goose. Bystanders on the sidewalks merely shook their heads. We'd enjoy a pasty or some bacon and eggs occasionally while I listened to my chums sing my praises. "What a nice guy Paulie Maki is," the barflies would say as long as I kept the beer flowing—everything's on me, boys—the beer, the pasties and the bacon and eggs. They tried to brighten my day with corny stories, many of which I'd heard before.

I'd be glad to get out of town. I'd blown blowing most of the pay I'd accrued in boot camp supporting these hangers-on. Once they realized this, they began to disappear. "Time to go back to the cemetery and dig some more graves," one said. I'd spurned my friends. Good old faithful Hicks. Hicks tried to talk to me into getting control of myself. He and Rita invited me over for dinner, and after accepting their invitation, didn't show up. Most of my other acquaintances studiously avoided me and I likewise avoided the people I knew and respected. Outside of the hangers-on in town, the only guys glad to see me were the boarders at Hell's Gate Ranch when I pulled in with a case of Bosch or Stroh's after the bars closed. I spent nights in the barn sleeping in the hayloft, always available to me for a night's rest. Wrapped in a horse blanket and bedded down on hay I slept cozily. Humble Huhta and I broke away for an outing by ourselves, and even though I had the money, he nonetheless cadged two bucks from the hapless Carmen Ulizzio. I spent little time at home.

My parents finally talked me into quitting the bars. I had only two short days left of liberty to recover from worsening hangovers before I left town to report in at the Coronado Naval Base near San Diego.

Still in a fog, those two days were barely enough to get rid of nausea and the shakes before I left for California.

My orders were to board the USS *Holgate* in Sasebo, Japan. From the U.S. Naval Base in Coronado, California, a number of first class seamen were flown to Tokyo, and those assigned to the *Holgate*, a landing ship dock or simply an LSD, then boarded a train for a six-hundred-mile journey to Sasebo. LSDs are an integral part of the amphibious or "gator" navy. The primary function of an LSD is to assist in operations of landing troops on unfriendly shores during wartime. A ballast-controlled large well in the hull of the ship accommodates numerous smaller craft deployed for carrying the troops to dry land. A large, hinged stern gate is opened, which enables these craft to exit the flooded well and embark on their operation.

The view en route revealed a country largely ravaged by war very much in a postwar stage of recovery, particularly in the cities. The countryside, however, seemed tranquil and practically undisturbed as though the war had not been fought at all—viewing the magnificent oriental style architecture and farmers placidly working the rice fields as our train swept south evoked surreal thoughts. Amenities included comfortable berthing and excellent food and beverage. Instead of sake or Nippon beer I opted for tea. The fog, the cobwebs in my mind caused by the week-long binge disappeared. I felt at peace.

Sasebo would be our home port while the *Holgate* operated in the Far East. While the city itself saw little of the devastation experienced by many major cities in Japan during the war, its surrounding hills bore witness to the state of preparedness of the Japanese military and the home populace in anticipation of an invasion of their homeland. Strategically placed guns in hillside dugouts and in caves could still be seen, long immobile and corroded.

Routine life aboard ship agreed well as it had at Great Lakes. Assigned to the gunnery division, I had a lot to learn in maintaining and servicing the twin 3"/50 caliber anti-aircraft weapons. A complex mechanism of parts involving breech blocks, levers, pins and retainers had to be cleaned and lubricated immediately following firing exercises and done periodically thereafter. A first class seaman striking to become a gunner's mate learned how to disassemble and reassemble these parts to an extent he could almost complete the task robotically. Lowering heavy breech blocks tethered to a line and an eye bolt made everyone safety conscious. During periods of inactivity the mounts were covered with heavy conformal canvass tarps, and tompions placed in the muzzles kept rain and dust out of the barrels. Routine duties included early morning "clamp downs" of the weather decks, which meant grabbing a mop or a swab. Daytime activities involved constant rust removal and the priming and painting of metal surfaces. Although often humdrum, I didn't mind routine work. And I didn't mind learning basic skills which might someday come in handy.

Sharing a common berthing space and working together, the gunner's mate and fire control technician enlisted men formed a closely-knit unit. The gunner's mates were the work horses of the outfit keeping eight three-inch fifty-caliber mounts operable and the fire control techs were the brains, having received a solid schooling in electronics at a naval facility. The fire control techs were responsible for maneuvering and firing the guns remotely when the mounts were in "automatic" control. "Manual" control, or direct firing from the mounts, saw crews competing for the most hits at a target, generally a canvas-sailed sled in tow at a safe distance by an auxiliary craft.

We got along well both on board and off the ship. When in port we spent many a pleasant evening at the Enlisted Men's Club, where we could buy a fifth of Seagram's V.O. or Canadian Club for only a buck and a quarter. Excellent imported Dutch and German beers as well as premium American beers were available at token cost. For those with a weekend pass the sybaritic pleasures offered by our Japanese hostesses at the Shiwada House, situated on a verdant hillside on the outskirts of the Sasebo, could always be afforded. Food, drink, music, baths and hostesses tending to every need cost a tad under four thousand yen per sailor. At the time a US dollar exchanged for three hundred sixty yen.

I had no time for prolonged benders nor did I have impulse to drink as though there were no tomorrow. Being constantly on the go in a regimented life, functioning within strict limits of military decorum, kept not only me but shipmates with similar proclivities to binge to excess out of trouble, at least most of the time. Those maybe four or five shots of V.O. or perhaps a couple of Heinekens at the E.M. Club sufficed for an evening. One notable exception occurred.

A lousy day to go on liberty, Knute Haugland and I suffered in the heat of a sweltering day in Hong Kong where the temperature reached one hundred fifteen degrees. The USS *Holgate* just finished participating in a joint naval operation near the Philippines. The ship would be anchored in the harbor off Hong Kong for an entire week.

Neither of us could endure much heat. Knute, hailing from a family of lumberjacks in northern Minnesota, like me acclimated well to cooler, more temperate climes. His grandparents emigrated from Norway to the states in the late eighteen hundreds.

"If you plan to own a suit, Maki, now's your chance to buy one," Knute, a second class gunner's mate, said.

"I don't really need one as I don't wear them, but what's so special about buying one in Hong Kong?"

"The best quality at the lowest price. I don't really need one either but if you're going to own one you'll never find a better price."

We'd ventured forth early one morning on a one-day pass. By eleven in the morning the temperature already neared a humid one hundred degrees. The humidity had to be as stifling as the air inside a foundry operating at maximum capacity. "Why don't we simply go back to the ship," I grumbled. "This is too much heat for cold-weather guys like us. The hell with those suits."

We nonetheless trudged on. Nearly defeated, clammy with sweat, we finally arrived at a tailor shop in the opulent metropolitan area of Hong Kong. Furnished with comfortable lounge chairs, the tailor shop air-conditioned at a crisp, dry seventy degrees, provided immense relief to the suffocating swelter.

"Would you sailor boys have something to drink while I take measurements?" our Chinese proprietor asked.

That's all the convincing we needed. "Please take your time. I need a perfect fit," I replied while imbibing a stiff bourbon and soda served over plenty of rocks. I'd selected worsted English wool in charcoal. The price, paid on the spot was twenty-two dollars, a bargain by any standard.

After measurements were taken and arrangements made to have our suits mailed to the *Holgate* Knute Haugland and I had each polished off three stiff drinks, courtesy of the house. We would have gladly remained in the tailor shop had the drinks kept coming. The outdoor temperature had risen above one hundred degrees, but fortified by the drinks, refreshed, we were prepared for adventure in this mysterious city. The torrid heat would not dissuade us.

"Let's take a look at Hong Kong," Knute suggested, "We've still got a lot of time on our hands."

We hailed a cab in the bustling, glitzy center of the city and gave the driver uncertain directions.

"We'd like to see more of Hong Kong and we'd like to make some stops along the way," I told him. "Show us where the working people live," I added, keeping in mind drinks would be a lot cheaper in a working-class neighborhood.

While the cabbie waited outside, we stopped at two bars for a couple quick highballs en route to a neighborhood appearing to be a vast slum. Not a skid row but simply a slum.

"This is where the working people live," our driver said.

"Let's take a look around," I suggested to Knute, who agreed.

"Be careful boys," our driver advised after dropping us off. "It's easy to get in trouble. Most people here are honest but there are also a lot of pickpockets and thieves."

"We won't be staying long. We're going to walk around this neighborhood for a little while before heading back to the ship. Besides there's still plenty of daylight so we don't expect trouble," Knute said. Warnings posted aboard ship urged caution to those going on liberty, and while recommending Hong Kong as being relatively safe, sailors were strongly warned to keep out of neighboring, communist-plagued Kowloon. There would be no trouble for us on that score.

"Just the same, be careful," the cabbie reminded us before driving off.

The disparity between the opulent metropolitan area at the business core of the city and this slum neighborhood could not have been starker. Clothing and textile outlets, precious gem brokerage houses, major financial institutions and diverse commercial enterprises flourishing in modern high-rise buildings contrasted vividly with block after block, row after row of closely spaced tenement buildings, most of which were at least four stories high, and while mainly of stone construction, not a few of the tenements appeared to be built of wood. The most visible sign these buildings were occupied were lengths of clothesline strung with drying laundry, hanging at every level from the ground floor to the top level. The entire complex impressed me as a large tinderbox ready to burn. How occupants avoided a mass conflagration over the years remains a mystery. The tenants obviously are extra careful with flame.

Most of the men living in the many tiny apartments in the slum, instilled of a strong work ethic, worked as dock hands in the busy port. Some worked as laborers in a large produce district while many pulled rickshaws. Both men and women assisted in managing small grocery outlets and laundries. There were few idlers.

Good intentions failed us. Sure enough, the lounges we patronized in the neighborhood offered drinks at very affordable prices. Hitting one joint after another, events became sketchy. The large amount of liquor we'd consumed exacerbated by the intense heat had taken its toll. My mind had become blurred.

We met a prostitute. At her invitation Haugland and I entered one of the tenement buildings where we bickered over price. The strange thing is I could not remember how the woman accosted us to begin with, yet some of the memories of our encounter remain surprisingly sharp. Her small drab apartment contained only barest necessities, and the entire setting of her living quarters seemed to be cast in yellowish brown hue. Spare of build and seemingly depressed, the woman stood passively by a sink with a single faucet. She did not protest when we'd offered her a rock bottom price for her services. Her expression resigned and devoid of animation, she projected pessimism, as though only more drudgery lie in store. "A syndrome peculiar to many Asiatics who've lost hope, particularly women," the *Holgate's* chief corpsman later told me.

Neither of us took her up on the reasonable terms she abjectly accepted; at the last minute we both backed out. One small grain of sense remained. We'd been warned by the chief corpsman of a high incidence of venereal disease in Hong Kong. Anyway we were both mokus, blind drunk and stupefied from the heat.

I still find it strange I can remember everything that transpired in her apartment with clarity and little else afterward. For the first time in my short drinking career I experienced what I refer to as an "ambulatory blackout." Still on my feet, able to converse to some degree, I had an almost a complete memory lapse of subsequent events. Our weird day in Hong Kong remains in my memory as a bad dream come true.

Now well into the evening, the streets were dark. Knute and I had somehow found ourselves in a large outdoor merchandising district.

"We're being followed," Knute said.

We were walking through dimly lit narrow lanes. Various goods were displayed on each side of the lanes, which appeared as arms of a vast labyrinth. I turned about to see three tough-looking oriental men trailing us, not too far behind. They were not young, at least in their late thirties. Obviously Knute and I were the objects of their attention.

"Just keep moving," Haugland said.

As in a nightmare, we could not shake them off. Our legs failed us. We tried as hard as we could to run in our thoroughly inebriated condition, but no matter which way we turned or tried to duck, there they were, right on our tail. We had no one to turn to—most of the shoppers in the district were elderly men and women who paid us scant attention.

Everything went blank. Neither Haugland nor I could recall much that ensued. Barely at best. We both remembered being pursued by the sinister trio after which matters turned black. I have a vague recollection of being herded into an empty shed. Later, we somehow fell into the hands of the Shore Patrol who escorted us to the landing where we boarded an LCM, which took us safely back to the *Holgate*.

We escaped bodily harm but we were both robbed. By whom? Were we drugged? Perhaps. We were both very drunk but not delusional. The next day we could only surmise the trio of men had somehow subdued us and then relieved us of our wallets and IDs. What actually happened and how this happened remains a mystery. Knute Haugland and I were both confined to the ship for an entire month until new IDs could be processed.

We were grateful to be alive. We never did get the suits.

I made Third Class Gunner's Mate. After the harrowing adventure in Hong Kong, I settled back into routine life and got the single red stripe on my sleeve with the crossed cannons emblem designating my new status as a third class petty officer. The consequences of what had happened and what worse could have happened on that torrid afternoon and evening remain etched on my mind; I vowed never again to lose such utter control of myself as I and Knute Haugland had allowed. Our guardian angels must have been with us.

My buddy Knute didn't have to worry anymore about being careful in strange places as he'd practically completed a second four-year hitch. Eight years in the navy would be enough for him. He had only two months to go after our escapade in Hong Kong.

"So long, Maki. Take good care of yourself," he said when he left. "And if you ever make it to Minnesota, look me up. There's some great walleye fishing up where I'm going." Knute left to become a partner with his father in a family logging business.

Was it possible I would keep my vow? I did not stop drinking, however, much of the time immoderately. Especially at the E.M. club where those four or five shots from a fifth costing a measly buck and a quarter would become a dozen or so. More than once I'd had one too many and wound up crapped out at a table before the evening ended. But there were no two or three-day binges; I became a lot more careful of places where I spent time while enjoying a liberty. Knute Haugland and I simply got careless in unfamiliar circumstances. There were no such worries at the E.M. club.

But there were watchful eyes, their gaze upon me.

The USS *Holgate* continued amphibious operations in the Far East with the naval Seventh Fleet for the next two years, during which time I got my third class stripe. Unbeknownst to me, our gunnery officer, Lieutenant j.g. Harry Pence, had some words with one of the older gunner's mates and some of the fire control technicians.

"Do me a favor and keep an eye on Maki," he advised them. "He shows signs of having good abilities but he doesn't control his drinking very well. At first the higher-up officers were going to ask him to apply to the Naval Aviation Cadet Program. I put in a good word for him. He learns fast and applies himself well when he's not drinking. He's got a mind of his own and he's not a toady, which we like a lot about him. But for now we're going to see how that dog sleeps and wait to see how he shapes up."

Indeed, Wally Grimes, also a second class gunner's mate, had mentioned the cadet program in Pensacola, Florida. "Maki, have you ever thought about becoming a naval pilot?"

"No, I haven't, Wally. Right now it's putting in this hitch and then getting back to my engineering studies. But thanks for asking."

"Just between you and me, Maki, Lieutenant Pence brought this up to me and a couple other guys. The officers apparently think highly of you. So do I. Think about it."

Me a navy pilot? I'd never thought of becoming a naval pilot. Flattered the officers thought so highly of me, this would take some serious thought.

But I had priorities.

"Three weeks at sea. It gets awfully dry out here," I told my closest shipmates. There were four of us: a cook, two fire control technicians and myself. "What do you say we make some white lightning. I know just how to keep this a secret from anyone on board the *Holgate*."

No one expressed contrary views or fear of what would happen if our top-secret operation were disclosed. As the man in charge I designated responsibilities.

"Guys, here's what we've got to do. Stew burner Johnny Landover is going to furnish the ingredients. It's not going to be difficult for him to comshaw corn meal, apples, sugar and yeast from the galley. Being a third class cook makes things easier. He can also lay his hands on a five-gallon crock. We just add the right amount of water."

Landover and the fire control techs listened closely.

"I'm going to be the brewmaster. We're going to ferment this stuff in the gun locker on the topmost deck of the ship. It's always kept locked but I've got access to the keys. The locker is vented high to the outside so no one should get a whiff of what's going on even if they're up there.

"Now here's where the brains come in," I continued, "I'm talking about Jerry Babcock and Ben Goodnough, our two smartest fire control techs."

"I don't know about the brains," Jerry Babcock ventured, "but Ben and I've got this big percolator coffee pot we can rig into a still. Ben says we can run the mash Maki's fermented and get at least one hundred fifty proof alcohol. We think we've got the thermostat adjusted to distill the batch at about one hundred eighty degrees. Just about right."

Ben Goodnough claimed alcohol distills at one hundred seventy degrees, maybe a tad higher.

"Maybe one twenty proof," Goodnough added. "Here's the way it works. We can seal the lid with a removable clamp and adapt a copper tube to the spout. Everything is leak proof. Then we plug it in and let it go to work. The way Jerry and I have got it figured, if we're careful, we should be distilling better than fifty percent alcohol once we fill the pot and plug it in. We shouldn't be cooking off too much water which boils and makes a lot of steam at two hundred twelve degrees."

Ben Goodnough had patiently encouraged me to learn to play chess. As a beginner and a slow student, almost bored, I pushed pawns aimlessly before graduating to fork a pair of rooks with a knight, and afterward, learning the rudiments of piece development and positional strategy. Once I learned the game I became addicted. But I had to play Ben, an imaginative coffee-house style player, at least a hundred times before I even won a single game. Even then I believe he eased up a bit because he facetiously announced "I'm starting this game with my knights facing backward." Playing chess proved to be a stimulating pastime during the long hours at sea.

Make white lightning? Just as good as playing chess, maybe even better. "Blue water moonshine," Jerry Babcock called it.

"The rest is easy," Ben continued. "The tube's got a coil that's immersed in a bucket of cold water. And guess what? Drip, drip, drip, and out comes the good stuff which we collect in some quart bottles Johnny's provided."

The operation proved to be a complete success. I managed to get the batch fermented in the gun locker without detection. It took less than two weeks before the fermentation stopped. I closely monitored the bubble activity in the brew before stirring the batch with a ladle several times. The vigorous fermentation at the outset slowed to a barely perceptible bubble formation at the end of the process. The coffee pot still worked splendidly. From a five-gallon batch of fermented mash we distilled three full quarts of high proof blue water moonshine. It mixed very well with orange or grapefruit juice supplied by Johnny Landover. We successfully fermented and distilled a second batch with an even better yield and with no unwelcome intrusion. I'd added more sugar to the second batch.

"Just what the hell's going on in here," the first class boatswain's mate bellowed. Standing watch and making a routine round, he'd intruded on our party. We were roaring drunk. Loud music, raucous voices and uproarious laughter caused him to look in on matters transpiring in the fire-control room where we'd gathered. Present at the scene were Wally Grimes and a couple guys from the deck force in addition to the four of us responsible for the product. Two quarts of the moonshine were already gone and we'd just got started on a third. The stuff had to be at least one hundred twenty proof—easily from the way it hit us. One of the guys from the deck force provided the music, and paying no attention to the first mate, continued to vocalize and thump chords on his guitar.

His unwelcome intrusion put an untimely end to our operation.

"You guys better get this mess cleaned up before the exec or the captain finds out what's been happening. And pronto. Let this be the end of it. Rumors have been spreading fast. There's a lot of talk of some bootlegging going on. Clean it up and there'll be nothing said to anyone," the first mate told us before returning to his post on the quarter deck.

Rumors indeed had spread, and had spread to the top.

"It's too bad those guys quit their bootlegging operation," the executive officer jocularly said. "I'd like to have tried some of their stuff myself. If it was any good I might have given them a fulltime job."

After three years in the Far East the USS *Holgate* returned to the states. I had a year to go on my enlistment.

"There's some nasty business that's got to be attended to," Wally Grimes said to me shortly after we got back. The *Holgate* would be anchored off Long Beach for two weeks after which it would go into a dry dock in San Francisco for maintenance and repair.

I listened closely.

"Jim Rawlings got beat up in a bar in San Pedro. For no good reason he says. His aunt and uncle living in San Pedro told him about the 'Proud Parrot' during a visit. That's a bar in San Pedro where they've got a parrot the owner claims is sixty years old. The bird is supposed to talk fluently for a parrot. Mostly longshoremen and merchant marine sailors go there to drink."

"Just be careful, Jim," his uncle advised him before he left to see the parrot. Despite his uncle's warning Rawlings did not expect trouble. He never thought he'd get beat up.

As a studious, young inoffensive yeoman, Jim Rawlings' main interests outside of reading included studying wildlife. He only wanted to see the bird. A quiet evening at the Proud Parrot, there were no more than six patrons on hand when he entered. Except for two, they were elderly men. Shortly after Jim ordered a beer a big lout at a nearby table started taunting him. He ignored the taunts as he intended to have just the one beer and then leave after seeing the parrot. But the bully wouldn't let up.

"What's a punk like you doing here? I suppose you think you're the defender of our shores in your spic-and-span uniform and those shiny shoes."

"I'm not looking for trouble, I only came to see the parrot."

"Did you hear that, Snake?" he said to his companion, a wiry, tough looking man with a perpetual sneer on his face. "A friggin' bird watcher. This kid came to see the parrot. Can you believe it?"

"Bingo, I think maybe he's a cheese boy."

"Well maybe cheese boy is looking for some action. Let's see if he'll oblige us."

"You guys can go to hell," Jim replied, losing his temper and rising to leave.

"Not so fast, cheese boy, you're going to make us happy," Bingo said, grabbing him by an arm.

"Let go of me. I'm going to leave. I said I'm not looking for trouble."

Jim tried to defend himself the best he could. As he struggled to free himself the big lout punched him squarely on the cheek. "Bingo," he said as he hit him. Jim reflexively struck back but only succeeded in getting hit again, after which Bingo forcefully kicked him on his buttocks.

"Now beat it, you pantywaist. We don't cotton to bird watchers here. Don't show your face here again."

Rawlings returned dejectedly to his relatives' home, the entire left side of his face bruised and his left eye swollen shut. It took days to heal.

We'd better go check this place out," Wally said. I agreed. Jim Rawlings insisted on coming with us, despite our reservations of having him along. "I'm demanding an apology," he said, "and I'm not looking for anyone to fight my battles."

"You'll get your apology once we settle matters there," Wally promised. "You've already fought your battle."

Second class gunner's mate Wally Grimes, a ten-year navy veteran, considered himself a member of the "Old Navy." He once believed if men aboard ship could not settle their differences with words, the swiftest path to a resolution required a duke-out in the ramp room, with or without gloves. The ramp room, an enclosed storage area located above the forward end of the large well, provided ample space for weight lifting and a general workout. A speed bag and a heavy bag were available for those wanting to improve their boxing skills or simply as aids to be used in maintaining overall conditioning. Wally had become my closest friend onboard the USS *Holgate*.

Wally and I'd both stayed in top shape using the equipment in the ramp room and doing hundreds of sit-ups and pushups while at sea. We often put on large, padded sparring gloves and headgear and went a few rounds. Sometimes we went at it with other shipmates. We'd build up endurance by skipping rope for at least ten minutes at a frenzied pace. Jim Rawlings used the ramp room chiefly for calisthenics.

"Let the best man win and let bygones be bygones," Wally would say recounting his earlier years in the service. He had been to ramp room three times and emerged victorious twice. His bouts took place before 1950, when according to Grimes, a new Uniform Code of Military Justice absolutely prohibited fighting to settle disputes on board ship or on any other military installation. Not that anyone had previously approved of "settle things yourselves," but authorities then were more apt to look the other way. Going a few friendly rounds in a gym using the headgear and sparring gloves, however, met with approval and was even encouraged. But the new code restrictions did not stop Wally from avenging wrongs done once off the ship.

"Fuck you. Stuff it up your ass," were the first words we heard when the three of us entered the Proud Parrot. It came from the parrot himself, perched on a spindle in a roomy cage. The large mangy bird appeared to be as old as the owner claimed. His once glorious plumage had faded from a bright green to a drab, grayish-green hue. His feathers appeared to be in a state of continuous molt. Just a few feathers of what once must have been a splendid tail remained. Only his protuberant beady eyes had not dimmed with age. They were as clear and perceptive as ever as he imperiously looked over the customers in the bar.

"That's the two guys," Jim Rawlings said quietly. A large potbellied man seated at the same table as before scowled menacingly at us as we ordered beers at the bar. His companion attempted to stare us down with hard intimidating eyes. Bingo and Snake to be sure. And this time a large crowd of merchant marine sailors and longshoremen were present and not just a couple of old men when Jim got beat up. They were a tough, formidable bunch of guys. They did not seem to resent us, however, and some even acknowledged our presence with a nod.

None of them exhibited the slightest bit of hostility at our being there. None except Bingo and Snake.

"I thought I told you to keep your butt out of here," the larger man told Rawlings. "And the same goes for your punk pals. Now get moving—all three of you—before I have to throw you out."

He remained seated as he spoke. Other patrons sat in silence for several interminably long moments. "Fuck you," the parrot squawked from his cage.

"We're staying," I finally replied. "Maybe you ought to get your miserable ass out of here. You and your crony are the only ones here who seem to have any problems." Obviously there would be no apology from the pair or even an explanation.

At five-eleven and one hundred eighty pounds and in top physical condition, I had no fear of this guy even though he stood three inches taller and had at least fifty pounds on me. If it came to a fight I just had to stay out of his reach and trust my reflexes. And although this oaf appeared to have had quite a bit to drink, I could not count his state of inebriation as an excuse for letting him off the hook after what he'd done to Jim.

Snake sneered as though relishing what lie ahead.

"Well, well, well," Bingo said to Snake, "we're going to have some fun," as he slowly rose from his chair. The fact there were only two of them against the three of us did not seem to cause him or his partner any concern.

"Sit down, Jim, Wally and I will handle this," I said as Rawlings started to get up from his bar stool.

The big lout hesitated briefly and even showed a tinge of alarm as I cleared a space between the bar and their table. After the pause he regained his confidence, his face a mask of irrational, brutish rage as he came toward me. Prepared and alert I'd sized him up as all brawn and no brains. No more than three feet away from me, he balled his right fist and cocked his arm well behind his shoulder after which he launched a tremendous haymaker. That's what I'd anticipated, and in my heightened awareness I saw the punch coming almost in slow motion. At the last instant I ducked and threw a right cross that landed squarely on his left temple. I'd countervailed the leftward momentum of his lunge by thrusting my full body weight in the opposite direction, loaded in my right shoulder and arm.

He crashed across his table and landed on the floor where he lay unconscious. I thought I'd smashed his skull. He did not move. In my still heightened state of awareness to protect myself I felt but scant relief when he staggered to his feet and sat down.

Wally had his hands full. Not wasting any time, Snake got into it with him right away and appeared to be getting the better of it. Although holding his own a cut appeared above Wally's right eye and started to bleed. Emboldened, Snake launched a flurry of punches, most of which Wally blocked. But some got through and Wally wobbled a bit. Snake thought he had him beat. He became openly defiant, and with both arms spread out at his sides, he began to jeer. "C'mon, punk," he snarled.

That's all Wally needed, now steady on his feet. He shot off a straight left, his full power packed behind the punch. I heard a very audible "splat," the sound of bones smashing as Wally caught him flush on a prominent nose, now flattened grotesquely off to one side of his face. Snake slumped onto a chair, blood streaming from the ruined proboscis, where he remained seated in a stupor. No longer were his eyes hard and intimidating: they looked small, weak and defeated. His mouth slack, he reminded me of a servile bookkeeper who'd just received a stern reprimand from an overbearing superior.

"Police," someone yelled.

Hearing the loud ruckus, two burly policemen walking their beat entered the Proud Parrot and instinctively directed their attention at Wally and me as being the instigators of the trouble. "Just some more trouble-making sailor boys," one of them remarked to his partner. The cops were getting ready to escort us out when three of the longshoremen who'd witnessed the proceedings intervened.

"Self-defense," the biggest one told the cops. He further related the circumstances leading up to the fracas. His companions backed him up. Bingo and Snake claimed innocence of having started the fight, but to no avail as the policemen handcuffed them and began to lead them away. "Any more trouble from you creeps and what you got here tonight will seem like a game of patty cake," a merchant marine sailor told the hapless pair as they were being escorted out of the bar. The policemen said nothing.

"Fuck you. Go to hell," the mangy parrot squawked loudly and clearly as the louts stumbled out the door.

After the Proud Parrot incident we spent most of our remaining time in Long Beach. We returned to the tavern only to spend a pleasant evening of camaraderie with the longshoremen who'd interceded with the law on our behalf. They were a great bunch of hardworking and fun-loving guys. "Sorry about your buddy getting roughed up by those two creeps," one of the merchant marine sailors said after hearing an account of why we'd come to the Proud Parrot. "Those guys give longshoremen and the merchant marines a bad name," another said. "Both of them are nothing but drifters looking for a quick buck. We won't be seeing those bums for a while, if ever. The judge gave both these guys thirty days in the can after they got patched up. And they won't be welcome here."

We experienced no further trouble following the Proud Parrot incident while anchored off Long Beach. After we left Long Beach the USS *Holgate* stayed blocked up in dry dock in San Francisco for nearly two months undergoing hull inspection and overall repair. This gave us a lot of time for liberty. We needed some good relaxation after the extensive junket in the Far East. It also meant we had to make our limited funds stretch between paydays. Wally Grimes, a single man, and I were content just going out for some inexpensive food and then some beer while on liberty. Forget trying to meet women, at least for the time being. Dating could wait; we could attend servicemen's dances later. For the present the grub and the beer would suffice.

Almost always running low on pocket money, we found the best bargains for food and refreshment near the intersection of Third and Howard Streets, a focal point of several greasy spoon restaurants and dives.

"Sailor boys, you don't want to eat here. This is a real skid row joint," a lone counterman advised us as Wally and I entered a shabby restaurant.

"All we need are some eggs, toast and coffee. Can you manage that?" Wally asked him.

"Well, the eggs are OK. They come out of the chicken's ass. Nothing gets through that hard shell. Coming right up, boys."

He surprised us each with a decent omelet. The coffee wasn't too bad either. Not bad at all for a fifty-cent breakfast. After leaving generous tips, Wally and I repaired to the Green Pump, a skid row bar near the corner of Third and Howard where one could still get a draft beer for a dime. After two hours we hadn't even spent two dollars between us. And we did not have to forget meeting women; a timely fate intervened, at least on Wally's behalf.

"You boys looking to have some fun?" a woman's voice resonated. "My name's Gretchen."

There stood a fiftyish woman who had to weigh two hundred and fifty pounds. Maybe even more. I had the impression she had once been attractive and slim but now she appeared coarse and seedy.

I said nothing.

"How much?" Wally asked.

"For you only ten dollars. I've got a room upstairs."

"Too high. How about five?"

They settled on seven dollars.

"You might as well come along too, sonny. If you're bashful you can just look the other way."

More than glad to accompany them as there were some tough looking customers at the bar, I followed the twosome upstairs to a sparsely furnished room. I wasn't about to stay in the tavern by myself; I had enough barroom brawling at the Proud Parrot.

Wally and Gretchen got down to business immediately while I stood near the door close to the foot of the bed. There I stood guard just in case the guys at the bar downstairs decided to hatch up some funny business.

Gretchen appeared even more imposing once she'd removed her underwear. Her thighs were as thick as stumps. Her immense balloon of a belly shook mirthfully when she laughed and she laughed loudly and often.

Matters were not progressing well for Wally. The couple had parked themselves too close to the foot of the bed. As he attempted to gain purchase, Wally's knees dangled over the end and his feet thrashed wildly at air. I had to make some deft moves to avoid getting kicked.

"What's wrong, tomato, haven't you ever done this before?" Gretchen puffed at him as he fumbled about on top of her. Despite his trim physique she called him a fat ass. "You can't fuck, you can't fuck," she added.

He ultimately managed to shuffle her hefty torso higher on the bed where matters improved significantly.

"Come on, tomato, let's go alligator," she started yelling. She shook like a massive jello in response to Wally's spirited buffeting.

Of course, I laughed.

"What's so funny, kid?" she asked.

"Nothing much, I just happened to think of some old jokes."

Gretchen did not budge from her spot when Wally got off the bed.

Like some big, contented seal she lay immobile in her abundant nudity. She smiled invitingly at me. One of her incisors I noticed was missing. Other teeth still in her possession stood in need of repair.

"How about you, Buster? Are you ready for a bit of heaven?" she asked me. "Only five bucks for you, kid."

"No thank you, ma'am, I'm broke. Perhaps some other time," I lied.

"Hey, alligator, you know where to find old Gretchen if you need some more loving," she said to Wally as we departed. "And bring your buddy with you. That bargain I offered still stands."

"It's no secret, Maki, we want you to give Pensacola a try. As I mentioned earlier to Wally Grimes and the fire control techs, you've got a good chance of getting into flight school. The officers are of one accord you can succeed," Lieutenant Pence told me a couple of months before my enlistment ended. "We stand ready to offer our recommendation if that's what you decide to do."

I'd moderated my drinking going out to have a few brews with Wally Grimes during my last year in the navy. This did not go unnoticed by Pence and the non-coms. Wally, Jerry Babcock and Ben Goodnough had quietly put in good words to Lieutenant Pence after noting the progress I'd made.

"Maki seems to have his drinking under control. He's a smart guy. He could go far," Grimes noted to our gunnery officer.

"Thanks for your consideration, Lieutenant Pence, but I've thought matters over carefully since Wally first brought this up to me. I'm going to stick to my original plans of becoming an engineer. I'm truly honored you even had me in mind for flight school. Thanks again."

Deep down inside I wasn't sure of myself. I'd done well handling my drinking during the past year but I still stood on shaky ground. I had many inner doubts. I had many questions needing answers. Me a pilot? How long would I last in flight school before I went on a big bender? Am I a coward for letting a splendid opportunity like this slip away so easily? I hated saying I had low self-esteem. Maybe I simply lacked courage; it made me sick thinking this could be the case. Anyone else would have jumped at the chance of becoming a navy pilot. Maybe if I'd had a longer period of sobriety under my belt I might have decided differently. I recalled my ROTC experience, my attitude toward military life. Didn't I conclude then I'd function better as a grunt rather than becoming a leader? Or at least be more comfortable.

I did not need major responsibility I finally decided. I would instead go back to college where everyone knew me and I'd be doing everyone else a favor. I'd be a straight-ahead, humble college-boy drudge. I wouldn't be crashing a plane and getting myself killed.

CHAPTER 8

An Engagement

"I'm giving it another try, Hicks. I might have to bother you once in a while with this calculus."

"It'll come back in no time flat, Paulie. Once you've understood the fundamentals of math and get them down pat you'll never forget them. Maybe you'll just be a little rusty to start with."

Here I was, nice little Paulie Maki back at da Tech—nice little Paulie Maki despite his one hundred eighty pounds. This time I contended without "Chump" Maki or ROTC as my hitch in the navy took care of having to reenroll in the program. Except for one big bash during a summer break I refrained from hard drinking and eschewed bumming although I enjoyed a few brews occasionally. Hard painful study instead occupied my spare time. Hopefully, everyone would be glad I was "doing the right thing." I'd become a worry-wart of what my well-meaning neighbors were thinking.

"Paulie's got the brains but he gives up too easily," Jake Bloomdahl had remarked to Pastor Henry Bylkas. "I wish I could help him," typified remarks of well-meaning townspeople. "He looked so sincere when I tried talking to him," Gladys Bloomdahl said, "but then he went out bumming and drinking some more. He didn't show up at home for three whole days. He had his parents worried sick."

My parents remained skeptical. My mom could only pray.

"You've got a roof over your head if you keep straight and buckle down to what you're supposed to do," my dad assured me when I'd reenrolled. "But any more horseshit from you and you're out of here for good. Keep up the booze and you'll wind up like Willard Janke."

I'd long forgotten the vow I made never to become a drunkard like Willard.

"Have you heard about Aldo," Hicks asked me. "He's going to be a priest."

I couldn't believe my ears. My worldly-wise friend a priest?

"You've got to be kidding me."

"He'll be entering a seminary in Cincinnati. Right now he's back at Northern University finishing his undergraduate work in preparation for the seminary. I got to see him quite a bit and talked to him before he left for Marquette."

I thought his wanting to become a priest to be nothing more than a young guy's fancy, perhaps something to do to please his parents. I even placed a bet with Hicks he'd not go through with this. Aldo couldn't be serious. I would find out.

We got together with Aldo over the Christmas holidays at Hicks and Rita's home. They were still renting. Rita had written and invited Abby to spend the holidays with them. To Rita's disappointment Abby couldn't make it. Her father, still in recovery from a back injury, had taken a nasty spill on a slippery December sidewalk.

There were now three children. A baby sister and brother joined young Alfred Maurice Huhta. Rita tried to keep them occupied in the kitchen while the three of us conversed in the living room. Not very successful at holding their interest, however, they ran back and forth fascinated by Aldo and me. The trio hopped up and down in front of us, waving their arms and babbling.

"You don't look like a priest, old buddy," I joshed.

"I'm not a priest yet. Far from it; I'm still a college boy. What's a priest supposed to look like?" he quipped.

I'd quite frankly expected to see a man of serious mien looking at me straight in the face with an unfaltering, solicitous gaze. Instead he looked more like a con man or a gigolo rather than a prospective man of the cloth. His dark full mustache complemented his likewise full head of dark, wavy hair, swept back on each side of his head and over the top in perfect symmetry. Still full of mischief, his large eyes darted about while his broad lips smiled even more knowingly and vulpine-like than ever. If he perceived awkwardness in a young newcomer he'd cause one of his cheeks to flutter. "What are you trying to keep from me, chum," his actions intimated. If one didn't know him, he'd impress his audience as being a wise guy until they saw through this humbug.

"Why the priesthood," I pressed on. "You were never an altar boy or were ever active in the church. You owe us an explanation."

"Give me a break. I'll get around to letting you know eventually but there's no need for heavy stuff tonight. Let's have some fun. All I can say for now it runs in the family. There has always been at least one Vella in the cloth going back generations. We've seen a couple bishops along the way in addition to priests and even a cardinal three hundred years ago. So you might say I'm maintaining a longstanding family tradition. Who knows, I might even become a bishop myself."

"You know what that means, pal. No girlfriends, no wife or family and celibacy forever. Do you think you can handle celibacy? You once told me you were going to spread yourself around and give all the girls a break."

"I've given enough of them a break already overseas. Just like you must have done in the Far East. And a few here in the States."

"I still don't understand why you want to be a priest. I never thought of you as being the religious type."

Celeste Vella secretly hoped one of her three sons would become a priest. But she did not apply pressure on any of them. Aldo, her youngest, would become her genius to fulfill the secret wishes of her heart without any persuasion. Despite his mischief, his tendency to always look for fun and his knack for sometimes getting under one's skin, Celeste perceived a very serious bent in her son's nature. She watched him mature from a lad mainly caring about the treatment of animals to a young man sensitive to people in distress, whether they experienced physical or mental pain. He truly wanted to help people. It took some serious thought before he decided on a course of action to best implement this aim. For Aldo, it would be the priesthood.

I finally asked the question Rita had been waiting for me to ask.

"How about Abby? What is she doing?" I asked nonchalantly.

"We still keep in touch," Rita said. "We've been writing often ever since we met several years ago at the Emmaus Hall Christmas party. You must remember that.

"This Heights Bunch is a pretty smart bunch," she added. "Abby graduated summa cum laude from Michigan State and look at my Phillip. Top honors in the chemistry class."

I'd already heard she taught philosophy and some courses in American history at a small private downstate college. "Was she dating, engaged or already married?" I wondered; I could not forget her.

Rita read my mind.

"Abby's still not married nor is she going with anyone," she said while searching my facial reaction for clues—she had to find out how I still felt about her. "And Lucas and Roxanna got married."

"It's getting late. I've been keeping everyone up and it's time for me to go. I've got some studying to do before I turn in." With the fall quarter over I still spent time brushing up on math.

Rita told me she'd arrived in town. She would be staying with an aunt in Calumet for two weeks. That's the first I heard about her coming. Abby made no previous effort to contact me as I had not corresponded with her since she'd last written more than four years ago.

I had a hard time convincing myself I'd lost interest in Abby. Like so many men of Finnish origin, I possessed a stubborn streak I let stand in the way of seeing her, even if only to exchange a friendly greeting. Many a Finnish man would sooner walk off a cliff rather than admit to his shortcomings, particularly if he believed he'd been offended by one close to him, however insignificantly. Some called us immature—even childish—for having this attitude. The accusers were shrugged off.

I'd not by any means lost interest in her but I resolved to be manly and tough. Not be like my sad, old great-uncle Sam, a bachelor brother of Grandma Maki, who got jilted as a young man. He never got over it and would weep while playing a mournful love song on the piano. There would be no weeping for me should separate ways for us become permanent.

Manly and tough it was. The mountains I'd manufactured from molehills when she showed up in town with Lucas Wagonhoffer still proved enough slight for me to avoid her. No matter what, I had no intention of seeing her, even though Lucas Wagonhoffer had disappeared from the horizon with Roxanna.

She found me instead, early one afternoon. I'd just stopped in at Toof's Café. While shooting the bull with some of the regulars I heard a voice from the past.

"Paulie Maki," the voice cheerfully said.

I knew the voice and from where it came without looking.

She had come alone. I admired her closely, trying not to gawk after I slowly turned around from where I sat at the lunch counter. But gawk I did, and I did not speak at once. A host of impressions of Abby flooded my head as I gawked:

Imbued with a beauty stemming from poise and dignity I found her more attractive than ever. Even more comely than when she appeared at the Emmaus Hall with Lucas. Her intelligent blue eyes quickly lit up when she smiled—her smile pleasingly accentuated the dimples on her cheeks. Shapely and trim, she appeared taller than I'd previously perceived her to be. I noticed a slight difference in her appearance since I'd last seen her more than four years ago: very faint creases were beginning to appear in the corners of her eyes. For me, this did not detract from her appearance in any way, but made her even more attractive. A perfectly natural lady-like charm she projected appealed as her most desirable trait. Abby impressed me as being totally devoid of affectation.

Stumped, I'd certainly not expected to meet her under these circumstances, if at all. Here I sat attired in a coarse outfit reeking of fish. I'd just got back from an all-morning fishing trip on the Traverse River when I stopped at Toof's for a cup of coffee. I'd limited out on speckled trout. I stunk more than ripe, for as anyone knows who's gutted a mess of fish, the odor does not easily wash off one's hands. But far worse, I'd got fish blood and some of the offal on my trousers from being in a hurry to get back to town. The speckies were iced down in a chest in the trunk of my car.

Toof, the proprietor of this small restaurant in Calumet, did not mind my smelly presence, and accustomed to having stinking fishermen as mainstay clientele, welcomed everyone whether they smelled or not. Other customers did not even take notice. The restaurant, although clean and noted for quality short-order preparations, stood low, shabby and dimly lit. Toof kept bottomless coffee cups full. Shuttered front windows blocked the harsh glare of the afternoon sun shining directly upon them. Cigarette smoke almost always filled the air. In order to get to the toilet one had to go down a narrow staircase and then navigate through a cluttered basement dimly lit by two light bulbs to get to a single stinking john at the far end. The john, situated in a tiny cramped space, provided facility for both men and women. One could often see feet protruding from under a small door secured with an eye hook, a door which had at least a foot cut off its bottom. A sighting of bloomers lowered about ankles was common. But no one complained too much of having to find his way to the john; ample servings of decent quality food offset this inconvenience. Even the health inspector overlooked the shortcomings of Toof's Café.

A fastidious dresser? Not me. Clothes do not make the man. Attired in my well-worn fisherman's outfit, Abby would not be impressed by a man who dressed up like some self-important small-town mayor. Hadn't I defeated all comers in a dirty-shirt contest in high school during a lengthy three-week contest? I'd come to believe casually worn dress should comport well with Abby or any other worthy girl. How a man should appear, even if ripe, would be of minimal concern to them. But a man reeking of fish? Too much to expect of anyone, particularly Abby.

Surprised but inwardly rejoicing I ventured, "What brings you here, Abby?"

"Just a hunch I'd find you somewhere in town. Rita told me what you're driving and I spotted your car in front. Right here on Fifth Street."

"Let's get a table if you don't mind sitting with a smelly fisherman. I just got off the Traverse River a little while before you came and if you've noticed by now, I smell of fish."

"You don't smell any different than you did before," she laughed.

"We've got a lot of catching up to do," I said.

Bringing each other up to date on what had transpired in our lives, both of us delighted at long last to be together, we talked for hours over coffee.

"How about getting together this evening? Maybe take a ride and have some dinner after I've had a chance to get cleaned up. How about I pick you up at five o'clock?"

"I'd love that."

We drove to Rabbit Bay which is located on the more placid south shore of the Keweenaw Peninsula. The oft-times blustery north shore features lengthy expanses of pebbled beaches, punctuated by sweeps of sand dunes and stretches of rocky and rugged shoreline, which contrasts noticeably with long, low-lying and sometimes wet areas near the lake front of the peninsula's mostly sandy south shore. Earlier in the day while on the Traverse River, muggy air, an overcast sky and a warm, a drizzling rain created ideal fishing conditions. Now the air was brisk and the sky clear. Very few mosquitoes and no deer fly swarmed about to bother us. We sat near a small bonfire on a broad, sandy stretch of beach, away from a small settlement of cottages. We had the beach to ourselves.

We would have fish for dinner and toasted marshmallows for

dessert. Abby set up "housekeeping" making coffee, heating a pot of green beans and slicing a loaf of Thurner's Crusty bread to go with the speckies I'd caught. "If you want to be busty eat Thurner's Crusty," a distributor would tell women on his delivery route. I fried the fish in a large heavy cast iron skillet. Sizzling in deep butter, the fish only took minutes to fry. We'd come prepared. In addition to paper plates, utensils and napkins Abby had supplied I'd brought along a substantial wire-frame grill to support the skillet plus the pot of beans and the coffee pot. The aroma of freshly brewed coffee filled the air. We'd arranged a couple of logs to sit on and an overturned cardboard box would serve as our table. Ten speckies, the limit for most Michigan trout streams at the time, curled in the sizzling skillet as only freshly caught fish will do. The fabled King Midas whose own breakfast of brook trout, transmuted into gold as a result of his cursed golden touch, would have slavered at the sight of these ravishing comestibles. Brookies fried in butter, nothing better.

After our feast and a toasting of Campfire marshmallows, we "outened our fire," as we say in Heights, and strolled a length of beach further away from the cottages. We did not walk arm in arm or even hold hands. My ingrained Finnish reserve prevented me from doing that. Yet, walking closely side by side, every so often our hips would brush. Intensely conscious of the contact, our faces flush with color, we continued to walk in silence, a silence which neither of us minded. I made no attempt to hold her nor did I utter to her muted whisperings of endearment. For a proud stubborn man of Finnish descent what foolishness this would be. No gushing sentiments or a hasty outpouring of words of love were necessary from two kindred minds at peace.

Visibility waned in the ebbing twilight. Summer darkness comes late in the Keweenaw, which is situated at the far western end of the Eastern Standard Time zone, the same time zone as New York City. The Keweenaw is one thousand miles west and five hundred miles north of New York City. On our way back to the campfire site Abby tripped over a log half-buried in the sand. I swiftly reached out and prevented her from falling.

"Are you OK? I asked her solicitously, drawing her close to me.

"I'm much better now," she replied softly as I pressed her body to mine.

Her upturned face drew close to my own, her lips parted. Discounting the one or two baby smacks I'd given her years ago, I kissed her for the very first time. She did not resist as I drew her even closer to me. I looked at her in the fading twilight as I had done on the way back from the Moose Lake Bible Camp in Pastor Bylkas's car. Her eyes were closed as they were then and her face serene. The angelic child's face I'd gazed upon so long ago had now transformed into a woman's countenance of ethereal beauty. I studied her long and intensely before I kissed her again.

"It's time to go," I finally said as we reluctantly loosened our embrace.

She did not demur. We slowly walked back to the camp site, arm in arm. We did not speak. On our drive back to Calumet she sat close to me, her head nestled on my shoulder.

"What about those snakes?" I asked her.

Although it could not be proven, Aldo, Hicks and I knew who put them in our lunch buckets. But it had never been explained to us at any time how the snakes got there. No one squealed. The hysteria erupting in Miss Kentala's third-through-fifth-grade classroom happened a long time ago.

"I knew you'd get around to those snakes someday," Abby replied. "Shirley and I learned a few tricks from you guys. As much as we hated snakes we had to get even for what you did to us."

We made the most of our two weeks of our free time together. It would be a well-deserved vacation for Abby after a busy year of teaching, with summer courses to follow shortly. Abby brought good news of her father who'd recovered completely from his fall. She'd devoted her Christmas vacation to his care. I would be busy as well. After a third-quarter break from Michigan Tech in early June, in July I'd be starting a summer job managing a motel in Copper Harbor when the tourist business began to peak.

We visited old sites. One afternoon found us at Big Rock where we reminisced on our childhood days. That's when I resurrected the snakes.

"Remember how we used to go to school early, about fifteen minutes before classes started," she continued, "well Shirley and I captured a few snakes of our own. Once we handled one or two it wasn't as bad the next time. We each got bitten once or twice but the worst happened when they managed to coil about an arm and then poop all over it. I found out later that stinky white poop is one of their main defense mechanisms. But with a little practice we got quite good at grabbing a snake behind its head and holding the other end just above the tail. We discovered keeping it stretched out prevents bites and poop altogether.

"We kept the three largest ones and put them in a sack just like you, Aldo and Hicks did. We just had to get them inside and put them into your lunch buckets without being detected. But we did manage to keep the snakes concealed. No one saw the sack which I'd placed in my book bag. Anyway, with everyone on the playground Shirley and I managed to sneak into the classroom and put the snakes into your lunch buckets. We hid them under Miss Kentala's desk. Everything worked perfectly. You know the rest."

"We knew it had to be you and Shirley but you really had everyone else fooled. You sure got even with us. Aldo and I cleaned blackboards for a whole week. We didn't mind the spankings so much as the loss of our free time after school. As I recall we broke out laughing at the spanking poor Hicks got. By the way, did Miss Kentala ever discover the truth of the whole matter?"

"I got to see her when I came to visit with my family and Lucas. We both had a good chuckle, especially when I told her about the box of "hazelnuts and blackberries" you guys presented to Shirley and me."

"I'd have done the same thing if those lads did that to me. Hazelnuts and blackberries. Good grief!" she exclaimed. "They gave you good reason to bring the snakes to the classroom. If I'd known what really happened at the time I'd have doubled up on the spankings they got."

We rented a boat and did some fishing on Lac La Belle. Trolling close to the tall reeds on the south side of the lake, I offered to do all the rowing but Abby insisted on taking turns. I expected our small craft to go in circles when she took the oars but she did a commendable job closely following the edge of the weed bed, where northern pike waited in ambush for the smaller perch or minnows of any species. We had not gone far on my second shift at the oars when she hooked and landed a nice northern weighing at least five pounds. I looked ahead to another fish dinner.

"Make sure you don't hurt my fish," Abby said apprehensively. She watched intently as I disengaged the treble hooks on her daredevle spoon from the gaping maw of the pike. I used a pair of long-nosed pliers to do this to avoid the seemingly countless rows of back-slanted, razor-sharp teeth. I did a good job of extricating the hooks but before I could put the uninjured fish on a stringer, Abby intervened on the pike's behalf. Feel sorry for a fish?

"Let's let this one go. I don't think we ought to keep any fish today," she insisted rather emphatically.

I grumbled as I released the pike and watched it slowly swim away.

"You'd never make a good fisherman's wife," I spouted. I'd taken up the oars again and she let her spoon back into the water. The daredevle wobbled slowly out of sight.

"What makes you so sure? Did you hear me complain when I stopped to see you at Toof's Café? Who put up with your stink? And do you think you'd make a good husband for a wife who knows how to fish?" she shot back. "After all, who caught that big northern pike?"

We were getting into it deep. An awkward, silent moment ensued. Abby pretended to be studying a frog sitting on a lily pad just outside the weed line. I broke the silence, exerting an extra hard pull on the oars.

"Pay attention," I barked. "Reel in some line. We're coming into shallow water and I don't want you getting any snags. There are a lot of sunken logs on the bottom through this stretch. They've been water-logged for years. Be careful."

"OK, boss," she said, reeling in a good length of line.

I kept my mouth shut about that "big" pike. Twenty-pounders are common enough.

Abby's vacation neared its end. She would be leaving and I would be starting my job in Copper Harbor. We made the most of our remaining time together. We kept everything simple, visiting with Rita and Hicks, and spending much of our time together outdoors. Abby's aunt accepted an invitation for a dinner with us at a first-rate restaurant in Copper Harbor near the motel I'd be managing. Every time I stopped at her home on Eighth Street to see Abby she always had a cup of freshly brewed coffee and some home-baked pastries waiting. I stood in good favor.

We roved in the "Centennial Heights Mountains" as Abby and I came to call a ridge running in a northeasterly direction between Centennial Heights and Allouez. The big bulrush swamp bounded the eastern base of the ridge. The gently rolling slopes of the ridge, populated with stands of hardwood and fir, were by no means mountains and hardly even hills. But for Abby and me they were our mountains. Small sunny glades carpeted with grass and thick, soft patches of moss interspersed stands of maple and oak trees, mostly of tertiary growth.

No trails existed so few ventured into these woods. Summer months found outdoor types on the beaches, trout streams or on hiking trails in the Keweenaw. Only during winter when a thick layer of snow covered the ground would cross-country skiers venture through the Centennial Heights Mountains. Today we claimed this Eden exclusively to ourselves.

We lay comfortably reclined on a carpet of grass in one of the small glades of our paradise. The morning sun had dried the dewdrops, which had formed during the chilly dawn. I cradled her head on my chest. We did not speak. Only the buzzing of dragonflies and the low drone of traffic on a distant highway could be heard. We did not make love.

"Why are you grunting?" she asked.

Abby would be leaving in the morning. We took a ride through Keweenaw County to Grand Marais. Grand Marais is a small inlet on the north shore of Lake Superior. I parked at a remote spot overlooking the inlet. On a high sand bank one hundred feet above the surface of the lake, we had a magnificent night view of our surroundings in all directions except for the densely wooded area behind us. The aurora borealis appeared above the horizon in the clear night sky. Earlier in the evening we had a picnic on the beach. We had enough daylight left to clearly see Isle Royale on the horizon while we roasted a few hotdogs and toasted some marshmallows. No clouds or haze had obscured our view of the island. Now we sat alone in the darkness. I'd been holding her hands. I'd become introspective as our time together approached its end. Moreover, I'd become pensive and remote. In such a state I grunted involuntarily.

I gradually released her hands. Sensing my disquiet Abby moved closer to me.

"You'll be leaving tomorrow. There's a lot on my mind." I replied. Molehills once again were becoming mountains. Maybe there were real mountains.

"Well, that shouldn't be a problem," she answered cheerfully. "I'll be coming back more often now. We've had such a wonderful time together."

I struggled to contain churning emotions. Relating my innermost thoughts to anyone always presented a most difficult task; until now I found it impossible. Yet I had to get a lot of stuff off my chest.

"The past two weeks with you have been the happiest of my whole life. But do you know what? If we hadn't met in Toof's Café I would have made no effort to see you at all. Once I've made my mind up about something I can be very stubborn. But let me say this: 'I'm truly happy we met'."

"I don't care—you're quite a softy once you've doffed that mantle of stubbornness."

"Abby, there's a lot you don't know about me. I'm still carrying a lot of baggage. It might not be a bad idea to clear the air before we go any further. Believe it or not I've put you on a pedestal—you deserve better."

"Paul, I don't understand."

"Abby, I failed miserably at many things. I don't want to fail you."

"I know about the problem you had with drinking. What I heard wasn't mere hearsay either, coming as it has from those we've known all of our lives. These people are genuinely concerned for Paulie Maki, a good person we care about. And you're certainly not failing now."

"I've got to prove myself to you. This may take a long time."

"Paul, you don't have to prove anything to me or anyone else. You've only got to prove yourself to you."

"There's no one I care for more than you. I care for you more than anything else in my life. I never want to lose you. But I'll feel a lot better if you can hear me out—I'm quite a stranger at opening to anyone. You, if anyone, deserve to hear what I've got to say."

Abby listened as I struggled to find words. I had never expressed myself uninhibitedly to anyone before. Hopefully this would be the last time I would open to anyone. I strove to be objective.

"Abby, you're right about having to prove myself only to myself. But I've got a long way to go. I believe anyone who drinks the way I've done is afflicted with a gross sense of inadequacy. This I know certainly has happened to me. You might call it low self-esteem. And please believe me when I say I'm not looking for sympathy."

"I don't understand," she said again. "I remember you as one of the healthiest persons I've ever known, not only physically but mentally. You've always been intelligent and spontaneous. From our experiences of our past two weeks I would not have guessed anything has changed.

And now you've got your drinking under control; just keep it up. You do not strike me as a man who has serious problems."

"I try hard not to show them. I've allowed things to happen in my life which may seem unimportant and even trivial to others but when I look back they are very important to me."

"I don't know of anything you've done wrong. You've perhaps made mistakes but from what I've seen these past two weeks you're doing great."

I went on to relate my enrollment in the ROTC program. I felt rather foolish relating this but I had to get this out. I explained how I made a decent acclimation to the program after encouragement from Colonel Huntington and how I'd won his confidence in me, and then I went and buggered things up.

"That's the tough part—I couldn't look him in the face. I'd become a creep. Not only that, I was failing my courses because of the booze—I'd become a big drunk."

Abby listened in silence.

"I got weak. The more I drank, the weaker I got—no surprise there. I became humble, obsequious to the point of making people feel uncomfortable. People dislike a Uriah Heep character, always bowing and scraping. On the other hand some of them mistakenly took my false, abject humility as a sign of improvement in my character. What a laugh."

"Paul, I've never known you to be obsequious. Perhaps humble but not in a sense one associates with an apologetic drudge. You've always been genuine. I just can't see you being obsequious to anyone. Help me out with this. I'm dumfounded."

"I got into a fight not long before I quit school and joined the navy. This happened at a drinking party not far from town close to the Laurium dump. Cops didn't bother us too much there. This lout wouldn't stop picking on a girl who'd come along with us. Nice girl, but not too attractive physically—thin and had some bad teeth. He called her names like *"kana paska,"* which as you might know translates from Finnish as "chicken shit." I told him to stop it. He kept it up and we finally got into it. Even though I had quite a bit to drink I gave the bastard a good drubbing and made him apologize to the girl. Then instead of letting matters rest I apologized to him! I even started to weep in my drunken condition telling him what a shameful thing I'd done by fighting. And this even though he richly deserved the drubbing. We exchanged a maudlin round of handshakes but the truth came out shortly. 'Maki's a phony,' I overheard him say to one of his pals. 'He thinks he's Jesus. Did you see him bawling with a long, sad look on his face?' So I tried to justify my drunken behavior by assertively trying to solve problems and being humble at the same time. I'd lost my sense of direction. That's just one example."

"You did the right thing by standing up for her—most guys would have let the matter slide."

Abby listened intently as I continued.

"During my last year in the navy I cut way back on my drinking. But way down deep I still lacked confidence in myself. I turned down a chance of a lifetime to become a navy pilot. I've often regretted the choice I made by not giving it a try. So I settled for college. Many times I've asked myself if I were an outright coward for playing it safe by not pursuing such a promising opportunity. Maybe I'm boring you with this introspective stuff. But that's the way I've got my situation sized up. Fear has been in the driver's seat for too long."

"I can understand you as a man conflicted in doubt but I don't think you made a bad choice by going back to Michigan Tech. What's so wrong about that? Engineering is an honorable profession. From what you've told me about your drinking problem you made a wise decision. And you have nothing to fear."

She sat closer. I had nothing more to add. We embraced for a long while, struggling against lust. I could only say her name. Too weak to say anything else, I said it repeatedly.

"We'd better leave. It's getting late," I finally said.

"Are you sure?" she teased. She nudged me gently in the ribs after we'd released our embrace.

"You'll be leaving tomorrow and you need to get a good night's sleep." I replied as I reluctantly started the car. "I trust we'll be seeing a lot of each other."

"Paul, I'll be waiting for you."

I lay awake for hours after I'd seen Abby to her aunt's home, long reflecting on the events that had transpired on the sand bank. I felt much better having cleared my mind of highly personal matters, and more importantly, immeasurably relieved Abby had shown such understanding. The doubts, the insecurity and my failures I'd unsparingly related did not cause an end to a relationship as I had feared, but only helped clear the path for one which already had significantly matured. Having Abby in my life meant everything.

I saw her off from her aunt's home early the next morning.

Abby and I got engaged. Our relationship deepened since we'd met at Toof's Café. She traveled to Calumet twice a year during breaks from teaching. In return I'd made trips to Flint where I stayed with the Tulppos. Her relationship with my parents had also grown.

Bundled in warm winter clothing, the night crisp and clear, we sat in silence on the old stone battleship looking at the bright starlit sky. The Little Dipper could be plainly seen, an infrequent occasion even in these smog-less northern climes. I broke the silence.

"Abby, will you marry me?"

"Yes."

More words were unnecessary. After long embraces we left the battleship to visit with Hicks and Rita. They would be the first to hear of our engagement. An ecstatic Rita and a well-wishing Hicks effusively congratulated us on our decision to marry. We chatted and exchanged well wishes well past midnight.

Abby and I did not make definite plans except we agreed to marry once I'd graduated and settled into my new profession. I made a vow to keep our relationship chaste. Just as we'd managed to maintain chastity in the Centennial Heights Mountains and on the sand bank at Grand Marais. Ultimate intimacy could wait until we were finally married, I'd determined. Celibacy would be appropriate until then. "We can wait a bit longer until we're married," I said to her. Abby voiced no objections to this and had little to add, but I had the impression she did not necessarily agree with me. I did not press the matter further. Had I become imbued with purity? Had I become a Sir Galahad?

Time passed. I'd reconciled my doubts whether I deserved Abby. Totally. I cringed every time I thought I about spilling my guts out to her. Why did I blab to her? Blabbed for the whole evening. I didn't have to do relate my failings—she would have accepted me without any explanations or reservations. How could I have been so stupid? Getting those things off my chest amounted to nothing but a momentary catharsis—feel good for a day or maybe a week or two and then retrogress to become my true self again. Whining about flunking out of ROTC and bawling after I'd given an insensitive lout a drubbing at the Laurium dump. How could I have been so weak? Only a bum could've blubbered worse than I did, or maybe not even as bad. And what else had I told Abby? "I believe anyone who drinks the way I've done is afflicted with a gross sense of inadequacy." Had I become some sort of a bush-league psychologist? One matter I held with certainty: there would be no more sniveling, bawling or confessions made to anyone. Not even to Abby.

The nagging memory of not trying for naval flight school faded. My life had become much easier; I no longer felt impelled to be humble and a promising future lie ahead. Graduating from Michigan Tech as a mechanical engineer held a lot of promise—I'd become an important man. I caught a glimpse of myself in the mirror and saw a smug, determined and superior look. Previously I'd only seen one person who could match my smug reflection and that was old Smelly at the bible camp, the guy making a big stink with Donald Boltz about Farmall and John Deere tractors. Rolfe Ellefson called Smelly's expression a "Junior Chamber of Commerce" look. An incident at the bible camp involving Smelly came to mind:

Young Bobby Olson stuffed himself with Spanish rice, his favorite dish, and seated later about the campfire, he'd let go a good one—a loud, resounding and stinking fart. A few of the campers backed away. Everyone laughed except Smelly.

"That wasn't funny. You ought to be ashamed of yourself," Smelly admonished him. This coming from Smelly who had sour balls. No one ever got too close to him. Smelly seldom failed to look for a youngster to reprove for some minor offense as he went about wearing his unctuous, self-righteous expression. "A strange bird for a farm boy," my pal Rolfe said. He said he had too much religion. No one prayed more fervently at the prayer bench following an evening service than Smelly.

Another glimpse in the mirror convinced me I had the ingredients requisite for success. Unlike Smelly, there were no youngsters to reprove and I had no problems one way or the other with religion. A new man. That's what I was, a new man—all my problems were licked and I would be happily married in the not-too-distant future.

Happy lives lie ahead for Abby and me.

CHAPTER 9

The Heart-Shaped Emblem

I lost my bet with Hicks. Following his graduation from Northern Aldo enrolled in the seminary in Cincinnati and initiated his study for the priesthood. We did not see him often. During his summer vacations he'd volunteered to participate in student missionary activities, mostly in Central American countries. We saw him during Christmas holidays when festive celebrations were observed at his parent's home. Fun loving, mischievous and serious without trying to be, Aldo hadn't changed. The basic personality traits instilled in his mischievous nine-year-old head were still there. Maybe this constancy helped give him the strength to stay the course in a life demanding sacrifices of the most basic sort.

Hicks's family had grown to a thriving brood of five healthy children in short time. That number would increase to eleven as the years passed. Three young sons and two daughters kept him and Rita busy. The most recent arrivals were twins, a boy and a girl. His academic career also prospered. Small, spare but of a dynamic persona, Phillip Huhta advanced to become a full professor in the Chemistry Department at Michigan Tech. In addition to teaching, his involvement in research projects, mostly in biochemistry, appeared to lift his energies to new levels. He thrived on new challenges and never tired of classroom activity. On casual-dress days he could always be seen in a flannel shirt and dungarees. His clothes were loose fitting, concealing his lean torso. He gave the impression of a scarecrow staked in the garden to ward off varmints. Most conspicuous of his loose-fitting attire were his trousers, the crotch of which bagged almost down to his knees. This style of wear is known to some of the locals as a "Chicago Drape."

With major studies nearly completed and waiting to wrap things up with final exams, I found more time to relax during the final winter and spring quarters before graduation. I'd made new friends, mostly with Keweenaw local guys in our senior class. No big beer bashes, we'd spent much of our leisure time enjoying winter sports and following Tech's hockey team, which was having a successful season.

Finishing my last quarter, I'd earned a solid B average throughout my four years of study. Best of all I landed a job in the booming aerospace industry. I began an interview process during the final months —job opportunities were excellent for almost everyone. I'd interviewed a half dozen prospective employers and had no problem securing an offer. I accepted one from an aerospace company after considering three offers. Alameda Aerospace, located in Newport Beach in Southern California, would be my employer. I'd begin work in July, a month following graduation with a Bachelor of Science degree in mechanical engineering. Not too shabby.

Nothing could go wrong now.

The Michigan Tech Huskies hockey team defeated the Northern Michigan Wildcats in a thriller. At the end of regulation the score was tied, three to three. Four minutes into the first overtime period the Huskies scored on a breakaway. Tony Chikula took a lead pass from Jim Kokko and sped in alone on the Northern goalie leaving the Wildcat defenders stranded in the neutral zone. A left-handed shot, Chikula closed in on the net, and circling to his right, deftly flipped a backhand shot past the goalie who'd sprawled down in front of his net to challenge him. The puck sailed high into the net, barely clearing the goalie's up-reached glove. The Huskies would roll to a ten and two season.

I attended the game, played in Marquette, with a couple of college buddies. I'd replaced Aldo's old Ford. The three of us rode in my '51 Chevy I'd purchased soon after being discharged from the navy. After the game we drove to the Beef-A-Roo, a fast food restaurant just outside of Marquette, and one of several restaurants in a small Midwestern chain of eateries. We'd just been seated when I recognized a vaguely familiar face. I could not quite identify its owner. At a table across the room along with another young woman sat a slender dark-haired girl who'd been regarding me inquisitively. Initially I paid no attention to this but as she continued to look at me I could no longer ignore her. I ventured a guess.

"Marie Loonsfoot?"

"That's my name."

"Paulie Maki from the Moose Lake Bible Camp. Come on over and join us."

"That was many years ago," she said as I drew two extra chairs to our table.

"Marie's an old bible camp buddy." I told my friends. "We met one summer at a camp in Minnesota when we were still young kids."

No doubt her recollection of the drubbing I got from Donald Boltz remained vividly in her mind. The one of boogers and tears. How could she forget the boogers? By ignoring her at the Moose Lake Bible Camp I'd played no small part in causing the ignominy she experienced during the full-body-immersion, humiliating baptism Abby had wrought upon her, not only once, but three times at the Berquist Beach. Then I realized we'd departed Moose Lake on rather friendly terms after a few hugs.

"You've grown a lot," she said.

Her full-length lustrous black hair, parted down the middle, fell straight over her shoulders onto her back. Large dark eyes carrying a hint of mischief complemented by a faint smile enhanced her puckish expression. A graceful slightly arched nose perfected her beauty. She reminded me of a spritely Pocahontas or a Nokomis still in the spring of her years. Perhaps a year younger than me, she stood nearly as tall.

"I spent two years at Northern as an English major before I decided I had enough college," she continued. "More college can wait if needs be."

"I quit Michigan Tech after one year but now I'm back at it. In a few months I'll graduate as a mechanical engineer."

"Since I left Northern I've been doing odd jobs, mostly waitressing. Right now I'm a barmaid at the Ore Carrier's Restaurant and Lounge in downtown Marquette."

"Any future in that?"

"Sure. One of these days I'm going to have a restaurant and lounge of my own. I plan to start out small and then go for something bigger as business expands. I've saved a lot of my earnings and the tips haven't been too bad."

We talked long hours over some hallmark Beef-A-Roo roast beef sandwiches and several root beers.

"It's time to get back to Houghton, guys. It's getting late," I finally said.

My friends had accommodation in the Douglass Houghton Hall,

the major student dormitory on the Tech campus at the time. Strict rules had to be observed.

"Here's my phone number," Marie said as we rose to depart. "It's been good talking to you and maybe we can talk some more."

I gave her my number in return but not without some misgivings.

Marie had not called me any time soon after our encounter at the Beef-A-Roo nor had I called her. A couple of months elapsed. Then several days before our graduation ceremony I received a call from her.

"We're planning a party. A beer bash. I thought you might like to join us."

"I'm busy right now. I'll be graduating within a week. It might be tough for me to attend."

"That shouldn't be a problem. It won't be held until two weeks from now, on a weekend. You can come on Friday then. Think of it as a graduation party for you."

My interest piqued, "It wouldn't hurt to attend the party and have a few brews after all the hard work I'd done getting through Tech," I reasoned, "and I'll make sure there'll be enough to drink. I owe myself at least one good party." Besides Marie had made a good impression on me.

"We'll be having the party at my dad's hunting camp near Humboldt. It's not a fancy place but it's a comfortable lodge in the woods away from town. Bring your friends if you like," she encouraged. "And plan on staying for the night. There's plenty of room for everyone."

The timing could have not been better. Abby mentioned she'd be arriving in Calumet on the Monday immediately following the party, which would give me plenty of time to get home and rest before she arrived.

I accepted her invitation after which she gave me directions to the camp she'd described in detail. The camp would be easy to find after an easy eighty-mile drive mostly through small towns and a wooded countryside. A small community isolated in a wilderness of lakes and forest, Humboldt served as a railroad stop at the time, still in use.

Expectant of new adventure three of us left for Humboldt early in the afternoon on a perfect summer day. The same guys who'd attended the hockey game in Marquette accompanied me. Johnny

Alatalo, a mechanical engineering major, and Rick Smith, an electrical engineering major, were both Copper Country boys and senior classmates of mine. We'd graduated from Tech the previous week. Carefree if only for a short while, eager to join the party, our spirits were high. The fun would begin early Friday evening.

Three guys from Marquette arrived along with Marie and four of her girlfriends. They came in two cars. Her father's camp accurately fit the description she'd given me—a clean rustic lodge, tidy and of log construction. Without plumbing to a water main or electricity, a well-primed hand pump instead drew ice-cold water from a well and kerosene lamps provided lighting.

The main space in the lodge, containing a large, long oaken table fabricated with sturdy benches on either side, impressed me as being Nordic in aspect. Of elegant craftsmanship the table and benches comprised a single unit sitting on a heavy planked floor. A large potbellied stove sat offset from the center of the back wall of the room. In addition to three small bedrooms in the main lodge, three outbuildings including a sauna accommodated additional guests, providing ample room for everyone. Toilet facilities consisted of an outdoor john, a two-holer. An addition of lye suppressed stink. Mr. Loonsfoot insisted not only on cleanliness but on tolerable air. The entire complex sat on seven acres of ground populated with a growth of magnificent pine. The lodge invited one as a hunter's paradise or a haven of retreat for any seeking relief from a busy life in town. And an ideal place for a party.

We'd arrived with three cases of Bosch beer. The Marquette contingent brought four cases of Detroit-brewed Stroh's Bohemian beer, another great favorite of Yoopers, noted for its almost orange color, its deep flavor and a dense creamy head. Marie and her girlfriends brought food, which they provided in abundance, from customary hotdogs and potato salad to the pièce de resistance consisting of several pounds of lake trout, which had been caught and smoked by Marie's father. Cut into chunks, the fish would be served with hardtack, onions and sour cream.

Eleven of us: six guys and five girls. Not a bad ratio for bush country boys. Our beer bashes in the Keweenaw saw about six guys to one girl if even that. Most of the time there were no girls at our Keweenaw outings. The guys at the Air Force base kept them well occupied. And the twenty-to-one ratio of men to women at the Tech didn't help matters. It took a lot of effort to keep our beer bashes from becoming desultory affairs. Picture several guys with earnest expressions on their faces trying to keep things going by discussing techniques for catching speckled trout or trapping beaver in some remote camp in the bush. At times moods soured and scuffles ensued. At the Loonsfoot lodge, the party would be a novel experience for Johnny Alatalo, Rick Smith and me.

One extra guy. It didn't take long to realize this would be a problem. It wouldn't be a problem for Alatalo or Smith but only for a fellow named Luke Garber. It would also become a problem for me. Garber's greetings were perfunctory when introductions were made. When my turn came to be introduced he merely grunted while looking askance. "What's wrong with this guy?" I wondered. "Maybe he's just had a rough day." Afterward he acted nonchalantly but didn't have too much to say. A lean, wiry tough-looking guy, perhaps a year or two older than me, he related sparingly that he'd spent two years sailing on ore carriers on the Great Lakes after which he avoided further conversation with me.

Except for Luke Garber who remained quiet everyone else appeared carefree, relaxed, and the party proceeded well. We made friends easily. There were horseshoe pitching contests and a bocce ball competition on a large makeshift flattened expanse of turf beneath the widely-spaced pine trees. The carpet of fallen needles and the trees did not serve as impediments to the game but merely added to its challenge. Bocce ball? A novelty for us Keweenaw guys.

After the outdoor fun we repaired to the cozy confines of the lodge. The late Upper Michigan sun had set and the evening air grown chilly. We basked in the comforting warmth emanating from the fired-up potbellied stove. Most of us sat at the rustic table while Luke Garber and a couple others sat apart in lounge chairs. Well fed, we began to drink in earnest—the guys and even the girls from Marquette were certainly no slouches when it came to drinking beer. Luke Garber was particularly impressive—each bottle of Stroh's slid down his gullet as though he were taking small cups of water from a fountain. I and my pals somehow managed to keep up with him.

It became obvious Garber considered himself to be Marie's beau. He could not keep his eyes off her but she did not appear to reciprocate his attention. He began to frown and not because he'd had a rough day. "Why did Marie have to invite these guys in the first place?" he had to be thinking. Marie had undoubtedly related to her guests how she came to know me and why we were invited. Told them just enough to arouse Garber's suspicion.

Garber's directed his frowns at me. He had to regard me as a rival for Marie's attention. Did he think she favored me? I'd not gotten any special treatment from her as she'd only undertaken to meet small needs of her guests and did so without showing any noticeable partiality. Nor had I in any way shown her undue interest. As with my friends, I'd merely accepted her favors as tokens of hospitality when she unobtrusively served a delectable treat or uncapped another brew to fill an empty glass. Most of the time we helped ourselves.

He frowned more intensely, attempting to fix me in an icy glare. Knowing we'd be leaving in the morning I simply ignored his senseless posturing. I could put up with this crap a few more hours. Everyone else appeared not to notice his sullen features as they were too busy having a good time laughing, telling jokes and drinking more beer. Or if they did notice it no one said anything. But evidently I'd really gotten under Garber's skin. For what? I had no intent of imposing myself on Marie or otherwise intruding on a possible if not probable romance between the two.

"So you Keweenaw guys think you can drink," he declared, joining us at the table. "Let's find out who goes under the table first."

The reputation of the Keweenaw had to be defended. For no self-respecting Keweenaw lad, especially a Finn, could take such a challenge lying down. I set out to prove equal to the task as did Johnny Alatalo and the non-Finn, Rick Smith, who claimed substantial Chippewa blood.

It became obvious we were not to be easily defeated after three quick chug-a-lugs although we as well as our competition were becoming quite drunk. Only Garber appeared to remain sober, his demeanor grim. His frowns, focused on me, deepened into scowls.

"Alright, you roundhead, this is just between you and me," Luke Garber blurted angrily. "Step outside."

In no mood for anymore nonsense from him, I drew him aside from the rest.

"You talk like a man with a paper ass. What's the problem?"

"I've had enough of your bullshit. Let's straighten this out outside."

No one protested as Garber and I stepped out into the night. Marie, I noticed, appeared to be non-committal. I could not tell where her sympathies lay. Whatever happened, this time there would be no boogers or tears.

We proceeded to the bocce ball court. The sun had set and the night sky clear. Dim light from the stars and the glow of a waxing gibbous moon provided us enough visibility as we maneuvered our way through the shadowy pines to a large swath of open ground. There were only the two of us. Garber had advised everyone else to stay inside. "This is a personal matter," he said.

"What's this all about?" I asked.

"You know damn well what this is about."

"Not really, although I might guess. Why don't you tell me?"

"OK, roundhead, it's about Marie. She may not be my girl now but she will be. The way I see it you're standing in the way. I don't like the way she looks at you."

"Look bud, there's nothing of the sort between us. So why don't we just shake hands and go inside and have a few more brews."

"That's not good enough for me. You're one too many here so why don't you and your pals hit the road."

"We'll leave on our own terms. Besides were not taking any chances on the road tonight with the state troopers out there. We're staying for the night."

The fellow gave me no quarter and he only became more truculent. He swaggered close and glared at me.

"You're leaving right now," he said, giving me a shove.

Although in no mood for a fight I had to protect myself. I seized his wrist and held it tight. With an arm free, he punched me on the chest and aimed a kick I barely sidestepped. To avoid further punches I moved about in a circular fashion while maintaining my grip on his wrist. In the meantime everyone else had come outside upon hearing the ruckus.

I caught him off balance and managed to secure him in a headlock. He was not as strong as I thought he would be—perhaps the drinking affected him more than me. He flailed wildly with both fists, but by bending and twisting my body, I thwarted most of his blows. The few blows he landed had little impact. I'd momentarily release my hold and then apply even greater pressure on his neck. He stopped struggling altogether.

"I'm going to let you go but no more funny business."

Luke Garber had enough. "We're out of here," he said to his buddies and two of the girls.

"I'll be talking to you soon, Marie," he bristled just before they drove off.

"That won't be necessary," Marie replied.

That left six of us. Everyone experienced great relief. The tension had evaporated. The night still quite early, not yet midnight, ensured plenty of time to continue the party. A lot of beer had been consumed yet still three full cases lie in reserve. But I'd had enough.

"I'm turning in. I've had a long day. How about if I stay in one of those guest cottages outside?" I asked Marie. "We've got to be leaving in the morning." I kept in mind Abby's expected arrival in town on Monday.

"You can sleep in one of the bedrooms here. I'll feel safer with you here in the lodge just in case Luke decides to come back and make more trouble."

Luke Garber did not return. I got undressed and turned in between clean cool sheets in a bedroom most removed from the main space. I could hear the hubbub of revelers as I looked out a single window at the tall pines, visible only by the light of the moon. At peace, I lay awake for a short while listening to the proceedings at the long table. My buddies laid it on thick to Marie's two girlfriends who had chosen to stay behind with Marie. There were no dissertations on chemistry or chromium plating of steel washers.

"Actually I'm the son of a chief," Rick Smith boasted to one of the girls in response to her query of his Native American ancestry. Smith, like Aldo, displayed a big rack of horsey teeth that gleamed as the polished ivory keys on a grand piano when he spoke. Outward-thrust, his buddies kidded him he could bite a sandwich through the open vanes of a set of venetian blinds.

From what I could hear, Johnny Alatalo, a son of a logger from Misery Bay, acquitted himself well for a usually taciturn Finn. He kept Marie's other friend entertained with droll stories of life working in the woods with cousins and uncles. He mentioned something about farting contests. The babble continued until I fell into slumber.

I awoke, the night dark and still. It had to be at least three in the morning. As though in a dream I felt a warm presence. Naked and awake, a real-life Marie Loonsfoot lay facing me, her expression intense, her large eyes luminous in the soft moonlight admitted through the window. She pressed her body against mine. I held her close. We did not speak—words were unnecessary.

I removed my underwear.

The party in Humboldt lasted nearly two more days. We'd planned to leave early Saturday morning after a night's rest but none of us had a care of leaving. The lodge had become a Bacchanalian paradise. Three couples reveled without restraint or intrusion. Just Alatalo, Smith, Marie and her two friends and I participated. We eased up on the drinking; more than two cases of beer left over from the first night of partying proved ample to sustain us for the rest of the weekend. We left the lodge only to buy staples from a small store on US 41. Bacon and eggs, a loaf of bread and some beans sufficed. We made good use of the sauna, bathing communally in the old country style once practiced in Finland.

Sounds created by squeaky mattress springs permeated the confines of the lodge. From the bedroom that had become a roost for us, Marie and I could hear Alatalo and Smith carrying on with their lady friends once the squeaking stopped. Alatalo kept his friend regaled with jokes he told in a basso profundo voice with a heavy Finnish accent. Smith bragged some more about his Native American heritage. Discuss techniques for catching speckled trout or trapping beaver as we did during previous outings in some shack in the bush? Forget that.

It had to end. Well into Sunday evening we said our goodbyes, but not before I professed love to Marie who promised to see me before I left for California. Happily she'd not once mentioned Abby during our outing. Most likely her memories of her had faded. If she had any recollections of the dunking she received at the bible camp Berquist Beach, she did not bring it up. Abby had to have long disappeared from her mind.

There were complications. Once home and refreshed after a sound sleep, I got some rather disturbing news on Monday morning—Abby had already arrived. After Marie and I snuggled together in bed and while the revelry continued, I'd totally forgotten about her—I'd never had such a good time. Abby had managed to come on Saturday—she planned to surprise me by arriving earlier than planned—two days earlier. Now she worried whether something had happened to me. Still away on the following day, my parents could only tell her I'd been invited to an out-of-town graduation party with friends. I'd not given them particulars and I'd not told them when I'd be returning except to say I might be late and would be playing it safe. They found nothing amiss when I returned home past midnight on Sunday after being away for two days. But Abby thought it quite strange I wasn't there to greet her.

During her short years at her downstate college Abby received a promotion as an assistant to the head of the philosophy department at Three Oaks College, where her reputation as a teacher flourished. Tough, demanding, but fair she'd earned the respect of her students and the administration alike. Not a large school, no more than twelve hundred students were enrolled at Three Oaks when she accepted a position with its faculty.

Three Oaks College, while regarded largely as a being conservative institution embracing traditional values, did not remain immune from the trending social unrest pervading universities during Abby's early years on the campus, when the free-wheeling, fun-loving lifestyle of beatniks in the 1950s transitioned into a mass movement of chaos and wholesale confusion promoted by malcontent youth of the 1960s. At Three Oaks, however, most students were still of a serious mindset, eschewing booze and drugs, while camp followers along for the free ride promised by those advocating drugs and promiscuous sex were in a vast minority, and for whom Abby lacked patience. She did not abide fools well.

Abby peremptorily dismissed arguments made in her classroom by Vietnam War protestors against US involvement in the war and refused to discuss the merits of flower children glamorized on widely-read magazine covers. Her answers to them were terse and dogmatic if a student strayed from the subject of philosophy. Many found it too easy to get off subject in the '60s when public debate heated to a boiling point on the merits of our involvement in the war. She made it her mind only to teach her subject matter and not take left-leaning political positions, which had become popular with administrators and faculties of many universities during the '60s. Yet, as the protest movement of the '60s accelerated, students had a lot of tough questions requiring satisfactory answers.

A frequently asked question provoked lively discussion on the philosophical foundation of objective truth. "Why is philosophy important at all?" a young hippie asked her. "The arguments I've listened to at the corner bar seem equally relevant as the statist views of Plato or the logic of his student, Aristotle. What the world needs is social justice, not just empty words."

"What do you mean by social justice?" Abby replied.

"Everyone should have food, shelter and clothing and an equitable income. Behavior should not be dictated by outmoded mores. If a person practices indiscriminate sex or takes drugs it should be no one else's business but his own. A benevolent government, not tyrants, should stand as a guardian of one's rights."

"You already have rights. You have the right of life, liberty and the pursuit of happiness. You can prosper according to your abilities and your willingness to assert them."

"Those are platitudes. How can I prosper if my talents are ignored by oppressors, the powers that be? Corporate bigwigs and their lackeys have made it impossible for me to succeed."

"You can start by getting an eight-to-five job and then going on from there. No one is forcing you to make decisions for you in your life. You may succeed or you may not. It's up to you. It's a matter of being responsible to one's self. But if you apply for a job in your slovenly garb and long hair employers will think you're nuts."

"Why should I be responsible? I did not ask to be born."

"You are being absurd. No one asks to be born. We're here whether we like it or not. Your parents only have the responsibility of raising you properly. That does not mean booze, promiscuous sex and drug abuse. It means hard work, energetic play, assiduous study and earned periods of relaxation. All of the time. No one owes you a damn thing. And if more people thought before bringing children into the world and raised them in a light of reason neither they nor their children would be asking others to carry their weight. Only then can one rightfully proclaim a birthright of which he can be proud."

"What about the weak and the indigent."

"What do they have to do with you? The best way of caring for them is by first taking responsibility in your own life and setting your own course straight. You will eventually become equipped to meet the needs of those truly in need of help. Then you can help them if you choose to do so without having to ask anyone else to pinch hit for you. But not one red cent for the able-bodied shiftless. Remember that. And don't go frying your brains with drugs and expect to make it in life while others feed you."

"You are being very judgmental."

"Of course I am. And so are you. You've just indicted a nation, a way of life, which has flourished for two hundred years. You'll not find a system that works and has worked as well as ours does. Opportunity is here for those willing to grasp it. It's all up to you," she reiterated.

Not impressed, the hippie quit Three Oaks College for the sanctuary of Haight Ashbury in San Francisco. Some but not too many of the malcontents heeded Abby's stern admonitions. Most of them went on their way as though some magic would occur to ensure a carefree existence. No one bothered to spell out the means of how they'd be sustained or who would sustain them. In their minds the emotional highs induced by love fests and the hype of mass gatherings would carry them through. With strength in numbers; there would simply be a revolution and everything would be fine. But the noise they made, the miles they marched, did nothing in the end but exhaust these failures in life. The mass gatherings degenerated into small enclaves of hapless individuals more at sea than ever before.

Abby had no tolerance for those merely trying to keep out of the rain. She failed without regret students derelict of academic prowess regardless of personal beliefs, whether they were saints or sinners. Strict standards had to be met. As a result, only the serious-minded opted for study at Three Oaks College. The school prospered even more and enrollment increased.

I made excuses. Abby did not press me for details. I told her I'd only spent the weekend at an out-of-town lodge with college buddies celebrating our graduation and had decided to lay over for the weekend after two days of hard partying. "Wouldn't some recuperation be the sensible thing to do?" I rationalized. I hadn't expected her to arrive until Monday and we'd only played it safe.

"Paul, you seem distant," Abby said.

"I've got a lot on my mind. I'll be leaving shortly for California where I'll be a long way from you. An eight-to-five job in an office will be a brand-new experience for me."

"We've still got a lot of time to spend together. Let's make the best of it. What's the worry?"

I still had better than two weeks before I would start at Alameda Aerospace after the Fourth of July holiday. Not enough time needed to be spent with one I loved and respected more than anyone else, but too much time for a man with a guilty conscience.

I'd known Abby all my life and our relationship had remained chaste. I knew Marie as an urchin at the Moose Lake Bible Camp and nothing came of it but trouble—I can still picture her gloating after Donald Boltz gave me that drubbing. When we met in Humboldt after running into her at the Beef-A-Roo the "think of it as a graduation party" collapsed into an unbridled two-day orgy, initiated without preliminaries. Talk about an irony: I'd remained chaste for one with whom I intended to spend the remainder of my life, and on the other hand, copulated without restraint with one I barely knew. I'd even promised her my love.

What should I have done? Pack it in and let's go home boys? I tried unsuccessfully to absolve myself of blame for what happened with Marie. After all, she'd warmed my bed after I'd had quite a few brews. What would any red-blooded male have done if he were in my shoes? Admonished her for being a bad girl? Most guys I knew would have been envious of me. Alatalo, Smith and I bragged about our exploits all the way home from Humboldt.

The guilt I'd tried to expunge suddenly vanished. A grim reality struck me at once. Marie and I had not taken precautions. What if she was with child? "He planted his oats and then he prayed for a crop failure," Pohjola, one of my dad's long-time friends, quipped while discussing one of his buddies who'd gotten a girl in the family way. Would I face a similar dilemma? Now I had a real worry, a potential problem that could destroy our plans. I could only hope there would be no complications and I would leave town for Newport Beach as though nothing had happened. Abby and I would then be married.

I tried my best to reassure Abby I had no problems or distant thoughts. During the remainder of her stay and before my departure to California Abby and I did things together as we had done previously. There were picnics, hikes in the Centennial Heights Mountains and visits with Hicks and Rita. Still very much conflicted, I felt matters with Abby were not quite right. No one except Rita, however, suspected anything. Abby in a trustful manner simply thought I had too much worry on my mind about my new job. Rita took me aside.

"Paulie, you look afraid of something. You don't act the same with Abby."

"What do you mean?"

"You're trying to be too nice to her. That's not the Paulie I knew. You're acting as though you've only met her for the first time."

"Well, I've got a lot on my mind, leaving home and my family and friends to go to California. I should be extra nice to her, don't you think?"

"You'd be nicer if you were yourself."

I looked down at my polished shoes. I could almost see my reflection.

In three days I would be leaving. Abby and I sat on the rock battleship early on a warming summer afternoon. We had the ship and the field in which it permanently resided to ourselves. The ship sailed due east. From where we were perched near the bow of the ship, I noticed the large emblem made from Lake Superior beach pebbles, cast in cement. It sat just off the bow on the port side, and lay as a final touch to the battleship scene fabricated by the WPA gang. Heart-shaped, I'd kept the emblem clear of weeds. "What a fitting symbol for our love," I thought.

"Paul, we ought to be firming our plans for our life together, now that you're back on your feet and doing so well."

"I agree, Abby. Once I get established in California we'll get married as I promised you. Hopefully getting settled won't take too long."

She clasped my hands. We made small talk. I'd lightened up. I recalled an incident I'd witnessed as a seven-year-old. Willie Juntunen's cousin Rudy claimed he could eat all the bacon in the world. Families in the slowly fading depression days and the early war years did not see much of this commodity. Rudy made his proclamation standing fifty feet due east of the bow as he faced uphill north. I got off the east-headed ship, and standing on the exact same spot declared, "I could eat all the bacon in the world." Abby laughed delightedly.

I mentioned Hicks's experiments.

"Farting into mason jars and balloons. Good grief," she exclaimed. "I can't conceive of such an experiment as even being possible."

Abby recalled childhood memories of her own. She resurrected the skirt hikings. I remembered them well.

"Hicks claims after these many years he can still taste those clammy bloomers. And Aldo claimed those face sittings ruined his looks."

I omitted mention of my personal sittings.

"If anything they improved his looks. Aldo's not a bad looking guy when he's not gawking or chortling through those big white teeth of his. Shirley and I just needed to slow him down for a while."

"How about the rest of us?"

"Little boys had to learn to be nice to good girls. Isn't that what Shirley told you? And if you've got to know, our underwear had to be much cleaner than those swampy drawers you guys most likely wore when we played football."

We talked for hours on the old rock ship as the afternoon wore on. In no hurry to leave, time sped by. The guilt of being unfaithful to Abby vanished. Even my fears whether I'd impregnated Marie Loonsfoot diminished. I reconciled my doubts by convincing myself I deserved at least one last fling as a single man. And besides, I fondly recalled my experiences at the Shiwada House in Sasebo and a few other flings on the West Coast when the USS *Holgate* returned to the states. I had no regrets whatsoever. Everything once again looked promising. Once happily married to Abby, I would go on to prosper in my career and accomplish many wonderful things as a mechanical engineer.

Happily musing on how well matters appeared to be working out, I received a jolt. The sand castles I'd built in my head came crumbling down.

I'd just got up to inspect features of the rock ship near its stern when I saw a vaguely familiar car rounding the corner of First and Jefferson Streets near the old Centennial Heights school, less than one hundred yards away. Then it struck me where I'd seen it before—I'd seen it at the Loonsfoot lodge in Humboldt. I watched with a sinking feeling in my gut as the car slowly proceeded down Jefferson Street as though its driver were seeking an address. The car moved even more slowly until it finally rolled to a stop near a garage across the street from the ship.

A sole occupant emerged from the car. For a moment I refused to believe my eyes. Had Marie Loonsfoot come to tell me I would be a father? Good news for me? Poor Hicks, or should I say Happy Hicks?

I'd forgotten she'd promised to see me before I left for California. But why hadn't she called first? This did not look good.

My mind operated in a peculiar mood. Abby and Marie passed into oblivion. I had a flashback. It involved the garage. Recollections of proceedings in the garage stampeded my head, blocking out any other thoughts.

The garage, once owned by Jake Bloomdahl, and presently owned by a logger, provided cozy shelter for many a drinking party once the bars in town closed at two in the morning. I'd participated in many of these festivities, which sometimes would last until daylight. Even during my recent years at Tech I often attended the parties, but confined a moderate participation only to Saturday nights after my studies for the coming week were completed. Among the Heights Bunch imbibers, Aldo joined us during his winter breaks. Except for an occasional beer or a glass of wine Hicks had become an abstainer and did not attend any of these gatherings. My memories are good ones—a bunch of amicable guys sitting around a wood-fired stove working on a keg or a couple cases of Bosch. Best of all were the early morning parties during winter months when the wind blew hard and the snow swirled, creating a comforting isolation from the outside world.

Not only just guys, Mabel Lahti, a widow who lived nearby the bulrush swamp, could be counted present nearly all the time. Dressed in fatigues she'd purchased from an army surplus store in Houghton, she held her own with any of the guys, matching them beer for beer. The outfit she wore had been used. The vendor forgot to remove a name tag sewn on one of the pocket flaps. It read "Sgt. Benson." Pretty, demure as a young woman and now in her late forties, Mabel's once attractive looks had weathered but she still considered herself seductive. She'd leer mischievously at a young guy, and if she perceived an interest, would plant a big slobbery kiss on him while catching him unaware. She'd become uninhibited and ribald. Once she had a dozen or so brews in her she regaled us with stories of a wanton existence as a younger woman. "We screwed like rabbits," she announced on one occasion, describing an affair she had with some guy from Tamarack. Mabel knew how to keep things going.

The flashback ceased. A happily smiling Marie Loonsfoot approached the boat. I noticed she carried something under an arm.

Still sitting at the bow, Abby barely paid any attention to Marie as she approached the battleship, thinking perhaps someone just needed to inquire about an address. I watched apprehensively from the stern.

"You forgot something. You left this behind," she said cheerfully as she drew near.

"Thank you."

She held a jacket I'd worn to Humboldt. I hadn't even missed it as the weather had warmed.

I'd of course made no mention of Marie to Abby in relating the proceedings at the lodge. I'd only told her there were some guys I knew from Marquette who had access to the camp.

Marie perceived nothing amiss as Abby remained seated at the bow, thirty feet from where I stood.

Abby did.

"Hello Marie," she said, recognizing her old nemesis from the Moose Lake Bible Camp after brief scrutiny.

Marie's smile vanished. Puzzled, she looked at Abby a long while before she finally spoke. Memories had to come flooding back to her of the dunking she'd received at the hands of Abby at Moose Lake.

"Am I interrupting anything?"

"Not really," Abby replied. "If it's OK with you, Marie, perhaps we can have a talk."

Marie no longer puzzled merely looked strangely at me.

"I agree. We need to talk. I'll drive if you want to go somewhere else."

"We can talk later, Paul," Abby said gently before driving off with Marie. Marie did not bother to look at me and acted as though I wasn't even there.

Neither Abby nor Marie were catty women. Both possessed dignity. Except for some small talk they rode in silence as Abby gave her directions to a small restaurant. Three elderly men sat chatting at a lunch counter. The women chose a booth in a corner, removed from a low din of conversation and the humming of an overhead fan. The old timers gawked at the two attractive women but the mention of fish dispelled their fascination. "I hear old Heikkinen limited out on brookies on the Trap Rock River yesterday," one of the men said. They forgot about Abby and Marie.

"Paul and I are engaged to be married," Abby said.

"I'm truly sorry for intruding," Marie replied, "but I understood Paul to be single and uncommitted to anyone."

"Marie, you don't owe me an explanation or an apology. You have no reason to feel sorry."

"Thanks, but I'll feel a lot better if I can get things off my chest. I can't gloss this over. I had no idea you were engaged to Paul, much less you or anyone else were even remotely involved with him. How could I? I promised him I would see him before he left for California and that's why I'm here. I wanted to surprise him. And despite our brief relationship, I expected much more from him after he left Humboldt. That's where we met."

Marie related in detail the events that occurred at the lodge. Neither boastful nor humble and omitting nothing, she told of our chance encounter at the Beef-A-Roo, my subsequent invitation to the party at her father's lodge, the trouble with Luke Garber and finally our brief but torrid affair.

Although devastated, Abby swiftly regained her composure.

"Paul puts demands on himself he finds difficult to keep. Even if they may appear trifling to others. Once he's made up his mind to do something he can be very stubborn—he's uncompromising and stern once he's taken a position on a matter. I've wondered whether the restraints he placed on our relationship were too great. He insisted on chastity and I respected him for that. Maybe he asked too much of himself. I might have known better."

Marie spared Abby of my declaration of love for her. In view of a long year's romance with Abby and compared with my brief affair with her at Humboldt, she believed her words would have fallen on ears as a lead block dropping from a rooftop to a sidewalk. A loud thud, coming to naught.

"I had to get this off my mind," Marie emphasized again, "not only for you but also for me."

The women talked for a short while longer before they left the restaurant. Both kept their composure, but on their way back to stone battleship, Marie broke down. Abby also was overcome. Marie pulled her car off the highway. Both women wept uncontrollably.

Paul Maki had deserted the ship when Marie returned with Abby, nowhere to be seen or missed by either woman.

"Please forgive me," Marie once more implored.

"There's nothing to forgive. I wish you well, Marie," Abby said before she drove way. There would no goodbyes or reproaches from her to Paul Maki.

"Paul, I'm releasing you from our engagement. I can't blame you for what occurred in Humboldt during your first night at the lodge. You had little control under those compromised circumstances. You are responsible for what happened afterward. You made a choice on your own, which I can't accept. I'm very sorry for the both of us."

We held each other closely and wept silently. I did not ask her for forgiveness for what I'd done. I would not beg for what I believed I did not deserve. Once again I stoically accepted my fate as a loser. With the game nearly won, I failed.

Abby returned to Lower Michigan after a short delay. Before leaving her aunt's home she stopped to say goodbye to her long-time friend Rita. Certain there would be hearsay and gossip but at least one trusted friend would get a straight story without having to relate to her the details. Distraught, Abby simply told her of our broken engagement owing to problems that had recently occurred, problems she regarded as unreconcilable. A visibly moved Rita did not inquire of the circumstances.

"I can't believe this has happened. I've always believed you and Paul were meant for each other and I still believe this way. I hopefully trust time will heal your wounds. Remember I'm always your friend and will always be here for you."

I had to get out of town. I left for Newport Beach the following morning. I'd spent a quiet last evening with my parents. They'd sensed something went wrong between Abby and me. They did not pry.

"Good luck, son. Our prayers go with you," they encouraged.

The heart-shaped emblem would soon be covered with weeds.

CHAPTER 10

Newport Beach

I arrived at the Alameda Aerospace facility where I would be situated after a lengthy, all-morning ordeal at an offsite processing center. I hadn't expected the processing. Arriving early at an unpretentious office in the business area of Newport Beach, I stood outside awaiting my turn to fill out numerous forms. Impatient, uncomfortable, I stood on the sidewalk looking down at my shiny black shoes I'd polished with extra care. A black suit in which I began to feel stuffy in the warming day matched the shoes. A starched white shirt and a tight-fitting necktie completed my outfit.

I could have sat inside. The wait seemed interminable. "Is this really worth it?" I asked myself. I'd never felt more uncomfortable. I lifted my arms and noted the resistance offered by the shoulder-padded suit jacket and the tugging of the suit in the armpits. I did not need padding in the shoulders. "How far is it to the Douglas fir and the Redwoods country?" I wondered. After I'd secured the job offer, out of curiosity I researched the logging regions in Northern California.

I made up my mind. If I wasn't called inside in fifteen minutes I would forget this nonsense and head for timber country. I remembered places such as Ukiah, Redding and Weaverville. This would not be a tough decision to make with Abby gone from my life. I'd been waiting at least a half hour and my name still hadn't been called.

The minutes ticked by: seven minutes, ten minutes, twelve minutes: only three more minutes to go and I would be a free man. I began to rejoice. But with less than a minute to go I finally heard my name called. My plans were ruined. Oh well, if matters did not work out in an engineering office, I could still quit and once again become a logger.

"Paul Maki," a pleasant woman's voice called out. "Come inside please and be seated."

Led to a private cubicle, it must have taken an hour to fill out the tedious forms. Names, dates, addresses and places of employment required for secret security clearance forms were a muddle of confusion which had me stumped. Why should anyone be obliged to remember this stuff? This made no sense. I made some wild guesses. The ordeal not over, I grumbled to the official taking fingerprints, "I'm an engineer, not a saboteur." "Just standard procedure for a security clearance, required of all new hires," he replied courteously.

Finally done at the processing center and nervous, I wondered if I'd made the correct decision. Felling pulpwood with Old Bones and enjoying a few cool ones at the end of a hard day would be much preferable than this rigmarole. That I could handle. Instead I'd be working in an office in the Alameda Aerospace Development Center without any idea of how I would manage that. This would be a discomforting new experience—fifty other guys, no doubt, and a harried boss as I once told Hicks. The Development Center, one of a complex of buildings situated on a spacious, well-landscaped acreage featuring a grove of eucalyptus trees, was new and modern, but for me, bleakly imposing. "Would I find meaningful occupation within this grim edifice? Would it be a prison?"

A smiling well-dressed man met me in the lobby.

"I'm Herb Mickelssen. I'm glad to have you aboard," a cheerful thirtyish guy greeted me. Blond haired, broad faced and of a robust physique, he'd been assigned to escort me about.

His smile genuine and his handshake firm, Mickelssen gave me a brief bio as we began a short tour of the facility.

"From Nebraska. Grew up on a farm not far from Lincoln in the corn country. I've been at Alameda for six years. It's a great place to work and we've got a fine bunch of engineers. I believe you'll fit right in with us. Midwestern boys with a strong work ethic are greatly appreciated here."

A nice Midwestern boy from the 1950s generation ready to embark on a challenging career. A nice Midwestern boy during my college days now attempting to simulate an identical persona as I stood shaking Herb Micklessen's large farm-boy hand. He could have easily been a good match for me in a bone-crushing contest. He did not sense my discomfort, for as far as I could tell, my humble demeanor and forced smile appeared to strike him as being perfectly natural, coming from one eager-to-please Midwesterner to another.

Despite my uneasiness I knew I'd get along with Herb Mickelssen, the test engineer on an earth-orbiting experimental package onto which I'd be assigned. The man impressed me as being sincere. We slipped into aseptic white coveralls and loose-fitting slippers that covered our entire feet before entering a clean, air-conditioned large room. Before we examined the hardware he introduced me to a couple of technicians. "We'll help you get started in any way we can," one of them said.

"This is it," he proudly announced. "It's called the *Orbiting Celestial Adventurer* or the "Adventurer" for short. It'll be transporting into earth orbit thirty scientific experimental packages installed into compartments. We call the compartments "bays." Thirty bays for thirty experiments. Most of the bays are unpopulated as we speak but we're starting to make good progress installing the experiments. Two additional bays are reserved for the batteries. I'll tell you about them in more detail after I've introduced to you to our staff."

There near the center of the clean room stood an octagonal structure six feet tall and roughly the same in diameter across the outer flats. Two rectangular panels, appearing as large flaps, were mounted at center height and outboard of the main structure diametrically opposed to each other. These were the solar panels, the power source for the Adventurer once stationed in orbit. Partitioned into four bays high axially and eight bays circumferentially at each axial station, the thirty-two bays housing experiments appeared to be concentrically mounted on an inner core cylinder. "That's got to be the structural mainstay," I surmised. I noticed devices which appeared as vanes on a set of venetian blinds installed on some of the external surfaces of the bays. "What are these for," I wondered. A lot of questions remained unanswered.

After introductions were made Herb assigned a cubicle, or as he put it, a work station. A desk, a table, a filing cabinet and a telephone—all for myself—at least I'd have a modicum of privacy.

"You'll be working for Doug Ridenbaugh. He's a heat transfer man, supervises thermal analysis on the orbiter," Herb said. "You'll be doing thermal analysis to start with."

Everyone appeared glad to see me arrive. I hadn't anticipated such a warm reception. Further, I'd naively expected to start working immediately on some aspect of the project but now realized my acclimation to the effort would be gradual. There would be meetings during which senior engineers would bring newcomers up to date on the Adventurer which involved the current state of the design, specifications and scheduling.

My apprehensions were beginning to subside. Fearful and anxious, I'd left the Keweenaw in a miserable state of mind. The apprehensions worsened once I got on the highway. I took my time. I had four whole days to reflect on how I'd messed things up with Abby. Out of my life for good. I had a very tough time handling that, but I kept sober as I traveled across the country in the '51 Chevy, and with plenty of time to think, I made up my mind before the trip's end to make the best of my new professional career. Being on the road a few days helped to clear my mind, and now at this journey's end, I started to feel at home at Alameda. The irritation I'd experienced in the processing center vanished and had resulted in nothing but some minor irritation. But if another minute had passed at the processing center?

"Come on in, grab a seat," Doug Ridenbaugh cheerfully said as he invited me into his office. "Let's go over a few basics now. Then you can spend some time reviewing what we've done and where we plan to go. First let's grab a cup of coffee."

A beaming Doug Ridenbaugh, clearly in love with his work, gushed over Grashof, Prandtl and Nusselt numbers, abstruse quantities particular to convective heat transfer, and terms familiar to me since I'd focused my studies on courses in heat transfer and fluid mechanics during my last two years at Michigan Tech.

"Feel free to ask questions."

"You mentioned the Grashof number. Doesn't this apply only to free convection?" I asked him hoping to make a good impression, as I'd already realized that in a highly rarified on-orbit atmosphere free convection would not be too significant. "The buoyant driving force for free convection depends largely on air density and gravity. And of course temperature differences," I added confidently.

Ridenbaugh looked approvingly at me. He may have been testing my knowledge in an indirect way by throwing in the Grashof number. In any event our discussion proceeded well.

"We don't worry too much about natural convection since there exists a near-zero air density and gravity field when the Adventurer is in earth orbit. We do have some hermetically contained forced convection apparatus installed for heat critical experiments, however, and we size the pumps sparingly since we are power limited. The solar panels you saw provide power during daylight operation and the surplus is stored in batteries for operation during darkness. An orbit only takes one hundred minutes, which as you can see, "day" and "night" have a whole different meaning from our customary twenty-four day. Thermostatically controlled resistance heaters are energized to maintain temperatures above a limiting cold case value during darkness. During daylight the opposite is true. We can't let the experiments get too hot."

"How about thermal radiation," I ventured. "We should be able to profit from that."

"Good point. Indeed we take full advantage of thermal radiation for both daylight cooling and keeping the equipment warm during the night when the Adventurer is in darkness. Remember those shiny vanes resembling venetian blinds Herb may have shown you? They are technically called louvers and are spring activated. Temperature sensitive, the louvers open during sunlight and close during the night. The vanes have a very low emissivity, which as you might guess, preclude radiation loss from the bays to space once the louvers are in the closed position. Keeps things warm in other words. During sunlight it's just the opposite—the vanes open permitting radiation from the panels to space, thus keeping the equipment from overheating. I forgot to mention a lot of the equipment requires a fair amount of power for operation. At the same time, a substantial portion of the power is dissipated as heat. If you've noticed, the exterior surfaces of the equipment bay panels are coated with a high emissivity black paint which means excess heat from the equipment gets dumped to space through the open vanes. Other than the forced convection I mentioned it's basically conduction and radiation from a thermal viewpoint. And done within a tight weight budget."

"I noticed two bays in particular having larger sets of louvers."

"They're the battery bays where we've got to maintain tight temperature excursions. Note the redundancy. We've got backup. The batteries are most important elements on the Adventurer except for the solar panels which keep the batteries charged. If both batteries fail, the mission is over."

We discussed matters such as battery life and efficiency. Ridenbaugh cited examples of the experimental packages designed to conduct various scientific studies. Some of the bays contained highly sophisticated optical instruments to be used for the celestial probes, which would be the most important aspect of the mission. Others contained medical experiments configured to determine how biological cultures would behave in a zero-gravity field.

"Do you have any more questions?"

"How about the launch phase of the Adventurer?"

"Thermal problems are not too significant during launch as this portion of the mission is relatively brief. The entire complex is shielded from the external environment inside a cargo bay in the launch vehicle. Temperatures remain fairly constant then, and if heating is needed on cold spots, resistance heaters kick in to keep things stable. It's a different story for stress and vibration. Structural integrity against rocket thrust and motor vibration must be demonstrated.

"There's a lot more stuff to go over," he added. "But for now why don't you get settled in. There's a lot of material for you to review. We're in it for the long haul. And don't hesitate to ask questions of anyone here. They're a helpful crew."

By the end of the day I felt relieved. Alameda Aerospace portended a promising career. The people I met impressed me as being knowledgeable in their disciplines and professional in their deportment. I even made a hit with the secretary.

"The new guy is cute," I overheard her say to another girl as I left. "He's got a few rough edges but he's still cute."

"Yeah, he's cute but he sure has got a funny accent."

The Douglas fir and the Redwoods could wait.

What a pleasant surprise.

"He must be punished severely and sufficiently," I heard a voice say during my second day on the job.

It took but a brief glance to recognize my old bible camp buddy, Rolfe Ellefson. He had not changed much appearance-wise as I recalled him from Moose Lake. There he stood at the entrance of my cubicle, a lantern jaw protruding, his flaxen blond hair combed to one side of his head and a devilish smile on his bony face. He'd grown tall and lanky.

"Tell me everything you know about Zoroaster and his ideas," I replied.

Rolfe had been at Alameda for five years and had attained a position as a first level manager directing test and analytical activities in the area of stress and dynamics. The group in which I'd become a member consisted of both test and analytical engineers. Approximately half the members were heat transfer engineers while the others were structural engineers. Members of each discipline monitored the testing of the Adventurer.

"What are you doing here?" he asked, acting surprised.

"I'm going to be a thermal analyst. I'll be helping on a project involving heat transfer between adjacent experiments. Doug Ridenbaugh calls it inter-bay heat transfer."

"We'll be talking a lot, Paul. Real glad to have you on board. I'll catch up with you later," he said before leaving as one of his engineers came by to ask him a technical question.

I'd be busy reviewing specifications, current drawings and observing some of the testing being done. This occupied much of my time to start with. I found out later through the grapevine that I owed my acceptance at Alameda in no small measure to Rolfe Ellefson who'd interceded on my behalf. Shortly after I'd undergone the interview process at Michigan Tech and upon seeing my name on a list of potential hires, he'd put in a good word for me to his superiors.

Memories of the Moose Lake Bible Camp flashed in my head. And the surreal encounters: first Marie Loonsfoot and now Rolfe Ellefson. My fortunes took a dramatic turn for the worse after meeting Marie. I'd lost Abby as a result. Working with Rolfe promised a turn for the better. Now I just had to perform my job well.

I heard nothing from Abby, not that I expected to hear anything from her. Neither did I hear anything from Marie—how could she contact me—she didn't even know where I was. But I had no doubt she would've found me had there been complications. My fears vanished.

After six months and some confusion over my addresses of residency I obtained a secret clearance that allowed access to information I previously had limited permission to view, which entailed important data necessary for doing my work. My task became a lot easier.

The job proceeded well. I came to appreciate the logical process involved in engineering the Adventurer. The vital importance of thermal analysis, which contributes significantly in effecting a mature design made an ingrained impression—correct analysis assumptions and the rigorous application of theory helped transmute numbers into a tangible entity.

I found the work challenging, exciting and rewarding. The

Adventurer had to function in a harsh on-orbit environment. Thermal analysts had to see that temperatures of critical heat-sensitive components remained within a somewhat narrow band. Temperatures could neither be too hot nor too cold for optimum performance of the experiments. During daylight the Adventurer is exposed to full sunlight, making it possible for powered components to overheat due to direct solar radiation impinging on the spacecraft. During darkness, the craft views deep space through a frigid window, which without a heat source, causes temperatures to plummet. In this case, power from the solar-charged batteries is supplied to keep components "warm." Insulation blankets and resistance heaters were installed as necessary to maintain temperatures within limits for both hot and cold conditions.

Numerous challenges arose, including compliance with a stringent weight budget, which is the case with any flight vehicle. If temperatures were proven to be excessive, as indicated by both analysis and testing, hardware modifications implemented had to be light-weighted as much as possible. The heat dissipation of experiments drawing high power could be quite significant and simple means for heat removal were often not feasible. Elaborate but relatively heavy devices for cooling then had to be configured. As Doug Ridenbaugh had intimated, one such device involved an addition of a forced convection apparatus, whereby a liquid coolant is pumped through a closed loop of tubing. At one "end" the tubing interfaces with a plate supporting the hot equipment where it picks up the heat. The excess heat is then transferred by the coolant to an external array of high efficiency aluminum fins, which radiate the heat to space. Compatibility between temperature, system weight limits and structural integrity ofttimes required ingenious but time-consuming modifications made on complex hardware.

At first everyone in the group applied classical or textbook formulations to determine temperatures of critical components. Temperatures predicted in this fashion, however, are at best approximations due to complicated geometry. More exact solutions were therefore needed.

Computerized software was still in its nascent stage when I checked in at Alameda. "Finite difference" programs or "codes" as they were sometimes called, however, were being developed. Application of these programs, implemented by technologically galloping high speed computers, facilitated the solution of complicated heat transfer and structural problems.

We eventually created "thermal models," whereby actual flight hardware is numerically simulated in terms of its geometry and its material physical properties. Heat sources and the environment to which the hardware is exposed complete the "input" for a heat transfer problem. These data form a large array or matrix of unknown temperatures. Once formatted into the program and keypunched into a high-speed computer, a rapid solution to a difficult problem is realized, taking the sting out of cumbersome, time consuming calculations done with a slide rule or a rudimentary calculator. If one fully grasps the underlying principles of heat transfer and is assiduous in constructing a thermal model of the hardware, accurate temperature predictions can be expected. Far more exact solutions than those previously obtained ensue.

Analytical or computer solutions are almost always corroborated by testing. Comparable results from at least two tests validate the thermal model; otherwise, modifications to the model are implemented as necessary—testing most often supersedes analysis. The relationship between analysis and testing is thus an interactive process, and eventually, without too much trouble, a reliable, high-fidelity analytical tool is obtained. A reasonably close agreement between test and analytical temperatures ensures that the thermal model can be used with confidence in future applications which brackets the entire spectrum of flight conditions, thereby saving everyone time and money. The scope of qualification testing is correspondingly optimized, anomalies in the design are economically detected and modifications to the hardware are accordingly made. Ultimately a design configuration is realized whereby product specifications are met.

I flourished in my work. Both mind and matter in the bush but now purely mind and it wasn't at all bad. Hunched over a desk with a cup of coffee, hours sped by as I tackled a challenging problem. The answer seldom came at once; a ten-hour day of futile effort often got rewarded by a solution popping into my head in the middle of the night. Long shifts thus became a twenty-four seven obsession.

My social life also flourished. I began to date.

"Where did you get that accent?" Katie Wills asked. "It's not quite Irish or Canadian or even Australian."

I'd been asked that question many times. At first I found it a source of irritation but later a source of amusement. I pulled her leg.

"Believe it or not it's a New Zealand brogue. Picked it up after spending only eight months in Christchurch."

"C'mon Paul, tell me the truth. You speak so distinctly, slow but kind of musical. I happen to love your accent."

"Actually my accent is peculiar to Upper Michigan where settlers from countries in Europe emigrated. They came to work in the mines, farm or to log the forests. The babel of tongues, of many different languages, resulted in the English you hear spoken by me. The Finnish immigrants including my grandparents played no small part in perfecting the brogue."

I thought of the two old friendly rivals, Niilo Kaipio and Jacob Binoniemi, and their contributions to the Upper Michigan or Yooper dialect. They omitted the articles and mangled the words, but their meaning remained nonetheless clear. Eventually with the aid of school teachers imported from the East Coast, the U.P. or Yooper dialect got polished to a comprehensible and more grammatically perfect form. Words are enunciated clearly with a slight lilt. However, heavy accentuation of spoken words remained. Indeed, the Yooper accent resembles the Irish brogue in some ways.

Katie Wills, the secretary of our group, and I began to date after I'd been at Alameda for four months. Librarian of aspect, bespectacled and reserved, her rather plain appearance belied her interests. An avid outdoors person, she spent much of her leisure time camping or hiking. She particularly enjoyed swimming.

An inlet at the Belmont Shores waterfront, marked by buoys, provided a safe site for swimming laps. A one-quarter-mile distance separated the endmost buoys. Initially I had a difficult time keeping up with Katie, an accomplished swimmer who went at least six laps during each outing. On leisurely days we both swam with snorkel masks enabling a clear view of the bottom. But after several sessions I gave her competition in the crawl stroke. Within a span of two months we both were easily swimming eight laps and sometimes more.

We were becoming a couple of health nuts except when it came to food. Good restaurants existed in abundance: Mexican, Chinese or traditional American. Our favorite, a smorgasbord in Belmont Shores, featured Swedish meatballs, imported Baltic herring smothered in a mustard sauce in addition to American favorites such as roast beef or chicken. Almost every conceivable salad lay splendidly arrayed on a large buffet, from hand-tossed Caesar to iceberg lettuce. For an average-size girl, Katie's appetite matched my own; it was refreshing to see her enjoy food without having to count too many calories.

We did some bar hopping later. Such a plethora of bars I'd never seen. "California dream bars" I called them. In the navy, my limited 3rd class-petty officer-means restricted my patronage to the vicinity of Third and Howard Streets in San Francisco. Here in Southern California among the many fine choices were Sileo's and the Hurricane Lounge in Long Beach and a place called the Salty Dog in Orange County. From one bar to the other we selectively made rounds. One stop during an evening sufficed. We imbibed in moderation.

Despite the good times we had together Katie noticed a restraint in my behavior. Something didn't quite click with her.

"What's wrong, Paul?" she asked as we sat in a cool air-conditioned lounge enjoying a couple of margaritas.

I'd heard this question asked several times before and never could quite get used to it.

"You sometimes seem abstracted, holding something back. Why don't you tell me what's on your mind? Remember I'm your friend," she continued.

After some hemming and hawing I finally came out with it.

"I intended to marry a girl I've known practically all my life. We broke our engagement just before I came to Alameda. Less than a week before I got here."

Katie, clearly perplexed, said nothing for a long minute. To her credit she did not pry—she may have regarded the issue as being too personal a matter for me to relate. Moreover, our relationship had not progressed far beyond a platonic stage; we were still not much more than good friends.

"You're a very strong person," she finally said. "The fact that you showed up at Alameda proves it more than anything else. From what I've seen no one has guessed that you had what must have been a most distressing experience. Especially when starting a new career."

"Very rough on me at first, particularly when I left Michigan and had time to think about matters on the road. But my mind settled once I got to California."

I did not mention the fifteen-minute limit I'd imposed on myself of not even starting at Alameda and heading for the timber country while enduring the wait at the processing center.

She looked at me quizzically, as though our breakup were no more significant than a date to a high school prom gone bad. "Was it that easy for you," she had to be thinking.

"She had nothing to do with what happened. I believe that's what eased the initial disappointment. It took me just a few short days to think this thing through. All I can say is she had no choice but to break off our engagement as matters stood. I think I can live with that."

"You obviously still think of her a lot."

"You're right. I do think of her a lot but now it's over and done. Life goes on."

We let the matter rest. Katie and I continued to date but a serious romance did not transpire. We continued our outdoor activities and did some more bar hopping. We eventually parted ways as friends. Katie would marry happily in just over a year. I would continue the bar hopping alone.

"You've done excellent work," Doug Ridenbaugh said. "We'd like to keep you here at Alameda."

I'd just had my first design review after nearly a year at the Development Center. With the aerospace industry booming and competitors seeking to pirate good people with generous offers, I'd been approached and tempted with good pay. But with a little back and forth negotiating I received a hefty fifteen percent pay raise from Alameda. I would stay with Alameda.

"We don't like to lose good people. Keep up your good work and you should be in line for a promotion maybe as soon as next year," Ridenbaugh added. Rapid advancement up the ladder for motivated engineers could be expected in the bustling aerospace days of the 1960s.

Headway on the *Orbiting Celestial Adventurer* progressed noticeably and substantially. Many design modifications had been implemented and the design approached its final stage. Most of the specifications were met. Simulation of on-orbit conditions would be underway in a cryogenic low-pressure test chamber in the not-too-distant future. A silent but palpable excitement mounted as that day approached, with final configuration testing anticipated in less than a year. The engineers and technicians involved on the project pitched in feverishly, many offering gratis services during evenings and on weekends at times when the budget ran low. Yet the project continued to be well financed as the Adventurer promised to be a first of its kind. Lots of money, much of which came from private entities and leading universities, had been put in and investors were eagerly awaiting the mission's success.

Success often generates more success. In my case it bred complacency. After more than a year at Alameda and having earned the respect of my fellow workers I sat on top of the world. I'd renewed my friendship with my old bible camp buddy, Rolfe Ellefson. I spent many pleasant evenings and some long weekends visiting with Rolfe and his wife Muriel, both from the Duluth area in Minnesota. They'd attended the same church and had wed in their early twenties shortly after Rolfe obtained a Master of Science degree in mechanical engineering from the University of Minnesota.

Earning a decent salary and situated in a comfortable apartment with its trappings in Newport Beach, I could not have been happier. The unit I rented came fully furnished, the rent modest and a large swimming pool handy. I only had to step out a sliding door from my first-floor living room and jump in. In the mid-sixties, developers in Southern California built an excess of units in anticipation of a continued influx of population to the greater Los Angeles area while the aerospace, aircraft and defense industries were booming. This meant low rent, short-term leases and the first month of occupancy sometimes offered rent free to attract a more permanent stay. I took full advantage and rented such a unit myself.

I traded in the old '51 Chevy for a brand-new model. I had money, top transportation and an apartment with amenities. Time had come for celebration. The Southern California dream bars were waiting, just as the Foxhead Tavern in Chicago awaited our presence when Boats Finerty and I went out on a bash while on leave from boot camp. And celebrate I did.

The contrast between my hometown bars and those I frequented in Southern California could not have been starker. Appropriately lit modern lounges of various motifs still smelled of cedar fresh from new construction. Among them were pirate dens, grottos, sophisticated piano bars and elegant nightclubs advertising the best show talent in the greater Los Angeles area. Some of the taverns featured hanging plants to keep the air fresh. Unlike the bars back home most were air conditioned. Ceilings were low and facilities were kept spic-and-span, almost aseptically clean. Additionally, many places offered good food.

Back home many of the taverns were of pre-prohibition construction and décor. Bars of heavy expensive wood fabrication, expansive back mirrors, glaring lights, high ceilings and stinking toilets characterized most of them. Old fashioned trough-type urinals stained a dark rusty yellow from years of use and overburdened johns most often awaited weary patrons—a vigorous flush was a boon. Spittoons could still be found in some of the older bars, at least for some years following the end of prohibition. If a drunk puked on the floor the bartender kept a mop and a bucket of chlorinated water handy for the offender to clean up his slop. According to one of the patrons at the North Country Tavern, putting "chunks" on the floor won him an unspoken badge of honor and provided evidence he'd had a good time. One could always expect loud hillbilly music or a Frankie Yankovic polka coming from the juke box. A sour, moldy smell of stale beer that had saturated the floorboards over the years combined with the heady fragrance of a freshly drawn draft created an inviting homey ambiance for loafers and hangers-on. Almost all the customers kept their cigarettes or their pipes lit. One did not have to function within the constraints of a rigid social decorum to have fun in these establishments.

The Salty Dog became my favorite haunt, where I became a fixture. I could be seen there parked on a bar stool almost every evening after work. Truck drivers, local businessmen and blue-collar workers alike found this tavern a most hospitable retreat. Oil-drilling riggers drove in from places such as Signal Hill in Long Beach. Renditions of popular contemporary vocalists such as Roger Miller and instrumentalists such as Al Hirt were piped in on a sophisticated sound system. As evenings progressed the lighting became subdued and mood music became the order of the day with Sinatra most often heard by a relaxed patronage. Elvis and the Beatles were heard less frequently. Few Elvis fans patronized the Salty Dog.

Meeting people there as elsewhere in Southern California was easy. A lot of the patrons, eager to establish new friendships, were widespread migrants from the country who'd come to live in what they regarded as a promised land of opportunity. I did some bass fishing on weekend outings with a guy from Nebraska on Lake Havasu. Along with some Okies I fished for corvina on the Salton Sea. We pitched horseshoes or played softball in the early evenings, after which we'd refresh ourselves at the bar with a few draft beers. Some of the friendships I formed were lasting.

Things got even better. I met Erma Jamison early one midweek evening.

"May I join you," a cheerful voice said.

It came from a woman sitting opposite from me at the Salty Dog's horseshoe shaped bar. Older than me, I guessed she had to be somewhere in her late thirties. A mother hen type I figured come to chit-chat. She'd been smiling at me for a while but for the most part I'd ignored her. Attractive and of a slender physique, I noticed she walked with a skip in her step as though ready to dance.

"Be my guest," I replied as she waltzed over, "please have a seat."

I knew right away she lied about her age. After exchanging names and a few pleasantries we discussed personal matters. Her actions were direct and she did not mince her words.

"How old are you, Paul?"

"I'm twenty-nine. Can I guess your age? I'd say you're no more than thirty-four."

"You hit it right on the head."

Right on the head, baloney. Her hair I noticed had been skillfully dyed to a pleasing auburn shade. Still it could not conceal a few strands of hair, which had begun to turn gray, however slightly. A hint of crow's feet showed about her eyes. She had a slight hook on her nose peculiar to Americans of Cornish extraction. Originally raised on a farm in New Hampshire, she'd indeed informed me her grandparents on both sides of her family had emigrated from Cornwall. Slight creases had also formed near the corners of her mouth. High cheek-boned and with a well-chiseled chin, by the time she hit forty-eight she'd have an authentic grandma appearance.

Large blue eyes were her most distinguishing feature. Frank and inquisitive, she arrested my small Finnish eyes in a steady gaze whenever I had anything to say. Initially I didn't know what to make of this; my responses to what she had to say were sparse. It became obvious she wasn't a barfly, or even worse, a hooker. Such characters would have received a cool reception at the Salty Dog in any event. I warmed to her. Erma Jamison became a more fascinating woman as the hours sped by.

"I'm a divorcee. I've been divorced for two years. I've got an eighteen-year-old son who's just joined the army and a ten-year-old daughter."

"Your daughter must keep you busy."

"Not at all. She's living with her father who's remarried. He's a marine stationed at the El Toro Marine Air Station."

I did not reply. For her to be thirty-four she had to marry at sixteen at the latest.

"Just in case you're wondering, I'm a working girl. Forty hours a week minimum. My ex-husband and his new wife have custody. I get my daughter on weekends."

She worked for an electronics firm involved in aerospace projects, manually soldering components to circuit boards, where she'd been employed since her divorce. Her tedious and demanding work required assemblers to work to exacting standards. Later, sophisticated automated procedures would supplant much of the labor-intensive manual effort. Matter of fact in discussing her employment she claimed her supervisors praised her nearly flawless work, and after one year, gave her the most demanding assignments. I had no reason to gainsay her claim and later discovered this to be true. She'd received commensurate pay raises, strictly based on merit.

"It's getting late. How about if I see you here tomorrow evening," I suggested.

"I'll be waiting. It's been a very pleasant evening."

After several meetings at the Salty Dog we began dating frequently. Our relationship became intimate. Our age difference made no difference to me at all. Nor did it make any difference to her. Appearance-wise, Erma Jamison's bona fide thirty-nine-year-old form and features appreciably vindicated her fib of being only thirty-four.

The more I became involved with Erma Jamison, the more Abby became a distant memory. I thought less and less of her. Yet I could not quite forget her. Except for a letter from Hicks on rare occasions, I knew little of her life. I began to smile as I read a recent letter:

Paulie:

Aldo is now an ordained priest, having fulfilled his requirements for that office in divinity school. Like yourself who lost our bet on whether he'd even enter the seminary, long skeptical he'd go through with his plans, I remembered he told me he'd be in it for the long haul.

The theological seminary hasn't in the least way diminished his ebullience. When he stepped off the greyhound bus in Laurium, a huge rack of gleaming white teeth flashed through wide lips lit up in a knowing grin. Aldo to be sure. He's the same old guy—that pencil thin line of fuzz he had on his upper lip when he taught us the facts of life has now matured into a magnificent mustache. Right off the bat he told some funny stories as we sat down to glass of Mr. Vella's most excellent wine.

When it comes to his vocation, however, he's all business. Few I know in our Lord's calling have been able to establish the rapport the way he does with parishioners, especially with those who are down and out. He's made himself available to always be on call to discuss needs of his flock, regardless of how large or how small their demands might be. They all love him. I don't see how he stays on his feet because the guy hardly gets any rest. He doesn't impose time limits on hearing any of their concerns, which he listens to and advises with sincerity and humor.

He's got a couple of habitual drunkards who've come to trust him implicitly. Regardless of their failings and broken promises he's always there for them, at times sharing a glass of wine or a beer as he listens to their stories. He does not give up. He's given them hope—our Heavenly father must have had plans for his life when he guided Aldo's steps into the priesthood.

Magooch always speaks well of you. He trusts one day your life will be most fulfilling. He says to take it easy on the beer.

Rita and I are both prospering. Can you believe there are seven of us now? There are four fine young boys and three lovely daughters. The twins are doing great. Two of our lads are exact replications of myself. They're going to be homely little runts like me but they're both smart as whips. One thing they've got going for them is there are no fearsome tomboys in the neighborhood to sit on their faces. Fortunately the girls resemble their mother.

Did I mention we've got a brand-new home on Third Street? Had it built by one of the local contractors a year ago. There's plenty of room for our family and even more should it come to that. It seems I can't even look at Rita and she's pregnant again. "There were six when I left home," I replied to a Tech professor when he'd asked earlier how many kids I had. And remember, you'll always be welcome to stay with us when you visit your home town.

My career at Michigan Tech is going well. I'm being considered for an administrative position, most likely department head, but I'm going to turn it down. There's nothing I like better than teaching except maybe research. Handling administrative duties would only get in my way. The Chemistry Department has got enough grant money for various studies and I'm presently involved on a bio-med project which has to do with strengthening body immune systems. We've come up with some promising results thus far but we've got a long way to go before we can show anything conclusive.

Now look, you roundhead, pardon me if get a little personal. Rita and many others including myself were truly saddened when we heard of your broken engagement with Abby.

As I continued to read I stopped smiling. In the solitude of my apartment my breath quickened and my heart beat faster. I felt a bit ridiculous, just as a teenager might be, wondering if he should ask a girl he liked to go on a date:

Rita and Abby correspond regularly. I must say Rita remains totally enamored of her. And I guess when you get right down to it it's quite understandable for Abby is truly a gem. We get to see her often during her summer vacation. She's now occupied as the head of the Department of Philosophy at Three Oaks where her career is prospering as an administrator, professor and as a part time consultant for setting up curricula for outside educational institutions. She's still unmarried.

Rita insists you are the only man for her and I tend to agree. Look, Fartblossom, get your act together and make amends. We're both positive Abby remains most amenable to that. You've got everything to gain.

Lucas and Roxanna are both doing well and are now the proud parents of a baby girl. Other than that, things are the same in old Centennial Heights. Everyone sends you their regards.

Hicks

Erma had always been a social drinker who imbibed with restraint. Now we were getting drunk together—just the two of us. There were fewer trips to the Salty Dog. We began to drink a lot—no hard liquor or wine—just beer. By ourselves in her cozy apartment, we reveled in long hours of carefree relaxation and looked ahead to our weekends spent in a drunken euphoria. Nothing else mattered. She even let slide her custodial arrangement to have her daughter on weekends just so we could spend the entire time together lapping up a case or two of Budweiser's or Lucky Lager's. Buffy, her cat, a tabby upon which she doted constantly kept us company. On one occasion when the cat disappeared for a couple days, she became very distraught. After making a frenzied but unsuccessful search of the landscaping surrounding the apartment Buffy returned after two days, much to our immense relief.

Erma Jamison, not a slouch, had few peers of similar physical dimensions when it came to drinking. For a petite woman weighing no more than one hundred twenty pounds, she could put the beer away with few visible signs of intoxication. Occasionally her generous Cornish mouth slackened at the corners and oozed spittle if she had one too many, but never once did she fall or otherwise appear sloppy. She always acted ladylike. What I did not yet know, when drunk she could on rare occasion become coarse and surly.

We made no long-range plans. Content to remain uncommitted, we allowed no permanent strings to be attached. "This is just what I've always needed," I smugly reasoned after we'd been together for three months. Come and go as I please with my wants satisfied—maybe she felt the same way.

I began to take her for granted. "Bag your bloomers and drag your bum to the Salty Dog," I phoned her on one drunken occasion.

Erma seemed more than happy with the way things were going. But cracks began to show in our cozy relationship. For one thing she had no interest in outdoor activities. I suggested spending a weekend at the Big Bear Lake resort area where we could do some hiking and boating and spend a night or two in a rustic cabin. We were rapidly becoming a couple of slugs from the self-indulgent weekends spent doing nothing but lying around and getting drunk.

"I don't like hiking and neither do I like riding in boats," she said peevishly after she'd had a few brews. "And I'm perfectly happy staying right here in my own apartment." I could only surmise she had to be getting tired of me.

But I would tough it out some more with her.

We visited with Rolfe and Muriel Ellefson on a couple of occasions when we were not drinking. Our hosts, both teetotalers, served coffee and pastries. During our first visit Erma sat throughout the entire evening without being very communicative. She had little to add to our conversation, mostly small talk, except to relate circumstances regarding her job. Polite and ladylike, however, she did not leave a bad impression with her hosts. The Ellefsons probably took her silence for shyness at meeting new people.

"Erma doesn't say too much but she seems very nice," Muriel told me afterward.

During our second visit, Erma resumed her ladylike pose. Again, she acted in a proper and polite manner when Muriel attempted to draw her into conversation. Though still somewhat withdrawn, this time she tried to be more communicative as our gracious hosts made every attempt to make her comfortable. At times, however, I noticed she sat stiffly with her hands folded. I had no idea what caused her discomfort. In particular, she seemed apprehensive of Rolfe and even appeared to be somewhat afraid of him. Even though a genuinely solicitous and friendly person, remnants of his old, wise guy bible camp persona rubbed off on a newcomer at times to cause uneasiness. And as a guess, maybe Erma believed she might be too old for me and my friends, being at least ten years older than the rest of us. For on one occasion I managed a peek at her driver's license while she napped, passed out from having too much to drink. Thirty-nine years old, just as I'd thought. Ten years older than me.

I'd previously not seen her uncommunicativeness. Judging from her behavior at the Ellefsons', it seemed her social skills were limited. In a barroom or in our sole company one could expect a gay and gregarious person; visiting with my staid teetotaler friends she behaved in a stilted manner. I found this disturbing. We rode in silence after saying goodbye to our hosts, but not before Muriel gave her phone number to Erma. "Why don't you give me a call when you get a chance," Muriel said to her. "Let's get together for a cup of coffee." While somewhat taken aback, Erma graciously thanked her.

Although late in the evening, we stopped at a roadside tavern to have a beer. We did not stop at one or two even though both of us had to work the next day.

"What's wrong?" I asked when we got back to her apartment.

I'd guessed correctly. No longer silent, her tongue loosened after a half dozen beers and as the hour grew late, she became maudlin.

"Please don't ask me to visit those people again. I'm nothing more than a little gray-haired old lady. They're very nice people, especially Muriel, but they're way out of my class. And maybe you are too."

Why do you say that? Our age difference is not a problem. Besides you're only five years older than me," I lied. "I believe we've got a pretty good thing going."

"Thirty-four years old, bullshit. I'm thirty-nine and it's time to stop kidding ourselves. I'm beginning to feel like an old dog in heat just for you to come around and keep happy."

I dropped my solicitous facade.

"Keeping you happy, what's wrong with that? And did you think I couldn't see those gray hairs under that dye? Not only that, I took a good look at your driver's license when you were passed out. I knew your age all along. Do you think I'm a fool?"

"I don't think you give a damn what I think. Right now, I'm sick and tired of your syrupy assurances everything is OK. What business do you have in the first place running around with a little old lady, or more to the point, an old bag?"

"Remember the little old lady having a few drinks at the Salty Dog? If it hadn't been for your asking to join me I'd have finished my beer and gone home."

"Finished your beer and gone home? Hell, knowing you, you were just getting started."

Neither I nor Erma were to be pacified. We continued to fuss over more beers into the early hours of the morning. With nothing resolved we both passed out into a fretful slumber. I could hear her snoring and mumbling incoherently all night long. At mid-morning we aroused ourselves from dense stupors. Erma called in sick. Offering no excuses, I phoned Alameda to say I'd be in for the afternoon and evening.

After near-perfect work attendance with but minor absenteeism, Erma called in several times offering lame excuses for missing work due to our prolonged binges. Before I met Erma my own attendance had likewise been very good; I'd missed an occasional day due to a severe cold. During the last several months a lot had changed.

We'd each missed at least six days of work over that span. I called in claiming a minor health problem, generally a cold, with nothing said. Allowed some flexibility I made up for lost ground by working late into evenings. No questions were asked. Twice I'd shown up on weekends. Management had no problems with this, and overall, the Adventurer proceeded well on track toward completion. The group had settled back into a forty-hour work week with overtime optional so missing a day of work occasionally did not cause any difficulty. Nearing its final design stages assembly was underway. A simple phone call—good to go to work without complications.

Erma did not get off so easily. She began to receive reprimands for her absenteeism. At first a solicitous supervisor offered help with whatever problems she might be experiencing. Like me, she continued to offer excuses for missing work, but the stink on her breath from having too much beer the night before became quite noticeable to her coworkers who suspected she might be having a drinking problem. More importantly, her job performance began to slip and not a few parts failed to get passed the inspector as a result of her impaired workmanship. Not heedless of repeated warnings to correct her problems or else face disciplinary measures, she'd go a week or two without serious drinking, during which time the quality of her work improved to the guarded satisfaction of the management.

After the debacle following our second visit with the Ellefsons we made peace. We both decided to "cool it" and do less imbibing. We took in a movie or two, dined at some upscale restaurants and spent time at the beach, most often near the Huntington Beach Pier. These outings were the best times we had when we were not drinking. We did not involve ourselves in any physical activity but simply lazed about, mostly at night. Sitting on a wicker mat we'd spread on the soft sand, we'd have contests at seeing who could spot the most ships, boats or watercraft of any type in the darkness. Erma, gifted with excellent eyesight, won these contests hands down spotting with ease remote ships' lights on the horizon. This eyesight enabled her to do well at soldering small components to circuit boards, day in and day out.

All this wholesome activity only went so far. We began to get bored. I experienced a tremendous relief when we went back to Budweiser and Lucky Lager. Once again we started binging heavily and missing work. I still managed to stave off explanations of my absenteeism with excuses of illness and I continued to work late evening hours. Erma, not as fortunate, got a three-day severance without pay after which both of us did not drink or miss any work for a whole month.

Then everything fell apart. Sobriety once more had become tedious; we loafed restlessly in her apartment, enduring a slow Monday evening. "Let's have some fun," she said. I agreed. We put caution aside and what started with a few brews wound up in a wholesale binge. Neither of us showed up for work the next day or the day after. We kept things going.

By now it had to be Thursday. Her supervisor decided to check on her after she'd called in the day before claiming a case of the flu. Highly skeptical, yet solicitous of her well-being, he paid a visit to her apartment. Waiting many long seconds before he rang the doorbell, he listened for noise. He did not have to prick his ears. Roger Miller could be heard blasting on a stereo above drunken, querulous voices. Whatever euphoria the occupants may have savored had vanished:

> *... woman sittin' home with a month-old child*
> *Dang me, dang me, they ought to take a rope and hang me,*
> *high from the highest tree*
> *woman let you weep for me ...*

"High from the highest caca in this toilet, woman let you weep for me," he heard a male voice bawling in an off-key falsetto after Roger finished.

"Shut up, Paulie, why must you always be so crude."

The supervisor listened more closely, positive it was Erma's voice even though it sounded very slurred.

"Look around this dump. It might as well be a toilet with this rubbish scattered every place you look."

A neat person, Erma's apartment had always been kept tidy. Now a complete mess, beer bottles, half-eaten sandwiches, newspapers and magazines lay scattered all over the floor. Dense odors created by unfinished, skunky beers that had sat out for days augmented the fouled air from numerous cigarettes and cigars almost always kept lit. Erma chain smoked cigarettes while I enjoyed cigars. Ashtrays were full of cigarette and cigar butts. Buffy occupied the only clean space in the entire unit—the bathroom.

"Thanks to you it's become a dump. Why can't you get off your lazy butt and start straightening up this place."

"Show some initiative yourself and maybe I'll pitch in and help. After all it's your apartment."

The woman, defeated, began to whine.

"Paulie, why don't you love me anymore."

"I never said I loved you in the first place."

"You're nothing but a bum who thinks he's a hot shot engineer."

"Look, you old bag, get me another beer."

Some more whining and grumbling followed. The supervisor heard enough. After Erma failed to respond to the ringing, he pounded on the door.

"Don't answer it," I cautioned. Nothing good could come of this. There we were, disheveled, and clad only in scanty bathrobes.

Erma could no longer endure the loud pounding. She opened the door and admitted inside a very serious, stolid Midwestern-looking man.

As he suspected no bedridden patient with some tipsy friends looking after her answered. Instead a slack-jawed, stone-drunk Erma and her similarly disposed male companion looked insipidly at their uninvited guest. The supervisor did not act surprised.

"I'd like to speak to Erma privately if you wouldn't mind," he said to me. "I'm Erma's supervisor."

I clumsily got into my clothes and left for the nearest bar.

"Would you please excuse me for a few minutes while I get dressed," Erma said after I left.

"Of course, please take your time."

After she dressed, she scrambled about stowing empty beer bottles and tidying the major trash. She made coffee, offering a cup to her supervisor which he declined. Taking some herself, she managed to sweep enough of the cobwebs out of her muddled head to face what undoubtedly would be most unpleasant consequences of her continued absenteeism.

"Erma, you were indispensable to our company at one time. Your work was of the highest quality and the products you helped to produce exceeded warranty. You'd have been difficult to replace when you were at your best.

"The company now finds itself slipping schedules due in part to your absence. And in the past several months more of the boards you've worked on failed to pass inspection and had to be scrapped. Given these circumstances we'd have no choice other than to replace you. But we're going to give you one last chance.

"You've got two weeks of vacation coming. Ordinarily you'd take it with the rest of the assemblers during plant shutdown. I've persuaded management to allow you to use it now to get your affairs back in order. The choice is yours to make.

"And one last thing: I have no business advising you on your personal affairs but let me put in my unwanted opinion anyway. From what I've just heard and seen here, I'd dump him. He's no good for you and as far as I'm concerned he's nothing but a user. And what's this stuff singing about crap in the toilet? That guy's nuts. You can do a lot better."

Erma called me the next day. There were no pleas from her to get back together for a fresh start or recriminations how I'd messed up her life during the past months.

"I'm going back east for a week to spend time with my parents. I've got a lot of thinking to do. I'll call you when I get back," she asserted, her voice clear, determined.

When she returned she phoned me, not wasting words.

"It's best we don't see each other anymore. I've still got my job, I'm sober now and most importantly I've got my daughter to help look after. Paul, we've had a lot of fun together and I wish you luck. There's a lot more I could tell you but let me just say I'm going to miss you very, very much."

"It's been great knowing you. Erma, please don't put yourself down with that little old lady stuff. You've got a good life left ahead of you before your hair turns gray and a lot more after that. Give me a call from time to time—I'm going to miss you too."

During the time I spent carousing with Erma I considered myself immune of any consequences of absenteeism. But I'd been kidding myself with excuses of illness. After some prolonged absences, concerned supervisors not only once but twice paid a visit to my apartment when I'd called in sick and afterward had not reported in. Too busy hitting the bars, on neither occasion did they find me home.

"Doug, Paul is most likely at the doctor's office," the ever-trusting Herb Mickelssen said to Doug Ridenbaugh when I failed to answer the door. Phone calls were unanswered.

"I sure hope he's OK," Ridenbaugh replied.

When I finally arrived at the office late in the morning of the next day neither man said anything to me of their visit except to express concern for my wellbeing. Haggard and hungover from carousing I'd missed three straight days of work. No prying questions were asked.

"Thanks, I'll make it," I told them.

"Are you sure, Paul?" Herb Mickelssen asked, his face a mask of genuine concern.

My face puffy, ashen and my eyes hazy, I suffered deeply.

"I'll be OK. If I feel any worse I'll leave early," I mumbled.

"It's good to have you here," Doug Ridenbaugh said. "You've really had a rough ride these past months. Just let us know if there's anything we can do to help."

A rough ride indeed. Alone at last in my cubicle and guilt ridden, I felt like a complete ass. "How long can this go on before the truth is exposed," I wondered.

Getting off scot free, my guilt short-lived, I went on another drunk, a big binge starting during the weekend and lasting for five days, just three weeks after Mickelssen and Ridenbaugh paid their first visit. Having no intention of going to work, I called Alameda early on a Monday morning claiming a recurrence of the flu. Phone calls unavailing, the men waited until two days had passed before paying another visit to my apartment. After ringing the doorbell and waiting for a few minutes, Herb tried to see if I were inside, perhaps too weak to respond.

I'd left the curtains to the kitchen window open. Mickelssen did not see an incapacitated man in a state of feverish oblivion but only a total mess, stretching from the kitchen into the living space visible just beyond. A disarray of at least twenty empty beer bottles cluttered the countertops and the floor. Sundry garbage lay strewn everywhere.

"Doug, you'd better come and take a look," Mickelssen said.

Again my supervisors said nothing after I showed up for work in the afternoon of the following day. Nothing at all.

"Paul, can you come to dinner?" Rolfe Ellefson asked me later the same day. "It's very important. There are some personal matters we have to discuss."

His voice sounded troubled. I sensed something very wrong as the cobwebs in my mind cleared. With no small feelings of guilt, I accepted his invitation.

"Try to relax," Rolfe told me after dinner. Muriel had left to visit with friends. "You most likely know what this is about."

"I do," I replied humbly. I could not look him straight in the eye. "Please go on."

"Let me say everyone in our engineering group has been happy with your performance on the Adventurer," he said after relating the details of Mickelssen's and Ridenbaugh's visits to my apartment.

"Even when you started missing work you managed to do well

by working the late evenings and showing up on weekends when you really didn't have to. The Adventurer is still progressing on schedule and there's been no major slippage," he continued. "But Herb and Doug have asked me to talk with you so we can straighten things out. Neither thought it necessary to go through formal channels and to higher management at this point. As your friend they thought you and I could best handle this informally.

"Everyone in our group is pulling for you. Those who know of your drinking problem are willing to help you in any way they can. Quite frankly, it's been public news for some while in the group. Some of the engineers suspected a drinking problem but everyone kept it quiet. The fact no rumors were spread says a lot not only of our group but also of you."

There were no recriminations from Rolfe. He tried to make me feel better by reminiscing on our Moose Lake Bible Camp escapades. He brought up the dunking Abby had given Marie Loonsfoot. This only made matters worse. I chortled feebly at his droll stories, but inwardly I failed to suppress a deep sense of shame. Not so much from being exposed as a drunkard, which had to happen eventually, but from the realization of my acceptance by the group after the outright lying I'd done. That's what hurt the most. I could have been fired for faking my absenteeism and in most places I would have been for even lesser offenses.

When I returned to work, no one in the group acted as though nothing had happened nor did they over-shower me with words of encouragement and commiseration. Instead, they did nice little things to let me know I still belonged. The women in the group unobtrusively left cookies or donuts on my desk and the men likewise included me in their activities such as flipping coins at the coffee machine to see who'd buy. They did not try to be too casual or overtly friendly and there were no sneering looks of contempt from anyone. Maintaining my composure at work I later broke down, and alone in my apartment, wept.

I looked up my old navy buddy, Wally Grimes. Wally did not wait for an enlisted man's retirement. After his third enlistment ended he accepted a position with a real estate firm erecting modern homes in the suburban regions of Southern California where the industry flourished. Now prospering as a married man with a two-year-old son and settled into a family routine, Wally nonetheless enjoyed having a few brews with his old navy chum. A few brews would be it.

I spent considerable leisure time with the Grimes. The freeway drive to Wally's modern new home in Inglewood, no more than an hour away from Newport Beach, made for convenient visits where we reminisced while enjoying a backyard barbeque. We did no heavy drinking, limiting our refreshment to a couple beers. I established a limit of four beers. Delighted at the professional stature I'd achieved, Wally greeted me warmly. I did not mention my troubles at Alameda.

"Hey, Paulie, took the bull by the horns, didn't you, you old gunner's mate. Lieutenant Pence and us non-coms were hoping to make a pilot out of you. Anyway it's good to see you doing well as an engineer. I always told Pence you had the brains."

"It's been a long haul since the *Holgate* and the Green Pump, hasn't it, old buddy."

"The Green Pump? What's the Green Pump?" Wally's affable wife Karen asked.

"You've got to understand an enlisted man's salary. Much of the time our wallets were skimpy and we had to learn how to stretch a dollar. Wally and I found a place in San Francisco where we could still get a draft beer for a dime. It's called the Green Pump. The restaurant next door wasn't too bad either. The guy running the counter really knew how to fix an omelet."

"Those were the good old days," Wally replied. "Almost as good as the old navy."

"Wally's talked about you a lot, Paul. And he's had nothing but praise for you. I'm glad to finally meet you in person. We hope to see you a lot now since we live in the same area. You're always welcome here and don't be bashful about spending a weekend with us," Karen said. "Look at little Henry. He'll be glad to see you come too."

Henry, their two-year-old toddler, tried to untie my shoelaces after sitting happily on my lap.

"We sure lapped up our share of draft beers at the Pump. A buck went a long way then," Wally said. "And it's great to see you practicing moderation. Which I've doing myself ever since I met Karen."

"As far as that goes we didn't overdo it at the Pump."

"It's too bad about the Green Pump and the restaurant close-by," Wally said. "I've heard the mayor of San Francisco and those on his council are beginning a clean-up of the area near Third and Howard."

My skid row sentiments kicked in. "What a shame," I replied nostalgically.

I'd been at Alameda for almost two years. I'd won back the respect of my fellow engineers. Returning to work after the five-day binge, I worked harder than before, a fact that did not go unnoticed by my supervisors, and was given more challenging assignments which I acquitted to their satisfaction. Minor slippage of the flight schedule for the Adventurer occurred owing to some problems discovered during final testing, but overall, the project progressed well.

"There's nothing more gratifying than knowing one has done a job well, done to the best of his ability," Doug Ridenbaugh said.

"Paul's work has been most satisfactory," Herb Mickelssen said, nodding in agreement.

Several months passed since the second visit of Mickelssen and Ridenbaugh to my apartment. Everything had gone smoothly on the job and I'd regained my stature as a reliable, productive engineer. My friends, almost anyone, would have envied a man in my position. I owed nothing to anyone. I had money, a job anyone would have been proud to have and had established several new friendships. But with things now going my way, free of self-imposed difficulties and not missing any work, my inbred complacency once again kicked in.

I happily began to hit the bars. "Why not receive my due reward for all the hard work I've done?" I ruminated over a few brews. "There's nothing to worry about; this time I'll handle the drinking." And with good reason, I surmised—I did not have any major hang-ups—I'd licked tough problems before. Wallowing in a deep mire, did I not wrestle with demons of self-doubt and gloom believing I'd irretrievably lost Abby to Lucas Wagonhoffer? Did I not emerge from the mire victorious after being long afflicted with morbidly introspective thoughts? Manly and tough it had to be then and it would be no different this time. I would enjoy well-deserved, pure relaxation after a hard day's work.

I abstained from going to the Salty Dog simply to avoid complications should Erma be there. Although we'd parted on good terms, I thought it best to avoid contact with her altogether. Later, however, I received a couple phone calls from her. She'd quit the bars altogether and enjoying favorable standing on her job, remained on good terms with her daughter.

The Keona Room, an old-fashioned tavern of pre-prohibition vintage not far from the Signal Hill in Long Beach, suited me perfectly. An inviting ambiance reminded me of hometown bars in the Keweenaw. No fancy frills, no hanging plants, just a plain old tavern with a sturdy bar and a large back mirror. Most of the patrons were hardworking individuals and businessmen, including pilots flying small craft out of the Long Beach Airport. At home with these guys, I sat at the long bar where I gazed smugly into the splendid full-length mirror while shooting the bull with them, evening after evening.

"The Focke-Wulf 190 could fly circles around the Messerschmitt 109. The best prop aircraft the Luftwaffe had. Lot better than our Lightnings and just as good as any Spitfire in the air," one of the men at the bar in the Keona Room declared.

"But no match for our P-51 Mustangs," another answered. "It's too bad we didn't have the latest models earlier in the war."

A chance had come to fly. One of the men involved in the discussion of the WWII aircraft had become a recent patron of the Keona Room, and himself a pilot, offered flying lessons in his Cessna 140. Only ten dollars for an hour of dual instruction, not bad. Previously I hadn't given much thought to flying but why not give it a shot. Taking him up on his offer I progressed to the point where it neared time to fly solo. I'd also completed a mandatory course in flight ground school.

"A couple more hours in the air and you'll be ready to fly solo. You're doing well enough but you still need more practice at maintaining altitude," my instructor warily said. "Otherwise you're a little slow at takeoffs and landings. Maybe need another hour or two at crosswind landings. But first keep your ass off that bar stool."

Solo flying did not transpire. Even though I progressed adequately enough, I knew I did not belong in the air. Imbibing again almost to the point of excess had begun to affect my coordination. Wisely, I took the hint and gave up the flying lessons before I'd be flying solo and risking grave danger.

"What do you think? Would I have made a good pilot?" I asked my instructor after I'd quit the lessons.

"I'll give you a frank answer, not a friendly one. From what I've seen you would have been barely average. Average at best under present circumstances.

"Just one more thing, Maki," he continued, "You'd have made an excellent pilot except for those dozen beers I see you guzzling every night and those highballs at the Keona Room. If I'd known that in the first place I'd never taken you up. Pack it in, pal, and maybe we can start again."

"Keep it up and you'll be an alcoholic," the bartender at the Keona Room said to me late one afternoon. I'd come to get my car I'd left in the tavern parking lot the previous evening.

I'd spent long hours at the bar the previous evening. "Why do you drink so much?" he'd asked me.

"I'm just trying to have a good time like everyone else," I muttered through a drunken fog. After a few more highballs I passed out, my head resting on the bar.

"Wake up, Maki, it's closing time. You know what the routine is. Hand over your keys and I'll call you a cab. You can pick up your car tomorrow when you're sober enough to drive."

I made no attempt to moderate my drinking. My habit became even more intemperate—passing out at the bar and handing over my keys to the bartender had become a ritual. Yet throughout this self-inflicted ordeal I managed to struggle in to work on time, hailing taxis as needed. I did not worry anymore about a beer-stinking breath as I'd switched to vodka. Anyway, the dozen or so brews that once slid down so easily no longer agreed—I'd begun to suffer bloat—there were no such problems with hard liquor.

Almost always hungover when I went to work, I began to make mistakes, most of which I corrected before the checkers spotted them. But in my foggy head, I made a serious mistake I didn't catch to the potential detriment of the project.

Assigned to a thermal analysis of a circuit board clustered with resistors, capacitors and transistors, I'd grossly underestimated the temperature of a high-power transistor, integral to a control mechanism used for deployment of the solar panels. Maneuvering the panels depends on a proper functioning circuit board, which means temperatures must be moderate. During peak operation the transistor dissipates substantial heat, and I had not allowed for adequate conductive grounding on the board, the absence of which would cause a drastic increase of the transistor's temperature. Unchecked, this would cause excessive over-heating that diminishes functionality of the board and which significantly impairs positioning of the solar panels due to concomitantly faulty controls signals. Reduced power to the batteries from the panels would be the net result. The transistor itself would fail outright under prolonged operation, bringing the Adventurer to a halt. A redundant circuit board of identical design would also experience the same fate.

"Are you all right?" Doug Ridenbaugh asked me after he discovered and corrected the mistake. "You don't look well, Paul."

"Yeah, I'm OK." Extremely nervous and suffering inwardly, my face, I thought, felt disoriented, like a huge glob of jelly about to form a puddle.

I did not receive the promotion brought up earlier at my first design review.

"Are you sure you're OK," Wally Grimes said on the other end of the line. "Paul, you don't sound well at all."

"I'm as fit as ever. Never felt better," I bawled drunkenly into the pay phone in the Keona Room where I'd spent an entire afternoon drinking rum and coke. "Thought I'd come up for a barbeque if that's all right with you and Karen. I'll pick up some porterhouses and a six-pack."

It was a Wednesday evening. I'd missed two days of work, my first absence since the five-day spree when Mickelssen and Ridenbaugh last visited my apartment. I'd spent the entire afternoon at the lounge and had caught Wally just as he'd got home from his real estate office.

"You're always welcome here, Paul. Just be careful driving. Are you sure you're OK?" Wally repeated.

"How about seven o'clock? This will give me time to pick up the steaks and yourself a chance to get cleaned up. Get that charcoal grill going."

I'd driven the freeways in the greater Los Angeles area many times during rush hours and late evenings. This time it would be no different. Dead wrong, I swerved in and out of traffic, and ultimately got pulled over by a state patrolman who gave a sobriety test. Upon successfully counting numbers backwards and walking in a straight line putting one foot directly ahead of the other, I took a pratfall when asked to raise my feet after placing both my hands atop the roof of the squad car. Expected to jump simultaneously with both feet I failed to do so. More to the point I failed the blood alcohol test miserably when asked to blow into a breathalyzer.

A stinking jail cell awaited. I fell off into a drunken slumber immediately after filling out some routine paperwork. The urine-stenched mattress I slept on competed with my boozy exhalations, which I didn't notice until much later.

I awoke in the early hours of the morning in a tormented state of mind after being passed out for a few hours in a drunken oblivion. I'd become nauseous during the night, making a big mess, my head pounding and my stomach in turmoil. My thoughts were feverish as though I were in a living nightmare. I'd seldom experienced such misery as a result of my drinking. At first, I didn't even realize I'd been locked in a dimly lit jail cell. Nodding in and out of wakefulness, it took me several minutes to get my bearings.

"What time you got, kid?" an older cellmate, a shabbily dressed, bearded and scurfy looking man asked me. His hair and beard appeared to be flaked with dandruff. The "dandruff" turned out to be small chips of paint which had molted from a bulkhead next to his bunk where he lay propped on one elbow.

"Hell, I have no idea. Go back to sleep."

"Sleep? I've been trying to get some sleep for the last three hours. You've had some weird dreams, boy, some powerful stuff. Kept me awake for hours."

"I'm sorry, I really tied one on and got hauled in here for drunk driving."

"I'm also sorry to see a young guy like you getting into such a mess."

Despite being locked up with some character who puked all over the place, the guy seemed eager to talk. What time? It had to be in the wee hours of the morning.

"Me, this is my second home," he continued. "When I'm broke and need a place to stay I get drunk and create a noise and disturbance just on purpose to get hauled in. A bunk, a couple of squares and when they turn me loose I'm as good as new. Works every time. But you, you're too young for this shit. You don't look like a bum."

"I might not look like one but I'd have to guess that's what I am."

"Who's this Loonsfoot character? And someone else you called Abby. You must have spent a whole hour babbling about the thickness of the sunshade. What in hell is the sunshade?"

"Has to do with the project I've been working on. I'm an engineer."

"Whew. That's great. Take care of yourself, young fellow. You've got a long good life ahead of you. Don't wind up like me."

"Thanks, my friend. Maybe we can have a cup of coffee together some time."

"The name is August Palosaari," he said shaking my hand. "I hang around not far from here at Yesterday's Saloon. It's just around the corner. You can find me there."

"You can make one phone call," the officer in charge informed me later in the morning.

Who could I call? Wally Grimes would now be at work. I could not drag Karen into this mess and after considering everyone else I knew I called Rolfe Ellefson. I had no choice but to phone him at work. He appeared to post bail of two hundred dollars after some short judicial proceedings. Fortunate not to lose my driver's license I retrieved my car which had been impounded.

Appearing at Alameda the next day, Herb Mickelssen and Doug Ridenbaugh asked me to join them privately in a conference room. Both men were downcast. There were few words of encouragement or commiseration this time.

"Paul, we've no choice but to terminate your employment with Alameda," Ridenbaugh said. "This is a higher management decision. Herb and I asked them to give you one last chance but we were overridden and their decision is final."

"I fully understand," I said humbly.

There were papers to be signed after I'd cleared my cubicle of personal belongings. I read them carefully, searching for mention of drunkenness. Almost absent of this, the reason for my termination struck hard: "Failure to perform assigned tasks."

Short and sweet. In other words, incompetence. This hurt a lot more than if my record of drunkenness were spelled in full as being the reason for dismissal.

After I'd loaded my belongings into my recovered car and signed some papers, Herb Mickelssen escorted me out of the building. I'd let this good man and the others down.

"Paul, I only wish you the best in life," he said, looking at me squarely through tear dimmed eyes while firmly shaking my hand. "I'll be praying for you."

I stood in the grove of eucalyptus trees outside the facility and took one last look at the building before driving away.

Alameda Aerospace was not a prison.

CHAPTER 11

Lumberjack

"What happened? Karen and I have been trying to reach you for the past two days. Is there anything wrong, Paul?" Wally Grimes called me one evening shortly after my firing from Alameda.

"There's a lot wrong, Wally. A lot more than I can handle right now."

"Is there anything I can do to help? Why don't I take a ride to your place if you're up to it? Anything you need?"

"That's fine, don't need anything. I'll be home all evening. Come on over."

"Be there in an hour."

I'd straightened up my messy apartment as soon as I got home after my firing to keep my mind off the dispiriting reversal of my fortunes. My head in a whirlwind of confusion, I made no attempt to decide on a course of action. In a fit of disgust, I poured the contents of a half-full bottle of whiskey and a few remaining beers down the sink—something I'd never done before—even now doing something so rash seemed inconceivable. Nervous, shaky and still sick to my stomach, I would tough it out without the whiskey and beer. Fortunately I found myself comfortably solvent although my drinking put a huge dent in my pocketbook and my savings. Almost a thousand dollars left in the bank should tide me through for a while and I'd paid my rent for the next month. But I had no idea of what to do; gloom set in swiftly to become an unaccustomed, unwelcome companion in my life.

"Man, you look terrible. Looks like you've had a tough go of things," Wally said. "When you didn't show up for the barbeque, Karen and I started to worry that something went wrong. You didn't sound well when you called."

"Have a seat, good buddy. First let me put on some coffee."

"What happened to you, a case of the flu or something even worse?"

"Something worse, something a lot worse. I got fired from Alameda. My very first engineering job," I said without hesitation.

"Just a couple days ago, but I expected it to happen sooner or later. The firing was long overdue."

Wally Grimes shook his head in disbelief. For a long minute he said nothing.

"Tell me, Paul, I hate to pry but I thought you were doing well on your job. You've always said you enjoyed your work and how about your supervisor? As I recall, didn't you mention you were being considered for a promotion?"

"I complicated the hell out of everything. They couldn't have a drunk onboard who missed days of work every two or three weeks. A drunk calling in to say he had the flu every time and finally getting caught up in his own lies. And that wasn't the end of it."

"You a drunk? I can't believe it. On leaves from the *Holgate* we tied on a few good ones but there were never any problems. Maybe Lieutenant Pence had some concern about the flight school. Didn't he ask if you were interested in Pensacola not long before you were discharged?"

"You haven't heard the worst of it, out on a big binge when I called you. On my way to your place I got pulled over for drunk driving, lucky I didn't kill someone on the freeway. I spent the night in jail and had to call a coworker to post bail. Made it to work and got terminated after many opportunities given to save face. Yeah, Lieutenant Pence mentioned flight school. I thanked him for considering me but told him I planned to go back to school.

"They'd put up with my drunkenness for a long time and more than once offered to help me with my problem. Can you beat that? But under the circumstances they had no choice but to let me go. There you have it, missing too much work for being a drunk. And yeah, my supervisors had me in mind for a promotion before I started drinking too much."

Wally again remained silent. He looked guilty, avoiding my gaze. Maybe he wanted to say he shared the blame for what happened. I broke in before he could speak.

"Listen, pal, I know what you're thinking, maybe you were a bad influence on me during our hitch in the navy. But it wasn't that at all, just the opposite. The good times we had together then were some of the best periods of my drinking career, in my whole life. No heavy binging, no being AWOL, we always managed to have some fun and still be shipshape. That's the way it should be. Physically, never in better shape—both of us I'd say. Wally, believe me, you had nothing to do with my getting fired. After I got out of the navy college kept me busy and there were no problems at all. I stayed practically sober for three years beating my brains out trying to pass tough engineering courses. But my problem with alcohol goes back a long way."

"I would have never guessed it. You don't appear to have any problems at all. You're a likeable guy who makes friends easily. Buddy, is there anything I can do to help?"

"Thanks, Wally, but this is something I've got to work on myself. You know, I never drink because I'm depressed or even feeling down. Sounds strange, doesn't it? But I love the stuff, even when I'm all alone and once I get started I just can't seem to get enough. You might call me a happy drunk."

I went on to relate the bash at the Hubbell Hall with the Independents where Eugene Seppala got me sobered up and the bender at Rice Lake when I sat alone in the night silence, perfectly content. Come to think of it, I didn't mind drinking in solitude. I didn't need any company to be in a complacent, euphoric mood. I'd become a solitary drunk; maybe I known this all along despite whatever company I happened to be with. Excluding, of course, Erma's company; I did not mention our days-long binges.

"Whatever it is, pal, remember I'm always your friend. You've got too much going for you just to throw everything away," Wally commiserated.

"Thanks, Wally. I'll probably be around for a while until I figure out what I'm going to do."

"You can look ahead to some barbeques. Probably dry ones," Wally said before leaving.

Rolfe and Muriel invited me to dinner at their home. Not without misgivings I accepted their invitation. After all, Rolfe's recommendation in no small measure ensured my hiring at Alameda. Then I had to go and mess things up. "Look, Paulie, why couldn't you be a man. Just show up and do what you were hired to do." But there were no such recriminations from Rolfe. Chatting outdoors while Muriel kept busy with dinner preparations, he only offered words of encouragement.

"Everyone at Alameda asks about you and wishes you well. They want to see you lick your problem and succeed."

"How about the project? I feel like I've left everyone in the lurch not completing my work on the sunshade."

"Right now we believe we've got most of the bugs out of the system and matters are proceeding on schedule. Herb and Doug finished your effort on the sunshade. You had matters well in hand on the sunshade making the job much easier for them to complete. Final testing ought to be done by the end of the next quarter."

"Rolfe, I feel like such a complete ass letting you and everyone else down."

"What's done is done. It's not the end of your career. You can make a bright future for yourself. And Paul, I really don't understand your problem. Since I've known you you've been a bright and spontaneous person, nothing like the drunks I've known," Rolfe said, echoing what Wally had told me. "Everyone we know respects you. That goes back to the Moose Lake Bible Camp. What's this stuff with getting drunk? I've got a tough time understanding that and I hate to see you punishing yourself. Me? I only tried a few beers while in college."

"A few beers in college? Only a few beers? Looking back I wish that's only what I would have done," I said anemically.

"Let me relate my brief experience getting drunk, for what it's worth," Rolfe continued. "One of my college buddies had a camp in the woods on the north shore of Lake Superior near Silver Bay. I should say his father's hunting camp. Three of us spent a whole night working on a case of beer. I must admit I got to feeling pretty good after the fourth bottle. We didn't know any girls to brag about so we spent the whole night blabbering college talk. "The fundamental theorem of the integral calculus," I declared to my pals. "Have any of you gone through the rigorous proof applying Riemann sums or were you only exposed to the heuristic proof?" A long windy discussion ensued, a lot of smoke coming from a trio of amateurs. Not too bad at math, I did understand the proof, however.

"After the eighth beer I got sick and puked up my guts. The next morning I woke from my messy bunk with a splitting headache. Cured my appetite for beer or anything else containing alcohol. I called it quits and settled for fresh air for good."

I found the realization comforting that Rolfe and his friends were also college prigs. It wasn't just Diggy belaboring Maclaurin series expansions or Max making a fuss over the valence of magnesium while enjoying a few brews on some bush road. And how about Louie questioning our pedantic display of German?

After dinner, Muriel left to visit friends. "Are you still seeing Erma?" she asked before she left. "She seems like a fine lady, always quiet and dignified."

"We parted ways," I told her bluntly. I did not equivocate. "We spent all our time getting drunk together and she almost lost her job. 'Am I an alcoholic,' she once asked me of herself. But now she's quit drinking and straightened out her life. I'll always think well of her—calling her an alcoholic might be a bit harsh."

"Good for her. I wish her well," Muriel replied.

"Am I an alcoholic?" I wondered. I dismissed the thought. A drunkard no doubt, but certainly not an alcoholic. A big difference existed between the two in my opinion. Once I began to drink I saw no reason to stop. Why go home to bed while still having fun? That's foolishness. On the other hand, I could count many long periods of going without a drink. And I never kept a bottle handy at my bedside in order to take big swigs throughout the night that by morning the contents would be drained. Only alcoholics kept a bottle handy. Me an alcoholic? Forget it.

Rolfe and I talked well into the evening. I'd long come to appreciate the cynical side of his nature. I resurrected Bible camp memories.

"What were you trying to do, frighten little Bobby Olson and the farm boys? How about that 'He died, He died,'" I asked, recalling the first night at the Moose Lake Bible Camp when the lights were turned off in the boy's tent.

Rolfe became serious. "Remember old Smelly?"

"How could I forget him. Couldn't handle Bobby letting one go at the campfire. And him and Boltz making a big fuss about tractors."

"Well, he cracked up. As you know in our faith, we're supposed to get 'saved,' which as you know, means asking Jesus to forgive your sins and accepting Him as your personal savior."

I'd heard this preached many times at the Emmaus Hall and had no problems with it. I considered myself saved.

"What happened? What's Smelly got to do with this?"

"He went holy-hopping around asking everyone if they were saved and he could never be saved enough himself. Smelly got re-saved at least once a month. Always the first one to flop at the altar and ask for forgiveness after the evening service. No one in the church had the good sense to tell him not to worry. One of the elders in our church even had the gall to tell Smelly he wasn't saved in the first place after he got saved for the sixteenth time. "You're going to go to hell, Smelly, unless you get right with God," this ignoramus told him.

"Smelly had a nervous breakdown, just an eighteen-year-old kid. He wound up in a mental institution for two years before going back to the farm. He married a plain, stout farm girl from Hibbing. He's doing OK now with a family of six kids."

"Then who died? Or were you just a joking?"

"Of course it was Jesus who died. And for a long time I believed He stayed dead. A hard time believing what's right when it didn't make any sense. Too much confusion if you asked me. A twelve-year-old expected to believe this stuff? How could I? Look at Smelly and that elder."

"So you're OK with it now?"

"Until I got to know Muriel, Jesus's death and resurrection made no sense. She convinced me otherwise even though I've still got a lot of questions needing answers. Theology can be challenging. But yeah, I'm OK with it."

"It's a wonder you didn't wind up a drunk like me."

"I might have if I hadn't slept in puke."

The cobwebs in my mind disappeared. I began to take long walks and by the end of a week my strength returned. One day I walked for more than twenty miles. I spent two weekends camping out in the Big Bear Lake resort area where I did some challenging hikes on trails in the surrounding hills. The swimming pool outside my apartment came in handy for doing hours of laps. It wasn't long before I could do three under water laps without coming up for air. Some of my neighbors called me "The Seal of Newport Beach."

I had to make plans. But what should I do? I still had the better part of my thousand dollars left and could perhaps count on some help from home if worse came to worst. But nothing came to mind.

Then I remembered.

August Palosaari. At least that's how I remembered the name. Another Finnish name. In my drunken stupor I couldn't have been sure I heard it right. My recollections of our conversation in the jail cell are sketchy. Despite his talk of getting drunk just so he'd get tossed in the can to dry out for a couple days and get some square meals, in the foggy recesses of my mind he impressed me as being more than just a plain drunkard. Curiosity piqued, I had to see this guy.

Yesterday's Saloon as Palosaari had said was a short distance from the jail and I had no difficulty finding it. I entered the tavern through a sturdy swinging door. "To hell with the dream bars," I thought as I surveyed the interior surroundings.

An old-fashioned tavern of pre-prohibition vintage, Yesterday's Saloon could have been a transplant from Calumet, Michigan. Like the Keona Room in Long Beach or the North Country Tavern in Calumet, the saloon had the classic features of a tavern of an earlier era. A long, heavy wood bar of expensive fabrication, a correspondingly long mirror behind the bar, a high ceiling finished with square metal panels scrolled at the perimeters, booths along the side wall, and some tables on the main floor space conduced to make an old-timer feel at home. Long absent from use, a brass spittoon sat off in a corner. Instead of a target for nasty yellow slugs, the spittoon, polished to a high degree of luster, stood enshrined as a trophy in a thick-walled glass box. The trophy resided five feet off the floor atop a sturdy pedestal.

Old-timers seeking respite from energetic young professionals buzzing about as bees, putting on the dog with their colleagues or seeking romance at their fancy watering holes, found refuge in Yesterday's Saloon. These grizzled patrons thumbed their noses at contemporary bars that featured hanging plants, frills and fancy food. No piped in loud music, lights controlled to an appropriate dimness or any other artificial distractions vitiated their sanctuary. Let the younger set have a fabricated ambiance with palm plants and sophisticated sound systems. Instead, an old-style jukebox provided music and harsh glaring overhead lights made it possible for a patron to see everyone else within. Comestibles were limited to Slim Jims and pickled hard-boiled eggs.

The toilet stunk. A large trough-type urinal, yellowed and rusty from years of long use, and reeking of ammoniac fumes, overwhelmed the olfactories of the occupant. Streaked with excrement, the john at best delivered a weak spluttering flush as I soon discovered. The drain in the center of the dank cement floor, rusted and clogged with cigarette butts, spelled certain disaster if the anemic toilet overflowed. If one stood in need of relief, he took his chances. The ladies' facilities were not much better according to one of the patrons.

There he was, seated alone at the far end of the bar. Another Finnish-American, I surmised, attempting to assert himself in a strange, rapidly changing society. Would he boast of having "Sisu" after he had a few beers in him? Sisu is a trait claimed by many of Finnish extraction meaning fortitude or just plain guts. Few of the sober minded Finns I knew bragged of having Sisu themselves. They just kept quiet. For these stalwarts, Sisu meant one's determination to meet obstacles in life head-on, paying one's debts and succeeding at a task once started without ever acknowledging defeat. This is the classical meaning of the word. But at times Sisu is mistakenly considered as bluster coming from one half in the bag. On one occasion at the Houghton County Memorial Airport in the Keweenaw, I remember a visitor from Finland, a young guy in his mid-twenties, getting ready to board his flight back to Helsinki. A sturdy fellow of medium height, his chest thrust forward and square of face, he stood looking straight ahead and blustered as though he were addressing a large audience. From what I could make out he bragged about what the Finns did to the Russians in Finland's Winter and Continuation Wars against the Soviets during World War II. Obviously, he'd had quite a few brews.

"Tartar, we destroyed you when you crossed our borders at Suomussalmi," he exclaimed defiantly in a thick brogue. In the Winter War, the Soviet military directed one its major attacks against Suomussalmi, a municipality in central Finland on its eastern border with the Soviet Union. Everyone in the terminal heard his boasting. "One Finn is as good as twelve Russians. And we'll fight you again if we have to." Although vastly outnumbered, the Battle of Suomussalmi resulted in a major victory for the Finns.

Palosaari appeared to be sober and not as old as I'd visualized him during the night we spent together in jail. Freshly shaven and casually but neatly dressed, he wore a flannel shirt and trousers of a coarse denim. His boots, made of full grain leather and laced with buckskin, were meant for outdoor work. A lumberjack's outfit. Clear-eyed and steady, by no means the man I remembered in jail.

"August Palosaari," I ventured. "Remember me?"

"How could I forget that noisy snoring? I lost a lot of sleep that night. By the way, you're looking great, kid. You ever get the sunshade figured out?" he asked, extending a hand.

At least I got his name right. "I'm Paul Maki," I said, reaching for his handshake. "I never got to finish the sunshade."

"Maki, did you say? Another *Suomalainen poika (Finnish boy),* hey? Don't run across many of them in these parts. That's assuming the name is spelled M A K I, which it probably is since you even look like a Finn. Bartender, bring my friend a schooner and bring me another."

"Make mine a seven-up."

Palosaari looked at me questioningly.

"I've been dry ever since I spent that night in jail."

"You caught me at a good time, catching me sober. Got locked up one other time since our night in the can. I'm glad to see you come, just getting ready to tie on another one. Why the seven-up, if I might be a little nosy?"

"I got fired from my job. There'll be no more sunshades or any other engineering for me, at least for a while. It's got to be seven-up."

I sensed Palosaari as not being an ordinary bum or a con man. He listened intently as I related the circumstances of my firing from Alameda. I opened to him, telling him my history of growing up in a small Upper Michigan town and how I'd messed up the engagement with Abby. Sharing a common bond in drunkenness, we talked for many hours.

"Me? I had a happy marriage once until I let drinking get the best of me. Had a wife and two great kids but am now divorced. Things went great for the first several years but I let life in the logging camp put me on a slippery downward slope. Or I should say life after work. Instead of going straight home with the money after a two or three-week run in the woods, I started hitting the bars with my logging buddies in Weaverville. Just a few beers at first and then going home but I started spending a lot more time in the bars. Then I forgot to go home altogether. The bars became more important to me than my family. My wife put up with this for well over a year until she finally decided she'd had enough of me so she up and left with the kids. I can't say I blame her. No money for anything, even lost the house which was the final straw. Here, Maki, is a picture of my family in my better days."

He'd kept the picture in good condition in a lined pocket of his wallet. It showed a handsome family, an attractive wife and two bright kids. An all-American family: a strapping and fit husband, a svelte brunette wife with a young son and daughter, both animated in appearance. August Palosaari appeared lean and spare without an ounce of fat visible on his sturdy frame. I studied the picture for a long while before handing it back.

"Right now she's working as a receptionist at one of the aerospace outfits in Pasadena. She never did remarry. She and the kids are doing OK especially without me around blowing the hard-earned dough on liquor. Yeah, I started hitting the hard stuff too.

"It's great of you to come and see an old drunk. I had a gut feeling you might show up. Like I said I was getting ready to go on another bender. Make a little noise, start a little trouble and then get some free lodging and a couple of squares in the can."

"A logger did you say. I worked the bush for a while in Upper Michigan, mostly cutting pulpwood for the paper mills. A lot of small stuff but kept my partner and me busy and in some spending money. Learned a lot from my old-timer partner, Riisto Salmi, about felling trees, clearing trails and skidding logs. Another Finnish guy by the way. And I really enjoyed the work and the six-packs at the end of a shift."

"I got started in Maine. That's where I met my wife. Elise is French Canadian. There were still a few stands of pine and lots of pulpwood. From there I moved on. Even hit the Upper Peninsula for a season. You must know of a place called Seney. A lot of flat land but lots of trees. Used to be a lot of white pine but when I worked the area, we cut spruce and balsam. From what I saw before we left for California a lot of the land turned swampy from too many trees cut down. Things went well in Northern California where I got started on the big trees, the Douglas fir, ponderosa pine, some redwood and some big cedar. A whole different ballgame out here—had to learn from scratch almost. Didn't see spars, block and tackle, donkey and guy wires in Seney or even in Maine. Here we worked on a lot of rough terrain, not much flat land but lots of steep slopes in the higher regions. Couldn't be too careful out there. Wasn't much more than a water boy to start with, the guys really kept me busy just being a "gofer." Once the foreman saw my willingness to bust my butt he eventually gave me more responsible tasks. Bucked and cabled logs for dragging them out, drove the 'cat and eventually got involved with the actual felling of trees. The big thirty-two-foot logs in California made the nine-foot pulpwood sticks I cut in Seney look like pencils. After a few years in the big conifers I became a tree climber or a "topper" as we were sometimes called. Just like an ornament on top of a Christmas tree. As good as any of them, but it's been a while. Then I messed everything by hitting the bottle too hard," he said, falling silent.

His hands were gnarled and calloused. His wrists were not large but looked sinewy and strong. Although somewhat careworn he still appeared to be in great shape. Losing a wife and two great kids had to really be tough on the guy. I said nothing. Plaintive hillbilly music wailed from the jukebox as we both sat in silence.

"I've got to go," I finally said. "You said you were starting another bender. Why don't you try holding off a day or two?"

An idea came to mind and I began hatching a plan.

"Here, take this twenty. Should buy you a few meals the next couple days. Just try to stay out of the can in the meantime."

August Palosaari started to object when I handed him the twenty. "Hell, Maki, you don't have to do this. I'll be OK just the way I am. That jail's not a bad place."

"You can pay me back later. I've got an idea which may help both of us. You can wind up in the can later if you want. I'll be busy in the meantime. What do you say we get together here on Thursday, say early afternoon? Hear me out on what I've got to say and if you think I'm full of shit there's no big loss."

I didn't want to take any chances by revealing what I had to suggest to Palosaari right away. He'd probably think I'd spew hot air, a lot of nonsense, about some impulsive scheme. And with a couple days to wonder what I had in mind with a twenty in his pocket should reveal whether he had any interest in my idea. No big secret what I had to say—I intended to suggest we partner up as lumberjacks. It would be a way for both of us to get some solid ground under our feet. With Palosaari employed once again as a full-fledged lumberjack, I would be his helper.

I returned to Yesterday's Saloon. Seated on the same stool as before, Palosaari still looked fresh and sober. After a quick beer and a seven-up we left for a lunch at a nearby restaurant.

"What's on your mind, Maki? This had better be good. Staying sober the last two days has not been easy."

"Ever thought about going back to the woods?"

"A lot of times I do, almost every day, but now I'm dead broke. Besides I sold off my equipment for liquor. Sold everything cheap, too—the two best heavy-duty chain saws money could buy plus my tools, sharpeners, picks, axes and wedges. One still needs picks and axes in the Douglas fir country even though it's not like lopping branches off a balsam. And as I said, my two chain saws were the best money could buy. Making matters worse I sold a heavy-duty pickup. No transportation at all."

"Mr. Palosaari, here's what I've got in mind."

"First off, Maki, let's get off this *Mr.* stuff. Call me August."

"Great. What do you say we partner together? I've got a few bucks and I can drum up some more to get us started. I've got the transportation so getting to the timber shouldn't be a problem. My car's still got a lot of mileage left on her; it's almost new. You tell me what we need and I'll see that we get it. Take another day to think about it if you've got any doubts. The sooner we can get going the better. Think of me as your helper. I'd like to learn the ropes logging in Northern California."

August Palosaari studied me closely.

"You're serious, kid, dead serious. Stop here tomorrow and I'll have a list of what we need. I've been aching to get back in the timber."

I discovered the conditions rough, hazardous—a lot different from working fifty-foot-tall spruce and balsams in the Keweenaw. The uneven, sloped landscape near Weaverville made the relatively benign terrain in the Keweenaw compare as a well-groomed municipal park. One had to be careful. Rocky outcroppings, thorny vines, steep embankments near raging rivers and hoofing the steeply sloped ground did not make for easy going. One misstep could mean a sprained ankle or even worse. Yet I felt at home in a timberland populated with large conifers, many of which towered above two hundred feet. The forest seemed endless, its silence surreal. This rugged forested landscape in Northern California struck me as being as close to a wilderness paradise as I could envision.

I had no trouble borrowing extra money from my parents, despite the fact both were deeply disturbed when I told them why Alameda let me go; I held nothing back. They had a difficult time accepting what seemed an early end of a promising career after my very first engineering position. Going back to the woods made no sense to them at all. My mom wept in disbelief for days. My dad tried to be philosophical. "Try to stay sober and make the best of it. If it means the woods, then so be it," he said in resignation when I phoned him for money. Up until then I'd kept them in the dark as to what happened at Alameda.

"Seven hundred dollars ought to put us in business, maybe even more than enough," August said upon reviewing his list of equipment we'd need. "At least enough to get us started."

I had enough money to buy a top-grade, heavy-duty chain saw and a lighter, more portable saw for limbing and topping trees. Auxiliary equipment included a power sharpener, a couple of hand saws and some axes. There was enough money for boots and to put some warm clothing on our backs.

"Maki, you don't know how much I appreciate this," he said shortly before our departure for Weaverville. "I'm going to make it up to you after a few paydays."

Palosaari had called a major logger whom he'd worked for during his previous stint in the woods. The owner of Brickhouse Logging had thirty guys working for him and owned a fleet of trucks for hauling logs. Brickhouse, an old navy man, welcomed August back.

"I'll be bringing a helper," August told him. "Hasn't had any experience in California but he's a sturdy guy with some experience working pulpwood in Upper Michigan. I think he'll work out well for you."

Before vacating my apartment in Newport Beach we had a small going away party. In addition to August Palosaari the only other guests were the Grimeses and the Ellefsons. Wally and Rolfe both agreed I'd made a wise choice after I told them I'd be partnering with Palosaari, now completely dried out and sober. Articulate and knowledgeable of logging he made a good impression on my friends. I did not tell them how we'd become acquainted—I mentioned our commonalities—August an experienced logger and myself one of limited experience.

"This may be a good thing for you. You're cut out for outdoor work." Wally Grimes advised. "Palosaari seems to know what he's talking about."

Rolfe Ellefson concurred. "I envy you. I wouldn't mind doing a season in the woods myself," he said. "You can always go back to engineering and make a fresh start. And despite what happened at Alameda, you've made some good friends there. Doug and Herb wish you the best."

"Just remember to go slow," August advised me the first day in the woods. "Never hurry. Once you get into the swing of things you'll develop a good rhythm making your job a lot easier."

I did not partner with Palosaari right away. "Might be better for

Maki to do odd jobs so he can see what's going on here," Brickhouse recommended to August. "Get a general feel for the operation and what's involved. I'm going to show him around first and have him do some basic work before he partners with you. He can work in gradually and then learn to do other jobs as well."

"High lead logging is coordinated operation which involves many skilled tasks," Gary Brickhouse told me. "I want you to take a good close look before you get started on anything."

August had mentioned spars, block and tackle, donkey and guy wires when I met him at Yesterday's Saloon. Brickhouse still logged with a "donkey," a steam-powered engine system, widely used from the turn of the twentieth century through the 1940s, and currently being replaced throughout the industry with modern equipment. Having inherited Brickhouse Logging, a 1920's enterprise, Gary Brickhouse opted to keep the donkey system which he maintained in good running order. His trucks for transporting logs, however, were new.

I saw everything first hand as I accompanied Brickhouse through an area being logged. Basically a complex of cables, pulleys and the donkey facilitated moving felled logs to a loading zone where they would be transported away. At a prominent location the largest and most sturdy tree called a spar tree, supported with guy wires and rigged with a pulley and cables, served as an anchor point for the donkey-powered cable system.

More new words found their way into my vocabulary: A "choker setter" wrapped a "choker" or a cabled noose at one end of a log, which facilitated the lifting and transport to the loading zone by way of the donkey-powered cable system, but not before a "whistle punk" sent a wired signal to the donkey operator to safely proceed. A loud "whistle" from the donkey resounded.

A college of learning unto itself, the entire operation required not only significant physical prowess but also good judgment. New guys had to learn things correctly. Safety first—Brickhouse took his time with a new hand and it eventually paid off— fewer accidents and fewer new guys quitting after a week or so because of being pushed too hard. As such, being not much more than a water boy to start with, I ran errands for the loggers doing the simplest tasks, perhaps getting a tool they needed or delivering a message to them from the foreman. Even though I hadn't done so much as put my hands on an axe during the first couple of weeks, just keeping up with the guys meeting their various needs kept me going as I hopped about the rough terrain. One could not be too careful on steep ground.

The loggers were an amiable bunch, always cheerful and mischievous. There were the invariable tricks to be played on the rookie. It made no difference whether a kid graduated fresh out of high school or a college boy in his late twenties like me wound up in the bush. Being a college boy made me a favorite target for their mischief.

I was reminded of Bobby Olson at the Moose Lake Bible Camp when Rolfe and I sent him looking around for striped red and white paint for painting our daredevles. My turn came to be sent on a wild goose chase: cosmic justice one might say. They didn't try to pull the "sky hook" routine on me, an old favorite of the crew trying to dupe a newcomer. They at least gave me some credit with my hard science education. Instead they connived to have me run around looking for a "root badger," a device supposed to crunch up the roots of small underbrush and vines making it easier to clear trails. "Let's see if this mechanical engineer can find one," they chuckled to themselves.

I feigned gullibility. Little did they know they were dealing with a knowledgeable man of college who knew when he was being spoofed. I had to go along with these guys.

"Isn't it just as easy to whack the stuff with an axe?" I asked. "A root badger, that seems like a lot of trouble for nothing."

"It's got steel teeth, chews up roots and spits them out. Real simple to operate, it's a small mechanical device, runs off gasoline. It's a lot faster than using an axe. Really makes it easy for clearing brush. You throw the saplings on the brush pile once the roots are gone. A very neat and sophisticated operation."

I began asking about for the root badger. What I got were vague answers from everyone as to the whereabouts of the device. I got sent from one man to another. They acted serious and none of them laughed. Each guy directed me to someone else, usually far removed. "The last time I saw it old Pete had it. Go check with him." I did a lot of walking. I spent a good half hour of bootless inquiry before I pretended to be at a total loss. "I give up. I can't find it," I lamely admitted. "You're a good sport, Maki," they said, taking turns slapping my back. "We had that college boy going," they laughed. Young innocent Bobby Olson only took fifteen minutes looking for the striped paint before Brother Rigo saved his day. I made it look good; the 'jacks were none the wiser.

Given more responsibility as time passed, I moved up from water boy, having been replaced by Bob Hazlitt, a twenty-year-old kid from Redding. Brickhouse kept a close eye on me until he finally partnered me with August. Experienced helpers assisted August while I gained familiarity with the overall operation and learned basic skills. Brickhouse believed in a fluid, flexible operation; permanent members of his crew were expected to learn each aspect of logging and to multitask. Lumberjacks working on contract had to have all the requisite skills before he took them on board, which meant operating the donkey and driving a truck, while at the same time having a lot of knowledge about first aid. Everyone on the crew had to be able to administer basic treatment in the event of an accident. Accidents were unavoidable but happily most of them were of a minor nature.

I bucked logs and choker set cables for towing. Dragging cables across the unforgiving terrain through a mesh of thorny vines taught me to be careful. Looking at my arms, heavily scratched from my hands to my armpits after my first day of choker setting, made me wonder if I'd made the right choice. Learning to operate the 'cat came easy, which I discovered to be a welcome respite from clumping through undergrowth while dragging a heavy cable to a newly felled tree. Bucking the large trunks into logs and choker setting them for towing kept me going strong.

August acclimated rapidly to his skill after his prolonged absence from the woods. It did not take him long to regain his expertise as a topper. When not involved with actual felling of trees, he soon climbed the towering firs as though he'd not missed a single day of work. New hands watched as he scaled a Douglas fir, nearly two hundred feet tall, to be used as a spar. A daunting task, shinning up a Douglas Fir required considerable physical stamina. I'd never truly appreciated a lumberjack's coordinated skills until I watched him climb, his spiked boots digging into the tough bark as he shinnied skyward. A harness, a durable loop of stranded wire attached to his waist and circling the trunk, provided his sole means of safety. Dig in with the boots and up with the harness.

Slow, methodical, yet fast and purposeful, time seemed to stand still before he reached the top. A light-weight chain saw, tethered to his waist belt, served for removing limbs as necessary. Fortunately, most of the limbs on the spar tree were near the top of an otherwise naked trunk. Once he lopped the top, the spar began to sway considerably causing a lot of nervousness for everyone watching from below. How a topper avoids catastrophe is truly amazing.

"Why the wire rope," I asked Palosaari.

"There's always a chance of a of hitting the harness with an axe or a making a careless move with a power saw when cutting those limbs," he said. "With pure hemp, one's dead. Chances of staying alive are a lot better with wire when you're one hundred fifty feet up."

Among various tasks as his helper, I had to make to make sure his gear remained in perfect condition. Everything down to his hard hat. Palosaari, born to be a lumberjack, taught me how to sharpen the saws and axes to a honed perfection. Maybe I'd become a lumberjack.

The Grizzly Den outside of Weaverville boasted status as being the favorite watering hole of the 'jacks. Every Saturday night the Brickhouse crew as well as crews from other logging companies could be found there creating a riotous scene of fun and camaraderie. A portly woman, a widow by the name of Thelma Longfellow, owned and managed the Grizzly Den. Her former logger husband claimed kinship with the famous New England poet. While on the job, he was killed instantly when a large dead limb falling from a redwood tree struck him on his head. He'd worn a hard hat. Amiable, brisk and homely, Thelma had a broad honest face featuring full red lips, which always formed a wide pleasant smile. Her face belonged on an oatmeal box.

"That stuff is rough on the constitution, isn't it buddy," a lumberjack from another outfit said to me.

"It could be better," I replied.

Seven-up still satisfied my thirst whenever I accompanied our gang to town. Hadn't had a drink since the debacle following my binge at the Keona Room. August also had moderated his habit, limiting his intake on any given occasion to a maximum of six beers, a regimen he observed religiously. "I'm not going back to jail anymore, come what may," he declared.

A shortage of girls seldom occurred at the Grizzly Den. The guys referred to Thelma and the girls as Mother Hen Thelma and her flock of chicks. Many of the young women twenty-one and older in the Weaverville area came to have fun. Single ones, divorcees and married girls were among the attendees. Younger girls not yet of legal age were accompanied by friends or their parents. The girls could always count on the generous, free-spending 'jacks to show them a good time. Not a few of them found husbands at the Den.

"You don't have to look for trouble. Trouble will find you," my dad once told me. "Especially if you're going to hang around the bars."

Lumberjack-weight lifter fit, Oscar Maki earned a reputation as a tough guy after putting on the gloves and getting into the ring with "One Round" Sammy Incapera, the carnival champ at the Legion Field in Calumet. At the urging of his best pal, Pohjola, and a couple other buddies he reluctantly decided to take on Sammy. Pohjola told the one about sowing the wild oats. They'd just attended a burlesque sideshow at the carnival featuring Dianne and her Monkey and were on their way out when Sammy issued a challenge to Oscar and his pals. "Who's the tough guy, give it a go with old Sammy," he yelled.

Once Oscar got into the ring, he overcame his apprehensions. Bombs away on radio Tokyo. My dad forced Sammy Incapera to quit with a broken nose after three rounds. "Kid, you're the first one to beat me," Sammy congratulated.

Word spread rapidly over Calumet of his feat and soon he became a target for every barroom tough in town. He got tired of this and he quit the taverns altogether when he and mom got married. Instead they enjoyed an occasional keg party with relatives and friends; my mom wasn't a prude when it came to having a few beers. Then they both got saved at the Emmaus Hall after six years of marriage and quit drinking altogether.

My dad was right. Trouble found me. The trouble occurred during a Saturday night outing at the Den while I chitchatted with a girl who'd initiated a conversation at the bar. Appearance-wise she struck me as being rather plain but impressed me as being quietly friendly and congenial. She apparently only wanted someone to talk to. August and the others were on the floor dancing with some of Thelma's chicks.

Suddenly I received a jolt from an elbow striking me hard on my right cheek. Stunned, I stood up from my bar stool to see a squat, sturdy young guy looking defiantly at me, right in my face.

"What's the problem? Why did you elbow me?"

"That's my wife you're talking to, you punk."

"You should have told me that before you gave me the elbow."

Broad of face, wearing a cocky expression, curly-dark-haired and built like a fireplug, he stood there sneering, no more than a foot away from me.

"Look, you pop-sucking candy ass, I suggest you beat it before I mess up your homely round face. You're one too many here." For emphasis he gave me a shove and looked ready to give me another.

I'd had enough. Attempting to restrain him, I got him in a bear hug. I really didn't want to fight. Maybe just get him calmed down and talk things over with a seven-up and a beer. Words would be wasted until then.

The fellow gave me no quarter. "I'm going to beat the shit out of you," he snarled.

Cripes, the guy was strong even though he obviously had a few brews in him. Perhaps just the right amount to be at peak performance. Even after the months of bucking logs and honing my physique to hard muscle he nonetheless managed to struggle out of my hold, and like the time Wally Grimes and Snake went at it in the Proud Parrot, he stood before me sneering and confident. "Now let's get down to serious business," he said. He stood relaxed, his arms thrust out at his side. Pop-sucking candy ass did he say? Exchange some nice words with this bum and then maybe start bawling like I did at the Laurium dump? My adrenalin pumping hard, he'd given me my chance.

I let go with a straight right and packing all my power behind the punch caught him smack-dab on his sneering mouth. He wobbled momentarily before toppling to the floor. His upper lip gaped wide like a split ripe tomato, and through the gory froth spewing from his mouth, I could see his front teeth were missing. I checked my hand which had begun to sting. Dark beads of blood forming rivulets dripped from my fingers. Wounds that would require seven stitches exposed the bones on my index and middle fingers.

By the time Thelma came out from behind the bar August and our crew members had drawn near to witness the fracas.

"Why don't you boys get this bum out of here," Thelma said to August.

"You've got a good right, Maki. And well used," one of the guys said.

Thelma agreed. "I'll see to it he doesn't ever come back."

The fireplug left on his own, still in a daze. I noticed his split upper lip had swollen to a large bloody red flap, which hung at least an inch below his lower lip as he shuffled out the door.

"I'm sorry this had to happen," I said to the guy's wife who appeared to be relieved.

"I'm not. That lazy bastard is no good. He's nothing but trouble and what you gave him he deserved. He just got out of jail and I hope he gets locked up for another thirty days."

"We're cousins," August said to me one night in our cabin. "Blood. Third cousins to be exact."

Four men shared a large cabin. The cabins were built in the 1920s by Brickhouse's father and his uncles. Rather than a large bunkhouse the logging company thought it smarter to have their crew enjoy more privacy and more square feet per man.

Initially there were six men to a cabin. This proved to be too cramped an arrangement; four guys per cabin of log construction proved to be optimum. As built, the cabins lacked conveniences and provided for only the barest essentials: a couple of double-tiered bunk beds and a potbellied stove. A nearby stream provided a water source. The men relied on kerosene lamps for lighting. They took showers under a rain barrel.

Modern propane-fueled ovens installed in each cabin eliminated the need for the long-gone bunkhouse cook or for relying on the potbellied stove for cooking. The potbellied stoves, however, were kept. Points were sunk and hand pumps for drawing water installed. The units, amply spread on an acreage several miles from Weaverville, had electricity. The men in each cabin were responsible for their own livelihood, which in addition to procuring their own food, meant sharing the cost of electricity and gas. Each cabin crew took care of minor repairs such as replacing a broken window or a torn screen door during mosquito season. Otherwise, Brickhouse let his crew have the places rent free. Most were occupied; a few of the loggers had homes in Weaverville.

Palosaari read the question mark on my face.

"Didn't you tell me once your grandparents came from Pudasjarvi? So did mine. When you told me your name at first I paid no attention. "Maki" is one of the most common Finnish names. My grandparents also came from Pudasjarvi and that's when I got curious. Could be a slight bit of a chance we might be related and sure enough we are."

We'd been seated around the potbellied stove with cigars lit one cold midweek evening. Our other two cabin mates were busy playing cribbage for dimes. Stunned at what August related I could not speak. Cause and effect. If I hadn't been locked up in jail with Palosaari this wealth of revelation would have resided undisturbed.

"What I discovered is we've got a cousin in Finland whose passion in retirement is genealogy. His name is Timo Hukkari."

I'd been unaware of my Finnish ancestry, aware only to the extent that I knew Grandpa and Grandma Maki had emigrated from Pudasjarvi. My maternal Koskinen grandparents had come from the Karelia, a richly forested region in southeastern Finland on the Russian border. The Russians grabbed the Karelia as well as a couple ports on the Arctic Ocean from Finland after World War II. I well understood the frustration and rage of the young Finn bellowing at the Houghton County Memorial Airport. Other than knowing my grandparents, uncles and aunts and numerous cousins, I'd been almost totally ignorant of my Finnish roots.

"Here, Paul, look at this. What do you think?"

August produced a thick volume complete with a family tree of the Palosaari lineage. An impressive result of an intensive genealogical study done by Timo Hukkari, the work appeared replete with names, dates and pictures.

"Before we get into this let me tell you a little bit about Timo Hukkari, a lifelong officer in the Finnish army who retired as a full colonel. Not too shabby. Hukkari had a distinguished career as a military officer and served as an aide to Mannerheim himself. Fought in many engagements including the ones at Raatteen Portti and Suomussalmi during the Winter War. Then later during the Continuation War he fought in numerous battles until Finland ceased hostilities with the Soviets in 1944. Colonel Hukkari finished his career as an ambassador in the Finnish Foreign Service after the war ended. He got to meet a lot of dignitaries: some of the top leaders from Spain, Germany and England among other countries. From what I gathered he didn't care too much about this activity but he took it in stride as he neared retirement."

Palosaari paused introspectively. "One of these days I'm taking a trip to Finland to meet him. Our Finnish relatives are talking about having a big reunion and are inviting relatives from all over the world to attend. Not only here, but places like South Africa, France and even Singapore.

"Now let me show you, cousin, how we're related. It starts with a great-great grandfather Palosaari going back to the 1850s. Here, take a look," he said as he flipped to an appropriate page in the genealogy.

"Our great-great-grandpa was Anders Palosaari. He and his wife Lena had seven kids, three boys and four girls. One of his sons became my great-grandpa and one of the daughters your great-grandma. His children had lots of kids of their own. Your great-grandma married a Maki, and as you can see, both your father and your mother and you yourself are named in the lineage. Likewise you can see my name, even got our family picture in Hukkari's book. That's me and my sibs with our parents. So on my paternal side I've managed to keep the Palosaari name down through the line as you did paternally through your great-grandpa Maki. Sounds complicated as hell, doesn't it? At any rate when everything is filtered out, we're third cousins, and like I said, blood.

"The way it's stated in Hukkari's book there are over three thousand descendants from just one man and his wife when spouses are included. And it makes you wonder how many more have come into this world since he had the book published just over a year ago. Small world, isn't it? And as far as you and I are concerned it got started in a Los Angeles County jail."

We sat in silence for a long while. Our cabin mates continued playing cribbage.

"I'd sure like to take that trip to Finland with you."

"The way it stands the reunion's still a few years away from now."

"Why so far off?"

"It's being planned to coincide with a special national holiday."

Our partnership prospered, our relationship perfect. We were more like friends than cousins. A third cousin? Which made it just about right. Back home in the Keweenaw we were always trying to impress our relatives—first and second cousins always trying to outdo each other vying for the top spot on the totem pole. Who got more toys at Christmas? My cousin Sparky got an extra-large set of tinker toys enabling him to build windmills and towers reaching to the ceiling while I got a small box of Lincoln logs. Build a small tongue-in-groove log cabin finished with green panels, made from a synthetic material, serving as the roof. Done. Oh yeah, I got a doctor's kit with a fake stethoscope and a phial of small cinnamon hearts for medicine. On Christmas day they were gone by noon.

August, more of a teacher to me than I a partner to him, and I flourished together as a well-oiled machine after I'd been on the job for six months. Once I'd acquired basic skills we were both putting good money in our pockets. The crisp, frosty early morning starts brought a carefree wellbeing such as I'd not previously realized. Choker-setting had become a second nature; inherent problems were resolved with patience. Most of the time enough clearance existed for securing the cable before the whistle punk signaled the donkey operator to haul the log to the loading area, but if a log lay too flat, tunneling a clearance meant dirty, fatiguing work. Careful but briskly efficient, I'd learned to avoid the dangers of an unstable trunk felled on a steep slope where a slight disturbance could cause a roll, slow at first but thundering as the timber gained momentum—little room existed for error.

We ate well-balanced meals every day. Not like the old logging camps in the Keweenaw where many of the pulp cutters subsisted on a rudimentary diet.

"Gimme a piece of punk, a ring of gut and a booze apple," one of the old-timers in the Keweenaw always would tell his grocer when he came to town to stock up on grub. Or in other words, a round loaf of sourdough bread, a ring of bologna and an onion. Other than the bologna and some oatmeal, flapjacks and coffee, these staples accounted for the main diet of loggers camped near the Bruneau Creek for a week or two before coming to town to get rip-roaring drunk and to look for barflies. Skinny and emaciated, by the time these guys were fifty years old they appeared as wire hardened skeletons with skin as taut as a drumhead. But they were still healthy and strong.

Our crew ate well: lots of bacon and eggs, pancakes and orange juice for breakfast and well-packed lunches. Roast beef dinners served with mashed potatoes and gravy were not uncommon as time permitted. Fruits and vegetables were available in abundance. There were few symptoms of emaciation; the guys were well-muscled and fit. All the 'jacks enjoyed salubrious health and regularity.

"If you've got to leave a shit in the bush make sure you cover it. We're not out here to breed flies. And remember to bring toilet paper. Dry leaves and moss are poor substitutes for cobbing those grimy butts," Brickhouse advised his crew.

Brickhouse, a man of faith, loved to read the bible. At times he'd share his favorite passages. He'd find a way to quote an appropriate scripture verse as occasion required. He read only from the King James Version of the Holy Bible:

And thou shalt have a paddle upon thy weapon; and it shall be, when thou wilt ease thyself abroad, thou shalt dig therewith, and shalt turn back and cover that which cometh from thee: (Deuteronomy, Ch. 23, v. 13).

"Did you know that a Finn developed high lead logging?' August asked me during a mid-morning coffee break. "A guy who came over from Finland by the name of Oscar Wirkkala."

Finnish pride in Finns of great accomplishment: Sibelius, Saarinen, Aalto, and of course Mannerheim to name a few. Pride heralded unabashedly by Finnish Americans in whose eyes their Finnish heroes achieved Olympian stature. Homes were painted blue and white, the same colors of the Finnish flag. Many can be seen painted in this simple décor this very day. While versed in English, the Finnish language remained the preferred language of choice in homes and on farms for years. And Finnish culture has always been a big part of life in Finnish-American communities found primarily in Maine, in Midwestern states such as Michgan and Minnesota, and on the West Coast, particularly in Washington and Oregon.

Finns of diametrically opposing views on life celebrate "Juhannus Paiva." Held in June, celebration of Juhannus Paiva, or St. John's Day, is their main cultural event of the entire year. For pious Apostolic Lutherans, Juhannus Paiva means week-long church services. Visitors and relatives from Finland invariably attend these services. It is strictly church and church fellowship for these sober-minded individuals. My departed grandpa and grandma Koskinen were among these. Alcoholic beverage in any form is strictly forbidden as are dancing, movie attendance or women putting on lipstick.

Juhannus Paiva means just the opposites for their imbibing counterparts. These are Finns whose favorite leisure activity is getting drunk—that means getting drunk during spare time when not working. Hardworking people, work is seldom missed by these doughty individuals on account of their habit. But they love to drink—some claim the predilection to get drunk resides in their genes—I'd often wondered if this were true of myself. I'd read somewhere how Nordics could not handle alcohol. "Maybe it's in my genes and there's nothing I can do about it," I'd thought at times of my own penchant for alcohol. "After all, I've got Finnish blood." This reflection gave me comfort instead of concern.

For the imbibers, Juhannus Paiva culminates in a couple days of unbridled celebration at some remote facility in the woods which has cabins and a main lodge for dancing and drinking. There is never a shortage of beer. Musicians, most often an accordionist, a stringed instrument and a horn keep things lively.

After completing my sophomore year at Michigan Tech I attended one of these festivals during a summer break with my college buddy, Johnny Alatalo, my Humboldt chum and son of a lumberjack from Misery Bay. This would be the sole occasion where I cast caution out the window to get rip-roaring drunk before returning to my studies. I dismissed qualms about tying one on—I looked ahead to the big bash at Otter Lake.

The fun started early in the afternoon. The Otter Lake Dance Hall handled a large capacity crowd of celebrants but most early-arrival revelers sat outside at picnic tables baking in the hot sun and swatting at deer flies and mosquitoes on a humid summer solstice afternoon. The real fun would begin in the evening when the musicians arrived. Featured at this event were two accordionists from Ewen, a string bass and a trumpet player. Johnny and I celebrated without restraint, putting down one beer after another, along with the farmers and lumberjacks from the Sturgeon River Valley. The celebrants spent the afternoon pitching horseshoes, playing softball on a nearby field, and for most participants, just plain getting drunk. A big truckload of Bosch and Stroh's had been hauled to the picnic—not content with a mere sufficiency of beer, only a riotous superfluity would satisfy the needs of these merry makers. Others brought a jug or two of whiskey to be passed around. The music started up early in the long summer evening and would continue well past midnight. As expected a few minor scuffles broke out with little harm done.

Dense clouds of smoke from numerous lit cigarettes and pipes saturated the Otter Lake Dance Hall as the evening wore on. The confines were stifling hot but no one seemed to mind. The celebrants appeared wraithlike in a dim, tangerine reddish-orange light. One could only discern a stranger from a neighboring farmer until he moved up close in the drunken fog. Of heavy log construction, the varnished walls of the building glowed dimly with a dark reddish hue despite being fouled by years of smoke and condensates that'd emanated from profusely sweating bodies. The proceedings in the large hall would have done justice to warmongering Vikings having returned home to the fjords, riotously celebrating their many plundering triumphs in a remote lodge. The musicians performed on a platform set up in the center of the spacious hall, leaving ample space for the dancers.

Round and round in the big dance hall the celebrants tramped to the lively peals of the accordions. The horn screeched and the base viol strings thumped. Polkas and humppas kept the dancers lively. A few old country haunting dirges played in a minor key slowed the activity periodically permitting the dancers a minute to obtain more refreshment. The Finnish farm girls might well have stepped out of the pages of *The Kalevala,* which is Finland's national epic poem. Mostly blonds and a few Mustalainens. A Mustalainen (gypsy or Romani) is a dark-haired Finn having roots mostly in northern Finland or Lapland. No insipid smiles from any of the blonds or the Mustalainens: jut-jawed and determined, hard eyes looking straight ahead and low-slung hips, latching a husband by whatever means stood foremost in minds as they grimly stomped the floor to a humppa, side by side with bawdy, drunken partners, equally jut-jawed and determined.

The lead accordionist, also the main vocalist, bawled out the lyrics in a sonorous gravelly voice, sometimes in Finnish. A tall lanky guy, broad red suspenders strapped over a time-tested flannel shirt held up his coarse denim trousers. A big helmet of swept back, wavy blond hair complemented his lean angular face. Outfitted with wire framed spectacles often worn by intellectuals, he inspired an image of a youthful Leon Trotsky striving to agitate the proletariat. He would have had no problems getting workers to strike. Bending his knees, bouncing up and down as he played, the music got louder and louder and the dancers stomped more vigorously.

"The accordion is the devil's instrument," old Finnish ladies used to say. They claimed its bold, pealing crescendos caused young men and women partnered on the dance floor to lose their inhibitions. "Too many shotgun weddings," these old ladies declared, "all because of that damned accordion."

They may well have been right.

"Let's get some fresh air, Johnny. We'll feel a lot better," I said in a state of drunken solicitousness as I led him outside the dance hall. Well past midnight and groggy I'd had way too many brews myself and needed relief from the stifling, smoky hall.

In an ebullient mood but too drunk to dance, Johnny got turned down by the unaccompanied girls. Unsuccessful, he barged in on a farmer from Toivola dancing with his wife. His luck improved. The wife didn't seem to mind the intrusion and neither did the husband. She stood waiting to stomp to a lively humppa with him. The farmer's wife, rejected but not dejected, watched as Johnny instead acted the part of a hussy and began to frolic merrily about the hall with her husband, who played along with the farce to the delight of a hooting crowd. After stumbling about the floor for a minute or two Alatalo became nauseous and spewed a torrential stream of foamy beer diffused with chunks of undigested hot dogs, which splattered the farmer's overalls.

"No problem, sonny," the farmer said despite the fact a drunken bleary-eyed Alatalo offered no apologies. "Piss will dry and shit will crumble and so will the puke," the farmer added.

The mosquitoes were out in full force. Although warm and close for a Copper Country summer night, I felt substantially cooler in the outside air than I did inside the smog-saturated, stuffy dance hall. "Let's take a walk to the lake. We'll feel better after a little stroll," I encouraged again. "That beer will be waiting."

We walked through the parking lot. A full moon made it easy to see. We both got steadier on our feet as we progressed down the middle of the lot toward a footpath leading to Otter Lake. Nearing the end of the lot we heard some noise coming from one of the cars: "Squeak, Squeak, Squeak, Squeak ..."

"Dog bite my pecker. We'd better check this out," Johnny Alatalo said. We'd both become quite alert.

We got a good look through a side window. "Stump Jumping" they call this peeping Tom activity. A couple going at it on the front seat arrested our attention. "Why they didn't use the back seat?" I wondered.

The guy failed to completely remove her bloomers. There they were, bungee-corded across her widespread ankles and logged down by her partner's legs, preventing her from kicking at the windshield and the upholstered roof. What had been a steady rhythm began to accelerate as revealed by the squeaking sounds and the motion of moonlit buttocks.

"The gun's going to go off in ten seconds. Something's gotta be done quick," Johnny Alatalo declared.

The fornicator neglected to lock his car, at least the passenger side door. Alatalo opened it with the authority of a cop nabbing some teenagers out having a few brews.

"Hey bud, you got a light for my cigarette?"

The guy bolted from his saddle as though he'd had his ass kicked out of it. "Let's go, Heikki, vee pedder get out uff here," the girl urged her partner in broken English. He needed no urging. He swiftly hauled up his trousers that had bagged loosely about his ankles, unlike his companion's taut, bungee-corded drawers.

We tried to get a better look at the fornicators in the full moonlight as they fumbled about in their haste to leave. From what we could tell they both appeared to be young adults. The girl made no attempt to pull up her bloomers as she'd covered her face with both hands. Despite her effort to conceal herself, a brief glimpse convinced Alatalo she was, of many, a Misery Bay cousin by the name of "Ihalempi." She did not have a husband. Ihalempi is a Finnish girl's name. Neither of us knew Heikki.

How the guy got his pants up to start the car and drive off in a jiffy left us bewildered with amazement. Alatalo's ten seconds had barely elapsed as Heikki and his companion scorched out of the lot, the tires spinning and spraying us with gritty sand.

"I might have staved off an unwanted pregnancy. Coitus interruptus," Alatalo said in his heavy Finnish brogue while I split my sides laughing. He'd noticed during their scramble to vamoose the parking lot the fellow had failed to put on a contraceptive.

"Shame on you, Ihalempi," he barked loudly as the car sped away.

All these reminiscences flashed through my mind, sparked by Palosaari's mention of Oscar Wirkkala the Finn.

What are you smiling about?" August asked.

"Nothing much, I'll tell you later at the cabin. What about Oscar Wirkkala?"

"Like I said, he's recognized as the pioneer of high lead logging in Washington. He invented the choker hook for cabling logs and secured a patent for a four-drum donkey engine. Where would we have been the last fifty years without the donkey dragging and lifting logs to the loading zone? He even had a factory in Indiana for manufacturing logging equipment. Wirkkala died recently, just several years ago in 1959. The man makes me proud to be a Finn.

Like most Americans of Finnish extraction, August Palosaari wasn't immune from his Finnishness. Besides the guy had real Sisu.

"I've got some good news," August told me during a coffee break.

"Elise and I are going to give it another try. This time I believe it's going to work out for good. There'll be no more benders being absent from my family. And our kids are happy, glad to see us getting together again. A lot of arrangements have to be made but that's the least of our problems as we've agreed to iron out matters, steady as you go."

They'd met on quite a few occasions, meeting at some halfway point between Weaverville and Pasadena where Elise resided with their two children. Palosaari still lacked transportation but that posed no problem as he had my car to use. He offered substantial money for wear and tear which I declined to accept. "Just keep the tank full and that'll be good enough," I told him over his protests.

A gorgeous woman, dark-haired and slender, Elise Palosaari's dark lustrous eyes sparkled with intelligence and humor. Favored with a flawless complexion and a generous mouth, a dimpled chin and a straight graceful nose perfected her beauty. I got to meet her when August invited me along on one of his trips. Now he invited me for another visit. It would not be an ordinary visit; this time I would be standing for him in a small chapel where the couple would renew their marriage vows. Once again they would become man and wife.

I could not help but feel a tinge of envy as I stood beside this handsome couple, their faces lit with a soft radiance. Grandpa and Grandma Maki looked the same way in their wedding picture, neither of them smiling, their faces composed and glowing serenely with happiness. Old Lady Mattila who eschewed inane smiles would stand for minutes admiring their picture. Their two children and a close friend of Elise were the sole attendees besides myself at the joyous nuptials. After the exchange of vows the entire assemblage including a young pastor who'd officiated the ceremony repaired to dine at a small Italian restaurant in the wine country.

I had difficulty believing August was the man I'd met in jail. Strapping and fit, this handsome man just above medium height looked years younger than the man in the slammer who'd asked me for the time. His rawboned face appeared leathery and wind-burnt from the many long hours of outdoor exposure; his once blond hair had darkened to shade of muddy brown with a hint of gray—not a gray associated with old age but a flinty gray identified with strength and vitality. Clear-eyed and confident he could have passed as a commander of a naval fleet out in tasteful civilian attire or the chief executive of a prosperous firm. No one could have guessed he once caroused as an inveterate drunkard and a jailbird.

August Jukka Palosaari had previously related to Elise Blanche Palosaari the circumstances surrounding our first meeting. "You've got to be an angel sent from heaven," she remarked not entirely facetiously.

"More likely a hobgoblin or some troll sent to instill some sense in him," I replied. "My angel got left behind," I added impulsively.

Elise noted a brief downturn in my mood from which I quickly recovered. She looked puzzled, and after a moment the expression in her lustrous eyes changed from a question mark to a look of tacit understanding. A woman's sixth sense perhaps. She did not press the matter.

"Have you made plans as to where you'll be living?" the young pastor asked the reunited pair. "I hope it'll be not too far from here. You'll not only be an asset to each other but also to our community. Your story, August, of how you've overcome your drinking problem and reclaimed your life and family is truly remarkable and one of inspiration. And I agree with Elise, Paul is an angel and not a hobgoblin."

The evening passed too quickly after a repast of delicious food served intimately in a private candle-lit room. We'd been invited to watch the chef prepare rollatini, the house specialty, through an open window to the galley. He amply spread ricotta cheese and spinach over a sheet of lightly textured pasta he then rolled up and baked like a pastry. A sauce of olive oil and clarified butter, subtly seasoned, perfected the dish. Caesar salads were hand-tossed at our table. This mouth-watering feast climaxed with tiramisu, the best I ever had.

I reluctantly refrained from sampling some of the finest Napa Valley wine as I eyed the glass of cabernet set before me. Temptation strong, the deep red wine glowed invitingly in the soft light of the room. I exchanged the wine for Perrier water.

I now fully understood August's fatalistic dejection after he'd lost his family and started to drink heavily. A beautiful wife and two intelligent and motivated children seemingly lost for good. Both children were not only intelligent but had plans for their futures. A thirteen-year-old daughter and an eleven-year-old boy, both interesting young people. Helen, their daughter, professed an interest in becoming a medical doctor and their son Carl planned on becoming an electrical engineer. A doctor and an engineer, most worthy professions.

"An angel did you say?" August commented. "I wouldn't go so far as to call him that. But providentially sent you might call it. And as for the jail, I now regard my old cell as a shrine, never again to be defiled by my presence."

"Can we talk," Brickhouse said to me. "We really need to talk. It's about you."

I'd been a member in good standing with Brickhouse Logging for nearly a year. I'd learned most aspects of ground operations and had acquired some experience operating the donkey. Bucking logs, choker setting the cables and occasionally driving the cat had almost become second nature to me. I'd always been a routine man, whether cutting pulpwood with Riisto Salmi, lowering and greasing breach blocks on the three-inch fifties in the navy or studying endless hours with my nose stuck in a book in college. Seldom bored, a routine life agreed well with me. Working the big conifers and some large cedar near Weaverville precluded boredom almost entirely. I scratched my head. "What would Brickhouse want to talk about?

Winter had begun to set in. Rain turned to snow. Worse yet, icy conditions curtailed logging operations—breaks in the weather could mean days of waiting before operations resumed. Unlike the Upper Peninsula winters seeing an average of four feet of snow on the ground, similar conditions in the steep terrain in Northern California meant costly work stoppages. Cutting and dragging logs on slippery twenty-degree slopes and on even much steeper ground posed too much danger. Wet slippery ground meant mudslides and avalanches. Full-scale winter logging in the Keweenaw is for the most part a flatland operation with some relatively minor sloped terrain, excluding of course, the Gratiot Cliffs and several other promontories. Snow, although deep during much of the winter, caused relatively minor impediment; melting didn't occur until spring. Our winters there were cold and dry. Many of the Keweenaw loggers preferred cutting in zero-degree weather with snow up to their butts rather than being attacked by swarms of deer fly on a humid summer day. Sweaty, running repellant applied to ward off the pests stung the eyes and fogged the vision, and many loggers regarded the sultry summer heat far worse than freezing one's butt in three feet of snow in the winter. Experienced pulp cutters had little problem with freezing temperatures; to keep warm one had to work steadily at a reasonable pace.

Out here in Weaverville we were spending more days off work in our cabins due to too much sloppy winter weather. Periodic cycles of freezing and thawing were bringing operations to a standstill. "Could this be the end of the line for me?" I wondered. "Am I going to be the first in line for a layoff?"

Gary Brickhouse like myself had also served in the "gator navy," as the amphibious fleet came to be widely known. He'd interrupted his logging career to enlist in the navy during WWII where he saw action at Tarawa and Peleliu on board a landing ship tank, commonly called an LST. He shared many of his experiences of his stint in the Far East, mostly on the good times he had there once the war ended. Like many surviving veterans of the war he said very little of the bloody encounters he witnessed in the Pacific. Thankfully I could relate only to the good times.

Married for twenty-years he and his wife were a childless couple. Broad of aspect, a solid man of medium height and high of forehead, his face congruently formed an almost perfect square. His reddish-brown hair, always tonsured in a crew cut, showed no sign of graying. He'd been talking of retirement for the past five years but always managed to put it off.

"You didn't go to college to get dumb," he told me after pulling me aside. "You didn't become an engineer to become a choker setter, although you're a damn good one. Palosaari could not have brought a better helper. You learn fast and should you decide to stick around I've no doubt you'll become an excellent topper, maybe as good as August himself, though he's the best I've ever seen.

"But I'm a lot older guy than you and you should be what you set out to be. So here's what: take some time to think matters over. My advice to you is to pursue your profession. If after mulling it over and you decide otherwise you'll always have a job here. I just hate to see true talent go to waste.

"And just one more thing, I'm going to invite Palosaari to join my outfit as a junior partner now that he's got his life straightened out and has got his great family to look after. I've been the sole proprietor of this logging operation ever since I bought out my brother's interest some years back. He wanted nothing to do with logging and couldn't find it in him to put in the hours after he saw what it took to run this operation. I'm starting to get old even though I still feel pretty good. So I might hang in for another five years or so despite the talk you may have heard of my retirement. I don't have any kids to inherit my business. My two nephews, my brother's kids, have both joined the beat or hippie generation or whatever you want to call it. "Free spirits," they call themselves, out smoking dope and composing mystic poetry. I can't make heads or tails of any of it. They both graduated from the university with good grades but so far they've yet to earn a dime between them. I wasted good money helping to put those kids through college. And gratitude? They think I'm just a dumb old fart raping the timber out to give everyone a screwing. But they're not above bumming a fifty or even a hundred from me when they're down on their luck. They're worse than my brother. Neither of them wants anything to do with logging so I've decided to count those moochers out. Yet I've set up undisclosed trust funds for these bums they can't touch until they're forty if they even make it that far. I just want to see the looks on their faces and hear their weasel words of appreciation for their mean old uncle when the time comes. The last time I saw the younger one he was standing on the corner smiling at the sky. Beatific—yeah, that's the word—smiling beatifically like some kind of a saint. I honked the horn and he didn't even notice me. So after some thorough head scratching August came up as the logical choice. I should have thought of him in the first place. It'll cost August some money if he wants to join me but I don't think the money will be a problem for him. He's a damn good man and I'm a reasonable man. Keep this quiet, at least for the time being."

"My lips are sealed on what you've just told me. I wish both of you the best if it comes to a partnership. I can't think of a more deserving man to assist in operating Brickhouse Logging than my friend August. Give me a week or two and I'll let you know my decision. It'll be a tough choice to make. You know, Mr. Brickhouse, I've always wanted to be a lumberjack."

CHAPTER 12

A Crossroad

I had plenty of time to mull over what Brickhouse told me. I had a lot to sort out. It would be tough to leave the woods doing the work I loved to do. I'd come to love lumberjacking as much as any other work I'd ever done. New friendships were a bonus I hadn't counted on when I arrived in Weaverville. The friendships I'd made were priceless; I'd never met men quite like George Carpenter and Abel Cooper. Carpenter and Cooper were the two cribbage players who shared a cabin with August and me. Both men were musicians who played together as a duo in their spare time away from the woods.

This evening George and Abel once again were occupied at the cribbage board. "Fifteen two, fifteen four, fifteen six and a pair is eight," Abel said as he tallied his score. August, who'd been busy with family matters, had retired for the evening.

I sat near the potbellied stove, basking in its warmth. Cold and nippy outdoors, the wind began to blow hard. The warm cozy cabin became a haven of relief from concerns of the outside world for the occupants inside. The warmth offsetting the frigid, blustering outside air engendered an ideal ambiance not only for sorting matters concerning a major career decision, but also for reminiscing on the camaraderie shared during many occasions with my lumberjack friends. These reminiscences for the present took precedence over my future concerns. How could I ever forget the great outings at the roadhouses and the wintry evenings spent in sheltered seclusion in our cabin? How could I ever forget the gig George and Abel put on at the Red Shingle?

I drew nearer the potbellied stove and reminisced long into the night.

"Dirty George has been inspired. Ladies and gentlemen, the Red Shingle is going to shake tonight. He's come up with a brand-new song and you're going to hear it very shortly. Let me first thank my good buddy Paulie Maki who's here with us tonight for providing the inspiration for this little ditty. Get off your duff, boy, and let these good people see who you are."

A hubbub of approving voices and some handclapping ensued as I arose and smiled at the crowd. "Thank you, thank you very much," I said in a muted Elvis Presley fashion after the "king" delivered a boffo performance before a wildly cheering throng of teenaged admirers.

"There's a good man, folks. One of the best young guys there is. Our song is called "Them Clammy Old Bloomers" and Little Ukiah and I are going to carry it away right now," Dirty George said when I sat down. "Let's hit it, Abel."

You with the bloomers, big baggy bloomers
you with the bloomers, clammy rank old bloomers
How do you do—boomp boomp—aha!
you had baggy bloomers on
I saw them—ha! ha! ha! Yes, I did,
La-la-la-la-la-la-la
Just me and you, la-la-la-la-la-la-la
you had them clammy bloomers on
Those nasty rank old clammy bloomers when you sat on my face
all my pals saw you do it, what a disgrace
Killed sixty million brain cells with that fat bum on my face
couldn't breathe, you ruined my looks, left a horrible taste
Now the gals won't kiss me, permanent bad breath
toothbrush, mouthwash don't cure it yet
Stinks to high heaven, lost my old gal Beth
just because, just because, ha! ha! ha!
wYou had them baggy clammy old bloomers on.

"What the hell, has that guy lost his mind?" a newcomer to the Red Shingle asked another newcomer companion.

"Let's stick around for a while, maybe we'll find out."

George Carpenter also known as "Dirty George" performed alongside his sidekick musician, Abel Cooper, or "Little Ukiah" as he came to be known in the roadhouses. Both men were decent vocalists and instrumentalists. During slow times in the timber the duo turned up at gigs on weekends anywhere along Route 299, sometimes pinch-hitting for other musicians who couldn't make it to perform. The Red Shingle Roadhouse, a favorite of Carpenter and Cooper, resided on Route 299 outside of Douglas City.

Abel fiddled while Dirty George played a guitar. They both vocalized. Them Clammy Old Bloomers evolved from my relating to Carpenter the numerous face sittings our Heights Bunch had to endure from Football and Rotten Mugga during our beleaguered childhood. Dirty George had a definite knack for improvisation. His melodies were comprised of snatches of tunes from various nondescript songs he'd strung together, and while performing, he transitioned from one theme to another as the wording and the rhythm demanded, a skill Dirty George acquired in his twenty years as a part-time musician. Arranging the music for Them Clammy Old Bloomers proved to be a demanding challenge for him, requiring all his talent for putting together the chords for this offbeat scatological ditty. His critics called these makeshift renditions idiotic, rubbish, and a lot worse. The newcomers were of this ilk. His fans called his improvisations vocalized jazz.

For standard fare George and Abel offered currently popular country and western songs along with occasional folk songs. Bluegrass and songs of depression day hardship were included in their repertoire. Gifted with a wide register, Dirty George could sing any piece whether in a lower key near the bottom of the register or in a higher key at the top of his range. But he always had one of his own ditties to sing, most of which he composed himself, and which often were of a scatological or bawdy nature. One of his favorites, a ditty he heard his father sing having origins in the Great Depression called "Can I Sleep with Your Wife Tonight Willie," drew considerable acclaim whenever he performed. George did not claim complete authorship to the song, sung to the tune of "Red River Valley", and where memory failed, he filled in with words of his own. To the merriment of the crowd he sang it as an encore to Them Clammy old Bloomers:

Can I sleep with your wife tonight Willie
it is cold sleepin' here on the ground
Just one night with your dear young wife, Willie
in that bed I'll be sleepin' safe and sound
I can hear the coyotes howlin' on the prairie
thin blanket don't keep this hobo warm

Imaginin' those lovin' arms around me
be keepin' me safe from all harm
Why are you frownin' old Willie
why do you turn your good friend down
Just remember the times we bummed the railroad
and that hoosegow in old Kearny town.

"Ladies and gentlemen, be sure to come back to the Red Shingle next Saturday night when that old skunk Dirty George and his good partner Little Ukiah will be entertaining you again. We'll spring a new song I've been working on lately."

"Can you at least give us the name of the song," someone called out.

"I Left My Gonads in San Francisco," he winked as he and Abel wrapped up their performance.

"That's more like it," the newcomer said to his companion.

Carpenter played a guitar in a small band during his college days. He'd earned a master's degree in English literature at a small school in Illinois, and bored after teaching for two years at a Midwest junior college, opted for the outdoor life. Working his way westward at odd jobs such as making hay for farmers in Nebraska and Wyoming he found his niche as a lumberjack in Northern California. A forty-year-old bachelor, he adapted well to the woods and settled well into a routine life. During off-hours his performances as an entertainer in the roadhouses drew substantial crowds and his reputation blossomed.

Abel Cooper, a native of Ukiah, had grown up in the woods where he spent his entire working career. He'd married young and raised a family of three children. Reliable a 'jack as they came, he claimed he'd missed but three days of work throughout his entire career and only when his children were born. Except for some minor bruises and scratches he'd not missed a day of work because of a major injury. He'd learned to play the violin at an early age.

Carpenter's physiognomy matched his bawdiness, which together fittingly validated the professional name he'd assumed. The man had a satyr's face: large leering eyes, a prominent hooked nose and a sloping bald forehead that arched and extended all the way back to his neck. Two wings of circus clown, bushy dark hair framed his shiny bald pate. A studiously groomed goatee and long high-mounted ears enhanced the image. Half clown and half satyr. Dirty George had no ass to speak of and his loose-flapping trousers failed to disguise his stilt-like legs. Except for broad shoulders atop a muscular but spare torso he might have been regarded as an undernourished tramp. His chest tapered like a "V" down to a narrow waste, and along with corded sinewy arms, gave an impression of a vibrant energy, which bespoke unmistakably of his rugged life as a lumberjack. And a good one too: Carpenter had been in the employ of various logging firms periodically for twenty years. His pile-driving meatless ass and skinny legs belied the man's prodigious vitality and his strength. His legs belonged on a long-distance runner.

Dubbed his professional name, "Little Ukiah", for being a respected lumberjack from the town of Ukiah together with his considerable musical talent, Abel Cooper, by way of contrast to his partner was a doleful-looking little man. Sad-eyed, weak-chinned, his sorrowful expression suggested he bore the weight of the world upon his shoulders. Cooper lived up to his name well. "Here comes Little Ukiah and his sidekick Dirty George," patrons would say as the pair entered a tavern to perform. Or sometimes the other way around.

As in the case of George Carpenter his appearance belied his strength. Although small of stature and in his early sixties the man could keep going tirelessly in the timber at a steady pace for the entire day. Called Little Ukiah in the roadhouses but affectionately known as "The Little Machine" by the 'jacks in our crew.

Both men kept August and me entertained during long evenings after a day in the timber when not at the cribbage board. This usually meant hillbilly music or some old-time hymns when they were not practicing their farces for the gigs. They saved their clowning theatrics for the road houses along Route 299.

My mind went back to one of the many evenings we'd spent in cozy isolation from the icy outdoors. "How about some picking and singing," I'd ventured during a stormy wintry evening.

Only the three of us were present, George, Abel and myself. August had left to take care of family business. Snow lay heavily on the ground curtailing logging operations and bringing traffic on Route 299 to a halt. The wind howled; the storm would last the entire night. Inside our cabin the stove kept us warm and relaxed. We'd kept the potbellied stove, casting a faint reddish glow, replenished with chunks of slow-burning hardwood. Earlier, we'd enjoyed a sumptuous roast chicken dinner Abel prepared with a savory oyster dressing. He'd picked up the oysters driving through Redding. They were not the big Pacific hawkers but the smaller, more delectable Chesapeake Bay variety. They were still fresh after being kept iced down for a couple of days. Abel, a devout Methodist, always asked the blessing before we ate.

After the dinner the three of us were in a laidback mood. Shut out from the world, well fed, we relaxed near the potbellied stove after we'd done the dishes and tidied the cabin.

"What about it, George, you in the mood for a few tunes?" Abel asked his partner.

"Might as well, Abel, not in the mood for cribbage tonight. Besides you fleeced me pretty good last night of all my dimes."

"What do you say we try the 'Wabash Cannonball?'"

Despite the fact the duo performed together for a long time these bosom companions always started off tentatively. They felt comfortable with familiar songs, emotively neutral, like the Wabash Cannonball. They seemed reluctant, almost embarrassed to play simple down-to-earth music, itching though they were to perform music from the heart. It took them at least a dozen songs before they got into the full swing of playing and singing without affectation or nuances. This evening it would be country and western songs. I joined them, singing along in a froggy voice, as they slowly evolved into the mood. In less than an hour both men warmed completely and their tentativeness vanished.

"Why don't you give me 'Wasted Love'?" I requested. "Wasted Love," in my opinion reigns as being the most plaintive and heart-rending hillbilly song ever recorded. A long-time favorite of mine, and also a favorite of George and Abel's, the version of Wasted Love we'd listened to had been recorded by Hank Snow.

They sang Wasted Love twice. George Carpenter and Abel Cooper waxed even greater the second time. Carpenter's satyr face softened, and from what one might assume, a practiced leering aspect of his visage vanished. Dirty George became St. George, rescuer of damsels and a slayer of dragons. His face radiant, Abel Cooper looked twenty years younger and saintly. From the way Brickhouse described his beatifically-smiling nephew Abel would have made the nephew look like a chump. George sang the melody in a mellifluous tenor while Abel provided harmony in a soft yet resonant pitch-perfect voice. No doubt they mooned over a lost love as I mooned over Abby while they sang and played, at least Dirty George. The violin sobbed; George came in with contrapuntal melody on his guitar during instrumental breaks from the lyrics. Totally rapt I sang along with them the best I could, groaning orgasmically at critical junctures in concert with the sobbing violin. I felt ten feet tall, exhilarated and important. "Women would swoon if they could see me now," I fancied without reservation.

Then I caught my reflection in the glass cabinet window of Carpenter's stereo. Moonstruck, my mouth had formed a mawkish crescent smile resembling a quarter moon. My slack features and my utterly stupid expression accentuated the natural homeliness of my round potato of a face. Embarrassed to reality I plummeted back to earth. I realized then I belonged in the same league as Simple Simon, the bumpkin importuning the pie peddler for his wares on his way to the fair. Swooning women indeed. They would have a good laugh instead.

Abel and George, finished playing cribbage, retired for the night. I turned down the lights and added a few more chunks of wood to the stove. It cast a pleasant soft glow in the dimly lit cabin. The wind blowing more tempestuously sent piercing blasts through the tall pines and about the eaves of the cabin. The windows shuddered and I inched closer to the reddish glow of the fire. Comfortable, content, my mind wandered some more as I basked in the warmth of the stove.

My mind drifted. "How's Abby doing?" I wondered. I still had no direct communication with her since I left Centennial heights for Newport Beach nearly three years ago. Except for an occasional letter from Hicks in which he let me know Abby still taught at Three Oaks, I'd heard nothing. Rita continued to postscript Hicks's missives and she always reminded me of her still unmarried status. Hicks and Rita were now the proud parents of nine children; it got to the point I couldn't even keep their names straight. Another set of twins joined the family. With each new birth I asked my mom to take care of the baby gift. "Just let me know what you got for the newborn so I'll know what to say if Rita brings it up."

I became nostalgic. My dear good mom. The pretty mustalainen-haired Elsa Koskinen who wrote the class song for the high school graduating seniors, her class of nineteen thirty-four. The one who stood by Oscar when out carousing in the bars with his carnival buddies. My mom Elsa, the one who fervently prayed for me when she and my dad got saved to lead a simple Christian life. Faithful and forgiving she'd attained the stature of a saint in my eyes.

As a teenager and an athletic young woman she could run faster than the girls and most of the boys and could climb trees like a bear cub. Elsa could skate like a dervish on blades: no fancy stuff like Roxanna Wagonhoffer nee Vella but with head-on speed, forward or backwards, and able to execute sharp turns in either direction. Most of the kids who only skated counterclockwise on the outdoor rinks only learned to execute a clockwise turn. My mom could do it both ways. And she learned to play hockey.

February 24, 1933. The Pine Street Lady Trojans on whose hockey team Elsa Koskinen played were vying to win the Kiesu Trophy. Their opponents were the Laurium Lady Bandits who'd won the trophy the previous winter having then defeated the Pewabic Indians. Neither team wore uniforms; clad in substantial winter garb in the near zero cold, one of the teams, in this case the Lady Trojans, wore broad white bands on each arm to differentiate the players. Except for the goalies very few of the women wore protective padding or gloves. Even the men played this way—at best some wore gloves and maybe shin pads or a cup during these sparse depression days. One played at his own risk; serious injuries, however, were rare.

Jan Beeha the longtime janitor at the Centennial School officiated the contest, played on the Trojan outdoor rink one short block from Pine Street. In this crucial game he overlooked minor infractions, only calling two penalties for tripping, one on each team. Knotted at zero-zero with only five minutes left in the game, tension mounted for both the players and the spectators. The Lady Trojans had peppered the Bandit Goalie, Bouncing Babe Barry, with thirty shots to no avail while the likewise formidable home team goalie turned away twenty-six Bandit shots. It appeared the contest would go to a sudden death overtime when suddenly a Lady Bandit broke loose with the puck. Only Fatso Lempea (there were a lot of Fatsos then) stood between her and the goalie. She moved in and at the last instant jolted the Lady Bandit with a heavy body check. Fatso then managed to shovel the loose puck ahead to Dashing Kallio who in turn sent a cross rink pass to Proceeding Koskinen, leaving her Bandit pursuers well out of reach near center ice. Waltzing in alone on Bouncing Babe Barry, Elsa beat her with a nifty shot that zipped between Bouncing Babe's pads as she sprawled to the ice to better defend her net down low.

One to nothing in favor of the Pine Street Lady Trojans. My

seventeen-year-old mom-to-be scored the one and only score of the game. Joy abounded in the Trojan camp. The victorious Lady Trojans took turns raising high the coveted Kiesu trophy. A welder at one of the car repair shops in town had a few years earlier burnished and gussied up a five-gallon milk container with tin angels and various hood ornaments from junk cars. This ornamented can became known as the Kiesu Trophy. One of the pictures taken of the victors remains in the Oscar and Elsa Maki household to this very day. Proceeding Koskinen is shown hoisted on the shoulders of two members of the men's Pine Street Trojans smiling happily with her dark mustalainen braids spilling out from her toboggan hat over the front of her parka. Also conspicuous are the wide ski pants she wore that flared from her maiden hips like a pair of Benito Mussolini riding britches.

Oscar and Elsa were married in the summer of nineteen thirty-four shortly after Elsa graduated from high school. My dad-to-be worked the night shift as a short order cook in a small restaurant in Chicago not far from the Loop. It would prove to be a brand-new experience for the twenty-three-year-old Oscar Maki, not only in the way of acquiring cooking skills but also in acquiring street smarts.

"Pull down your pants boy, I'm going to make you feel real good," the night cook told him after he'd been on the job for only a week. He had him cornered in the kitchen late on a slow night. For Oscar it could only mean one of two things to the cook: fellatio or sodomy.

"No thank you, I'm not interested. Besides I'll be getting married in a month. Let's forget you even brought this up."

"OK, boy, only kidding." Not once afterward did the night cook broach the topic or ever make mention of it.

Oscar Maki and Elsa Koskinen were married in the parsonage of the Moody Memorial Church in Chicago. Wee, cute little Paulie Maki entered the world the following summer, the "cutest baby in the whole world," at least according to his mom. And except for my maudlin reflection in Carpenter's stereo window I have no good reason to gainsay her claim.

I finally dozed off after the long hours spent before the potbellied stove.

I'd thought long and hard after Brickhouse gave me his advice. I couldn't afford to make another mistake and again let my family and my good friends down. More importantly I couldn't let myself down again.

There were too many questions on my mind. How do I explain to a prospective employer my abbreviated career at Alameda? "Oh, I just decided to quit after two years and do some lumberjacking. But here I am, fresh out the conifers ready to help you with your engineering problems." How could I tell them I got fired for being a drunk?

I needed help. After some brief thought I knew I had to talk with Rolfe. Who better than Rolfe? If anyone he would have suggestions as to how I could get back into the field. I had nothing to lose: I would surprise him with a visit—it would be best if I talked with him in person. I first called my good friend Wally Grimes to let him know I'd be in the area for about a week.

"Good." Wally replied, "And while you're here you've got a place to stay. Got an extra bedroom or the guest cottage outside. Take your pick, wherever you'll feel more comfortable."

"There's some business in Southern California I've got to take care of," I told Brickhouse. "I'll give you my decision when I get back."

With inclement winter freezing cycles causing sporadic logging operations I'd no difficulty getting his OK to be gone for a week.

"I'll let you know as soon as I get back," I reiterated.

"No problem, Maki, I just want you to do what's best for you."

"How about the guest cottage?" I asked Wally Grimes when I got to Inglewood. "Might work out better for the both of us since I'll be coming and going."

I gave Rolfe a call at Alameda the next day to his happy surprise. "Need some advice from you; I'm going back into engineering if anyone will hire me. But first how about my taking you and Muriel out to dinner?"

Later during the evening at the Ellefsons' I related my concerns to Rolfe of getting hired. My plight understandable, a lot of questions would be asked particularly if I were to remain in the Aerospace industry where my sparse two years of experience would be most applicable.

"I see what you mean but there are other avenues for you to explore. Right now the aerospace industry is still booming. Should help your cause a lot. Firms are hiring a lot of consulting engineers willing to work on a temporary basis. "Job shoppers" they're called. Most of them are guys preferring to move about rather than looking to become a direct employee with a company."

"Where do I fit in with just two years of experience? Even though I believe I learned a lot and buckled down hard on the job regardless of my absences."

"We've got job shoppers right now at Alameda helping to put the final changes on the Adventurer. Shipping containers, desiccants to prevent excessive humidity, drop testing, shock and vibration isolation during transportation, matters affecting the integrity of the final product. That's well in progress. By the way the Adventurer is set for a launch next fall when hopefully we'll send it into orbit. There's been a lot of slippage of schedule but that's not unusual for a project of this magnitude. Most of the guys we've got are long-time shoppers but there're a few with the same experience level as yours—fresh out of school—work as a direct employee for two or three years and then opt for temporary assignments. Mostly single guys by the way but there're some who travel with families. There may even be some longevity—some of the assignments can last for quite a while—we've got a guy that's been at Alameda for four years as an electrical engineer. You wouldn't know him, he works in another department. Job shopping may not be a bad way for you to get back into engineering. The money's not bad either."

"How do I get started at this?"

"Tell you what: I'll do some checking around the next couple days and get back to you. Give you a call at Wally's. Let's start with that."

"How's August Palosaari doing?" Wally asked after I'd brought him up to date on my logging experience in Weaverville.

I briefly mentioned his getting back with his wife without relating the problems which destroyed his marriage the first time.

"He's going to be a partner in Brickhouse Logging."

Mildly surprised, a question mark showed on his face when Brickhouse pulled him aside one early afternoon. "What could this be about," August wondered.

"I'd like to discuss an important matter with you. It might be better if we took a ride to town. There's an out-of-the-way restaurant where we can talk freely. Shouldn't be too busy now," Brickhouse replied to his puzzled companion. "I've got to keep him guessing," he thought mischievously.

"Why me?" August replied after Brickhouse stated his intent. "You've got guys with more seniority than me."

"More seniority perhaps but none with the all-around savvy and experience you have. As you know a lot of my guys are subcontractors and I don't think it would make any difference to them. They're happy enough with their piece work production."

"I can still see this as causing resentment amongst the old timers, guys who've been with you a lot longer than me."

"Don't think I haven't thought of that. I've already done some checking around and felt them out. Up front with them too, not that I had to discuss my business concerns with them at all. Almost to a man they've got nothing but high respect for you, August. Any man who can lick a drinking problem the way you did and works as hard as you do and gets his family back together is looked up to in their eyes. These 'jacks know what heavy boozing is all about. I listened to only a bit of grumbling when I told them I might be forming a partnership, bringing you into Brickhouse Logging as a junior partner."

"That's very generous of you, Gary, but right now Elise and I are just starting to get back on our feet financially. There's not much money."

"I've thought of that too and I may have solved the problem of any resentment anyone on my crew might have. It's quite simple for the permanent guys; I'm increasing their yearly bonuses. The bonus each man gets will correspond to his output in the timber. The price per stick each man gets will also go up, which should sweeten things for them. The piece work contractors will get a fair increase too. Look, August, Brickhouse Logging has been a flourishing enterprise for a long time and I trust it will continue to prosper in the future especially with your assistance."

"I don't mean to pry but how about your family? You must have family members to stand first in line."

"No family, no kids, bought my brother out years ago and his kids are not interested." Brickhouse repeated to August what he'd said to me about the nephews.

"Look August, I may be retiring in ten years or so. I want to keep Brickhouse Logging going and you're the best person I could think of to help me do it. You've still got at least twenty years of good legs under you."

Palosaari remained silent for a couple minutes. From his jail cell in Los Angeles County to the woods to getting his family back and now this: a junior partner in a prosperous logging firm—almost too good to be true.

"This is going to take some money and as I said right now I'm short. How's that going to work?"

"Like I said I've thought of this too. With my recommendation the people I do my banking with have agreed to arrange to a long-term loan at a reasonable rate of interest. I've told them it's a person I highly recommend and one I trust and will back up implicitly."

"So Palosaari is now a partner." Wally Grimes said.

"Yes, things moved fast once August accepted Brickhouse's offer. There are some logistics concerning his family but they're working out the details as we speak. For the time being his wife will continue her job as a receptionist at the company in Pasadena. I can't think of a more deserving man than Palosaari.

"By the way, Wally, did I tell you that Palosaari and I are third cousins," I added, mentioning Timo Hukkari's genealogical research of the Maki family tree.

"Let's hope some of that Sisu or whatever you call it rubs off on you," Wally Grimes laughed.

"I've got some information for you. Can you meet me this evening? Stop by for dinner," Rolfe called me. "We'll talk about it afterward."

"I'll be there. Thanks for the invitation."

"Phoenix Aeronautical Systems is hiring in St. Louis. They're having a difficult time of it staffing up for a Martian spacecraft project. That's right, a Martian project, they're in competition with two other firms to put a spacecraft on Mars. What it amounts to is both Phoenix and its competitors are looking to staff engineers. Aerospace engineers are in short supply with the industry booming across the board. Could be just the ticket for you. Your heat transfer experience on the Adventurer should be quite applicable to what they call 'the lander project'."

"What's involved? How do I go about making my presence known? And what's this stuff about a spacecraft on Mars?"

"Quite briefly it's a mechanized hardware that's called a "Lander."

It'll be deployed to collect soil samples and to do an in-depth study of the Martian atmosphere and its terrain. And to look for signs of life. As far as you're concerned you've got to put a resume together. I can help you with this, the sooner the better."

"If you don't mind Rolfe, let's start right now."

"I've got a lot of resumes in my file at work you can look over. Come to think of it I've got a couple here at home you can use as guidelines. That's where you start; I know a couple agencies here in the Los Angeles area that are submitting qualified people for the project. Your thermal analysis experience should be a good fit."

"How long should it be, and how much detail?"

"We don't want to overstate anything. Just highlight your strengths and educational background and you'll be in good shape. Don't exaggerate your experience like some amateurs do. Look at this one, this guy's resume is five pages long. You'd think he did everything under the sun. We brought him on board at Alameda and had to let him go after a month."

We got started right away. In a couple hours we'd come up with a respectable draft. Handwritten, short and concise, everything fit on less than two sheets of paper.

"Here's what, I'll first place a call to an agency I know best and we'll take it from there. Get your resume typed and the best thing to do is to take it to them in person. These people are only four miles from here. You'll get to meet the rep in person—helps a lot—a good representative can go to work for you right away. I'll arrange a meeting for you. One thing to remember—they'll be taking a cut of what they bill their client but these people aren't shysters. So you should come out OK once everything's settled. You'll be getting paid by the hour and the agency bills the client accordingly. And if you like I'll ask Muriel to type your resume. What do you say?"

"Thanks Rolfe, thanks for the help. Let's go for it."

Muriel typed the resume the very next day. Rolfe and I proofed it. There it read—**Paul Maki-Thermal Analyst**. Happily everything fit on one page. Clear and concise.

Opal Technical Services, a nationwide agency, had a branch office in Huntington Beach. Rolfe directed me to see a guy by the name of Bill Myers. A big guy, he looked more like an ex-pugilist than a professional type. About six-two and weighing in at two-ten, appearance-wise intimidating, his face bore some scars and his left ear looked like it had been half chewed off.

"Yeah, that's right, Maki," he said reading my mind after we'd been introduced. Did some boxing in my younger days. Still a young kid in my early twenties—nothing much professional in the ring, mind you—mostly barn fights. I was the champ for a while; the fights were all down and dirty. As you can see I got my left ear chewed off. Happened in a clinch. I managed to KO the guy but decided I had enough of this, and besides, I got cheated out of the purse too many times. I went to college like you, worked my way through and like you eventually got a degree in mechanical engineering. No spectacular grades but I made it. Care for a beer?"

"No thanks but I'll take some coffee if you've got some."

"Coming right up. Anyway a company back east in the Boston area hired me. They were doing a lot of defense work involving the design and manufacture of anti-tank and surface-to-air missiles. I did OK too, worked my ass off and got a couple raises. Then they started hiring temporary engineers and I left to become a road shopper myself for a couple years. Still single then and happy with the money coming in. It'll be the same for you if I get a fit for you in St. Louis. Later I got a promising opportunity to join Opal. I'm not a bad salesman as it turned out and right now I'm their top rep in Southern California."

"What do you think my chances are?" I'd apprised Myers of my working as a lumberjack for the past year.

"I think they're pretty good. Rolfe Ellefson has put in some good words for you. A couple of my guys are at Alameda now as we speak. Rolfe says you've got a strong work ethic and you catch on quick. What you've got to do is keep your nose clean. I'm aware of your circumstances at Alameda. All of them. And the fact you've still got a security clearance will help a lot although it may not be needed at Phoenix. We'll see. Also it might not be a bad idea to get some character references from people you've worked with on the logging crew."

"This sounds great but I'm kind of nervous. Two years of experience isn't a whole lot to brag about. What's the supervisor going to say when he sees me coming?"

"Look, you go in there and bust your balls. Pump some sunshine up his ass. Just hang tight for now. I'm quite sure I can find a position for you at Phoenix. If not we'll try somewhere else."

Two days later Wally took a message from Myers asking me to call him immediately.

"We scored, Maki. They'll be needing you in two weeks. Phoenix has some contractual issues to settle with NASA and then it's a definite go. So if you can hang tight until then you've got a job. I'll give you an exact starting date later."

"Let's meet at the Iron Horse in Orange. That's the fancy place on Harbor Boulevard. They serve some great open-face roast beef sandwiches. How about seven o'clock this evening?"

"That's sounds great Paul," Erma Jamison replied. "I'll be there at seven."

I still had a couple days of free time in Southern California now that I'd lined up the job in St. Louis. With plenty of spare time on my hands I gave Erma a call. She sounded great on the phone. Katie Wills and I had frequented the Iron Horse on a few occasions.

I ordered a beer for Erma and a customary seven-up for myself as we waited for our food. She looked younger than her forty years and even more attractive than she had when she floated off her bar stool when we'd met for the first time at the Salty Dog.

"I wanted to see you again as a sober man. I owe you and myself much after those many binges and the trouble I caused both of us. And as corny as this sounds I wanted you to see me as a man who believes he's got his life back on track. I hope this doesn't sound silly to you."

"Not at all, Paul, the feeling is mutual. I'm glad you called. I remember our last binge together all too well."

Erma received a promotion and presently directed a small group of technicians assembling circuit boards. Enrolled at a community college she'd undertaken study in basic math and fundamental electronics. "Passing everything and doing well. I'm getting straight A's; not too bad for a forty-year-old in a classroom with a bunch of kids."

Her daughter, also doing well, thrived in a sensible disciplined home environment during her stays with her focused mother. Erma had made an arrangement with her ex-husband to have her daughter live with her for two weeks each month during the school year. During the summer months her daughter enjoyed even longer stays.

"How about you, Erma, met anyone else yet?"

"Not really. I've done some occasional dating. Remember that supervisor who paid us a visit?" After we'd each missed a couple days of work?

"You mean the guy who barged in while we were listening to Roger Miller?"

"He's the one. He's a single guy who's asked me out a couple times. A straight arrow. He's still my supervisor. Not many sparks flying but he always treats me well. An old-fashioned type, he always opens doors for me and makes sure I'm safe in my apartment after a date. Who can tell? He even asked me what happened to you. I just told him I lost track and hadn't heard from you in quite a while. I didn't know you'd left the area to be a lumberjack."

"It's a good thing that guy's disappeared. He's sure a strange fellow," he said.

"I hope he's not the jealous sort, come snooping around the way he did."

"He's really not. He means well but he's of the junior chamber of commerce variety. Always out to do good. At least he saved my job and I'm grateful for that."

"It's getting late. I'd better be going. I've still got a lot of things to do here and when I get back to the logging camp before I leave for St. Louis."

"Let me get something off my chest if you can spare a couple hours. Why don't you come to my place where we can talk for a while? If we stay here much longer they'll be asking us to leave."

Her apartment, spic-and-span, stood in stark contrast with the mess we'd created the last time I'd been there. After checking on her sleeping daughter she put on some coffee. We made ourselves comfortable in her living room. Buffy lay curled up on my lap, purring contentedly.

"Paul, I've never told you this before, but I can say I loved you. Maybe I should have told you this a long time ago. I loved you sincerely and without regret. On more than one occasion you mentioned that our age difference made no difference and I'd come to believe it myself. Being ten years older than you began to seem as a trifle. We had a lot of good times together between the binges and I'll always treasure the memories. I remember the happy times we shared, sitting on the beach at night spotting the ships or simply going out for a dinner. You might have thought I was bored at times. Whiny, perhaps, when I had too much to drink but never bored. I can even smile whenever I think of the times we got drunk. We had a lot of fun even then despite our few squabbles. There's something to be said about letting the hair down every so often and letting others keep the store. How does it go? I'll spin while you toil.

"But I realized you had someone else in your life, someone very important to you. Call it a woman's intuition if you like but there's more to it than that."

"I don't quite follow you, Erma. Please tell me what it is."

"Paul, whether you realize it or not you talk a lot in your sleep and you speak clearly. Especially after you've been drinking. One night you kept going on for at least a half hour about someone named Abby. And you mentioned a loon's foot. At first I thought you were dreaming about some hunting partner of yours when you brought up the loon's foot. Shows you how much I know about hunting. Never much of an outdoors person I found out later a loon is not even a game bird. But when you started talking about still being in love, I realized Abby was a girl. It wasn't mushy stuff either, maybe someone you'd hurt and felt deeply about. I didn't bring it up at the time. I thought maybe I still had a chance for a permanent place in your life."

"You're right Erma, in practically everything you've said. There is an Abby. But I believe my relationship with her is over for good."

She looked at me long and earnestly.

"It's a long story. If you've got the time why don't I tell it to you. But first, how about some more coffee."

At three in the morning I finally left. Talk about revelations—first Erma and then August Palosaari in the jail cell who'd shared my voluble dreams.

"By the way Erma, Rolfe and Muriel Ellefson both give you their regards. They think you're a fine lady. And you certainly are."

"I'm no longer intimidated by them, especially Rolfe. Muriel and I get together for lunch every so often," she replied.

Matters progressed well. The future bright once more, I'd got a brand-new opportunity, a reprieve, a new lease in my career and once again I'd be an engineer. I loved being a lumberjack, but I'd be denying myself of an even more promising future if I didn't try to live up to my full potential—I'd spent years of my life in preparation to become an engineer. Even without the alcohol, I'd already done enough dodging and shirking responsibility to myself.

All my friends in California were doing well. Rolfe Ellefson had recently become a second level manager. Erma had turned her life around and received a promotion. Wally Grimes prospered in real estate and took full advantage of the real estate boom in Southern California of the '60s. August Palosaari's meteoric rise from a jail cell to becoming a partner in a prosperous logging company suggested a success story that would have made Horatio Alger proud. My friends from the Keweenaw were also experiencing success in their lives. Not going to be left behind I'd now be rejoining them in the ranks of success and achievement. I would take my rightful place at the table.

My business in Southern California finished, I spent my last evening at a quiet gathering at Wally and Karen Grimes' home along with Rolfe and Muriel Ellefson. In the morning I'd be leaving to wrap up my affairs in Weaverville.

The mood festive, light, well-wishes for my success abounded. Karen and Muriel kept everyone refreshed with coffee and pastries. Henry happily slurped a mug of hot chocolate topped with marshmallows. He'd just turned four years old and had grown shyer since the time he tried to untie my shoe laces. Tentative at first in accepting my presence, I presented him with a heavy-duty toy truck I'd bought for him. Time for fun and games, he made startup noises—*Br-r-r-nn, Br-r-r-nn, Br-r-r-nn, Br-r-r-nn*—before he shifted into high gear. For the Ellefsons and the Grimeses I bought each couple gift cards for dining at an elegant restaurant.

"Be pulling for you, old gunner's mate buddy," Wally Grimes said. "Be sure to stay in touch."

Rolfe clasped my hand firmly. "Just remember who you are and Who made you. We'll be keeping you in our prayers."

I noticed Karen and Muriel weeping silently after they both gave me big hugs. After many goodbyes and more hugs I retired to the guest cottage for the night. I left early the next morning before the Grimeses awakened.

I gave my decision to Brickhouse when I returned to Weaverville. Gary Brickhouse and August Palosaari had both sent letters of recommendation to Bill Myers.

"As I told you, Maki, you've always got a job with us if you ever change your mind," Brickhouse reminded me. Packed and ready to go I'd received a definite starting date from Bill Myers at Phoenix

Aeronautical Systems. "Before you leave we're giving you a send-off party at the Grizzly Den. The guys have chipped in so it should be quite a spread."

I still had a few days left before I left for St. Louis. Logging operations were at a standstill, the weather still too inclement to resume. Most of the 'jacks sat around reading or writing letters to loved ones. The party would be welcome break for all.

Practically everyone attended, the lumberjacks, Mother Hen Thelma Longfellow and her flock of chicks. The hangers-on were present in number. Word spread fast of Brickhouse's party.

Thelma Longfellow greeted me broadly, her smile easily as wide as the Quaker's on an oatmeal box. I took turns dancing with Thelma's chicks who wished me well. They were quite impressed when they found out the reason for my leaving; I'd previously asked the 'jacks to play down the fact of my education, and although brief, my engineering background. The food was served buffet style at the expense of Brickhouse and his lumberjacks. "Make sure everybody gets plenty to eat," Brickhouse told Thelma, "and I'll cover the bar tab for the girls. Might as well cover everyone else too."

Thelma's kitchen staff had prepared a large vat of venison booyah as the main course. Loaves of whole wheat, rye and sourdough bread lay spread in abundance. Appetizers included slices of peerless cured Pacific salmon, served lox style with rye crisp, onion slices and cream cheese. No shortage of anything existed except an absolute dearth of canned speeches. Spontaneity prevailed.

"You sure had me going with that root badger," I lied graciously when the one of the 'jacks resurrected the matter.

"Maybe Paul will invent a real one," Brickhouse said. "Save you guys a lot of scratched elbows and asses when you've got to dump in the woods. Make it easier to clear a spot first." He quoted Deuteronomy Ch.23, v. 13.

The time arrived for ribaldry. Dirty George and Little Ukiah kept us entertained doing a repeat of Them Clammy Old Bloomers to the delight of those who'd not heard it before, especially Thelma's chicks. As an encore, Dirty George sang Can I Sleep with Your Wife Tonight Willie.

"Hey George, give us the one about the gonads," I yelled.

"I Left My Gonads in San Francisco," was a song about a man who'd vamoosed from a termagant wife. She'd deprived him of intercourse for six years, and once escaped from her, he discovered he'd become impotent. A solo performance, Dirty George readily obliged a noisy crowd.

Romance transpired in the Grizzly Den.

After his bawdy rendition, George Carpenter joined Abel Cooper, myself and Bob Hazlitt, the young guy from Redding who'd taken my place as a gofer shortly after I started to work for Brickhouse. A clean-living hardworking fellow well-liked by the 'jacks, Hazlitt didn't smoke, drink or swear but he seemed to be very shy. A young woman not yet twenty years old, sat at a nearby table with one of Thelma's chicks who may have been an older sister. It became obvious to everyone the girl showed more than a passing interest in Hazlitt. She managed her best to feign indifference to Bob but her blushing face became a dead giveaway of her true feelings. At first her glances were surreptitious but she began to gaze at him more openly.

One could not tell whether the girl's infatuation affected Hazlitt unless one looked closely at him. Like the girl, he also pretended indifference. Perhaps he thought he had to be manly and tough. He managed stoical looks, sat stiffly erect attempting to appear handsome and dignified, and while ignoring everyone else tried hard to engage in serious conversation with George and Abel. But he lacked a natural presence that became quite noticeable to his friends. His voice took on a forced pitch. "One of these days I'm going to be a topper like August," he proclaimed loudly in a crackling voice. He grew fidgety and started to fall apart. Manly and tough? Definitely not Bob Hazlitt.

Dirty George came to his rescue. "Hey, Bob, cut out the crap," he whispered to him. "Just go over there and say a few words to her."

"I don't know what to say," Bob confessed.

"That shouldn't make any difference. I'll bet she'll be glad just to have you come over. Say anything at all."

That settled matters for Bob. He stood up and drew himself to full height standing erectly and stiff. He heaved a big exhalation and strode over to the table, where without ado he mumbled an introduction and plopped down beside the girl without asking if he could join her company.

"What's there to lose," he reasoned, "what happens, happens."

She did not at all appear to mind his lack of social grace. Rather she lit up with a warm glow. Still I began to doubt whether George had given Bob good advice.

At first he hemmed and hawed. Then in hoarse strained voice he began to relate to her a string of rambling long-drawn-out events in which he'd been personally involved. None made much sense. He mentioned a funeral at which he'd assisted as a pallbearer. "How does she manage to put up with this stuff?" I wondered.

The young lady listened patiently to Bob's boring stories and only when Hazlitt realized she showed true interest in him did his inhibitions vanish. Her friend tactfully left the couple to themselves and joined some other people. The enamored young couple began to make small talk and chat merrily over soda pop. Giddy with delight Bob and the young lady remained oblivious to everyone else in the Grizzly Den. The hours sped by.

"Bob, it's time to be getting back to the camp," Abel gently intruded.

Bob reluctantly departed but not before he invited her to a service at a small Methodist church in nearby Junction City where he sometimes pinch hits as a Sunday school teacher. She gladly accepted his invitation.

Affairs went well for Bob after that. I later heard from Abel Cooper the young couple had married and were prospering. They were the proud parents of a baby girl.

"I can never repay you for what you've done for me," August told me later.

"It works both ways, cousin. I wouldn't be here without your help."

"Cousin, we've got to stay in touch. For one thing we've got to make it to our family reunion in Finland. I'm looking ahead to it and I know Elise and the kids would want you to come along."

"I'll be looking ahead to the reunion too. Count me in."

My time in Weaverville had almost run out—I had one day left in camp before I left for St. Louis. The weather had cleared and the snow had melted. The two previous nights were crystal clear and cold. By morning a heavy layer of frost covered the ground. George, Abel and August returned to work. I had to be alone for a while. I'd already said my goodbyes. I needed time to reflect on where I'd been and where I'd be going. After the guys left for the timber I took a drive westward on Route 299 toward Helena intending to find a remote spot in the forest. Not much of a town remained since Helena's early days. The population had dwindled to almost nothing. Some of the original buildings, mostly of log construction and relics of better times, were still standing. Other than that a gas station, two taverns and a restaurant spread along the roadside were still in business.

I stopped at the restaurant for breakfast before proceeding further west. Three men sat at the counter discussing the weather over coffee. Except for a low hubbub of conversation the only other sound came from the monotonous ticking of an old-fashioned clock on the wall. The low drone of conversation, the ticking of the clock and the aroma of freshly-brewed coffee had a soothing effect.

Driving west for several miles I exited north from Route 299 onto a secondary road leading deep into the forest through rugged terrain. After snaking around tortuous curves and roller-coaster-riding steep grades and dips in the road I finally found what I sought—a large pristine stand of magnificent ponderosa pine. Insofar as I could tell no one vitiated the scene except myself. Some of the trees looked to be over two hundred feet tall.

The sun had risen and at midmorning the frosty ambiance bolstered relief to my entire being. Deep inhalations of crisp air purged lingering apprehensions of whether I'd made the right choice. The frost-covered needles on the tall trees formed a stark contrast with the reddish bark of the stately pines. Shafts of sunlight penetrated the canopy creating an ethereal world of magic and wonder. Being in a great cathedral could not have produced the sense of awe and peace I experienced there in the forest. I meditated in solitude, undisturbed. Would a wise old man, a benevolent wizard of the woods, appear to offer words of encouragement? Would he solemnly say to me "Go forth, my son, and prosper? I give you my blessing."

I reflected not so much on my future but what had happened during the past year. I'd made new friends, solid reliable friends in the firs of Northern California with men who not only knew how to work hard but who knew how to play hard. These guys knew hardship and what it took to overcome it, never asking for quarter from anyone. They'd give you the shirt off their back if they thought you needed it more than they did themselves. Men who knew how to have a good time without worrying whether anyone thought them crazy. Where had I ever met anyone before like George Carpenter and Abel Cooper? These lumberjacks knew how to laugh spontaneously and laugh heartily. I did not hear much laughter like this elsewhere, certainly not in college. Nothing mattered, after one had paid his dues in the conifers minds were clear of petty thoughts and worry. I would miss these woods: the sweat, the toil, the immense carefree satisfaction and the good-natured camaraderie always coming after a grueling day's work. Memories of toppers scaling two-hundred-foot-tall Douglas firs would linger long. The all-clear signal from the whistle punk to the donkey operator would resound in my dreams long after I'd left the timber.

Was I doing the right thing in leaving this behind? Hadn't I found my niche in life as a lumberjack? Hadn't I always wanted to be a lumberjack? Leaving the woods was the most difficult career decision I'd ever made. I would be leaving a world of genuine friendship, absent of fraud and deceit, where men of good will still lived and flourished. I'd come to a crossroad.

No wizard appeared before me and no words of encouragement were uttered. Instead, the splendiferous rimed conifers illuminated by shafts of sunlight stood mute, their silence tacit approval of the decision I'd made to leave. I would be leaving these stately giants for good hoping they'd be spared the axe and the saw. I left this magnificent stand when the frost began to melt.

I departed Weaverville late the same evening. I checked the weather reports and the highways were clear.

I drove off into the night.

CHAPTER 13

Tragedy

The Phoenix Aeronautical Systems facility impressed me as being every bit as imposing as the Alameda Aerospace complex. Of modern construction, the main engineering office stood three stories high, and designed to feature openness, large windows copiously admitted sunlight to numerous offices inside south-facing walls. The surrounding grounds were expansive and well landscaped. Two large auxiliary buildings sat to the rear of the main office. Lush flower beds interspersed along wide walkways could be seen on the well-manicured lawn. The prime attraction to visitors consisted of a series of four large ponds about fifty yards away from the front of the main edifice, each featuring a gushing fountain. Ducks, geese and several swans could be seen swimming placidly. One could have mistaken the complex for an upscale resort.

This time no amiable Herb Mickelssen greeted me at the entrance. But I suffered an interminable wait in the lobby just as I'd experienced at the Alameda processing center. Not alone, three other shoppers also scheduled to begin working bore the delay impatiently alongside. We drew curious looks from employees of Phoenix Aeronautical Systems as they passed us on their way to respective destinations. "Some more damn mercenaries," I heard one of them mutter, most likely regarding us as nothing but money-grubbers.

After conversing with the trio it transpired that I had the least experience in terms of engineering as well as being the youngest of our quartet. The eldest, Al Dusterhoff, claimed twelve years of experience as a road shopper. The two other men, Fred Mercer and Charlie Eubanks, were not far behind, boasting of eleven and eight years, respectively. Dusterhoff and Eubanks were stress analysts while Mercer, like myself, would be a thermal analyst on the *Ares Explorer* as the Martian project had been designated.

I grew apprehensive as time passed. "How am I going to fit into this picture," I worried, despite assurances from Rolfe and Bill Myers everything would be OK. "Here I am with my meager two years of experience against three old pros."

After enduring an hour and a half Monday morning wait our supervisors finally showed. Wendell Sauer supervised the heat transfer group while Don Rubik assumed responsibilities for managing a large group of stress analysts. Neither offered apologies for the delay other than to mention they'd been detained in a meeting.

Wendell Sauer led Mercer and me to a large bullpen area situated near the rear of the building, arrayed with row after row of closely spaced desks. There would be no private spacious cubicle this time. The heat transfer group occupied approximately half the space while the stress group occupied the remainder where Dusterhoff and Eubanks would be working under the supervision of Don Rubik. Both Sauer and Rubik were longtime employees at Phoenix and had private offices.

"Let's get started," Sauer addressed Mercer, handing him a thick packet outlining a task after directing us to our desks in the bullpen. Mercer had just sat down at his desk.

"Maki, I'd like to speak with you privately for a few minutes," he said after I had scarcely settled into my meager space. My luggage for the most part consisted of a few heat transfer textbooks and a slide rule. Mercer had a rudimentary calculator, a precursor of the powerful Hewlett Packard or Texas Instrument desk calculators yet to come. He'd already started on his assignment.

A large man of imposing presence, Sauer did not waste words.

"You may consider your stay with us as probationary," he said without preliminaries once we were seated in his office. "Your experience is the base minimum accepted by our staff at Phoenix, and although Opal has provided us with a good recommendation, it's up to you to prove your worth. That means productive accurate work done within a tight schedule. We allow a grace period of two months for engineers of your experience level after which time we'll know whether we want to keep you. Just do your best, perform to the best of your ability and you should come out alright. And just one more thing, Maki, I didn't have to tell you this but it's for your own benefit," he added bluntly.

"Now let's get started on a problem."

The *Ares Explorer*, an ambitious NASA project, consisted of two primary subsystems: an orbiter and a lander. Just as Rolfe told me

Phoenix Aeronautical System competed with two other firms to build the lander, designated as the *Ares Lander*, or for short, the "Lander." The Lander itself resembled a big bug that had pockets or compartments for containing various instrument packages. Three other firms vied for the "Orbiter" contract.

Sauer gave me a brief description of the Lander and the harsh environment to which the hardware would be exposed. He handed me a brochure illustrating the *Ares Explorer* in various stages of its mission from an artist's point of view: from its launch from earth aboard a high-thrust multi-stage launch vehicle, its trek through space until the Explorer is correctly positioned in Martian orbit whence Lander separation from the Orbiter occurs.

Sauer's brochure contained a wealth of fascinating technical detail. A heat shield, fabricated from a phenolic heat-resistant material, protects the Lander from aerodynamic heating during its descent to the surface. Although the Martian atmosphere is substantially less dense than the earth's, aerodynamic heating is still quite significant. "Slow" landing onto the Martian surface is then facilitated via a parachute and reverse thrusters. A light-weight crushable aluminum disk of a honeycomb design attached to the base of the Lander acts as an energy absorber and is designed to minimize "g" forces during impact, which could otherwise damage sensitive instruments and thereby render them inoperative.

An exotic telemetry system incorporated jointly into the Lander and the Orbiter transmits information obtained to a NASA receiving station. The power source for the Orbiter consisted of an array of two solar panels while the Lander relied upon two radioisotope thermoelectric generators for its power. A redundancy of vital components vastly improved odds for mission success.

"Look at those brochures a lot," Sauer advised. "I found illustrations more instructive than specifications when I started working. They helped me a lot. In other words, a picture is worth ten thousand words. Of course you'll be looking at the specs later which formally detail the mission objectives. They're quite voluminous."

"Now let's get down to business. I've got everything you'll need to begin on a heat transfer problem," he said, handing me a thick folder. "Let's take a look."

I'd be working on a control unit for the soil sampler. Numerous temperature sensitive components mounted on circuit boards had to be qualified for operation on the Martian surface, not only electronically, but also from a thermal standpoint. For optimum performance, temperatures of a miscellany of resistors, transistors, capacitors and semiconductor diodes could neither be too hot nor too cold. Part of my job involved the sizing of strip heaters in terms of wattage and their placement on the unit's heat sink. Temperatures could not become too cold during the Martian night.

Sauer provided a preliminary drawing, which showed the unit mounted to the chassis while pointing out regions on circuit boards where significant heating occurred. Power dissipations causing heating of components are of vital importance I'd quickly come to learn at Alameda. For instance, some of the current passing through a resistor is dissipated as heat. Means for cooling obviously had to be defined to ensure the resistor does not overheat. Sauer went on to identify copper laminates sandwiched in epoxy circuit boards configured to transfer heat as well as serve their primary electronic function. A duty cycle defined for both daytime and nighttime operation in the widely varying Martian environment indicated when the powered unit operated. Auxiliary hardware including insulation and louvers controlling radiation were nearly identical to those installed on the *Orbiting Celestial Adventurer*. Sauer supplied enough information to get me started entirely on my own.

The instruments and experimental packages on board the Lander had to operate reliably and survive in a harsh Martian environment, an environment seeing sand storms and temperatures falling to a minus two hundred and twenty degrees Fahrenheit at night during the winter. Maximum temperatures only reached seventy degrees during the Martian summer. "And this is where our staff enters the picture," Sauer said, "We've got to configure the hardware to meet exacting specifications. And keep in mind a tight weight budget has got to be met."

"Now remember, Maki, the *Ares Lander* is only in the proposal stage. Phoenix is in competition with two other firms and we expect to win the contract to build the Lander. Our proposal has got to be completed by the year's end when a winner will be announced. That's got to be Phoenix.

"Good luck, Maki." Wendell Sauer said as I left his office.

The two months passed. "We'll be keeping you, hopefully until the end of the year," Sauer told me early one morning. "You've passed your probation."

This coming from a man two years my senior in age at best. "Stern but fair," the staff members called Wendell Sauer. So I'd be working at Phoenix for a while longer. "You've passed your probation." I'd never heard talk like this when working in the tall conifers of Northern California nor had I ever before listened to similarly patronizing gab from teachers while attending Sunday school. "You've been a good little boy, Paulie." Hogwash. And I'd yet to pump any significant "sunshine" up Wendell Sauer's ass as Bill Myers had advised. In the timber we were free and independent. I felt like a school boy having been given a gold star for good deportment. Would I be given a certificate or even a placard for meritorious performance? This talk reminded me of my bible camp days when Rolfe and I had received stern admonitions to behave, but no words of praise, from Brother Rigo. "Now here I am a grunt sitting in a big bullpen with fifty other guys just as I'd imagined." Fred Mercer had put up with this for eleven years. Grunts carrying out work assignments handed out by our direct employee superiors. "I'm still a junior engineer," Fred Mercer remarked, and from time to time he signed off on short reports accordingly: "Fred Mercer, Jr. Engineer." Most of the time we wrote "memos" documenting the progress of our efforts. Still I was glad to be at Phoenix.

Despite my lowly status, the job progressed well and the money coming in added substantially to my savings. Happy to be learning a lot, and except for some archness shown toward the shoppers by a handful of the direct employees, I could not complain. A good reason existed for the archness—a small minority of the shoppers *were* mercenaries who brought nothing to the game—they were just in it for a fast buck. They did not last long.

"You're doing well enough, Maki. I won't be spoon-feeding you anymore," Wendell Sauer said to me during a noontime stroll. "From now on you'll be hunting down information you'll be needing by yourself."

Glad to hear that, I'd been on the job for nearly three months and until then I'd sat at my desk practically all the time, where I had little opportunity to meet other engineers to converse freely. Maybe get a cup of coffee. I'd almost come to be a drudge.

"I want you to talk to our lead designer," Sauer told me as we returned to the office. "That'll be the best way for you to start interfacing with everyone involved on the project. He knows more than anyone else here how to configure equipment in tight spaces. You'll be analyzing a power supply package. Dissipates a lot of heat. You'll be needing heat pipes. Go see what he's got laid out."

Heat pipes for me would be a brand-new ball game. I had a lot to learn: a heat pipe as its name suggests is a cylindrical member, and in short, a pipe closed off at both ends. This device is used in situations where the heat source associated with equipment, such as the power supply Sauer assigned me, is too large to handle by conventional means—in most instances, simple conduction of heat through metal or natural convection from a surface to air suffices for cooling of equipment without involving any sophisticated mechanisms.

The pipe interfaces with the heat source at one end, and at the other end, with a heat sink. Highly efficient as a heat transfer mechanism a working fluid inside the pipe extracts heat at its "hot" end. The heat causes the fluid to vaporize, which then migrates through the center of the pipe to the "cold" end where the vapor dispatches its heat to the base of a heat sink. A one-piece unit, the heat sink for this application is nothing more than an array of highly conductive fins formed by machining parallel grooves into an aluminum plate. The finned surfaces are treated to enhance radiation heat transfer, which is the primary medium for dumping the heat to space. Once the working gas is cooled it becomes liquefied and returns to the hot end of the pipe by way of capillary action through a fine-meshed wick, and the process is cyclically repeated. Convection from the finned surfaces also comes into play but it is kept in mind that convection is a relatively minor player in the game due to the more rarified Martian atmosphere. Altogether very neat.

Technical challenges would keep me very busy.

The lead designer worked in a cubicle on the far side of the bullpen from where I occupied a desk. I hadn't yet met the man, and except for Wendell Sauer, I had no need to interface with anyone else in the group. Determined to do my best I'd kept busy humped over my desk during my probationary period—if I left my work station it was mostly to get a cup of coffee. Now I stood looking at the designer's name plate posted on the outside of his cubicle. "George Haagejndas" it read. "How in the world is that name pronounced," I wondered. Sauer had ignored mentioning his last name, perhaps just to see how I would react to it. "His name is George," he'd only said. "You'll find him at the other end of the bullpen." Indeed, Sauer now stood a short distance away affecting nonchalance.

The occupant of the cubicle had to be reading my mind. He did not disappoint. "It's pronounced 'Hăg-***gayn'***-dăs'," a sonorous voice replied from within. I still hadn't seen the person. "The 'j' is a 'y'. The two connected 'a's' are pronounced as a single short 'a' and are thus cheated of customary emphasis," the voice continued. He'd obviously encountered confusion many times previously and most likely had some laughs at newcomers wrestling with the pronunciation.

"George Hăg-***gayn'***-dăs," he once more added emphatically. "Please come in."

Haagejndas's utter lack of impressiveness impressed me the most as the man rose to greet me. Before me stood a man of medium height standing erectly, almost at attention. A very portly man, an enormous gut starting at his pectorals sloped at a thirty-degree angle to his waist where it reversed direction and arched inward to form a big bag hanging well down below his waist. He wore voluminous pleated trousers held up by a broad stretch band in lieu of a belt. Serious of mien, his dumpy torso caused him to appear shorter than he was.

The man had no neck. Immediately atop his ample torso sat a large concrete block of a head, devoid of sharp corners and edges. Standing erectly he gave the impression of a private awaiting orders from his corporal. When he stood in profile one perceived a look of grim determination on his features. George Haagejndas projected a bible camp look, coming as though from a well-behaved child too eager to please his elders. His lips, pressed firmly together, indicated resolve. Not one hair on his large head could be seen out of place. Except for a thick clumpy thatch protruding modestly above a square forehead his sandy-colored hair parted neatly. The parting line ran distinctly down the left side of his block-like head. A deputy dog hat sometimes worn by law enforcement officers, chin strap and all, would have perfected his big-bellied persona.

George Haagejndas wore thick-framed horn-rimmed glasses with a double nose band, the lower band of which resided on a conspicuous hump of an otherwise inconspicuous nose, just below the bridge. He always looked the same, erect and stolid, as though anticipating a call to duty. "Here I am; I am ready. Send me forth," his "I am here to do good" expression seemed to say. As it turned out, he never failed to heed the summons.

"I'm George Haagejndas," he once again repeated as I entered his cubicle. "What can I do for you?"

"Paul Maki," I said, shaking his proffered hand. "I'll be doing a thermal analysis on hardware needing heat pipes for cooling. There are a lot of high-wattage components needing an efficient thermal conductance mechanism for cooling. Wendell Sauer tells me you're the man I should see to get started."

"You've come to the right place, Maki," he said, after which he produced a preliminary layout for a major power supply unit Sauer had assigned him. Significant heat dissipation during peak sunlight operation required highly conductive and efficient heat pipes as a means for cooling. "We don't have much space to work with but I think we can manage it." Haagejndas went over everything in detail and provided me with a copy of the layout for his proposed design and a catalog spelling out the performance ratings of a variety of heat pipes. "Let me know which one you'll need and I'll get right to work on completing the installation drawing," he added.

"Civic responsibility, Maki, that's where it's at," he declared after we'd thoroughly discussed technical details and sat down for a cup of coffee.

Haagejndas, a Korean War veteran, had enrolled in a three-year curriculum at a technical school prior to his enlistment where he'd studied mechanical drafting and design. He married shortly after his discharge and had since been employed by Phoenix, where by dint of dedicated hard work, he'd risen to become the lead designer in the drafting and design department.

When it came to civic responsibility Haagejndas sat before a full plate as a Boy Scout leader, a deacon of a Lutheran church and a trumpet player in a group of veterans, which assembled to march in Memorial and Veteran's Day parades each year. He gave freely of his time to benefits organized for helping orphaned children and the homeless. If someone needed assistance at a bake sale or helping at a food kitchen for the needy they could always count on George Haagejndas. Asked often, the man stood ready.

The job, though demanding, proceeded smoothly. I interfaced well with other cognizant personnel and got the information I needed efficiently. I worked independently at last, the way I liked it. Life good, I'd managed a three-month lease on an apartment in Hazelwood, a suburb north of St. Louis and an easy drive to work. Month-to-month rental payments would follow. I had nearly eight thousand dollars in the bank, a very tidy sum for me. Flush, and like a miser reveling in his hoard, I smugly watched my bank account swell. Being a man easily adaptable to a routine life, eat, sleep and work agreed well with but minor distraction. I maintained my physical fitness by working out at a neighborhood gym through a vigorous routine of weight lifting, swimming and punching a speed bag to keep conditioned already good reflexes. Outside of an occasional movie with my partner, Fred Mercer, I participated in little social activity.

George Haagejndas invited Mercer and me to his home for a dinner one Saturday evening. Haagejndas had a reputation for looking after the "strays" that happened to be working at Phoenix on a short-term basis. As single men, Mercer and I qualified as strays.

An amiable family of "marshmallows" greeted us. The Haagejndas family members were fair-skinned and plump, indeed resembling marshmallows. In addition to George Sr. the family consisted of Haagejndas' wife, Dolly, and their two children, George Jr. and Annie, the younger child. Broad smiles lit up their round faces as they invited us into their home.

George Haagejndas and his wife Dolly were natives of North Dakota. They boasted of growing up in Lawrence Welk's home town of Strasburg, an early settlement of German immigrants. "What kind of a name is 'Haagejndas'?" I asked George Sr. during a hearty roast beef dinner.

"It's a Dutch name. I'm half Dutch and half German and one hundred percent American," he proudly declared. "Dolly's parents are both of German extraction. Our parents are still living in Strasburg."

I should have recognized the name as being Dutch. The pronunciation threw me off.

A cheerful portly woman, Dolly Haagejndas like her husband wore thick framed glasses. Her features were not prominent and what one mostly saw when looking at her were her round glasses and a compressed smile, not too wide but very cheerful. Her small twinkling eyes peered merrily through the glasses. When she smiled she resembled a happy cookie.

"Mommy, Daddy, Lawrence Welk is on," Annie called from the living room.

We'd just finished huge slices of homemade lemon meringue pie after generous helpings of roast beef and mashed potatoes with gravy.

"Bobby and Cissy are going to dance for you," Lawrence Welk's accented voice resounded as Annie turned up the volume on the TV. "A one-an-a-two-an-a."

"What do you say, gang, let's go watch some champagne music," George Sr. declared. "If I might say so, Lawrence Welk's the greatest."

We repaired to a comfortable living room to catch the tail end of Bobby and Cissy frolicking about. Then came some tap dancing from Arthur Duncan followed by Myron Floren and his accordion. The entire cast beamed radiantly except for Buddy Merrill who peeked up shyly as he flawlessly played his guitar. Everybody enjoyed a good down-home evening of wholesome entertainment.

My opinion of Lawrence Welk changed for the better that evening. Practically everyone I knew including myself considered him as an entertainer just for old retiring men and women. My taste in music became more "wholesome" as a result. I unapologetically came to realize Lawrence Welk's plain down-to-earth music did not require a nuanced understanding of musical complexities.

"Daddy, let's do the *Parade Man*," George Jr. piped up when the Lawrence Welk show ended. A chubby little rascal, and like Alfred Maurice Huhta, George Haagejndas Jr. thrived as a clone of his father, a root that had germinated from the stump of George Sr.

"Not now, son. Mr. Mercer and Mr. Maki wouldn't be interested in seeing the *Parade Man*."

"Aw, c'mon, daddy, let's do the *Parade Man* now."

"Don't let us stand in the way. Why don't you go ahead and do it," Fred Mercer said, surmising the *Parade Man* to be a game just to amuse the children.

"OK, we'll do it," George Sr. said, "but we're going to do it properly. Come on son, let's clear a space." Moving some furniture aside they cleared a swath running between the living and the dining rooms. "We've got to have space to maneuver. Pardon us, gentlemen, while Junior and I make some final preparations. Please excuse us for a couple minutes," he added.

Father and son went upstairs to make their preparations. Wearing costumes, George Sr. appeared in an outfit consisting mainly of a bright blue jacket which fitted snugly about his expansive torso. Epaulets adorned the jacket; additionally, gold braids and two chains of brass beads crossed his chest. My interest now thoroughly piqued I looked ahead to the *Parade Man*, reminded of a line from "The Observation Post", a limerick composed by my favorite comic strip artist, Walt Kelly, the author of the renowned strip, *Pogo*:

"Their plum plumed tops
and buttons bold
And braid of burning brass ..."

A hat he wore in military parades and his shoes completed his regalia. The shoes were conspicuously curled up and pointed at the toes. Tufts could be seen at the toe tips. He found it unnecessary to change his baggy pleated trousers. George Jr., similarly attired, tapped his feet in readiness to proceed. We noticed George Sr. held a trumpet while Junior had a drum suspended at his waist.

"Are you ready son?" George Sr. asked, facing us from the far end of the dining room.

"**Boom-Boom-Boom-Boom, Toot-Toot-Toot-Toot**," the drum and the horn sounded as the pompous pair marched in step, slow of pace, toward where we sat near the back wall of the living room. Pausing before us, their instruments silenced and marking time by tapping his feet in a slow rhythmic cadence, George Sr. began to sing in a loud voice:

The band strikes a chord and George Haagejndas sings,
little Georgie sings a lovely little song
He sees the people here, he sees the people there,
George Haagejndas sings a lovely little song
He's a parade man all day long so you can hear him sing
you can hear the tuba and his trumpet too
With an oompah, oompah here, and a tooty-toot-toot-toot there
I'm little George Haagejndas, here's my horn

Haagejndas, supplying mostly his own words, borrowed the tune from a polka I'd heard a few years back, performed by an amateur band from Milwaukee. It didn't make any of the charts. I couldn't remember too much of the original but I distinctly heard them vocalize "With an oompah, oompah here." I also heard them sing something like "Here's Joe Banana with his horn." Close enough.

Doing a precision about face father and son proceeded to march back to the dining room. George Sr. seized up his trumpet with a flourish and started to blast shrill notes, swinging his instrument from side to side as he blew:

> ***Bah**, bah, bah bah bup-bup **Bah**, bah*
> *Bah bah bah bup-bup bah bah bah*
> ***Bah**, bah, bah bah bup-bup **Bah**, bah*
> *I'm little George Haagejndas, here's my horn, **bup-bup bah b-a-a-a-h***

Junior, trailing his father, kept accompaniment with his drum during the entire performance. The parade came to a stop after several more excursions and many more flourishes, blasts on the trumpet and a frenzied beating on the drum. Fred Mercer and I laughed without restraint along with Dolly and Annie for several minutes. We finally settled down when Dolly served hot chocolate topped with marshmallows.

"Daddy, can we do *The Bread is Good*?" Annie asked.

"Well, I don't know," her father demurred, although we sensed he itched to perform some more.

"Encore, Encore," Mercer and I demanded.

"Just a minute," he said, "I've got to make a quick change. It'll only take a minute."

He reappeared wearing the same outfit except he'd exchanged his military topper for a Kaiser Wilhelm hat topped with a spike.

"Annie, this time you've got to help me," he said.

"I'm ready daddy," she said, carrying a loaf of whole wheat bread on a tray from the kitchen.

Strictly a vocal rendition, Haagejndas had composed *The Bread is Good* in German. He only recited the first two lines in German as they would not be too difficult for his listeners to apprehend and the rest in English. The drum and the trumpet were put down and Junior retired to the sidelines.

This time Annie marched in front of her father, holding the tray before her as though she were about to serve a group of diners. Taking short steps both marched lifting their knees high in precise measure. Annie's short plump legs resembled two large inverted bowling pins, swiveled at the top and hinged in the middle, as she pumped high her knees. The bread did not slide on the tray. Haagejndas' modified pace caused his baggy trousers to flutter apologetically.

Halfway down the swath George Sr. began to recite *The Bread is Good* in a clear stentorian voice:

Der Deutsche sagt, "Das Brot ist gut, ist das Brot gut, das Brot ist gut"
Der Deutsche sagt, "Das Brot ist gut, ist das Brot sehr, sehr gut"
(The German says, "The bread is good, the bread is good, the bread is good,"
the German says, "The bread is good, the bread is very, very good")
I work to feed my family working hard the whole day long,
I eat to fill my belly and to make my muscles strong
First I work and then I eat and then I sing a song
first I work and then I play, then one cannot go wrong
Der Deutsche sagt, "Das Brot ist gut, ist das Brot gut, das Brot ist gut"
Der Deutsche sagt, "Das Brot ist gut, ist das Brot sehr, sehr gut"

"Das Brot ist gut!" Junior piped from the sidelines.

There were other verses as well extolling the virtues of those involved with the bread, from the farmer who planted the wheat, to the miller who ground the flour and finally to the housewife who baked the loaf with loving hands.

The swath Haagejndas and his son prepared afforded barely enough width to perform intricate maneuvers. A wide hallway between the adjacent rooms at the mid-length of the makeshift course did, however, provide some extra room. On one of their back and forth excursions, as the two-people parade approached the hallway, George Sr. barked a command:

"Double to the rear, on the right flank, Hut! On the right flank, Hut!"

One two three four. Executing this maneuver caused the marchers to reverse their initial heading. Father and daughter had shortened their steps even more, allowing them to execute the move in the limited space with military precision. They'd obviously rehearsed this routine many times.

At the finale of their performance George repeated the opening stanza. "**Das Brot ist gut**!" he bellowed, slapping his big belly repeatedly with both hands. His huge bag of corpulence shook like a vat of jello disturbed by a nine-on-the-Richter-scale earthquake.

Das Brot ist Gut highlighted the evening of warm hospitality and fun. Other than realizing our host performed as a competent mechanical designer dedicated to his work, and discovering him to be a loving husband and father, I'd thoroughly underestimated George Haagejndas. Much more accrued to this very funny, self-effacing man than being a Boy Scout leader or an assistant at the soup kitchen who went about doing good deeds such as inviting strays to dinner. As an entertainer George Haagejndas dwelt in the same league as Dirty George. Recollections of "Little George Haagejndas" tramping across the floor while blasting away on his trumpet or bellowing and singing would never fail to brighten my day.

Except for a week spent in the Keweenaw with friends and family the memorable evening of delightful companionship spent at the Haagejndas home would be the last I would enjoy in a long time.

"We're going to be very busy the next half of this year. If you're thinking of taking a break now's the time to do it," Wendell Sauer told me during a late-May noontime stroll.

I'd been at Phoenix nearly four months. The job proceeded well and I'd completed the analysis of the power supply unit Sauer had assigned, during which time I'd selected the hardware needed for cooling. The heat pipes selected were neither too large nor too small but sized large enough to handle a worst-case heating condition. With an ample margin of safety ensured, George Haagejndas ably configured the power supply unit to be installed within a limited space. Sauer, happy with results, made his suggestion to take a break before I got started on a new task. I took him up on it. I'd miss a week without pay but I could now afford it.

Three years. I hadn't been home in nearly three years since I left for Alameda Aerospace. Time had flown by and I'd nearly forgotten the Keweenaw and my friends still living there but now I'd make amends. I'd neglected my parents. Previously outings with my buddies took precedence while my mom and dad remained in the background. Basically stay-at-home types they were delighted to be my guests at a quaint restaurant located on the shore of Lake Superior in Copper Harbor. I timed our reservation to be present for the main attraction taking place. Though early in the tourist season each evening toward sundown a sightseeing boat laden with a goodly complement of vacationers returning to Copper Harbor from Isle Royale would announce its arrival in the small harbor with a blast from a loud horn, at which point the signal would be acknowledged by the ringing of a large bell outside the restaurant. The wait staff composed mostly of a bevy of attractive girls would step onto an outside deck and initiate a lively high-stepping dance to the delight of the inbound tourists and the diners. The horn would sound again in appreciation. Pulchritudinous cheesecake remained on full display as the girls kicked high their heels.

"You're looking great," my dad said during a delicious dinner of same-day-caught fresh Lake Superior Mackinaw trout. "I'm proud of you, Paul," my ex-hockey player mom added.

A Bavarian cream pastry topped with berries, a house specialty, followed the main course. We talked for a good two hours over coffee following the repast. Our conversation lightened.

I'd never been able to defeat my dad at arm wrestling despite many attempts to do so.

"Now that I've been to college, worked as a lumberjack and am becoming a full-fledged engineer what do you say we give it a try. With all this knowledge I've got and strength I've acquired in the big timber I think I can beat you now."

"You've got me a bit scared," my dad said. "I've never been to college. But if you like let's go outside to the picnic table under that pine tree and give it a go."

My dad could go either way—right arm or left—strength-wise they were equal. I put my faith in my stronger right arm—we went at it with our right arms. Our arms were deadlocked for at least two minutes in grim silence with neither arm budging. But I felt my strength ebbing. I managed a final desperate thrust, which to my disbelief, availed nothing. My dad's arm stood unmoved, and sustaining an unwavering force, he pushed my arm slowly down until it finally gave out. My knuckles banged hard against the heavy planked table. A man twenty-four years my senior ignominiously defeated me. Blood blisters began to appear on my knuckles.

"Maybe what you need is a couple more years of college," my dad quipped.

"Now you guys cut it out," my mom admonished.

I found it comforting to realize some things never changed. Matt Roces spun tall tales at Jacob Binoniemi's sauna. There he sat upright, trying to steam young buck newcomers off the top bench and dousing them with icy, cold water if he failed in attempt. "Gotta get rid of that city slicker scum." Old Jacob still transacted his business with the women on their side of the sauna, peering through the same open window through which he only had access. "Now don't you be looking at my tiddies." Alive and well, Niilo Kaipio still boasted of his status of being a "high 'lass Finn" to newcomers obliged to hear him out. His board sidewalk in Centennial Heights remained for long in the planning stage. Old Lady Mattila and my mom continued their weekly afternoon coffee clutches. Sometimes they invited Jacob Binoniemi and Niilo Kaipio to enliven the discussion. Mabel Lahti had not abandoned her Sgt. Benson army fatigues, now well faded. Her presence at the Saturday night beer bash in the old garage could always be counted on after the bars in town closed.

What had changed in Centennial Heights was the size of Hicks and Rita's family. Nine children with another on its way as evidenced by her distended belly, seven months gone. They had a large new house built on Third Street to accommodate the expanding family.

There were five boys and four girls. Two of the lads, one of them his eldest son, were exact replications of their father, and as Hicks himself put it, homely little runts but both smart as whips. "At least one thing they've got going for them is there are no fearsome tomboys in the neighborhood to sit on their faces," Hicks pointed out to me as he'd previously written.

"Fortunately the girls resemble their mother," he once again emphasized. I agreed, upon paying a visit.

He'd turned down an administrative position at Michigan Tech and instead opted to continue teaching. Additional time-consuming involvement in a bio-med research project having to do with strengthening body immune systems only served to strengthen a resolve to succeed in his career under demanding circumstances.

Missing were Abby and Aldo. Aldo presently found himself at one of his missionary outposts in Central America, visits to which he'd continued from his student days, while Abby kept occupied wrapping up another semester at Three Oaks College.

Hicks and I limited out on brookies on Hills Creek downstream from Jack Raudio's farm. Koljonen's pool always yielded some nice eight-inch brookies. My dad, Hicks and I had even better luck on the Montreal River, deep in the Keweenaw, where the brookies were larger, up to eleven inches or more. Early one evening my dad drove us to his favorite spot on some slow-moving water called the "sloughs." Muggy air and an overcast sky following a warm drizzling rain created ideal conditions for us. The stream ran a little bit high from the winter runoff of melted snow, and altogether, made a prime time for catching brookies.

"Bio-med research, what's that about?" Oscar Maki asked Hicks. The three of us were seated on a bank near a deep hole in the sloughs my dad referred to as "The Pohjola Hole" after his carnival buddy first showed him the spot. Pohjola and my dad were long-time fishing partners. We'd each nearly caught our limit of ten brookies and finding time to relax, we'd lit cigars and poured strong coffee from a large thermos.

"It basically involves organic chemistry dealing with life processes. It's a study of substances vital to life such as proteins, nucleic acids, lipids and enzymes at either a molecular or at a compound level. These are some of the matter we are attempting to isolate and trying to acquire an understanding of their behaviors from a viewpoint of a chemically pure state."

"How does this affect the body itself? Does this perhaps mean that a shortage or an excess in the body, say an enzyme, can influence one's health?" my dad asked.

A good question coming from a guy who hadn't been to college which made me proud of my dad.

"That's quite true, Mr. Maki. I may have mentioned to Paul earlier we've made some fairly good progress in the field but we've got a long way to go. Researchers in bio-med or bioorganic chemistry still have much to learn. You can almost say our research is still in its nascent stage. The apparatus we're using must mature to obtain more conclusive results, but as we speak, more sophisticated means of analysis and testing are becoming available. There's a lot of talk of advanced apparatus appearing in the field which involves phenomena such as magnetic nuclear resonance and chemical mass spectrometry. What this simply means is bioorganic chemistry ties in with physics. We've been able to attract grants, mostly from pharmaceutical firms, to keep things going. Our research can be very frustrating at times but even the smallest breakthrough makes it worthwhile."

"How about a cure for cancer?" my dad inquired.

"That's still a long way off. Right now we're striving to find a balance between the chemical processes in the body that can either beneficially influence or harm one's wellbeing. Our studies entail malignant cell growth, viruses and hormonal imbalances. Regarding viruses and hormonal imbalance I believe we've made substantial progress. To a large extent we've been able to show how chemical imbalances in the body can adversely affect health. There's a lot of new stuff coming out now which can be used to check the harmfully invasive impact of viruses. Cures are being discovered which can alleviate the distress of a common cold for instance. Ailments such as herpes simplex affecting a large portion of our population are being treated successfully with over-the-counter pharmaceutical products. These products were practically nonexistent ten years ago. But coping with growth of malignant cancer cells is the greatest challenge in our field of research. Insofar as cancer is concerned universities are coming at the problem from every angle. We've got a highly respected professor in the Chemistry Department, a Dr. Portugal, who's dedicated his life to finding a cure for cancer."

"You're doing a great job, Professor Huhta. Keep it up," my dad said appreciatively.

The days sped by idyllically. A gathering at Hicks and Rita's home included our parents and Armando and Celeste Vella. It would be my last night in town. Their children were bright, mischievous and well-behaved. Hicks had not misstated his eldest son's appearance: a duplicate of his father, feature-wise and in stature, Alfred Maurice Huhta followed in his father's footsteps, and now a senior in high school, had achieved academic excellence throughout.

I reflected on how this all began. If it hadn't been for the month spent picking strawberries at my Uncle George's farm where would we be now, especially Hicks and Rita? Cause and effect—it gave one pause to contemplate.

There were babies everywhere I looked—the kitchen, the dining room and the living room. They took turns sitting on my lap. This came to a stop after one of them, a chubby little rascal, fell asleep and dampened my trousers. I joined the kids in playing games, one of which required identification of creatures roaming the earth, both extinct and extant. Illustrated in a glossy book were dinosaurs of various sorts.

"Can you tell me what this one is?" Calvin, a bespectacled, owlish four-year-old chap asked me. He pointed at one while concealing its name.

I played dumb. "It's got to be a brontosaurus."

"That's a tyrannosaurus rex, silly," he corrected.

The evening passed by too swiftly. Before I left the Huhtas' with my parents, Rita drew me aside.

"Listen you round-headed Finlander, it's time I gave you some straight talk. There's only one person in Abby's life who's meant to be her partner and that person is you. You've now got your life straightened out and I suggest you'd better see her. And the sooner the better. Don't let her languish at Three Oaks."

I replied only to thank her for her concern and for a fine evening.

I sat alone on the rock battleship after the festivities ended and I'd seen my parents safely home. A clear night sky and a waxing moon provided decent visibility. Except for the dampened trousers the chilly night air did not bother me too much. Out of curiosity I checked the curved pipe on the amidships deck of the ship. Reaching under some empty cigarette packs, cigar wrappers and pop bottles I discovered the empty pint bottle I'd drained of whiskey before I got shooed off Old Lady Mattila's porch. "Yeah, I've got everything under control," I thought before returning the bottle to its hiding place.

I left Centennial Heights the next morning. Driving down US 41, Homer's Iliad I'd read as a preteen came to mind. Maybe what Rita told me about Abby caused this.

"An un-slain Hector still stands before the towering walls of Ilium. Am I that un-slain Hector?" I wondered. In my case no loving wife, an Andromache, sat at my side.

I chose an indirect route back to St. Louis, driving eastward toward Marquette.

I stopped at the Beef-A-Roo for a quick sandwich where I'd met Marie Loonsfoot after the hockey game along with my pals, Johnny Alatalo and Rick Smith. As I had an extra day to spare my plans were to take quick tour of Sault Ste. Marie, a historic town on the eastern end of Upper Peninsula I'd never visited. Everyone calls the town the "Soo." This would mean extra miles of driving but with a long weekend at my disposal I'd have plenty of time for the travel and to rest up before returning to work on Monday.

I remembered I still had Marie's phone number in my wallet. It would be as good a time as any to give her a call. Perhaps she might join me for a root beer. After all, our parting of ways at the rock boat in Centennial Heights when she surprised me with her impromptu visit transpired to be far from what she'd expected. She'd only hoped for a pleasant visit but only received a bitter disappointment. She'd left without a word. Maybe I'd manage to make amends.

With nothing to lose, I fished the phone number she'd given me from my wallet and crossed my fingers as I called from a pay phone outside the restaurant. Hopefully she'd be home. A male voice answered the ringing, "Brian Loonsfoot."

"May I please speak to Marie? This is Paul Maki, an old acquaintance of hers."

An eerie silence followed, portending gloom. Brian Loonsfoot cleared his throat. I thought I heard a muffled sob. I began to feel uncomfortable. Why had I bothered to call in the first place? I felt like an intruder. Brian Loonsfoot finally spoke.

"I'm Marie's father. Marie is dead."

Stunned, I could not find appropriate words. I finally mumbled, "I'm terribly sorry, Mr. Loonsfoot. I don't know what to say."

"Neither do I," he replied. "But Marie spoke well of you."

I did not probe him for details. Sorrowfully, I said I would remember her and her loved ones in my prayers.

"Marie was murdered," he added in a choking voice after a pause.

I fumbled for more words. Too shocked to weep, I briefly mentioned the fun times we had together at the Moose Lake Bible Camp and told him what a fine girl Marie was. I added that I'd been on the West Coast since I'd last seen her, and for the past three years, heard no mention from anyone about what had happened to her. If Brian Loonsfoot had any knowledge of the party at his lodge he did not mention it nor did I bring it up.

Another silence ensued. "Paul, you will be in our prayers as well," he said graciously after the pause. We said final goodbyes.

I aborted my plans of driving to the Soo. Overwhelmed with disbelief I had to find out what happened to Marie. I had plenty of time to do a search. I thought of the newspaper. Locating the Marquette newspaper office, I asked a clerk if I could see the archives. She led me to a large room containing many filing cabinets stashed with back issues. Some of the papers were rolled on spindles.

I soon discovered what I needed—Marie Loonsfoot was strangled to death by Luke Garber after being severely beaten.

A totally rotten apple, Garber had a criminal record of stalking women and on two occasions had beaten them severely but only suffered minor consequences for his actions. He'd married as a late teenager in Lower Michigan and divorced his wife after one year. He'd served time in prison for assaulting a girl, an acquaintance of his former wife, and granted parole for good behavior after spending just a year in prison, resumed his pattern of preying on women.

According to the newspaper account he turned abusive toward Marie following a brief acquaintance. She ended the relationship after which she'd been incessantly harassed and stalked by him. Convinced she had no other recourse she obtained a restraining order preventing him from seeing her again or contacting her in any way. Nonetheless Garber kept up his harassment. Like a hound relentlessly pursuing a rabbit, he kept track of her whereabouts day and night and harassed her with phone calls while either at home or at work. Complaints to law enforcement officials failed to bring her respite.

It got infinitely worse. One night in a drunken rage, Garber lurked in the darkness as she finished a late shift at the Ore Carrier's Restaurant. Except for a few wait staff members the poorly lit parking lot outside the restaurant had emptied. He'd concealed his own vehicle off on a dark side street. While Marie stood unlocking her car door in the darkness, he stealthily attacked her from behind and clamped her mouth shut to prevent her from screaming. He beat her unconscious and strangled her with his bare hands. Authorities apprehended him shortly afterward. A check of a later edition of the newspaper revealed that Garber received a sentence of life in prison.

The murder occurred two months after the party at the lodge in Humboldt when I'd already begun working at Alameda.

"Are you alright sir?" the clerk asked solicitously as I left the archives, ashen and trembling, fraught with sorrow and anger.

"Yes ma'am," I replied, "I'm OK. Just a little upset stomach."

Shaken to the core I headed south and drove nonstop to St. Louis. My mind in turmoil during the entire drive, I barely recognized the towns I'd passed. Focusing on driving did little to alleviate my growing distress. I only became more introspective and depressed.

Why hadn't I heard of this? I could only suppose no one else knew of my involvement with Marie other than Abby, Johnny Alatalo and Rick Smith so there would be no reason for anyone else to inform me of her death. News of her murder, while undoubtedly well publicized throughout the Upper Peninsula, may not have reached quite far enough to make headlines elsewhere. Abby had returned to Three Oaks College while both Alatalo and Smith accepted positions with East Coast firms almost immediately after graduation following our weekend party in Humboldt. Being away from the area absent of publicity had to make it almost impossible for them to hear of the murder. No one else I knew including Rita and Hicks had any awareness of my brief relationship with Marie.

A beautiful trusting young woman snatched from life because of the vile action of a wretch. Two short months. Would this senseless tragedy have happened had I not decided to join the party at the Loonsfoot lodge? Was I either directly or indirectly to blame for inflaming Garber's insane rage which led to his slaying of Marie? Would events have otherwise been different if I hadn't gone to Humboldt? Cause and effect. Except for the lunch stop at the Beef-A-Roo and my phone call I might have never known of her murder or at best would have learned of it at some indefinite time in the future. Would time have then expunged the guilt I now experienced? I could not help but hold myself being at least partly responsible for what happened to her. And I didn't even bother to give her a call before I left for California. These reflections would continue to haunt me.

I played devil's advocate for myself. What business did Marie have in inviting me to her party in the first place? Didn't she already know enough about this lout before the party? "She had to be totally naïve in inviting me along knowing Garber would be there," I thought, not in an entirely cynical frame of mind. Did she secretly hope for another Donald Boltz-type bible camp drubbing I'd receive at his hands? Who's the toughest of them all? She must have had some idea of his behavior, his character, and there could only be trouble, particularly with everyone busy getting drunk. Who knows? I wrestled with these demons long and hard but eventually dismissed any untoward thoughts of Marie.

Years later I found out from one of her friends who'd attended the party that Marie had known Garber for just a short while before the outing at the lodge. They'd met at the Ore Carrier's Restaurant. She filled in the gaps of what happened to Marie which the newspaper had not detailed in their account of the murder. Garber had moved from Lower Michigan to the Marquette region six months before he met Marie. Initially impressed with him, Garber had managed to keep his past hidden and he initially came across to her as being charming and mannerly, but soon afterward began to show some rough edges. She invited him to the party anyway as a friendly gesture not realizing then he could become jealous, possessive and abusive. After his boorish behavior at the lodge she told him she'd no desire to see him again. Only after the party did he begin to stalk and threaten her and that's when Marie had the restraining order placed against him.

Marie's friend also told me Luke Garber had vowed revenge against me for what'd happened at the lodge. He would be in prison for many years.

Brooding in my apartment after the long drive my guilt worsened. Hadn't I professed my love to Marie during our weekend of unbridled festivity at the lodge? Did I not accept her gift of love to me at the lodge without reservation? Despite being drunk for almost the entire weekend the sentiments I expressed to her did not seem hollow then.

Unpleasant memories came to mind. Alatalo, Smith and I bragged about our exploits all the way home from the party, and after the fiasco at the rock battleship I'd resigned from the scene like a defeated dog. Was I a coward? I'd accepted without protest Abby's pronouncement our engagement had ended, freeing me of further obligation to her. But how about Marie? She'd left before I'd had a chance to say a word. She had to be too hurt to stick around to talk to me, even to give me a piece of her mind. I'd made no effort to offer an explanation to her afterward. I owed her much more. I only had to make a call before I left for California and I failed to do this. Too late, too late, the door had closed.

A beautiful gracious woman, intense, free-spirited and trusting—gone forever. Because of one terribly bad relationship with a cowardly lout her she lost her life and her dreams were shattered forever.

There was nothing I could do. I did not make a phone call to Marie three years ago which might have altered her fate. She might be alive today. After Humboldt conversation between us ceased. Her smiling face would remain as a lasting remembrance when she appeared in Centennial Heights with my jacket. "You forgot something. You left this behind," were her final words to me. At the rock battleship while I sat with Abby, Marie exploded out of my life.

CHAPTER 14

Buck Rogers

"We'll be working seven days a week from now until the end of the year," Wendell Sauer announced to his group of thermal analysts early one Monday morning. This means ten hours a day Monday through Saturday and eight hours on Sundays. We've got a lot to do yet if we're to win the Ares contract. That includes everyone, the direct employees of Phoenix and temporary employees here on contract."

I'd been back on the job for three weeks since I left the Keweenaw. With work proceeding well and money rolling in, my bank account swelled due in large part to the fact a premium topped our wages, at least for the job shoppers, on our earnings for hours worked above forty hours during a week. We'd already been working a fifty-six-hour weekly shift, ten hours a day Monday through Friday and six hours on Saturday, which left little time for activities of my own choosing.

The hot sticky summer had arrived and the short weekends spent before we started on a seven-day work week provided opportunities for some sightseeing. Fred Mercer and I invited George Haagejndas and his family to an outing at the St. Louis Zoo after which we hosted them at a restaurant on the Mississippi River waterfront. On the following weekend we toured the Onondaga Cave State Park, resplendent with stalagmites and stalactites, particularly in the vast Cathedral Cave, and of course, Eero Saarinen's St. Louis Gateway Arch. Restraining an urge to boast I avoided mentioning its main architect was of Finnish extraction. Afterward little time existed for anything else but work.

I buried myself in my work. Try as I may, however, I could not get Marie's murder off my mind and neither could I expunge feelings of guilt of whether my actions led to her death. But the seven-day work week without doubt helped more than anything else to keep thoughts of her passing suppressed.

"You're doing a great job, Maki," Sauer told me a month after we'd been on the accelerated schedule. "We'll be starting some serious testing. I'm assigning you to assist in monitoring thermal testing. Once you've gained enough familiarity with our procedures you'll be helping me to write plans for the final tests."

Acquiring hands-on test experience supplementing the analyses I'd done would look good on my resume. Thermocouples and thermistors would be a brand-new experience. Efficiently locating these instruments to obtain the most data and the most typical temperature response always presented a challenge. A judicious placement of thermocouples on the hardware being tested required not too many thermocouples or too few—predictions made as a result of exhaustive heat transfer analyses provided guidelines for locating the instruments. Most of the analyses we performed were thermal transients, which involve time-varying temperature changes. Would a critical component overheat? How long would it take to heat cold hardware to reach a safe operating temperature?

Phoenix had a sound system in place whereby an operator monitoring the test gave a blow-by-blow account of what occurred during a thermal transient test. "We're approaching the yellow limit" or "we're only five degrees below the red limit." A temperature stabilized at or below the yellow limit indicated matters were thermally satisfactory and component temperature specifications were thus met. The red or upper limit could not be exceeded, and if it was, quite often required modifications to the hardware, which could result in costly delays. Improved cooling schemes or more heaters for cold conditions would then be implemented. For the most part, however, the design progressed on schedule. Schedule slippages were modest; any modification made conduced to optimize the design. Again, as at Alameda, test results corroborated our analytical models—a standard practice throughout industry—testing always superseded analysis. Yet the invaluable contribution of analysis to the design process cannot be overstated.

"Would you consider joining Phoenix as a direct employee?" Wendell Sauer asked me one day. "You have that option once mutual contractual obligations are met, which will be in another month. Think about it, Maki, you've got plenty of time to make a decision. We'd like to keep you on board here at Phoenix."

Sauer called me into his office to relate this after I'd been at Phoenix for nearly six months, the minimum time obligation required for my stay to remain with Opal. Phoenix then had the option of offering a contractual engineer a direct position. I could not have been more highly complimented for my efforts than having received Sauer's offer. I'd buckled down with little distraction and had formed no close associations with people I'd worked with except for Fred Mercer and George Haagejndas. I promised Sauer a decision after some time to think it over.

All the while I avoided patronizing the bars and missing work on account of getting drunk.

We'd visited many of the tourist attractions in St. Louis and its surrounding region. We'd yet to visit the Gaslight Square, an entertainment section developed in the mid-1950s featuring a variety of tourist attractions, which included cabarets, restaurants and antique shops. The overall décor and architecture quaintly reflected the riverboat era and streets were lit with gas lanterns. Some of the nightclubs attempted to capture a New Orleans-Bourbon Street ambiance. Ragtime, Dixieland and modern jazz performed by popular entertainers could be heard in the cabarets. Pleasure-seeking members of the younger generation, mainly young professionals, swarmed the numerous cabarets and taverns in Gaslight Square although a lot of older business types and hippies could also be seen there during its heyday.

"Come along, let's have a nice dinner and then we'll see what the district has to offer," Fred Mercer said. "I know drinking seven-up while having to endure a mob of topers isn't much fun but let's take a look anyway." Being a non-imbiber I had no previous inclination to visit the Gaslight Square despite its many attractions.

Mercer, one of the few single job shoppers in our group and a man in his mid-thirties, had never married nor had he ever aspired to take a spouse.

"I'm not interested in a long-term relationship. There's plenty of time for marriage," he said. "Anyway it wouldn't suit my lifestyle of being a road engineer with a lot of places to see and more adventure to come. How can I raise a family when I'm always on the move?"

After an excellent dinner at an expensive restaurant we stopped at one of the many flourishing cabarets in the Gaslight Square. We entered an establishment called "The Oliphant", advertised by a large horn affixed above a sign over the entrance. Walls inside the premises, along with another horn, featured weaponry from a medieval period: swords, lances, helmets and shields marked with large crosses.

"What a curious name for a place," I thought. "The Oliphant, what kind of a name is that?" I asked the manager. He informed me that an oliphant is a horn fashioned from an elephant's or an *oliphant's* tusk. Pure ivory. The ones above the entrance and on the wall were replicas fabricated from plastic.

"Maybe you've read *The Song of Roland*," he said. "That's the one where Roland blew into his oliphant during a battle. There's a synopsis of the Battle of Roncesvalles—take a look, right below the horn on that side wall."

I remembered I'd read an elementary version of the French epic as many other school children must have done from an Elson Reader. The synopsis revealed a description of how Roland defended the rear of Charlemagne's army returning to France from Spain after lengthy engagements against the Saracens or Moors. At the last moment during a fray in which the Saracens attacked his small group of defenders Roland took up his oliphant to alert Charlemagne and blew into the horn so hard it caused his temples to burst.

A timely blast on a third smaller horn roused The Oliphant's patrons to a greater camaraderie and more fun.

We were in for some entertainment.

The patrons, with a sole exception, were practically all neatly attired young professional types; in a few years they would be referred to as "yuppies." Very few wedding bands could be observed; most were single. Seated at a table near the center of a large floor space Mercer and I had an excellent view of the surroundings. A coterie of young men had arrived, among them a small, lean young man sporting a goatee. It did not take long for us to realize he was European, a young Frenchman to be exact as it transpired. Attempting to impress his buddies he went about accosting some of the young women present upon whom he exercised a vast bag of Gallic charm.

"Mademoiselle, you must come with me to my boudoir. You are a most beautiful woman. Zee big bad Frenchman wolf will make you very happy tonight. I will fulfill your many desires and you will not be disappointed."

The woman he addressed, a hefty tall young farm girl from Lincoln County, towered above him by at least five inches.

"How will a small man like you make me happy," she laughed, equal to the occasion.

"Ah, mademoiselle, I will eat zee pussy," he replied, totally unabashed. "Zen I will clasp you to my bosom and transport you to paradise. I have zee peerless penis."

The farm girl laughed some more. "A little pisswillie like you would have to put a board across my ass to keep from falling in."

Undeterred the Frenchman directed his attention to other girls with similar results. "You do not comprehend what you are missing," he finally said before settling at the bar with his chums.

His entertainment value held sway. The management did not ask the ribald Frenchman to leave. None of the patrons appeared to mind his indecorous advances toward the women.

At a nearby table were two young women somewhere in their mid-twenties, one of which appeared rather portly and plain looking but cheerful of demeanor. Shoulder-length brown hair parted down the middle adorned her attractive slender young companion. Both women were neatly dressed.

"How about some female companionship, Maki," Fred Mercer said. "I'll see if they'll join us for a drink."

"Go ahead. Good luck with them. A little conversation would be nice."

At least some conversation would be refreshing. We'd been working hard and long with little diversion outside of the sightseeing.

"Just one thing, Maki, if they join us, I'm setting my sights on the plain girl. You can have the good-looking one."

Mercer favored physically less attractive women, a well-known fact amongst job shoppers who knew him best. When asked why he related a story of advice he'd sought and had been given by an older man reputed to be a successful lady's man while out barhopping. Mercer had just got started as a contractual engineer in his mid-twenties. Up until then he hadn't had much luck in meeting girls and almost always got rebuffed by girls he considered pretty.

"You've got to try the 'GUE' policy," his mentor advised. "What you are is a nice hardworking young engineer but 'nice' won't get you far if you're just out for an evening of adventure."

"The GUE policy, what's that?"

"Go ugly early."

"Doesn't that backfire?" I asked Mercer after he'd explained his strategy to me. "If they found out what you're up to they'd slap your face or even worse."

"Look at me. I'm no prize either. I've got to take what I can get. What's even better is that a lot of these plain girls are intelligent and fun to be with. The GUE advice I got has worked well. The hell with the pretty ones. You can have them."

Fred Mercer's machinist father worked most of his life for one of the auto makers in Detroit, and determined to see his son received an education, worked hard to see that he got one. He sent his son to Michigan Tech in the early '50s maybe two years before I'd first enrolled as a freshman. Unbeknownst to me he graduated from Michigan Tech in mechanical engineering as an honor student having made the dean's list during his entire four years there as a student.

Not a prize, at least from a physical standpoint, short, stubby, bespectacled and bald by the time Fred reached twenty-five years, he easily could have marched in toot parades with the cadre of pimply-faced students pervading the Michigan Tech campus in the 1950s.

"Yeah, count me in as one of those guys wearing a beanie cap with a windmill mounted on top of it, one of those happy larks you told me about. I even smoked a pipe, an Oom Paul. In case you don't know, an Oom Paul has got a full-bent curved stem and a large bowl."

Mercer applied the advice his mentor had given him assiduously and it often brought results. Tonight at The Oliphant it would be no different.

At his invitation the girls joined us. Mercer ordered a round of drinks and a seven-up for me. In terms of "giving an earful of bull" to the young women neither Fred Mercer nor I could match the Frenchman. On the contrary Mercer presented a staid demeanor and appeared almost humble in his approach as he projected an air of genuineness toward them. I similarly dwelt, equally humble.

"So you're both engineers, how interesting," Adrian Parks, the plainer of the two, remarked after some rather awkward introductions. "Engineering certainly has got to be a worthy profession," her companion by the name of Juliette Campeau added.

I sat back and smiled politely after the introductions were made. Convinced our conversations would be brief, positive the women would leave as soon as they finished their drinks, I sat back and smiled some more. Everything seemed too perfunctory, too polite. From my previous experience more often than not "how interesting" nipped stimulating discourse in the bud. Conversation afterward deteriorated rapidly.

"What brings you to St. Louis?" I asked Juliette Campeau. I would be glad when what portended to be nothing more than a brief encounter ended. Nonetheless matters proceeded better than I'd expected. Juliette had more fuel in her tank than I'd assumed at first blush. And so did Adrian Parks. I'd underestimated them; I figured they were just a couple of nice young working girls out making the rounds for some relaxation and maybe have a few laughs after a busy day at the office. But they didn't seem to mind in the least the pedestrian conversation we had to offer. Perhaps they were tired of being hustled by roguish albeit amusing mashers like the Frenchman. Maybe they just wanted some small talk from what they perceived as a couple of harmless humble drudges.

"I'm from New Orleans," Juliette Campeau said. "I'm a travel agent for a company organizing sightseeing cruises on the Mississippi and in the Gulf of Mexico. Sometimes we venture into the Caribbean if we can attract enough moneyed clientele. Right now I'm stationed at a branch office here in St. Louis helping to arrange river cruises."

Mercer appeared to be making a good impression on Adrian Parks, a coworker of Juliette's, and a secretary at the travel agency. After the awkward introductions he came across to her as a courtly gentleman. He'd removed his glasses. Unaccustomed to having them off his eyes seemed to protrude and they looked wider, giving his face a naked appearance highlighting his baldness. Worse, he had almost no eyebrows to speak of, which coupled with his prominent convex baldness gave him a reptilian look. It made no difference to Adrian. She and Mercer were exchanging meaningful looks, gazing deeply into each other's eyes.

"You don't look like an engineer," Juliette Campeau said to me.

"What's an engineer supposed to look like?"

"Stolid, straight ahead, serious of mien and somewhat bookish. An engineer should look like he's always deep in thought over some weighty problem. You look more of an outdoors type. If you hadn't told me and if you don't mind my saying so I would have guessed you're a farmer."

I laughed at her openness. "That's not a bad guess and I accept it as a compliment. I've done some lumberjacking and who knows I might do some more." I related my experience in the woods in Upper Michigan and in the tall conifers of Northern California.

"So that's it. A lumberjack, at least close enough in pegging you as an outdoors type."

The evening turned out to be long and pleasant. Before Mercer and I left, Adrian and Juliette both gave us their phone numbers.

I called Juliette Campeau a week later. I arranged a date with her for the coming Saturday evening following another demanding ten-hour day. At least Sunday would only be an eight-hour shift. I'd made a dinner reservation at an upscale restaurant.

We hit it off well. She took no notice that I didn't order wine for myself during the meal or an after-dinner drink. I could not have asked for a better start. I'd been asked many times since my stint in a Los Angeles County jail why I didn't drink. Most of the time I simply said I wasn't in the mood for a drink, or I had pressing matters to attend. Since I didn't take wine Juliette abstained from having some herself.

Juliette had green eyes. Large wide green eyes that were rather closely set, which when narrowed and her curiosity aroused gave her a medieval appearance. Cast in this light she resembled a nosy witch bent on fathoming one's innermost secrets except she lacked a long, crooked nose and a hooked chin protruding above a grinning toothless maw. A beautiful girl, Juliette's features were refined, delicate, and her flawless fair complexion seemed almost translucent.

Curious of my background I related my Finnish ancestry, how both my maternal and paternal grandparents had emigrated from Finland to establish themselves in a small community in Upper Michigan. Her eyes narrowed as I told of the contrast between the teetotalers and the imbibers and how these two widely disparate factions functioned together.

"Basically we've got churches and bars, a lot of each in our small towns. While the church goers and the patrons of taverns are at great odds with each other concerning the use or abuse of alcohol they both share a common thread. All of them believe in hard work."

"Did she view me as one of the teetotalers?" I wondered. Probably not since I'd met her in a cabaret.

"My family ancestry from what is known traces back to Acadia. As you may know Acadia was an early French colonial settlement in The Maritimes off the east coast, mainly in what today is Nova Scotia."

Well versed in her heritage Juliette related the tumultuous conflicts between the French and the English culminating to a head during the French and Indian War.

"We were expelled from our homes in Nova Scotia at the start of the war. Not too long after the fall of Quebec many Acadians went to Louisiana to settle rather than remain and succumb to British rule."

"Was it any better for them in Louisiana? I thought Louisiana became a colony of Spain."

"You'll have to excuse a history lesson. As you undoubtedly know the French and Indian War brought about a great disaster for the French. Part of the redrawing of territorial lines following the War resulted in Louisiana becoming a Spanish colony. In the early 1760s as I recall. Insofar as my ancestors were concerned they made the better choice. Much better than living under the English whom they detested. So here we are today, still in Louisiana. We're often called Cajuns. I'm a Cajun."

Juliette invited me into her apartment, an invitation I respectfully declined when I drove her home. She'd made a good impression and I wanted to leave her with a good impression of me.

Fred Mercer had likewise begun to date Adrian Parks. I asked how things were going between them.

"Almost too good," he replied. "I've got to be careful now as I've got a lot more miles to travel and a lot more of the world to see. But if you've got to know Adrian's the finest young lady I've yet met."

We went out several times together as a foursome in the few hours Mercer and I had to spare after work when we attended a late evening movie or simply grabbed a bite to eat. Our social life had to fit in with our heavy work schedule. Although I hated the game we even went bowling once; I managed to bowl a personal high of one forty-six, which happened to be the lowest score of our foursome. Most of the time Juliette and I dated by ourselves.

Despite the long hours at Phoenix I managed to keep my schedules. But as for many involved on the *Ares Lander,* I'd begun to experience weariness and fatigue despite my best efforts to get some rest or opting for an occasional invigorating workout at the gym. And like everyone else, I grimly persisted.

You're tired, Paul. You seem to be awfully nervous and edgy too," Juliette told me after a Saturday night date. "I've never seen you like this before."

We'd been dating for over a month. Except for goodnight kisses we'd not become intimate. She'd leased an apartment in a high-rise building erected to attract young professionals near the downtown business district. After a dinner engagement we sat over coffee making small talk in the living room of her small but elegantly furnished apartment. She turned on her stereo and we sat back listening to a Mario Lanza album.

It wasn't just the exhaustive hours spent at Phoenix. The seven long-hour days a week of meeting the demands of a heavy work schedule were putting me on edge; the work alone I could handle as well as anyone else. Much more than meeting the demands of a heavy work schedule, I could not dismiss a growing emotional attachment to Juliette Campeau. Even though I'd known her for only a short while I'd let this beautiful intelligent young woman become increasingly more a part of my life. But despite my emergent attachment my feelings at the same time were conflicted. In evenings alone in my apartment I attempted to sort matters out.

A lot had happened in the past few years. Despite Rita's assurances to the contrary I'd destroyed a relationship with Abby set to become permanent. My affair with Erma Jamison I chalked up to a life experience and I had no regrets whatsoever it had happened—all the bad with the good—Erma proved to be a mature person and had set her course straight. We'd parted as friends. I had many happy memories of our involvement together and if I had to do it over I would not have changed a thing.

Three significant women in my life and now there would possibly be a fourth. The memory of the third woman, or should I more aptly say the second remained, I still could not reconcile with my actions. The fact I'd made no attempt to contact Marie Loonsfoot while I had the chance continued to haunt me. Had I missed an opportunity for a permanent relationship by not pursuing Marie? I compared her with Abby. Both were gracious beautiful women—one staid, most levelheaded and able to chart her course heading off harmful relationships before they ruined her life, and the other free-spirited, spontaneous and trusting—all too trusting, I reminded myself. I'd failed them both and try as I may I could not rid persistent feelings of guilt surrounding Marie's murder.

"I'm alright, Juliette. I've had a very busy time of it at work today and maybe I'm just not getting enough rest."

"Are you sure?" she asked, narrowing her green eyes. "If there's something bothering you, you can tell me. I'm your friend."

"Thanks, but I'm OK. Tomorrow I'll be as good as new."

Juliette went to her kitchen where she drew something out of a cupboard. When she returned she carried a bottle of brandy and two goblets. She splashed a generous portion, a good two ounces, into each glass.

"Here, why don't you try this. It'll help to settle you down."

I hadn't mentioned anything to Juliette of the self-imposed difficulties I'd incurred because of drinking and she'd perceived no reason to ask.

She set the goblets on coasters on the coffee table. Noticing my hesitancy to take one, perhaps assuming I might be a bit polite, she handed a goblet to me and took up the other for herself. I deeply inhaled the rich savory aroma of an expensive liquor wafting from the goblet. I'd never smelled anything so seductively fragrant.

"To our health," Juliette said, our goblets poised before us.

The brandy cast an inviting amber glow in the soft light Juliette had adjusted. What the hell. One little drink, I might as well go ahead and try it. Who knows? In my nervous and edgy state I had no doubt it would do some good.

No beverage I'd ever savored tasted as good as that goblet of premium brandy. The flavor exploded in my head as I tossed down the golden liquid in one go. The nectar of the gods could not have produced a more salubrious effect. I felt better immediately.

Let's have another," Juliette said as she generously refilled our glasses, this time close to the brim. We took our time with this one. It had been a long time since I felt as relaxed as I did then.

Juliette and I sat apart on a sofa. Mario Lanza had progressed well into the album, vocalizing soaring passages from the *Student Prince*. He nostalgically brought to life the romantic setting in Old Heidelberg in his clear, powerful tenor voice. I noticed her stereo was a KLH brand, designed by an engineer in Cambridge, Massachusetts, and at the time, regarded as one of the finest stereos available. The richly grained walnut cabinet evoked pleasant memories—my mom had an identical unit and for long Mario Lanza had become *her* favorite vocalist. She'd purchased every album recorded by him and would listen to him for hours while doing household chores. Pleased to discover Juliette Campeau enjoyed similar tastes would she at last be the one to have a permanent place in my life? *(I want a gal, just like the gal that married dear old dad...)*

She dimmed the light even further. Her large green eyes shone as lustrous emeralds in the soft glow as we gazed at each other. Her features were composed, radiant, her gaze not intense but rather that of a child viewing for the first time a fresh winter snowfall. Perhaps this was the first time we'd truly met.

"Come here," I said gently.

She did not hesitate. We embraced for a long while, our mouths deliciously, greedily coupled, our tongues probing, our bodies trembling. We slowly released our embrace as she rose to her feet. She took my hand and helped me to my feet. Still holding it she said nothing but guided me into her bedroom.

I awoke the next morning refreshed.

"The coffee is ready," Juliette said. "There's time for breakfast before you leave for work."

"I'll call you soon, dear," I said before leaving.

"Please do."

The six months had come and gone. Wendell Sauer approached me again.

"Well, Maki, have you made a decision whether you'd like to join Phoenix?"

"Yes, I have, and I thank you for considering me for a direct position. I'm honored that you would ask me to become a part of this company. But for the present time I'm going to continue working as a contractual engineer."

"Are you sure?"

"Phoenix Aeronautical Systems is a great place to work and I appreciate the leeway, the added responsibilities you've given me. I've tried to acquit the work assigned me to the best of my ability. Not only has the work been challenging and rewarding in what I've learned here but I've made some good friends. Aside from our professional relationship I consider you my friend. But frankly I've got a taste for contract engineering or job shopping as we like to call it. What I plan to do is see some more of the country and what else the aerospace and defense industry has to offer. I truly appreciate your offer."

I weighed at length what promised to be a flourishing romance with Juliette: should I risk a long-term relationship with her in view of what had happened with Abby and Marie? I spent long hours mulling things over. Why, I asked, should I even care what happened with them? They were gone. A very tough choice to make but ultimately I decided to play it safe and stay as a road engineer.

"Maki, let me know if you decide to change your mind. Phoenix plans to keep you here through Opal as long as there's a demand here for your services. Think it over some more."

I discovered Trixie's Lounge to be an ideal spot for quietude after a demanding ten-hour shift. A small retreat for an after-work crowd, located a half-mile north on Lindbergh Boulevard from where I lived in Hazelwood, I'd stopped at Trixie's a few times along with my buddy Fred Mercer and once when Adrian and Juliette were with us. The clientele included a bustling mixture of businessmen, young professionals and blue-collar workers. The dimly-lit piano bar provided a cozy quiet place for those seeking relaxation minus any loud conversation or grating music. Trixie's Lounge featured a pianist on weekends. Food offerings were tastefully simple. One could order a hamburger or an open-face steak sandwich, advertised as being the best short-order offerings in the St. Louis region. Now after a long day's work I began to stop in alone once or twice during the week. No longer seven-up, after the night I spent at Juliette's apartment I made it a quick shot of whiskey or two and then home.

Industry thrived in St. Louis, and staying open for long hours, Trixie's took full advantage of the activity. Trixie's Lounge opened early during the day to accommodate those getting off work from night shifts or anyone else moseying the bars to get a quick drink. One could always find a seat there. By ten in the evening the midweek crowd petered out but on weekends the lounge bustled until a 2:00 AM closing time.

Nobody called him "Mean Frank." No one in Trixie's Lounge called him that to his face; they addressed him merely as Frank. A very broad-shouldered guy in his mid-thirties just over six feet tall with arms long and muscular, sleek black hair combed straight back and possessed of steely blue eyes, Frank Ralls indeed impressed the crowd at Trixie's as a most imposing man. Bar patrons claimed Mean Frank could see right through a person. Mean Frank worked intermittently as a steel worker on high-rise construction projects, putting in long demanding shifts with crews erecting the skeleton framing of a building, followed by short periods of inactivity.

Habitués of Trixie's Lounge claimed Mean Frank had a history—a history of being a tough guy. Neither a troublemaker nor a bully Frank Ralls however became known as an enforcer. He'd come from a place in Pennsylvania called New Kensington, a locality not too far from Pittsburgh. Some claimed he once operated as a one-man mafia hired by small business owners to rectify wrongs caused by young punks vandalizing their operations. After positive identifications were made Frank would patiently seek out the culprits and would exact justice. This usually meant a stern lecture as a minimum with due recompense paid to the offended owner, and if not heeded, a broken arm or leg could be expected, at least according to Trixie's patrons. They claimed local law enforcement officials tacitly approved his actions.

Threats made on his life by young hoodlums did not materialize. Whether or not any arms or legs were broken citizens of New Kensington inspired by Frank's resolute actions formed neighborhood watch groups and saw to it no harm came to him. The problems the businessmen were experiencing eventually became sporadic at best. Once the vandalism stopped Frank left the area to work on construction projects in various cities. He'd been in St. Louis for two years.

I got to know Frank Ralls during my frequent stops at Trixie's Lounge. He proved to be just the opposite of a tough guy. Although physically intimidating he came across as being a modest congenial fellow, always gentlemanly and courteous.

"I'm doing the Lord's work now," he told me. "In my spare time between jobs I'm helping out at the downtown soup kitchen. There are a lot of down-and-outers needing a hand."

"By any chance do you know a guy by the name of George Haagejndas? I'm an engineer and I work with him at Phoenix. He's the lead designer on our project and is a damn good man. He told me he helps out once in a while at a soup kitchen. Maybe it's the same place."

"I sure do. I see George quite often and he helps there a lot. Keeps everyone entertained to boot."

"How about the *Parade Man* or *Das Brot ist Gut*?

"So you've seen him perform too. Every so often he brings his wife and his kids along to the kitchen. It's something watching George blasting away on his trumpet and his son beating on his drum in their costumes. And little Annie with her loaf of bread. He's also got another act you may not have seen. George is no slouch."

"Another one, how come I didn't get to see that?"

"This one requires extra people. It's about Lord Cornwallis surrendering his sword to George Washington at Yorktown. For this act he needs extra helpers and that's where some of the regulars dropping in for their soup come into play. Some of them play the role of Continentals and the better dressed ones act as British soldiers. A big guy with a long nose plays General Washington and George Haagejndas himself assumes the role of Lord Cornwallis. A fat General Cornwallis, can you imagine that? They really get into it. On one occasion he roped me into being a Continental with about six other guys."

"How do you suppose he comes up with all this funny stuff?"

"Good question. I've scratched my head about this. But with the surrender at Yorktown Haagejndas takes some poetic license. He's got Cornwallis himself surrendering the sword to Washington instead of their respective seconds-in-command who actually performed the ceremony. He says it makes for better entertainment with a humbled Cornwallis passing off the sword to a haughty Washington.

"Haagejndas brings along a cockaded hat for Washington to wear. And you ought to see him decked out as Cornwallis in a red coat and those baggy trousers. Little George, the British drummer boy, is beating away on his drum as surrendered English soldiers march between the files of Continentals. These "Englishmen" sure know how to play the role of pompous asses—these guys could do a lot better than the soup kitchen—maybe they should go professional. You ought to hear them sing "The World Turned Upside Down." Some pretty good voices in that motley group. The finale is the best of all after Lord Cornwallis brings his troops to a halt before Washington. The solemn expression on his face with his lips pressed together as he hands his sword over to General Washington is priceless. The whole routine is a riot and keeps spirits high."

We'd grown close. I began to date Juliette often. Time being of essence, we kept things simple. The Phoenix engineering staff saw no letup in the heavy work schedule so we had to economize our time together. After a quick shower and change of clothes it usually meant going out for a dinner at a good restaurant and then spending the rest of our evenings at Juliette's apartment just chitchatting or listening to an album on her stereo. Juliette's musical tastes were varied, consisting mostly of classical arrangements and some recordings of Gilbert and Sullivan works in addition to Mario Lanza.

I kept our supplies of brandy and other premium spirits replenished. And unlike my relationship with Erma Jamison we imbibed in moderation. Juliette limited herself to no more than three snifters of brandy, her favorite libation, or two stiff cocktails at the very most, and I did the same when together. Yet this didn't stop me from dropping in at Trixie's Lounge after a long day at Phoenix. Those two belts of whiskey were not enough, soon becoming three or four shots or even more at times. Still I believed I had everything under control. A half dozen belts would not hurt anything. I could handle that.

One Saturday evening after a dinner date both Juliette and I had a few too many. Our mood euphoric, relaxed, we were no longer strangers but lovers.

"What do you say to another," I said after we'd each had three goblets of brandy.

"That's a great idea, I'm all for it. We've both been working very hard and I think we ought to let our hair down a bit."

I filled our glasses from a fifth of her favorite brandy. A few more generous libations followed. It didn't not long before a mutually pleasant glow had become heady intoxication.

Juliette had never probed into my past love life or affairs. Now she'd become inquisitive.

"Paul, have you ever been in love, I mean seriously in love with anyone? You really don't have to tell me," she added noting a hesitation on my part.

"An engagement to a girl I've known practically all my life fell through. Just before I started a career as an engineer in Southern California. It just didn't work out for us. For one thing I didn't have any money. Plain broke," I replied, dissembling.

As Katie Wills had done she did not press me for details.

"How about you? With so much going for you, brains and beauty, there had to be men in your life."

"Thank you for the brains and the beauty. There have been some men but nothing too serious. I met a few dandy types but our relationships did not last long. I've learned to be careful. I fell for a passenger on one of our few cruises into the Caribbean, an older guy in his mid-thirties who promised me his love. Only twenty-one at the time, young and dumb you might say. Turned out he was already married.

"Also my career requires relocating, sometimes often, just as your profession may require. By the way, have you thought of settling into a permanent position with some company, maybe Phoenix? If you want my opinion, I'd consider that if I were you. And to tell you the truth there's been no one I've met quite like you."

"Juliette, you've come to mean a lot to me. We've come a long way even though we've only known each other for a short time. Let's see what happens. I'm hoping for the best."

I hadn't told Juliette how I'd turned down Wendell Sauer's invitation to accept a direct position at Phoenix although I'd recently begun to reconsider the offer. What happened between Julie and me had happened too quickly in the few short months I'd come to know her and I related this to her more than once. Marie's brutal death still very much affected me and try as I may I could not forget Abby. The three years since our broken engagement did not seem very long. How could I then do justice to Juliette carrying all this baggage? She deserved the best without complication. Or maybe by constantly dwelling on this I might be just plain foolish; perhaps I'd allowed guilt and a false sense of chivalry stand in my way. Still I needed more time.

After several more brandies we went to bed. No lovemaking followed. I fell asleep immediately. I had a fitful, tortured night, lots of crazy dreams. We awoke the next morning going on ten o'clock both of us groggy from severe hangovers. Late for work, this happened to be the very first time I missed work since I'd been at Phoenix or had not reported in on time. "Oh well, I'll get cleaned up and go in early in the afternoon and stay late."

Juliette did not look well as she prepared some coffee. Face ashen after a bout with nausea she complained of a throbbing headache. Faring not much better I woke up with sick guts, a splitting headache, frayed nerves and a hangover as bad as I'd experienced when getting thoroughly soused the very first time.

Juliette for the most part remained silent as we sat down for coffee. She did not serve breakfast as she always had previously. Although I found her silence a bit disturbing I attributed it to her headache and did not press her for conversation.

I managed to make it to work by noontime having phoned I'd be in late. With nothing said of my late arrival I stayed on a couple extra hours after everyone else left, which Wendell Sauer OK'd. Back on schedule on Monday morning, the job resumed well.

That afternoon somewhat surprised to hear from her so early in the week I got a call from Juliette. She'd never before called me while at work.

"Paul, can you see me? We need to talk, the sooner the better."

"How about tomorrow evening. I've got some catching up at work to do this evening. This sounds important; I can be at your place right after work tomorrow, say about seven."

"That'll be fine, Paul. I'll expect you then," she said. No further conversation followed.

"What could this possibly be about?" I wondered. Juliette sounded quite serious. "Has something happened at her sightseeing agency? Has she changed her mind about our relationship?" These and other questions crossed my mind. I assumed whatever she had on her mind could not be too serious. I put the matter to rest.

An apprehensive Juliette Campeau greeted me when I arrived at her apartment the following evening. Yet she looked great, having fully recovered from her hangover, but by no means did she appear to be the delightful woman I'd come to anticipate whenever I arrived for a date. Absent of her childlike absorbing look of wonder, she rather impressed as being neither unfriendly nor cold but somewhat distant. She got straight to the business on her mind.

"Who is Marie Loonsfoot?" she asked after we'd made ourselves comfortable on her sofa. No soothing background music contributed to ease our minds this evening; only the monotonous ticking of a clock could be heard. "And something about a murder. I couldn't make out all the names but you mentioned someone called Garber. At first I thought you were just having a bad dream caused by the brandies but everything sounded so real. After being passed out for a couple hours I couldn't sleep much and tossed and turned for much of the night, sick to my stomach. You talk very clearly in your sleep. I thought maybe you could clear the air on this. If only a bad dream then so be it. But after you kept talking in your sleep I thought it had to be a lot more than just a bad dream. This business about a murder has really got me disturbed."

"Juliette, you're right to bring this up. I haven't told you everything

I should have told you before. I haven't been fair to you. There's a lot more to what I've told you than a messed-up engagement."

Her eyes did not narrow this time. Nor did she gaze at me in her wonderful way with her large emerald eyes, a gaze I'd come to anticipate. Looking at nothing in particular, she appeared downcast. She did not speak.

"More than a bad dream, a real murder. Marie Loonsfoot was murdered."

I went on to explain my involvement with Marie going back to the Moose Lake Bible Camp as children to the drunken party at her father's lodge in Humboldt. Bringing Abby into the picture, I sorted through the multiple complications which had occurred in my life—my engagement to Abby—my brief but torrid affair with Marie during the fateful weekend at the lodge to her appearance at the rock battleship in Centennial Heights where Abby and I sat discussing our future and how our engagement came to be broken. I omitted nothing, from the unpleasantness with Luke Garber at the lodge, to her murder shortly thereafter at his hands and how I'd only come to discover the facts surrounding her death only after three years had elapsed.

"I learned of her murder from her father through a chance phone call I made only a few short months before I met you at The Oliphant. If it hadn't been for that call I'd still be oblivious of what happened to her. But now it seems her murder happened just yesterday."

I related my guilt for not having called Marie after she departed for Marquette from the battleship.

"One phone call might have made all the difference in the world. I lacked the presence of mind to do one simple thing. She had to die believing herself a complete nothing concerning our brief relationship."

What more could I tell her? Here I sat making a confession just as the time I vented to Abby on the sand bank at Grand Marais. I really didn't have to, but I got on to the drinking anyway—maybe this Pandora's box I should have kept and should always keep closed. I told her about flunking out of school the first time I attended Tech and how I got fired from Alameda.

"So there you have it, Juliette. Drinking—a lot of drinking—I allowed it to play a big part in messing up my life. No one to blame but me," I added lamely.

"Paul, I'm terribly sorry…if I had known …" she started to say.

"There's no need to apologize, there's no way you could have known this. I could have told you about the problems I've had with drinking long before. And I could have turned that brandy down."

A long silence ensued. Juliette did not speak and I had nothing more to add; I'd held nothing back. Here I sat with a woman with whom I'd become strongly attracted. She'd listened compassionately as I related the circumstances of Marie's death and how I'd lost Abby. Juliette looked withdrawn and appeared frail, small and numbed with defeat. She did not look at me. I could think of nothing to say; not even a single word of comfort came to mind. Because I could not find any. We'd again become strangers. Matters had become surreal. "What am I doing here?" I thought. A lesser woman might have asked me to leave. The ticking of the clock muted further discussion.

She regained her composure and broke the silence. "Paul, I need some time to think things over. I appreciate very much all you've told me," she said as I left.

We did not kiss goodnight.

Juliette phoned me a week later. I'd not attempted to call her in the meantime.

"Paul, we've got to talk some more. Can we meet this evening at my apartment?"

"I'll be there right after work," I replied with a sense of foreboding.

Having settled on her sofa after I arrived Juliette did not waste words.

"Paul, first let me apologize for offering you that drink. What I did, I did out of ignorance."

"What's done is done. Like I told you last week I could have turned it down. You're not to blame for anything."

"To me I'm still an accessory to what happened. But there are other things I've got to tell you. I've done a lot of sorting out matters this past week. Please forgive me if I'm a bit awkward."

"Juliette, there's no need to be uncomfortable; I'm here to listen and understand."

"Paul, I believe we need to end our relationship. As you mentioned before matters between us were proceeding too rapidly and I've come to accept this as well. I can't begin to tell you how much I appreciate your candidness in relating your affairs and your personal struggles. Hearing of the murder of one you held in high regard has got to be a heavy burden. And I can't begin to fathom the disappointment of your broken engagement. You obviously loved Abby a lot."

The telephone rang. She did not answer it. I made no attempt to gainsay what she related. Neither did I interrupt her with a profession of how much I'd come to cherish her. An anemic request for another chance would have sounded hollow and weak, almost a travesty. I regarded begging for love beneath me.

"I've had issues of my own regarding alcoholism."

"Alcoholism," I wondered, that's a new one to me. "There's no doubt I've been a drunkard, maybe I've even become an inveterate drunk despite going long periods without a drink. But an alcoholic? Does Juliette believe I'm an alcoholic? A drunkard perhaps, but an alcoholic, never."

"My father died an alcoholic," she continued. "A good kind man who took care of his family the best he could but he let drink get the best of him. Despite efforts to quit and seek rehabilitation he didn't make it. He died from a destroyed liver, a forty-year-old man, and me just fifteen years old at the time. In addition to my mother he left behind my brother and my sister. They're both younger than me. They're getting on their feet as we speak and are finally able to take care of themselves. I've tried to help them to the best of my ability since I've worked for the cruise travel agency."

I did not ask her to reconsider her stance. Carrying forward many unresolved issues would weigh too heavily on us. Our relationship finally at an end, I thought of our initial encounter at The Oliphant when I'd assumed a brief conversation with Adrian and Juliette would be the extent of our meeting—just a couple of unassuming guys chitchatting with two nice working girls—which turned out to be a lot more promising. A budding romance cut short, pleading with her would only make matters worse. I had no respect for anyone who pleaded for love when he did not deserve it.

"I can say my feelings for you run deep and despite knowing you for only a short while I've begun to love you. But I'm afraid. I tell you this, Paul, not because I'm afraid for myself; I'm afraid for you. Believe me when I say I want the best for you but you'll have to resolve your issues on your own. I can't help you with that. I have neither the strength nor the capacity to help you exorcise the demons from your life."

Weeping, we embraced for long minutes. We wished each other well.

"Hey bud, there's no sleeping at the bar. You want me to call you a taxi?" the bartender at Trixie's Lounge said after he managed to rouse me out of a drunken slumber. The dimly lit lounge and the soothing piped-in music made for a perfect atmosphere to ruminate on a quiet Tuesday evening. Again, without plans for the future, I'd a lot to consider.

"Look, I can handle this," Frank Ralls said. "Paul, why don't I give you a ride home. I'll drive you in your car so you can have it at your apartment tomorrow." Frank had come in for a nightcap after I passed out.

"How are you going to get back?" I asked in my stupor.

"You're less than a mile from here; I'll drive you home and I'll hoof it back. No problem."

"Thanks buddy." Frank safely parked my car after driving me home.

"Take it easy on the booze, pal," he said handing me the keys before he walked back to Trixie's.

The quiet Tuesday evening occurred two weeks following our separation. I went to Trixie's straight from work where I'd since become a steady patron. Few other customers were present. Only two couples had stopped in for a few beers and a quick bite to eat. Four shots of Canadian Club helped to clear my mind. Straight up, unmixed and no ice, chased by a slug or two of water just enough to curb the pleasant harshness in my gullet after I'd polished off the shot. After one of their nonpareil open-faced steak sandwiches, I relaxed and paid no heed to the humdrum of droning conversation.

I settled back to nurse some more whiskey. In no hurry to get home this evening I lazed self-indulgently in the calming ambiance of the dimly lit lounge. I'd have many more shots before closing time. What better time or place than this for serious reflection.

With Juliette out of my life I buried myself in my work trying to forget what happened. I'd grudgingly accepted her decision to break off our relationship—end our affair before we got too deeply involved. Though disappointed, Juliette did not say to me "Let's wait and see if you can defeat the demons haunting you and we'll see what happens then."

Equally disappointed with the way matters ended I nonetheless felt a grim satisfaction derived from the clinical parting our of ways; we'd managed a clean, surgical Midwestern-bible-camp separation. We'd wished each other well and had vowed to succeed in our respective endeavors. "I wish you the best," I'd told her, and thankfully there were no platitudes, there were no entreaties made by either of us to reconsider our decision. No promises were made to see each other again after some time had elapsed. Good old Brother Hoekstra, good old Herb Mickelssen and good old George Haagejndas would be proud of the professional manner in which Juliette and I parted ways. Surgical and clean? Humbug. With everything said and done this rationalizing amounted to nothing more than another major defeat for Paul Maki.

Juliette Campeau would undoubtedly go on her way succeeding in her promising career and Paulie Maki, if he so chose could likewise do the same, going about radiating a bible camp expression, glad to see his friends and smiling symmetrical smiles upon meeting new acquaintances, for I present a perfectly symmetrical smile to all and sundry whenever I feel obliged to paste one on my homely round face. That's exactly how I looked in my high school graduation picture and that's the way I smiled upon being introduced to Herb Mickelssen and Doug Ridenbaugh at Alameda Aerospace. "I'm happy to be here and meet such fine people as yourselves," my face-muscle-strained-symmetrical smile would suggest, enhanced by an eager-to-please Midwestern expression in my small imploring eyes.

All the guys I knew had hobbies or wholesome avocations. Maybe that's why none of them had any problem with liquor or even an inclination to tie one on occasionally. Wendell Sauer occupied his leisure time as a bird watcher in the Mississippi River backwaters. George Haagejndas put on funny little acts with his kids and the habitués from the soup kitchen. George Carpenter and Abel Cooper found an outlet for their immense energies through music. Rolfe Ellefson, who as a young person struggled intensely with the Christian beliefs he'd been taught, and although he held his views to himself, kept deeply engrossed in theology. Who knows what else? Some of the strait-laced guys I worked with were amateur photographers, coin collectors, model railroad buffs or were passionate about outdoor life: canoeing, skiing, hiking or going on camping trips with their families. None of this stuff interested me for long; how does anyone have fun paddling a canoe? For most of these activities I stood as a vicarious bystander.

What do I like to do? Drink, that's what I like to do—passionately, which deep down inside I'd known and practiced all along. Who doesn't like to get drunk? Throw those inhibitions aside once in a while—makes perfect sense to me—everyone should do it, go out and have some fun. The lengthy periods of abstinence in the woods and while at Michigan Tech served as nothing to end self-defeating behavior. I failed to cap the bottle for good. The influence of the many good friends I'd made had come to naught. If the guys at Brickhouse Logging could see me now they'd call me a charlatan and a bum. I would not be able to look them in the eye. So here I am at Trixie's Lounge with my miserable butt parked on barstool getting soused. Hell, I hadn't even given a single thought about Marie Loonsfoot.

My mind drifted back to early childhood. I had to go all the way back to the beginning. Me a big drunk? Life with the Heights Bunch always stayed simple, so uncomplicated then. Who would have thought Paulie Maki, that nice little boy, would turn out to be a big lush? How could he? His parents and childhood friends in the Heights Bunch were great if not the greatest. After seeing drunken old Willard Janke almost drown and then hear of him freezing to death in a snowbank Paulie Maki should be the last person in the world to become a drunkard.

How did I get into such a mess? What would the Heights Bunch think of me now? I ruminated long over my whiskey on my childhood friends and the good times we had together growing up—escapades at the rock battleship and Roundy Pond. How about those snakes? I had to laugh when I thought of the face-sittings we got from Football and Rotten Mugga.

My closest friends, Hicks, Aldo and Abby were succeeding in their careers. How about little Paulie Maki? What would he do now? Would he also succeed?

"Welcome, Paul," a new Herb Mickelssen would say as nice little Paulie Maki arrived at some other engineering facility wearing his symmetrical bible-camp smile. "We're glad to have you aboard." On and on, and after initial success, failure.

After those dozen-plus whiskies, I finally had everything figured out before I crapped out at the bar. In the dim recesses of my head a light began to shine. "Paulie Maki you're nothing but a bum," the light registered.

Take it easy on the booze? Hell, after Frank drove me home I shook off the grogginess and got started in earnest. I took a quick inventory of my larder I'd stocked since my breakup with Juliette. Drunk or otherwise I'd never take chances with a meager supply. I smugly surveyed my well-provisioned stash that included two unsampled fifths of fine bourbon. A fifth of premium brandy I'd bought previously for special occasions with Juliette stood in reserve. A cool case of beer, sixteen ouncers, lined the shelves of my refrigerator. After more than a year of sobriety in the woods and at Phoenix, beer once again agreed well—it would take some doing to again experience bloating. I rejoiced in my stock of potables—ensconced in my apartment and alone I would imbibe to my heart's content. Arguably relieved matters were settled with Juliette and content with the bar stool appraisal of where I stood, I deserved a day off from work.

Missing one day of work should mean nothing. But a stern, strait-laced, roast beef and mashed potatoes Midwestern outfit like Phoenix would show zero tolerance for a lowly job shopper who goes out bumming and getting drunk when he should be working on a critical project. Especially for a here-today-gone-tomorrow job shopper. Who could blame them? Phoenix knew everything what had happened at Alameda before they took me on. Almost a sure bet I'd be fired from Phoenix if I caused any nonsense even if they were presently happy with my work.

But then again, why should they make a fuss? Hadn't Wendell Sauer asked me if I'd like to join Phoenix as one of their own engineers? No longer as a job shopper? Wasn't he pleased with my work? Besides, the only work I missed, or should I say had shown up late for work, followed that minor weekend binge at Juliette's apartment.

I'd take my chances. I would not bother to call in saying something suspicious such as "I've got the flu" as I did at Alameda. Anyhow, the people at Phoenix knew too much about me already to listen to some flimsy excuse. So now it would be just me, the beer and liquor, and some plaintive hillbilly music. Good enough for me; I couldn't ask for more. Tempted to phone Juliette and invite her over after having had a few drinks I instead let my old stubborn streak kick in. I did not call nor would I call her—I had to be "manly and tough," just as I'd been when persevering the presence of Abby, seated next to me all the way to the Moose Lake Bible Camp when barely a teenager.

The one day of missed work turned into three days. On the third day I enjoyed an early breakfast of pickled eggs, sauerkraut and beans. The beans were leftovers from a previous meal and had been stashed in the refrigerator for at least two weeks after they'd sat out for two days following the first serving. Looking ahead to a long pleasant day, I had a couple beers followed by many shots of Jim Beam. I imbibed comfortably in an armchair listening to the hillbilly music.

I began to fart—deadly, rich sulfurous farts. "Just what you can expect from beans, sauerkraut and pickled eggs topped with a couple brews," I mused contentedly, steeped in my essence. I eventually dozed off in a drunken stupor, oblivious to the music and to my bodily functions.

The doorbell rang. In a daze I shuffled out of my chair to open the door. There in the hallway stood Fred Mercer and Wendell Sauer. Both men reeled back from the open doorway, involuntarily gagging. Because what caused them to gag was that I'd utterly and prodigiously lost control of my bowels while passed out in the armchair. I opened the door still too groggy to be much aware of my soiled drawers.

"May we come in?" Sauer gravely asked.

Although stone drunk, I felt a tinge of embarrassment. I'd not in any way expected callers from guys I worked with. At only three in the afternoon these guys should still be working to complete a late Friday shift. Both men were far more embarrassed than me; I slowly began to apprehend the purpose of their visit.

"Please excuse me, gentlemen, I've had an accident," I said after I grasped the enormity of what'd I'd done. "Some beans I had earlier must have been tainted. It must have happened while I slept. Please come inside, we can talk in the kitchen."

Empty beer bottles lay strewn about in my messy reeking apartment—the dense stink I'd involuntarily created overpowered the sour odor of stale beer. A half fifth of Jim Beam stood on a coffee table near my armchair. An unfinished tumbler of whiskey stood next to the bottle.

"I'll make this quick, Paul," Wendell Sauer said as he and Fred Mercer carefully followed me into the kitchen. "Please excuse us for this visit, but everyone at work is concerned for you. When you didn't come to work or call we suspected the worst," Sauer said quietly, "and not necessarily a binge. Right now I don't know what to tell you, but if you would come in on Monday we can talk some more. Late Monday morning would be fine."

Some small talk briefly ensued. The three of us were at a loss for words. Fred Mercer appeared downcast, unable to look me in the eye. After a few awkward exchanges both men left rather hurriedly. "Let's get some fresh air," I heard Mercer say in the hallway outside my apartment.

Finding scant relief after this awkward, bizarre episode finally ended, I undertook the grisly task of cleanup.

Wendell Sauer did not lie to higher management to coverup what happened. "Paul, we were aware of your previous problems at Alameda Aerospace before Phoenix brought you on board. The references you provided to Opal Technical Services while you were still working for Brickhouse Logging attested to your character and a strong work ethic. People you worked with at Alameda vouchsafed your work ethic. Those you cited as references on the logging crew were convinced you had your drinking problem licked and had nothing but praise for you. And we at Phoenix could not have been more pleased with your performance; your work has been more than satisfactory for one with less than three years of engineering experience.

"Now, regrettably, Phoenix has no recourse but to terminate your services. Let me say I've attempted just this morning to intercede with higher management to give you another chance and I say this humbly. But the company policy is firm regarding situations such as yours.

"I will ask one favor of you, and that is to stay on through the remainder of this week that we can transition your tasks to someone else on our staff. Upper management is OK with this. You were involved with a lot on the *Lander* and your help in tying up loose ends would be greatly appreciated. Otherwise you may regard your obligation to us as completed, and under these circumstances, would be understandable. The choice is yours to make," Wendell Sauer said.

Good old Wendell Sauer, stern but fair. After the binge I tapered off my drinking over the weekend, enough to arrive late Monday morning, shaky and defeated. Even before Sauer showed up at my apartment I had no illusions what Phoenix' decision would be regarding the continuation of my services; I'd already made this *fait accompli* decision for them when I started my bender.

"Of course I'll stay; I'll stay as long as needed to transition my tasks. I can start right now."

"Thanks, Maki, that'll be a big help."

And work I did. I buried myself in work, the only way I knew to keep my mind off the rush of what had transpired—two blown excellent engineering jobs, the very first in my brief career. Sober but still shaky, the first two days passed by tortuously slow but by Wednesday my mind pretty much resumed its normal function. The project proceeded well and it neared completion with the aid of a Phoenix staff engineer assigned in the transitioning. There were no supercilious looks cast in my direction or snide remarks heard from the staff, just as there were none when I received second chances at Alameda. I'd halfway expected to hear someone whisper "that guy shit his pants," but Fred Mercer and Wendell Sauer were mum on the subject. Neither told the staff the details of what had happened even though some had suspected drinking caused the problem, as had the staff at Alameda. Mercer and Sauer were decent, honorable men.

Late on Friday afternoon Fred Mercer and Wendell Sauer saw me out the door. Again, as the time when I was ushered out from Alameda, words were few. I thought I saw moisture appearing in Sauer's eyes as he firmly clasped my hand to wish me well. "I'll give you a call," Fred Mercer said. Other than that, George Haagejndas, standing as erectly and proudly as ever, came to see me before I checked out. "I and my family will be praying for you," that good man said.

The moderator's voice broke the scripted vocalizing on TV, tuned to one of the major networks. "We're taking you Cape Kennedy this morning to witness the launch of the *Orbiting Celestial Adventurer.*"

The scene at Cape Kennedy bustled with activity this early morning in October. The launch vehicle, with the Adventurer shrouded atop and fully equipped for flight into orbit, stood in readiness on the launch pad. The launch or supply tower, a huge latticework of beams, gussets and spars had been safely rotated and moved at a safe distance away from the launching pad. Launch was imminent.

I'd not come to Trixie's Lounge this morning to witness the launch; only by mere chance I happened to be there. I'd arrived at Trixie's early, barely a week after my firing from Phoenix. Being too busy getting drunk I'd completely missed previous news of the impending launch. I'd completed the transitioning of my activities at Phoenix and having lots of leisure time on my hands I'd become an early morning regular at Trixie's after a quick breakfast. Most of the time I had a few quick shots and then went back home to drink in solitude. Quite drunk on this particular morning, I'd been on a big solitary bender the evening before that lasted well into the wee hours of the morning, and upon awakening, picked up where I left off at Trixie's. Only a short walk, I had no worries of being nabbed for drunk driving as I'd left my car in the apartment parking lot. Seated at the bar were Mean Frank Ralls and a couple of tough-looking young guys at the other end. Both were big bruisers and they'd obviously been drinking a lot judging from their leering expressions and their coarse conversation. We'd not seen them before. Besides Ralls and myself they were the only other customers present. I sat chitchatting alongside Frank, drinking a coke. Little did I know he'd only come in to check up on me. Appearance-wise unkempt, I'd not bothered to shave, bathe or change clothes for an entire week.

Cameron Avery, the moderator, briefed his viewers on the proceedings readying the Adventurer for launch into earth orbit. In an avuncular voice he expatiated on the lengthy preparations made just to transport the launch vehicle from an assembly building to the pad. Footage showed the vehicle stationed on a large mobile, tracked platform. Called the crawler-transporter, this large rig stood more than twenty feet above the ground, and as it inched ahead slowly it bore its precious cargo from the assembly building to the launch pad, no faster than one mile per hour. Leveling devices kept the platform stabilized with but slight deviation occurring from the vertical axis of the launch vehicle. Once there, cargo loading operations were facilitated by use of the launch tower. In the case of manned flight, Avery instructed, the tower also facilitated the embarking of the crew. Numerous checkouts of the electrical, hydraulic and mechanical systems ensured complete readiness for launch. Hours of preparation were required from the time the launch vehicle left the assembly building until actual launch, only minutes away.

All the engineers and technicians at the site and those inside the blockhouse, although experiencing a controlled tension remained calm, while everyone else, the spectators who'd come to witness the event firsthand and TV viewers were electrified with anticipation of the forthcoming blast.

The countdown began: ten, nine, eight, … three, two, one, zero. "We have liftoff," Avery's assuring yet exited voice told his viewers. In a controlled but dramatic fashion he vividly described the thunderous, rumbling, earth-shaking wondrous beauty of the launch as the beast accelerated skyward. A deep rumbling, thrilling the spectators to the marrow.

I got into the act. "First-stage burnout of the Atlas booster will occur in about five seconds," I announced gratuitously to our small crowd in the lounge. Sure enough, Avery shortly afterward announced the jettison of the booster.

"Now the second stage Centaur is kicking in and will take the Adventurer into a five hundred fifty-mile earth orbit, or in more conventional technical terms, a four hundred eighty-mile circular orbit," I added. "That's nautical miles. The five hundred fifty miles are statute miles in case you're wondering."

The two toughs who'd come in didn't like it. They were not impressed first by my shabby appearance and were irritated by the matter-of-fact way in which I described the events. They were not in the least bit impressed that thus far my predictions were accurate, which only irritated them more. Trouble was brewing.

"Look, we got a rocket scientist," one of the guys said to his companion. "And this big brain must read the newspapers once in a while."

"I'll betcha he reads comic books," the other replied. "Hey, hobo, what comic books you been reading?"

"*Buck Rogers*," I replied. "You ever heard of him? *Buck Rogers in the Twenty-fifth Century*."

Buck Rogers became my favorite comic strip as a youngster, long before I got into *Major Hoople* and *Pogo*. In the '40s just after the war my dad subscribed to the *Chicago Herald American*, a now defunct second-tier publication, which featured *Buck Rogers*. Barely ten years old, I'd eagerly followed the daily exploits of its hero, Buck Rogers, out to establish peace and order in far-off astral domains. Sources of fascination included curvo-ray guns, back-pack rockets for hopping about from one point to another on alien planets, full-fledged rocket ships for intergalactic space travel, and of course, extraterrestrials.

"The *Celestial Adventurer* is now in orbit. The launch has been a success. What remains to be seen is *are all systems a go*," Cameron Avery announced.

"What do you have for us now, Mr. Smartass Buck Rogers," one of the toughs demanded.

"Be glad to oblige you. In a few minutes expect to hear the solar panels are deployed. That's a good sign the batteries are doing their job and the wiring is OK."

"The solar panels have been deployed. That's a very encouraging sign for mission success," Avery announced minutes later.

On and on it went. At timely intervals I provided the lowdown on the checkout phase of the control systems and the instrument packages. The toughs grumbled to themselves and were not happy. They were spoiling for a fight.

"How come you're not at the Cape directing the launch," one of them goaded.

"They sent me here to educate you," I responded, having got sick and tired of these bums ruining what should be a celebration of an engineering triumph.

"He helped to build the Adventurer. My friend is an engineer," Frank Ralls addressed the pair. "So let's settle back and have a drink. Here, I'm buying."

They were not appeased. Matters worsened. I did not need another barroom brawl. I looked at the scars on my right hand caused by the fracas at the Grizzly Den. I would bear them for life.

"Look Mr. Broad Shoulders, we can pay for our own drinks. Furthermore I don't like your looks."

The bartender intervened. "You guys can leave now. We don't go for your kind of trouble here. This is a peaceful bar. So hit the road."

"We're not going anywhere until we kick some ass," the larger of the pair said. "I'm going to start with Buck Rogers."

"That won't be productive. Why don't you just sit down," Frank replied.

The toughs rose from their stool and slowly approached us. I stood up, prepared to defend myself.

"Sit down, Paul, this is not your fight," Frank said, rising to greet them.

Action was fast, furious and accomplished in less than twenty seconds. The larger man lunged at Frank with the aim of grabbing him in a wrestling hold. Mean Frank Ralls deftly stepped aside and grabbed him from behind by his belt. He increased his opponent's momentum with a mighty heave, and thrusting him forward, sent him crashing head-first into a wall. Anticipating the other, Frank wheeled about to deliver a timely swift kick to the tough's groin as he moved in to help his companion, now slowly rising from the floor where he'd crashed. He balked as his crony howled with pain, groveling on the floor.

"No more funny business or it'll be a lot tougher on both of you than what you just got. Now as the bartender said, get your miserable asses out of here."

"You better get some rest, Paul," Frank said after the troublemakers left. "There's no need for you to be out punishing yourself."

He dropped me off at my apartment where I fell into a deep sleep. But not before I thought of the Adventurer. At least I could claim I played a part in its success.

I had no regrets.

CHAPTER 15

Three Oaks

A month passed since my firing. I had all the time in the world to do what I pleased. To start with, this meant doing nothing. After the fracas at Trixies's Lounge I made a feeble attempt to stay sober by limiting my intake to a modest six-pack a day, give or take a little, with maybe a shot or two of bourbon or a quick snort of vodka quaffed between the brews. Other than Frank Ralls and Fred Mercer stopping in a couple times I made no effort to see or contact any of my friends. Solitude agreed well.

I had a lot more breathing space in which to think things over than I did when I stood in the forest of ponderosa pine trees off Route 299. Only this time it would not be looking ahead toward advancing a professional career. Committed to no one I initially counted being a free man with a clean slate as a blessing, but trying to stay sober became a burden. Time oppressed heavily.

Then I remembered Morris.

"An amount I deem entirely insufficient," Morris, a notoriously vainglorious pedant, sniffed disdainfully as he sat above a serving of cornflakes. Once widely acclaimed for his fastidiousness in addressing each and every matter, whether of large or small import, Morris later faded into obscurity at an obscure date. "Only by being punctilious in facing minor difficulties can one be assured of success in confronting major problems," this pedant had repeatedly and gratuitously admonished.

While measly servings of cornflakes for Morris, for me it was beer. Hence, I deemed a six-pack a day an amount entirely insufficient. I thus increased my ration to ten beers per day before graduating almost entirely back to hard liquor. The punctiliousness I'd mustered in facing this problem, like Morris, faded away. (The last I heard, he's still alive and well.)

"What hogwash," I mumbled in a drunken fog. "I'd vowed to

succeed and here I am a big drunkard. Fired from my first two jobs after only three years in aerospace. Three measly years. What should I do? Maybe go back to college? Forget that. Go on smiling some more symmetrical smiles?"

Perhaps I'd been kidding myself all along of being an engineer, corralled for an entire day in a bullpen or, at best, as a cubicle zombie. Hadn't I dreaded that prospect before I even got into engineering while working in the bush? Right about the fifty guys and a harried boss. Maybe not so much the harried boss. What good would it do if some other outfit took me in with some smiling Herb Mickelssen happy to see me come and help them? The result would ultimately be more big benders and another firing.

Who would hire me as an engineer in the first place—two false starts and two failures—even if the aerospace industry, still thriving at a high level, stood in need of engineers? Eat crow and go back to Brickhouse Logging? Totally out of the question after I'd let those guys down who'd vouchsafed my character to Phoenix. How about the pulp bush in the Keweenaw, and being recognized as a failure, have to face everyone I knew in my home town? I could read their thoughts: "Paulie Maki just aint got it in him." Go back to college? None of these options made any sense.

Maybe I'd wind up like Crazy Charlie. A survivor of the Bataan Death March, and after a lengthy imprisonment in a Japanese POW camp, Charlie's mind was never the same when the war ended. Whatever family, whatever friends he had were nowhere to be seen. Still he managed to get along well enough living alone in a house trailer in Laurium.

Cleanly shaven and always appearing neatly dressed in a suit and tie a newcomer could easily have mistaken him for a businessman out on the town having a few brews. There sat Crazy Charlie at the bar at Haas's Tavern, just a short walk away from his trailer, minding his own business. But if a single woman happened to stop in for a drink or two he'd put a couple of quarters in the juke box and play some melancholy love songs. Charlie would then join in and harmonize in an insinuating, mellifluous voice, and at the peak of an emotive refrain, he'd cast an admiring glance at the lady in the full-length mirror behind the bar.

After catching her eye and convinced he'd made a good impression he'd begin to dance. Not with her: oh no. He did not extend her an invitation to join him, but instead he began to dance alone, all by himself. He glided gracefully across the floor—almost weightlessly it seemed—arms reached as though the lucky lady were clasped in his embrace. Beaming happily all the while the music played, he waltzed on and on, oblivious to the patrons at the bar. He wasn't a bad dancer either.

On one occasion Crazy Charlie left Haas's with a woman to the wonder of all the patrons. It's anyone's guess what happened after that.

Confusion had to be eliminated. All the well wishes, the admonitions, the prayers made on my behalf by those closest to me and from friends I'd made had come to naught. "We'll be praying for you, Paul" had fallen on deaf ears. "We're pulling for you; we want you to succeed," my parents and friends had encouraged. How many times had I heard that one? This had long become monotonous; I'd lost count I'd heard it so many times.

And the dreams—not only had Erma Jamison and August Palosaari been privy to my innermost concerns I'd babbled during drunken nightmares but now Juliette Campeau had heard everything. My vocalizing made Erma circumspect about a possible permanent relationship. While in jail I'd kept August awake for long hours babbling about the sunshade. In Juliette's case the exposure helped settle matters between us early on and no doubt circumvented future complications. They'd wished me well—I didn't need any more well wishes.

It would be better to avoid well-meaning people. "What then should I do?" I wondered repeatedly. Day after day of indecisiveness passed as I idled away time imbibing in my thoroughly cleaned armchair.

How about simply becoming a man of leisure? This made the most sense of all. The money I'd accrued would ensure a lengthy period of leisure should I be careful how my monies were spent. And that's what I decided I would do one afternoon, mellowed out after putting away a six-pack of Buds and a few shots of bourbon. How did Erma Jamison put it? Let others toil whilst I spin. Or something like that. Paul Maki—man of leisure.

I rejoiced in my hoard. Eleven thousand two hundred and eighty-three dollars, nothing to sneeze at, should go a long way. I didn't owe anyone a dime; my loans and car payments were paid in full. Prior to getting fired I hadn't given too much thought to my financial status except to watch my hoard grow. Now I smugly savored the prospects this tidy sum would bring. During the lengthy periods of sobriety while working at Brickhouse Logging and Phoenix Aeronautical Systems I'd lived modestly and my savings increased substantially especially while working the heavy overtime schedule at Phoenix. For a man who sometimes found himself strapped of rather limited means, in my estimation I'd become reasonably solvent. I could become a leisurely man, a most appealing prospect.

Not only would I be a man of leisure but even more so I could become a bum. A bona fide certified bum. I'd never looked down on bums: most of the ones I knew were an amiable bunch of fellows without a care in the world who came and went as they pleased. I thought of Humble Huhta, Hicks's uncle, who for practical purposes lived a bum's life and how he thrived on a meager pension and handouts. I remembered the stories I'd read of skid row bums who retreated to the gutter after being feted to all the food and drink they could handle in one day. No complaints about them from anyone—an enviable lot to be sure. Let air-sniffers find fault if they so wished.

There would be no expensive nightclubs, frivolous vacations to tourist traps, scenic mountains or beachside resorts or any such place I had no interest whatsoever in seeing. Let the eight-to-fivers with their wives and kids piled into station wagons go to swarm the beaches. I'd make my substantial savings stretch and what better way to do this than to become a thrifty bum, keeping a careful eye on where I went and seeing the monies were dispensed in a miserly fashion.

Most of my barroom buddies back home would drink until they spent every last dime they had. I could never understand that—the guys I chummed around with when home on leave from Great Lakes were always broke—they'd piss away their meager earnings made from raking leaves or shoveling snow and then they'd go out mooching drinks like they did from me.

Being broke in compromised unimaginable circumstances in an indifferent city with no place to go would not happen to me. I would remain solvent—that eleven thousand plus dollars in my hoard would go a long way. Thankfully I would be the last one to be caught short. A clear path lie ahead.

"Olkoon niin", sanoi Kieri, "kuin Naiset potki ja pieri." This bit of doggerel translates from Finnish as "So be it," said Kieri, "as the women kicked and farted."

Toivo Kieri, a bartender in the Keweenaw during the roaring twenties, frequented whorehouses thriving in the region at the time whenever he felt the urge to procreate. This became a fact well-known all over town. A bachelor well into middle age, he made his round to his favorite brothel, a cathouse west of town on the Canal Road along the Portage Canal. Also notorious as a voyeur, after Kieri planted his seed for a few extra bucks he gained permission from the madam to view the activities of her charges involved with other customers. From where he stood experiencing vicarious pleasure in a dark closet, a knothole provided him a clear view of the frolicking going on in an adjacent room.

Word quickly got around of his voyeurism and one of the habitués of the cathouse composed the doggerel in Finnish that would bedevil Kieri haplessly for the rest of his life.

"So be it" would also be it for me. Thank you, bartender Kieri. And thank you, Morris.

Frank Ralls and I sat at the bar at Trixie's watching a St. Louis Blues hockey game. The game turned out to be a desultory affair for the St. Louis fans because the Blues were getting trounced by the Montreal Canadiens. Big Jean Beliveau, the illustrious Canadien center ice man, had just scored on a power play making the score four to one, Montreal. I'd just got up ready to leave when I got a surprise. In walked Fred Mercer, Adrian Parks and Juliette Campeau. I'd not seen nor spoken with Juliette since we parted ways.

"What are they doing here?" I asked myself peevishly. I've already had enough trouble without Juliette showing up. Perhaps she's come to sympathize with my being fired. I did not need sympathy; I'd learned to eschew well-meaning remarks from people intending sympathy for me when the difficulties I experienced were caused of my own doing. That's the last thing in the world I needed. Still the constraints of social decorum had to be observed and so I did not leave.

"I've got some good news," Fred Mercer said after the five of us had seated ourselves at a table. I had no difficulty guessing what the good news involved as Adrian beamed with pleasure. She could only conceal the good news from those unaware of her romance with Fred.

"Adrian and I are going to be married," Mercer announced. "And my traveling days are over. I'm here to say I've accepted a permanent position as a staff engineer with Phoenix."

Petty thoughts continued to course through my mind after Frank and I offered our congratulations. "Had Fred Mercer been offered the position which had been offered to me? What would have happened had I not screwed everything up, and after more serious consideration of Wendell Sauer's offer, accepted it? Would Mercer be sitting here now announcing good news? Maybe I would be the one proclaiming good news."

Mercer seemed to read my mind.

"I've been toying with the prospect of becoming a permanent employee of Phoenix for the past few months. Sauer asked me to join Phoenix just weeks before my first six months with Opal expired."

That much settled, no need for further speculation on whether Mercer secured the position Sauer had offered me. We'd each been offered a direct position at the same time. Relieving myself of petty thoughts I remembered I'd turned my offer down. Mercer and I both could have become Phoenix staff engineers.

"This deserves a celebration. Bartender, drinks for the table and some open-faced steak sandwiches for everyone," I ordered impulsively. "Everything's on me," I announced over the protests of Mercer and Ralls.

Ladylike and demure, Juliette for the most part remained silent. "I'm so happy for Adrian and Fred," she only said to me.

I fumbled for words, experiencing an awkwardness. All I could muster were a few desultory remarks and questions concerning her career. Back to square one and then some; to me our meeting here at Trixie's seemed as tentative and as unpromising as it had when we'd first met at The Oliphant.

"Do you have any plans for the future?" she asked.

"Nothing definite, I've been thinking of going to Chicago. There're a lot of opportunities there. Maybe try something different from aerospace engineering."

"Why did Juliette have to come along with Fred and Adrian," I wondered, allowing petty, suspicious thoughts to again occupy my mind. "Does she intend to give me another chance?" Inwardly I experienced ambivalence should this be the case. Did she somehow know I would be at Trixie's and would tag along with her friends to catch me there by surprise?

"Paul, I tried calling you at home earlier to bring you up to date on the important matter involving Adrian and me," Fred Mercer said. "We stopped by your apartment to invite you along. We brought Juliette with us to hear the good news of our engagement even though Adrian suspected Juliette already knew this would occur despite Adrian's attempt to keep it a secret from everyone, even her best friend. Adrian has a hard time concealing her elation and it makes me quietly proud to be the inspiration of her happiness.

"You're looking better, pal. Chicago, did you say? Anything specific in mind?" Mercer continued.

"Not yet. I've sent out some feelers in response to want ads for engineers in the Chicago Tribune but I've heard nothing back so far. A lot of different outfits, mostly companies involved in industrial engineering and various sorts of manufacturing. I've had to tailor my resume to show how my aerospace experience is best applicable to their needs. So I'll just keep looking."

Actually I'd directed my resume to firms I believed would have low expectations of my services and would be OK whether hired or not. OK either way; I could lose myself in Chicago. I had no relatives or friends there. My plans were to find a low cost of living arrangement on West Madison Street or close thereby. What better locale than skid row to do some serious bumming and make my money stretch. Sending out a few resumes and landing some lowly job I didn't care two cents about would not stand in the way of my decision to be a bum.

I casually observed Juliette for her reaction and saw nothing discernable in her demeanor or facial expression indicating disappointment or even concern. For the most part she seemed detached but by no means appeared unfriendly.

After our sandwiches and another round of celebratory drinks Juliette drew me aside.

"Adrian and Fred asked me to come along with them. I strongly suspected they were going to announce an engagement. And I'm glad you're here. It's good to see you again, and it would be great if you can give me a phone call. Paul, there are some matters I'd like to talk about with you privately."

"I'll call you shortly," I replied.

Frank Ralls appeared to be somewhat nervous, seemingly out of character for him, when Juliette and I returned to the table. As usual he projected a gentlemanly and courteous mien but I couldn't help but sense a nervous edge. I hadn't noticed any discomfort as we sat watching the hockey game and when Adrian, Fred and Juliette arrived I was too surprised to notice if there were any change in his demeanor. No one else appeared to notice any nervousness on his part.

Frank had met us several times before at Trixie's while Juliette and I were still dating. We always welcomed his gentlemanly presence in joining us for a few drinks, sometimes with Adrian and Fred present. Oh well, probably nothing for me to worry about; perhaps something involving his current employment occurred on the construction site. Most likely some minor issue or otherwise he would have told me.

"Frank and I have begun dating. It's important to me you should know this."

Once again I sat on the sofa where Juliette and I spent our memorable evenings together. And this time, as it had been during the two most recent visits, no pleasant music emanated from her KLH stereo or soul-searching looks exchanged as we sat drinking coffee.

"I owe you this, Paul. Frank wanted to tell you of this himself and did not wish to keep you in the dark of our seeing each other. In his eyes he told me that would have been a betrayal of friendship and after some discussion we both agreed it best I tell you myself."

"You really didn't have to tell me this, Juliette; you don't owe me an explanation. It's your life. I have nothing but respect for both you and Frank."

"I told him how our relationship came to end. He'd asked me why he hadn't seen us together for a while. At first he urged we patch things up—Frank did not take lightly what he'd perceived as a growing love between us. After I related our circumstances, which I thought fair, did he ask me for a date but only when some time passed. Frank is aware of your difficulties and like Fred and Adrian wants the best for you."

"There it is again," I thought gloomily, "we only want the best for you."

Although deeply disappointed I felt relief. My relationship with a woman I'd come to adore and one whom I highly respected came to a stop for good. Terminated once and for all. How about Juliette? She could not have found a better friend, a better man than Frank Ralls—a better man than Paul Maki—at least better than the Paul Maki of the few past months. Had it been anyone else than Frank Ralls I might have felt a lot differently. Juliette had placed her confidence in a good man. Any lesser man and I would have had difficulty accepting her decision.

Before I left her apartment I wholeheartedly wished Juliette well and that her relationship with Frank would prosper into one of love and trust. She said nothing but only held me tight.

The Great Western Casket Company expressed interest in me as a possible fit. Two days after our celebration of Fred and Adrian's engagement announcement I received a letter from the firm inviting me for an interview in a month. They apologized for the wait citing a company reorganization in progress as causing the delay. I'd responded to their ad in the Chicago Tribune with small expectation of ever hearing from them. The ad merely stated "Mechanical Engineer Wanted. Must Have a Bachelor of Science Degree in Mechanical Engineering and a Minimum of Two Years of Experience." Good enough for me. I wrote back indicating I would be available for an interview. The prospect of being hired by a firm making caskets did not appeal; no doubt the work be a humdrum eight-to-five routine. The Great Western Casket Company—what use would they have for an aerospace engineer who could not hold down a job? Most likely I'd get a small paycheck but so what. No doubt I'd be fired again and what difference would it make?

I had the better part of a month before I left for Chicago. One more month in Hazelwood and I'd situate on West Madison Street or an otherwise low rent district, even if I wasn't accepted at Great Western. What to do? With a whole lot of time on my hands, a whole month, I grew tired of being a fixture at Trixie's Lounge and then coming back to my apartment to get soused. Fred Mercer and Frank Ralls stopped by from time to time to cheer me up. Outside of another invitation to dinner I'd accepted from George Haagejndas, also extended to and accepted by Mercer and Ralls, time weighed laboriously on my hands. Then one afternoon I got inspired, inspired by a dozen shots of brandy I'd savored in solitude.

Maybe they ought to call *me* Football. I'd bounced from one woman to another: first Abby, then Erma Jamison and eventually Juliette Campeau. Mention of Marie Loonsfoot would be a sacrilege. Where should I go from here?

I would bounce some more and surprise Abby with a visit. A short one-day drive from St. Louis to Three Oaks College located several hundred miles away posed no difficulty; let's jump in the car and go. "Let's find out what this strait-laced schoolmarm is up to now," I resolved over the brandy, "what could be better than that."

Rita had always insisted Abby was the one for me. "We were meant for each other," didn't she say? Well let her see me now. In my solitude I'd begun to entertain dim thoughts of Abby. How could this hen of a spinster, this old maid, go on and on and never once make any serious mistakes in her life? Why didn't she latch on to some respectable administrator with a nice modern home in the suburbs? She had to have a life outside of college. This erstwhile face-sitting girl had to have more going for her than trying to teach a bunch of dumb clucks philosophy and history. I would go to see her and find out for myself.

I did not have Abby's phone number or address so I called Rita.

"Paul, are you OK?" she answered after some glad exchanges. "Your voice sounds a bit slurred."

"I'm alright, I've got a bit of a cold. We must not have the best connection," I lied as I could hear her distinctly. "You're not coming through the best but I can still hear you well enough. Maybe we can try later."

"That's OK, I can hear you well."

"I'm sure Abby will be thrilled to hear from you once again," a delighted Rita said when I told her the purpose of my call. "And after all this time to think she'll be seeing you in person," she said after providing me with her address and phone number. She then brought me up to date on important events which occurred in her and Hicks's life.

"Hicks loves his research at Michigan Tech … Child number ten … keeping me busy along with the rest of our big brood … Gabriel Huhta already four months old … grateful for the help the older kids provide … don't know where I'd be without them … don't have much time for massage therapy … got some time for my clients here in Heights. Just think, Alfred Maurice is now in his first year of college at the University of Michigan. I can't say how much I cried when he left home for Ann Arbor."

"Lives in a house swarming with babies for sixteen years and then cries after the first kid leaves home? That's got to be a first," I thought drolly.

Thankfully she did not inquire of my employment status. Nor did I volunteer the circumstances leading to my dismissal from Phoenix. She most likely thought I still prospered in my career as an engineer, climbing the corporate ladder to success. Outside of mentioning Aldo would be climbing the corporate ladder to success. Outside of mentioning Aldo would be returning to Centennial Heights for a Christmas visit she wished me the best in my visit to Three Oaks.

A placid conservative town near the center of the Lower Peninsula of Michigan, I discovered Three Oaks to be as quiet a town as I'd ever visited. A modest roadside sign proclaimed its population as being seven thousand, four hundred and twenty-six inhabitants. All the streets ran north to south and east to west over an almost perfectly flat terrain making it impossible to get lost. A few stop lights at main intersections and stop signs in the quiet residential areas politely regulated the flow of traffic. The homes in the residential area were neat, maintained well and the picture-perfect lawns were studiously manicured. Groomed elms and maples lined the quiet streets. I noticed quite a few churches interspersed throughout the town, mostly of Protestant denomination. The number of churches, indicating a staid conservative populace, seemed disproportionately large to the population.

I checked the town for bars. There were very few neighborhood taverns and only a few steak and potato type restaurants licensed to sell beer, wine and liquor. Considering these dreary facts I found Three Oaks to be a rather depressing town. From what I observed on the sidewalks most of the denizens were clean-cut and well-starched in their dresses, suits, white shirts and ties. Clear-eyed studious-looking young people strolled purposefully toward certain destinations. Three Oaks College students no doubt. Long-haired hippies were far and few between although a few of them could be seen milling about aimlessly.

Situated a short distance away from the western side of the town the Three Oaks College campus appeared to be as austere and well-manicured as the upper-middle-class residential area. No surprise there—the way a conservative institution is supposed to look—stately red brick edifices planted on spacious lawns with a lot of shade trees lining the walkways. Most students looked to be clean-cut types, sober of mien. "These young men and women are aspiring to become industrious citizens upholding proven traditional values," I could almost hear some revered patriarch proclaim. "We instill in our students basic virtues enabling them to stay the course of our great nation," he might add. "No fooling around here with alcohol, drugs and illicit sex. Our students will succeed."

I did not call Abby at once. After I'd made a thorough survey of the town I took a room at a spic-and-span but economical motel on a highway leading out of Three Oaks. I planned to take my time getting in touch with her. Earlier I'd stopped at a state liquor store to stock up on potables to help make an adjustment to these sterile surroundings. Then after checking in I managed to find a tavern to my liking outside of town a short mile away from the motel. The clientele were a convivial lot comprised mostly of farmers of Dutch extraction, big jolly guys ready to chew the fat and make friends with strangers. I learned most of them were either growers of corn and soybeans in this most arable part of the state or committed to the husbandry of milk cows and hogs.

The drinks kept coming. Treated to one beer after another after relating to them my Yooper upbringing in the Keweenaw, I listened to story after story of week-long drunken escapades in deer hunting camps in the northern part of Lower Michigan or in the Upper Peninsula, both densely wooded regions providing remote hideaways for the weary seeking refuge from toil or city life. These big affable louts put down their dozen draft beers as though they were drinking soda pop at a Sunday school picnic. Just like my cousin Sparky who once drank fifteen bottles of Orange Crush at a family outing. These farmers showed little sign of inebriation.

"Us trolls ain't as dumb as we look," a big portly guy proclaimed. "Except for my uncle Johann shooting a cow somewhere near Escanaba thirty years ago we know what a deer looks like and we ain't shot any cows since. And as far as hunting goes we just join our Yooper buddies at the hunting camp to celebrate for a whole week."

"Go dance with my wife," another told me. "She's got me worn out." The wife, a good-natured sociable woman and I bounced across the floor to a lively Frankie Yankovic polka blaring from the jukebox. Even these Dutchmen liked Frankie Yankovic. The farmers finally let me reciprocate their hospitality when I got around to buying drinks for the house. Enjoying an evening of good clean fun, and as the evening wore on, I completely forgot the purpose of my visit. Refreshed, relaxed from the conviviality in the tavern I returned to my room and capped off the evening with a couple belts of brandy.

Despite the good time I had at the tavern I awoke the next morning with a miserable hangover. Nauseous and shaky, I discovered conditions outside were weather-wise equally miserable. Six inches of wet, slushy snow covered the ground on this dark, gloomy December morning and more heavy snow kept falling. I clearly wouldn't be seeing Abby today and I would not call her until I'd made apt preparation to visit her directly. Further, I had plenty of potables on hand; I'd stocked up well at the liquor store. From long experience with the bottle, as had become my wont, I once again thanked myself for never being caught short.

Conditions were perfect for getting drunk. I tidied my surroundings enough that the motel establishment wouldn't think they had a drunk on their hands. A couple quick shots stayed my frayed nerves enough to go out and have a breakfast at a nearby restaurant while the cleaning service performed their duties. The "Dutch Haus" happily resided a close walking distance from my room. Outside of the breakfast, I had a supply of Slim Jims and some smoked herring to sustain me for the rest of the day.

As the day progressed my mood grew as somber as the dismal weather. With a bottle always handy I wound up well soused by mid-afternoon and not in an amicable mood. Why did I come here in the first place? I'd naively imagined a happy reunion with Abby Tulppo. Abby would light up with joy when she met me; her wide-set eyes would glow with pleasure as those marvelous dimples formed on her smiling face. Then after spending a couple days getting reacquainted, we would go to visit her parents in Flint for an evening of fellowship and bring everyone up to date on what had happened in our lives. "Here we are, all is well, and everyone is glad Abby and I are back together again." "Isn't Paul a fine young man," Mrs. Tulppo would gush to her husband.

Instead of a joyful reunion I dallied about, plastered in a motel, drunk, but still possessed of enough smarts to realize these fanciful reveries were nothing but the dotages of a drunkard. I would pack up and leave tomorrow. I must have been nuts thinking of coming here. Forget Abby and forget her for good; why would she want to start over with a big drunk in the first place? "Look here, Abby, I tied one on with the farmers last night but I'll come to see you when I'm sober." What a crock of bull; nothing could come of this. I would leave this corn-and-pork chop town behind and never again come back. I would be gone in the morning. Half of a fifth of Old Crow lay within arm's reach alongside my bed. After polishing off the whiskey I passed out into a drunken slumber.

Events proved otherwise. I would not be leaving today; I'd slept in. Of more importance unfavorable driving conditions were forecast along the route I would be travelling back to St. Louis even though the roads appeared to be plowed clean in Three Oaks. Weather reports stated icy conditions over the entire stretch of I-94 west toward Chicago, the highway I would be driving. Several accidents were reported and motorists were urged to stay off the roads. A major winter storm swept south of us, affecting areas in southern Michigan, northern Indiana and

Illinois. Three Oaks and areas to the north luckily were on the northern fringes of the storm. So what to do now—I would have to hole up at least another day in Three Oaks. Nonetheless, I felt rather chipper after a big breakfast at the Dutch Haus restaurant. Back to the bottle, a full fifth of vodka stood close at hand. Refreshing myself with a couple beers and some vodka I felt even better.

Once again inspired, I altered my plans to leave. Why waste time moping in a motel room the whole day long? Why not pay a visit to Three Oaks College, there to see Abby in person? Wouldn't Abby be delighted at my spontaneous appearance rendering unnecessary phone calls and decisions otherwise to be made? Walking in and greeting her unannounced would be a genuine surprise.

I quickly showered and shaved and donning my best outfit prepared to set out for the college. I still had time for a few more bracers of vodka. "No one will be able to tell I've been drinking. The odor from those two beers I had will be gone by the time I get there and—ho! ho! —no one can smell the vodka." For insurance I would bring along a pocket-fitting pint of vodka convinced it would blend unnoticeably with coffee. Everything went my way—the motel provided a coffee brewer with large-sized paper cups, complete with lids. The day promised to be a great success; I would visit her early in the afternoon. Smug with my plan I only had less than an hour wait before I drove away to the college. A few more shots of vodka sustained my cheerful mood, and half in the bag, reinforced with Dutch courage, stood ready to go.

School was in session as evidenced by the parking lot filled with cars. It would take much more than bad wintry weather to shut down this bastion of higher learning. Not like future years when mere storm warnings and traveler advisories would cause closings and untimely delays.

"What can I do for you sir? May I help you?"

A hefty, broad-featured middle-aged woman cheerfully greeted me at the reception area in the Three Oaks College administration building.

"Yes ma'am, my name is Paul Maki. I'm an old childhood friend of Abby Tulppo. I'm passing through on my way to South Bend, Indiana and I thought I'd stop to see her and say a quick hello. Would you know I've been detained by the snowstorm and have had to lay over? Perhaps you can help me. I'd like to surprise her."

"Why of course, Mr. Maki, I'm sure she'll be delighted to see you. As we speak she's giving a seminar to senior history classes. If you can wait for perhaps an hour you should be able to catch her then. The auditorium in which she's lecturing is in the Ames Hall, just across the parking lot."

"Thank you, ma'am. You've been very helpful. Have a nice day."

"Why wait for an hour?" I asked myself. "Why not go directly to her classroom."

First I went back to my car and liberally spiked the coffee with vodka. Fully prepared to meet Abby, I took a couple snorts from the flask for good measure. I checked my appearance in the rear-view mirror, pleased to see I looked bright, cheerful and not in the least inebriated, and appeared neither bleary-eyed nor flush of countenance. Nothing could go wrong even after I took a pratfall on an icy patch halfway across the parking lot. Holding the lidded cup in precarious balance as I slipped the coffee miraculously did not spill and the pint of vodka remained safe in my suit coat pocket. I saw no one around to witness my accident. Off to the side of the main entrance to the Ames Hall I took another deep swig from the flask before entering the building. Once inside, no one seemed to pay much notice of me as I examined a list posted on a bulletin board. A young woman passed me in the hallway as I studied the postings. Well dressed and well-groomed I'd not given her or anyone else pause to question my uninvited presence. After exchanging polite smiles, she proceeded along the hallway. A notice posted on the board read "Andrew Carnegie and John D. Rockefeller—Men Who Helped Build Industrial America: a lecture by Professor Abby Tulppo, Main Auditorium, from 1:30 to 3:00 PM."

Professor Tulppo's lecture embraced a portion of a continuing series on men whose contributions significantly helped to industrialize America. Abby had just started to deliver a synopsis of a lengthy discourse on Carnegie and Rockefeller, the steel and oil magnates, and the evolution of their respective empires. From where I stood listening quietly outside the main door to the auditorium I could clearly hear everything she said. I dared not peer inside through a window. Taking an occasional sip of my spiked coffee, I found a chair close-by and sat down feigning interest in a magazine I'd picked up from a table. The young woman in the hallway passed by again and we acknowledged each other with a friendly nod.

"Yes, their methods may be considered ruthless by today's standards and even by many at the close of the nineteenth century," Abby began in summary. "Monopolies—certainly—Carnegie had control of a very large part of the steel industry and his Carnegie Steel would become the stimulus for the birth of the US Steel Corporation. Along came the financial wizard, J. Pierpont Morgan. After Morgan's buyout of Carnegie's steel interests and some other concerns in the industry, US Steel would become the largest corporation extant in the early 1900s with a market capitalization of over one billion dollars, a first. A very large sum of money then. Having a monopoly on an entire segment of American industry became even more pronounced in the case of John D. Rockefeller with his Standard Oil, an undeniably huge monopoly.

"Consider their beginnings: Andrew Carnegie grew up as a son of a Scottish weaver whose family, which later emigrated from Scotland to America, shared a dirt floor space with a neighbor. Although not similarly impoverished John D. Rockefeller grew to manhood under rather strained conditions. His father, William Avery Rockefeller, became known as a wheeler-dealer in his business activities and as a philanderer. Despite less than auspicious circumstances early in their lives both men rose to become titans of steel and oil by the dint of sheer intelligence, savvy business transactions and just plain hard work.

"Monopolies, yes. Yet where would this country be today without these men of vision? And these are but two of many men that unfettered rose to the top of the economic ladder by employing to the maximum their God-given talents. Their monumental achievements have lifted this country to unprecedented levels of prosperity, easing drudgery and making life better for everyone. Thank God for men of vision."

A question and answer period followed. I could hear Abby's clear voice calmly answering challenging questions posed by her students. Most of them seemed satisfied with elaborate answers she gave. One of Abby's students, however, less convinced than his classmates of her views on the matter, questioned her forceful summation.

"Professor Tulppo, I agree with you that both these men were great innovators and men of vision," I heard a cultured, well-modulated voice say as I listened carefully outside the door. "Their achievements in the industrial world cannot be confuted. Moreover, both men indisputably were philanthropists of considerable renown. One need not look far to see a Carnegie Library and who has not heard of the Carnegie Hall in New York City. Rockefeller's philanthropic works, while not as evident to the eye, are likewise noteworthy. His millions donated to charities and missionary causes have passed neither unappreciated nor unnoticed."

I listened more intently and despite the ample quantity of liquor I'd consumed I could distinctly hear everything he said, and I could not help but wonder on what ground this fellow stood. So far he'd done a fair job of covering his ass, no doubt as preparation to refute Abby's succinct apology for these tycoons. Despite the tipsiness, the fogginess of mind I began to feel, I had little problem focusing my attention. But his lengthy discourse made me irritable.

"Yet on the other hand," the voice continued, "too many minuses in my view have offset the plusses. By this I mean the untold strife, the untold suffering in the unheralded ranks of labor caused by disputes with management over unjust working conditions. I cite as an example the strike against Carnegie Steel in eighteen ninety-two during which episode seven workers and three strikebreaking Pinkertons were killed in bloody combat. Think of the untold suffering of their families in the aftermath. Despite the enormous wealth these men accrued and despite their philanthropic generosity they perhaps turned a too jaundiced eye toward the worker. Higher wages and improved working conditions would have raised all boats, not only yachts on which these tycoons luxuriated."

I began to get his drift; I smelled a skunk. Why does Abby grant him so much time to respond? Other students as well must be given an opportunity to express their views on the matter.

"Looking deeper, perhaps they pushed the country too rapidly into an industrial society. In my opinion, a more moderate transition from an agrarian to an industrial nation might in the end have better served mankind's ultimate purpose—social justice and equality for everyone. Instead of heedlessly pursuing avaricious schemes for one's self-aggrandizement, perhaps these men advisedly might have been coaxed to work together with committees—committees formed of responsible men who would implement a slower system of growth, but in the end, would redound to the benefit of all. And of course a benevolent government would approve and regulate the activities involved. After all, John D. Rockefeller, an intrinsically benevolent man, not only taught Sunday school but at times served as a lowly janitor in his church, indicating an altruistic spirit. The same spirit can be found in the clear unpretentious writings of Andrew Carnegie. And power would ultimately devolve to the workers, the people, where it truly belongs."

A blooming Marxist. Power to the people, like hell. What would he say next? Like Johnny Alatalo in the parking lot of the Otter Lake Dance Hall listening in the moonlight to noises coming from a car, something had to be done. I'd heard enough. My irritation, my Dutch courage, reached a new height. I forgot about Abby. I barged into the auditorium.

"**Dummen! Dummen! Dummen!**" I shouted.

The veil of fog in my mind lifted. In my heightened perception I managed a quick glance at the offender. Still speaking, he stood before a chair near the front of the auditorium. A neatly attired young man, undistinguished in appearance and except for the wire-framed glasses he wore, one could have easily thought him to be a typical clean-cut conservative Three Oaks College student. The wire-framed glasses reminded me of the Trotsky-like accordionist from Ewen performing at the Otter Lake Dance Hall that Johnny Alatalo and I listened to years ago. What respectable conservative college boy would wear wire-framed glasses? Only Trotskyites wore those. While the accordionist reminded of being a rustic sort, this student lent an impression of being a polished young man of class, polish rubbed off on him while perhaps growing up in a wealthy, influential family.

Covering her mouth with her hand to suppress the sound, Abby emitted a muffled cry. A profound silence in the auditorium ensued. I proceeded to deliver a tirade but not before draining the contents of the well-laced coffee. The offending student I noticed shrunk bewilderedly into his seat.

"Humbug," I loudly declared. "Carnegie and Rockefeller politely sitting in on committees being advised by charlatans? Humbug.

"Pig iron and coke and open-hearth smelters. That's the best you can expect from a committee. Maybe they would have dragged in Henry Frick to cart in the coke. And no doubt glowing reports of significant progress being made would be issued by the media to befuddle an amazed public.

"I can see it now. Vulcan at his forge as in fabled times of yore. Nothing but praise for these illustrious visionaries who'd condescended to the whims of benevolent men who know what is best for everyone. In the meantime the nation would remain impoverished but sustained by a Pollyannaish hope the future would become brighter.

"Committees did you say? A committee at its best is taxed to untold limits to organize a Sunday school picnic."

During the heat of my rambling I did not notice the hall-monitoring young woman looking in on the noisily disrupted seminar and then slipping quietly away to alert campus security. Within minutes I faced two sturdy men who ordered me to stop the commotion. They demanded I accompany them at once. I neither gainsaid nor resisted their demands and readily obliged them. During the heat of my outburst I'd removed my topcoat. I'd tucked it under my arm, and as they escorted me out of the auditorium, my nearly depleted pint fell out of its pocket and shattered on a hard-tiled floor. Shards of glass glinted in a small puddle of vodka.

The campus security guards swiftly remanded me to the custody of local police, who promptly locked me up after I'd signed some routine paperwork. I would be the sole occupant of a jail cell where nothing but a bare mattress and a single threadbare blanket were provided for my comfort. The clammy mattress had the stench of urine, just like the one I slept on in a Los Angeles County jail. A clean town and a filthy jail—my impression of Three Oaks and its facilities for confining obstreperous drunkards. These strait-laced Midwesterners did not pamper bums.

The heady intoxication I'd experienced on my way to Ames Hall had completely vanished. Reduced to a drunken stupor, I'd practically lost awareness of my surroundings and how I'd arrived in such a place. It made no difference—the jail would be as good a spot as any to spend a night. But it would be a long siege. Still early in the evening I had at least fifteen solitary hours of fitful sleep and misery to look ahead to until I had any chance of being released. I dozed off immediately on the putrid mattress.

After a couple hours of numbed sleep, I began to have weird dreams. The revered patriarch I'd imagined earlier when I arrived in Three Oaks appeared as a cadaverous old man. "Who do you think you are, young man, to come here and defile our sanctuary?" he cackled. His teeth I noticed were rotted. Real people got into the nightmares. The entire student body present at the seminar appeared as malevolent imps. They gleefully jabbed at me with sticks as they cavorted about. "Don't think you had me fooled dressed up in your fancy suit," the hall monitor sniffed. Even the amiable Dutch farmers I'd imbibed with intruded to let me know what a worthless fellow I was. More torment, more nightmares followed, after which I finally plummeted into a deep slumber.

Early the next morning the clanging of metal jolted me back to reality as the jailer opened the cell door. Weak, restive, but clear of mind, and after a meager breakfast of burnt toast and stale coffee, the jailer escorted me to a small courtroom to stand before a local magistrate, a justice of the peace. Hopefully I'd only get a small fine.

The magistrate did not proceed to lecture me on bad habits, no doubt sparing moralizing admonitions for the possible benefit of younger neophyte derelicts. "You are charged with public intoxication, disturbing the peace and creating a noise and disturbance," he coldly declared. "How do you plead to these charges?"

"Guilty on two of the three counts, Your Honor. Would Your Honor please advise me on the difference between disturbing the peace and creating a noise and disturbance?"

There would be no getting out of this one. "How do you plead to these charges," the justice of the peace, in no mood for semantics, sternly repeated.

"Guilty as charged, Your Honor." Sparring with this magistrate, a dour, grayish, grim-faced old man would be futile. Not expecting leniency I awaited his judgment with resignation.

"Very well. You are fined a sum of seventy-five dollars on each charge for a total of two hundred and twenty-five dollars, payable forthwith. I am otherwise sentencing you to thirty days in jail in lieu of full payment, however short the portion of the fine imposed you cannot meet. This means if you're even one dollar short you go to jail."

My heart sunk. I'd barely left Hazelwood with that much money. I now had less than one hundred fifty dollars in my wallet, and in hope for an abatement of the fine, futilely related this circumstance to an unmoved magistrate. About to be taken back to the jail I heard a familiar voice from the rear of the small chamber.

I turned about to see Abby. In my apprehension during the proceedings I hadn't heard her enter the courtroom.

"Your Honor," she said, "if it's not too late may I please intervene on behalf of the defendant, Paul Maki?"

The justice of the peace frowned. "Professor Tulppo, perhaps we can speak in privacy for a few minutes."

Left under the guard of my jailer I waited apprehensively while the magistrate conferred with Abby in a side room. They returned in less than fifteen minutes.

"Mr. Maki, after considering your actions at Three Oaks College I'd imposed the maximum sentence on you as already stated. Were it within my province I would have imposed an even stiffer penalty. Your behavior at Ames Hall was incomprehensible and utterly disgraceful. Nonetheless, Professor Tulppo has convinced me of your intrinsically good character. You are indeed fortunate to have had the lifelong acquaintance of such a sterling person as Professor Tulppo. She has magnanimously offered to pay your fine in full, an offer I've accepted. I trust you have the means to travel to your home. It is my understanding you presently reside in St. Louis. Godspeed, young man."

"Paul, I have a request to ask of you," Abby said.

After she'd paid my fine and I'd recovered my car from the college parking lot we sat together talking in a coffee shop. I'd not yet returned to the motel to change my clammy clothes. I would need my room for at least one more day before leaving Three Oaks. Abby had taken the day off from her activities at the college.

"I can't begin to tell you how grateful I am to you. You bailed me out of a lot of trouble. I'll pay you for your inconvenience as soon as I get back to Hazelwood."

"Thank you, Paul, you can take your time if need be. But you owe my students and everyone concerned at Three Oaks an apology—in person. I will reschedule the seminar group to appear tomorrow afternoon in the Ames Hall auditorium. The entire body of students present at the seminar should be there to hear what you've got to say. I've also spoken with the receptionist at administration and she wishes you well. Before you apologize, if you choose to do so, I will make the students aware of how you came to be at the auditorium in the first place. This should clear matters a bit for everyone. I'll call you at your room to confirm the time. Right now you're not looking well and you stink. You'd best go back and get some rest."

"Thanks, Abby, I'll be there. Thanks for everything."

Greatly relieved and fatigued I returned to my room. Despite the realization I'd perpetrated such a mindless act I rested well. First I sent my urine-stenched best outfit to be worn once again at the auditorium to a two-hour drycleaning service.

Still very shaky but clear of mind I sat apprehensively before nearly a hundred history students in the main auditorium. Before Abby turned a microphone over to me I waited off to the side of the lector's dais while Abby briefly told the students of our growing up together in a small town and our subsequent friendship into adulthood. She did not mention we'd once been engaged to be married.

The words for an apology came easily. I did not need a rehearsal and my apprehensions vanished as I rose to speak.

"My name is Paul Maki and I'm a drunkard. Many of you no doubt wondered how a total stranger off the street would barge into this auditorium only to rant in a drunken state. Why would he want to come to Ames Hall to do this? Randomly picking Ames Hall and then go about eavesdropping outside the door before storming inside is utterly surreal and mind boggling. I intended to surprise Professor Tulppo with a visit but I let drink get the best of me.

"I first must thank Professor Tulppo for helping to clarify to you who I am. Even more, I thank her for giving me an opportunity to apologize to all of you for my unwelcome intrusion two days ago. She is most gracious in explaining how our friendship began in early childhood and continues to this day. Yes, she is my friend, and her actions in mitigating a mindless, stupid act on my part which could have turned out much worse for me proves more than anything else I am still a friend. I otherwise would not be standing before you.

"How I became a drunkard is not important to anyone but myself. What is most important to me now is that I may be forgiven for my crude actions. It is easy for me to say I'm sorry for the distress I caused you and I truly am sorry. What will not be easy for me will be having to live with shame.

"In particular I apologize to the student I so rudely interrupted. He is obviously an intelligent and a highly idealistic young man. While we may differ in opinion on weighty matters I trust we are both of an accord allowing each of us to respectfully disagree. And after sharing our views, however divergent, in the end we can still be friends.

"To every one of you here today I say you are in the right place for learning. Professor Tulppo is the most intelligent person I've ever known and I trust a most excellent mentor.

"I thank you for your forbearance and I sincerely wish you the best in life."

My ordeal over, short and sweet, I prepared to leave the auditorium. But I did not anticipate the response of the students. To a young man, to a young woman, they stood and loudly applauded. This is not what I'd expected. I'd anticipated polite applause at best and the very ones I'd affronted were cheering me.

Abby strode over to speak to me. "Thank you very much, Paul. That was magnificent."

Well-wishing students gathered about to offer words of encouragement and to shake my hand. Awed by their magnanimity I had to muster all my emotional strength to keep from weeping.

"I'll be pulling for you, Mr. Maki," were typical words of encouragement.

"I must say I'm almost glad it happened, even though it must be very painful for you, sir," another said. "It has helped open my eyes to the real world and problems good people can face."

The student I'd cut off with my diatribe approached me. Fidgeting about uncomfortably, and quite embarrassed, I had a difficult time looking him in the face. I noticed he also fidgeted uncomfortably. It would have been easy to avoid him by simply walking away from the milling crowd. I had to do something and do it right—noble posturing would not suffice. I offered my hand, which he accepted, and before I could verbalize a personal apology, he thanked me for the kind words I'd expressed for him.

"I count you as a friend," he added. "What you did today took courage."

We briefly discussed his career plans. Like Abby, he intended to become a teacher. I thanked him for his patience and understanding and wished him well before I left.

The winter storm finally ended after a gusty three-day blow. The major highways south to St. Louis were reported as clear. I had an extra day to spend in Three Oaks before I left, and with the better part of a hundred dollars in my wallet and my lodging expenses paid in full, I invited Abby out to dinner at one of the better restaurants in Three Oaks. She offered to foot the entire bill realizing my presently strained circumstances, an offer I adamantly refused. I had to talk to her to get some weighty matters off my mind.

I didn't just come to visit Abby. Although inspired during a big binge I'd come to Three Oaks with a hope we might repair our broken relationship. We'd get off to a fresh new start. Instead I spent a night in a stinking jail for disturbing the peace while drunk. If it hadn't been for her intervention with the magistrate I'd still be in jail. If I'd felt awkward with the student I'd offended I felt even more so as we sat to dine in a private booth.

I struggled to find words. I could only thank her some more for what she'd done on my behalf. Sensing my discomfort, Abby eased my apprehension by reminiscing on old times. There were no words of reproach from her such as "Why did you come here, Paul? How could you have done such a stupid thing?" Anyone else would have left me to rot in the Three Oaks jail.

"We should talk some more," she said after I paid the tab. "The evening is still early, we can talk at my apartment."

"I'm glad, there's a lot I've got to tell you," I replied.

Us good old Finnish coffee drinkers. We easily drank eight cups apiece of full strength regular as we exchanged life's stories long into the night. I poured out my experiences, achievements and failures, which had occurred in my life during the years since we'd last seen each other. She listened intently as I recounted my happy days in the conifers of Northern California working for Brickhouse Logging.

"I met a distant cousin in a Los Angeles County jail where we were both locked up for issues related to drunkenness. Drunk driving for me. He traced our roots back to a common great-great grandfather in Finland. After straightening out his drinking problem he got back together with his ex-wife and they remarried. Now he's a partner in the logging firm. Talk about success. He's talking about a family reunion in Finland some day. Wouldn't that be a great trip for his family?"

Her mood changed perceptibly. Abby appeared noticeably downcast and did not reply.

"What happened to your hand, your right hand?" she asked after long moments of awkward silence, noticing the scars on my fingers.

"I got into a fight. Self-defense, I had no choice." I related details of the fracas at the Grizzly Den.

I forged ahead, impelled. Memories of Marie Loonsfoot remained foremost—I had to get the entire business of what happened to Marie off my mind regardless of how painful it might be to Abby. She began to weep as I related the details of Marie's untimely death.

"I'm very sorry, Paul. I've been totally unaware of this and didn't hear anything about this until now," she said. "I'm beginning to understand—no, I fully understand how devastating Marie's death must have been to you—and it is also devastating to me."

A longer, more profound silence ensued. Now we were both

carrying a lot of baggage. Add what I'd just related to what Marie had told Abby at the restaurant years ago. A lot for Abby to handle. Under these circumstances a "fresh new start" would be out of the question. And here I was: a failure in my career, a drunk and practically a full-fledged bum.

I rose to depart. "Abby, I'll be leaving in the morning. I have a prospect for employment in Chicago. It's far different from aerospace engineering but at least it should keep me going for a while until I can get my life back in order." I did not mention my plans of giving up and dissipating my fortune on skid row. "Please feel sorry for me Abby, here's what I'm going to do." In the intensity of this emotional moment I inwardly renounced this vapid scheme, this utterly inane scheme, which had no rhyme or reason. Who knows? Would I become successful? Or would it be another false start in Chicago?

She wept uninhibitedly as we held each other in a long embrace. I'd never seen this gem of a woman so devastated, so completely broken. Words of comfort did not come easily; I could only repeat her name as I held her close.

"Paul, promise me to always let me know where you are and how I can contact you," she said after she recovered. I gave her my promise before leaving.

I departed Three Oaks early the next morning.

CHAPTER 16

The Great Western Casket Company

"Don't I know you from somewhere?" Donald Boltz asked.

I was batting three for three: First Marie Loonsfoot, then Rolfe Ellefson and now Donald Boltz, three attendees of the Moose Lake Bible Camp. I sat uneasily before Boltz, the plant manager of The Great Western Casket Company, as he interviewed me for a position at the company. If it were anyone else besides Boltz I would've remained apathetic. Shortly after I got back from Three Oaks, I got a call from Great Western confirming the date and time of my interview. I'd grown impatient with a lot of idle time on my hands and the call came opportunely. Boltz directed the production facilities of the entire complex.

"I guess you do. Paulie Maki back then. Do you remember the time we spent at the Moose Lake Bible Camp? That's got to be twenty years ago."

The Moose Lake Bible Camp. Cause and effect. It never failed to amaze me how different **lives** might have been if the chain of events had been otherwise. I most likely would not be sitting here at The Great Western Casket Company being interviewed by Donald Boltz hadn't I attended the bible camp years ago. No doubt Boltz's path would have remained in a straight line leading directly to Great Western whereas mine would have been entirely different. Too much had happened afterward as a direct result of those two weeks I'd spent at the Moose Lake Bible Camp. The people I'd met there, the consequences of subsequent meetings with Rolfe Ellefson and Marie Loonsfoot, were too significant in altering the course of my life.

Donald Boltz hadn't changed much with passing years. Swarthy, of a stocky build, I recognized him as being much the same in appearance when he'd given me a drubbing at Moose Lake while my friends stood by witnessing my humiliating defeat. Although somewhat portly he still looked fit and trim as I studied his stolid broad features. A glow of recognition came over his features. He obviously remembered the scuffle we'd got into as he appeared somewhat abashed.

"Let me tell you what Great Western is all about and where we're at," he said, recovering quickly.

"Our main product is coffins and we also make large shipping containers and smaller metal cans. The metal containers are primarily used as garbage cans. The shipping containers or drums are synthesized from wood fibers in an adhesive slurry and are used for shipping and stowage of dry goods. You know the type, circular containers with clamping rings for the lids. You see them everywhere, very common. Right now Great Western is doing reasonably well in this product line, especially with the metal cans. We got into shipping containers three years ago and we got off to a great start. But we're starting to slip and our competitors are gaining ground on us in sales of fiber drums. We've been turning out some faulty products and we're starting to hear a lot of complaints from our customers. Our stuff is not holding up; we're seeing a lot of swelling and dry rot. The problem wasn't evident at first. I think the main problem is in the fabrication process of the material and we've got to get a better handle on what's causing the problem. Also the clamping rings for the lids aren't working as well as they should. Some of the clamps become too loose after the drums have been opened a number of times. And that's not a big number. The clamps have got to stay tight. So we're looking for someone to get rid of the bugs, mainly someone who will get to understand binders or adhesives used for fabrication of the synthesized wood or paper if you want to call it that. We think the glue has a lot to do with the problems we're having. Someone who can come up with the right matrix so to speak to ensure a quality product. And in case you're wondering we're good with coffins," he chortled.

"Wouldn't this be a better fit for someone with a background, say in chemistry?" I asked.

"We've thought of that. But there's a lot more involved than the fabrication process—drop testing, durability, handling loads, making sure we sell an undamaged product. A lot of our stuff is falling apart. That's why we think a mechanical engineer would be a better fit for multitasking. We're not looking for an experienced guy as you might be wondering. This will be a "learn as you go" position and Great Western is willing to compromise on schedule if the end product meets expectations. After the problems we've had we don't expect an overnight fix. Also I'm letting you know the initial salary we're offering is modest. Pay increases of course will depend on perfecting the product and increased sales. And we've got to keep the customers we've got now."

Frowning, Boltz paused to scrutinize my resume.

"Bachelor's degree in mechanical engineering … three years total of aerospace experience … H'm," he muttered.

"Tell me, Maki, why are you leaving aerospace to look for a job with us?"

I had nothing to lose. I halfway expected the interview to end promptly. One way or the other what difference would it make? But I began to hope I'd get the job; Donald Boltz impressed me as being a man I could trust. I held nothing back.

"I got fired from both jobs, from a staff engineering position with Alameda Aerospace and as a contractual engineer with Phoenix Aeronautical Systems. Fired from both jobs for being a drunk who didn't show up for work half the time." To my relief the questionnaire form I'd received from Great Western stated nothing concerning an arrest record. Thankfully there would be no complications on that score.

Tapping a finger on the table where we sat, Boltz said nothing for a long while.

"I can supply references if you wish. References from the very people who are most aware of my problems and the very ones who let me go."

"What do you think, Maki, got everything under control?"

"Right now, yes. I won't make any promises but I'll give you work to the best of my ability. Regardless of anything else I've always done that."

"Tell you what, let me think this over and I'll get back to you one way or another shortly. I appreciate your honesty."

A week later I got a letter offering me a position as a quality control engineer. As I suspected a modest salary quoted amounted to less than two-thirds of what I'd received at Alameda Aerospace. No surprise there.

I accepted the offer from The Great Western Casket Company.

With Christmas less than a week off I'd be starting at Great Western shortly after the first of the New Year. Rather than leave for Chicago immediately I opted to remain in Hazelwood through the holidays where I'd be with people I knew. Not knowing anyone in Chicago did not seem as appealing as previously. After returning home from Three Oaks, I'd tempered my fatalistic view to be a bum. I found the strength to begin life anew in sobriety even though a renewal of a relationship with Abby did not transpire. At least she acted on my behalf before the magistrate when I needed her most. I'd make the best of it in Chicago on my own.

I wanted to be with friends. Going home to Centennial Heights to spend the holidays with my parents remained out of question—how could I face everyone in my home town having been fired a second time—too much for me to handle. Sober during my last visit I at least still prospered in my occupation. Having convinced them then I'd finally be a success, I could hear everyone now: "That Paulie Maki will always be a bum. Just when he gets his feet on the ground he lets himself and everyone around him down again." Not in the mood to face them even if no disparaging remarks were said to my face, sidelong glances would indicate what they were thinking. If anything, the paranoia invariably resulting from the excessive benders practically gave me a sixth sense in reading my detractors thoughts, sparing me perhaps from their carping criticisms. Paranoia, I'd come to believe, is not always bad.

I received a surprise visitor. "Who could this be, another magazine salesman? Since living in Hazelwood I'd turned away at least three salesmen trying to sell me a subscription to True, Argosy or some other such men's magazine still in vogue. It couldn't be Frank Ralls or Fred Mercer coming to see me so soon as we'd got together for lunch the previous day. In anticipation of having to disappoint another salesman I finally responded to the solicitor's importunate pounding.

In the doorway stood a man with rack of horsey teeth who would have done justice to any salesman or hustler. A well-groomed dark mustache and dark mischievous eyes darting about completed the image. A tongue-in-cheek voice made clucking sounds. It was no salesman but my longtime friend Aldo Vella. Or since he'd become an ordained priest, Father Aldo Vella.

I hadn't seen my good friend in several years and we hadn't otherwise communicated for some time. Now here he stood at my door in flesh and blood, as hale and robust as ever. He hadn't changed much appearance-wise, except slightly tinted gray strands of hair sprinkled throughout his abundant and well-groomed mane began to show. I would have at least expected to see a pot belly on a man living what I assumed to be a sedentary existence but he looked fit and trim. Maybe wrong about the sedentary life Aldo appeared as fit as a fiddle, to use an old cliché.

"Can you afford a weary sojourner a night's lodging, as unto Chaucer's pilgrims seeking refuge on their way to Canterbury? Or perhaps a week's stay?"

"Come on in, you educator of naïfs on the facts of life."

"You've had pretty rough go of it," Aldo said after he'd brought in his luggage and we'd made ourselves comfortable.

"You might say that. You're looking great, pal."

"Look, I talked with Abby and Rita. They said you could use some help and for what it's worth, here I am. But let's give that a rest. Tough go of it at Three Oaks, hey?"

Unbeknownst to me, Abby and Rita had both called Aldo shortly after my visit to Three Oaks. Abby had not glossed what happened there to Rita. Both women had impressed upon Aldo to see his way to Hazelwood, which he did not for a moment hesitate to do. It meant a short day's drive from Racine, Wisconsin where he resided and currently served as a parish priest. I thanked my good luck I hadn't departed for Chicago.

"Don't say "hey", the hay's in the barn with the cows and the horses. Football told me that once just before she sat on my face. Still it's good to hear it."

Aldo brought me up to date. My old rival Lucas Wagonhoffer and his beautiful wife Roxanna were prospering while their young daughter, following in her mother's footsteps, showed a strong interest in becoming a vocalist. Roxanna became the choir director at a church they attended in Lansing. Involved in veterinary science Lucas directed a team researching livestock disease and its treatment. At times as his parish schedule permitted Aldo continued his missionary outpost work in Central America. Forgoing a planned holiday visit with his parents in Centennial Heights, he remained in Hazelwood through Christmas.

"Let's go and get some dinner. On you of course," Aldo said.

I wanted my friends to meet Aldo. I gave them a call. What better place to go than Trixie's Lounge. There we met Frank Ralls, Fred Mercer and Adrian Parks and George and Dolly Haagejndas where we dined on some excellent open-faced steak sandwiches. Frank, Aldo, Fred and George enjoyed a couple beers while the women and I drank either sodas or coffee. Juliette Campeau accompanied Frank. Adrian again beamed with pleasure as Fred related they'd planned a spring wedding.

Aldo and I regaled everyone with accounts of the face sittings our gang had endured at the hands or more aptly the buttocks of Football and Rotten Mugga. They laughed boisterously when we recounted our personal sittings.

"Aldo claims those girls ruined his looks. That's the main reason he settled for the priesthood knowing he wouldn't stand a chance with the girls after what happened to him. Football sat on his face for a full minute."

"The priesthood?" Frank said. "I served as an altar boy once. My parents wanted to steer me into the priesthood before I got into trouble. I grew up in a town with lots of hardworking people. But New Kensington had a few troublemakers then, including me. A rough place to live twenty years ago."

I did not mention how Frank helped to establish peace in the neighborhood.

"I can't picture you as a troublemaker," Aldo said. Frank's gentlemanly demeanor, his persona, for long held sway above his imposing physical attributes, which might perhaps intimidate an unknowing stranger, and sometimes for uncertain newcomers even of the caliber as the keen, forever streetwise Father Aldo Vella. "I spent a couple years in a reform school for boys. Even afterward there were some bumps along the road and I wound up being a strong arm for some of the merchants in New Kensington. I wasn't too happy with that either. Now as I told Paul I'm trying to help doing the Lord's work."

Frank and Juliette had continued dating. Free from reservations of whether she had a place in my life I found comfort knowing things were going OK for her. Juliette appeared to be happy, secure in Frank's presence—an intimidating man to troublemakers—yet a most gentle person with whom one felt completely at ease. Were Juliette and Frank falling in love? One sensed an aura. They were serene, in harmony with each other. Their tranquil presence reminded me of Old Lady Mattila admiring Grandpa and Grandma Maki's wedding picture, the one showing both their faces composed and glowing serenely. Had I experienced this with Juliette? Had our love progressed to this level?

While envious I could not find it within me to be resentful of their happiness. I inwardly and sincerely wished them well.

"George, you've got to show Lord Cornwallis surrendering his sword to Father Aldo and Paul," Frank said.

"We're getting set up for Christmas," George Haagejndas replied. "All of you come to the soup kitchen this Saturday afternoon. After everyone is fed that'll be a good time to perform. Of course Dolly and the kids will be there as I'll need my son to help out with this one. I'll make sure everyone's invited that enjoys our brand of humor. I'm sure Father Aldo will too."

If Aldo had "come to help me" it certainly didn't entail gratuitous advice or reproach. We only had good times throughout his stay. My friends in St. Louis took a quick liking to this man of the cloth with his easygoing ways. At the soup kitchen Aldo volunteered to act the part of a British soldier. Except for the aria from *La Traviata* he'd sung in my dad's old barn when three teenagers got drunk on his father's wine, he revealed a musical talent he'd kept hidden under a bushel by adding his mellifluous tenor voice to "The World Turned Upside Down." This followed a brief closeted rehearsal. A cockaded hat disguised his well-groomed wavy dark hair and his mustache powdered to a lighter cast enhanced a look better to play the part of an Englishman.

In addition to making a good impression on my friends, Aldo fit right in with the cast. The denizens of the soup kitchen also took a quick liking to this man of the cloth. After the performances he spent hours in light-hearted conversation with them. Some related personal concerns to which Aldo lent a sympathetic ear.

"What do you make of it?" I asked Aldo the following evening.

We were seated in the kitchen of my apartment over coffee. We had the luxury of an evening to ourselves. We'd got on to theology. I'd just related Rolfe Ellefson's struggle with the existence of God, or more to the point, the reality of Jesus Christ. He'd also taken issue with the literalness of the scriptures. I related how Rolfe and I had become bible camp chums and how he'd later interceded for me in securing my engineering position at Alameda Aerospace.

Although Rolfe's theological concerns were those of a young adolescent and perhaps reflective of immaturity, I still found his views intriguing. And although I myself had given little thought on abstruse theological matters I'd become more piqued with what he'd told me as time passed—Jesus dying and staying dead. What twelve-year-old with the church upbringing, the faith we shared, would have the gall to believe that? "He died, He died," I could still hear him saying at the Moose Lake Bible Camp.

I got to hear Aldo's take on the subject.

"Do his arguments hold merit or are they merely questions a young person at odds with his faith might ask?"

Aldo did not reply at once. Like myself I assumed he'd taken his indoctrination in his Roman Catholic faith for granted as I did mine in our Protestant faith at the Emmaus Hall.

"Your friend Rolfe Ellefson is an interesting man. I'd like to meet him someday. He raises serious questions any sincere believer should ask. If you don't mind I'd like to put in my unwanted opinion."

"Go ahead, I'm listening."

"Let's start with the Bible."

This ought to be interesting I thought. Some of the kids and even some of the adults attending the Emmaus Hall claimed Catholics didn't even read the Bible. Some went so far as to say they didn't know anything about it. On the other hand, many church members I knew had their nose stuck in the Bible constantly. They believed in the inerrancy of the scriptures, word for word, and they claimed events occurred exactly as described. I'd never given much thought to this one way or the other.

"I believe many of the names and events chronicled in the Old Testament are historically accurate. King Saul, King David and Nebuchadnezzar for instance are substantiated historical figures. The Jewish captivity by the Babylonians is of course factual. But I neither endorse nor gainsay as literal events such as Joshua commanding the sun to stand still or men living to be over nine hundred years old. The list is lengthy: Balaam's ass—an animal that talked, Jonah swallowed by a whale and the fiery furnace. These stories and many others as well found in the Bible are in my belief mainly allegorical accounts and not necessarily exact physical descriptions of what truly happened.

"I find it much more credible to believe these scriptures were inspired to present truth symbolically in ways easily understood by the common man, as opposed to portraying incidents exactly as related. Skeptics might certainly find fault with assertions made by some claiming preternatural events occurred precisely as stated in the Bible.

But God did not give man a childish mind. He therefore left it to man to differentiate, to filter substance found in stylistic narrative and to apprehend on his own the workings of nature. That's why He gave him a brain. It's inconceivable for me to think of life without a challenge.

"Loyalty, honesty, integrity and justice—these are the qualities found in abundance in God's word. And mercy. I believe the most instructive lesson to be learned from a bible study is being able to distinguish between right from wrong. The lessons are invaluable—an implacable righteous God bringing his wrath upon the unjust wicked while rewarding the just. The end results of infidelity, licentiousness and deceit are clearly spelled out. God does not abide folly. Remember Esau selling his birthright for a mess of pottage? Nor does He intend for man to be confused and to lead a dissolute life. If the Bible merely ended with the Old Testament a clear blueprint is established for nations to forge governance based on truth, justice and integrity. But as your friend may have discovered in his search it does not end with this."

"Well, what is it?" I asked.

"Jesus Christ rose from the dead after being crucified on a cross. I believe in the empty tomb and His resurrection from death on the third day, literally and implicitly. His resurrection is the cornerstone of our Christian faith. Without this belief we have nothing and everything written in the New Testament would have long since paled and become commonplace. The evidence in support of this belief I hold to be true is overwhelming as attested by His disciples and others such as Mary Magdalene who witnessed our risen Savior. And against overwhelming odds in an age of political suppression and the subjugation of entire peoples by Rome His church not only survived but grew and flourished down through the centuries. A risen Jesus Christ someday returning to gather His own to eternal life in heaven is the one great hope for all mankind.

"Jesus Christ is real, His divinity is real and most importantly, His resurrection from the dead ensuring eternal life for repentant believers is real. Proclaiming good news is why I am a priest."

I kept the coffee pot going, a long-ingrained habit. We talked long into the evening getting on to topics such as why does God permit suffering. A very serious person and one who took matters of his faith very seriously, Aldo's extraction of substance from what he regarded as mainly allegorical accounts in the Bible made good sense.

We later sat in silence. Aldo appeared troubled; something bothered him. He seemed hesitant to talk further.

"By the way, Paulie, Abby told me what happened to your friend, Marie Loonsfoot. Care to talk about it? He finally asked me.

"Not really, it's something I'll have to work out on my own."

We spent Christmas day at the home of George and Dolly Haagejndas. Dolly had outdone herself in preparing a sumptuous turkey dinner, replete with an oyster dressing, mashed potatoes with a giblet gravy and a host of savory condiments. In addition to Aldo and myself, Frank Ralls and Fred Mercer were present along with Juliette and Adrian to participate in a joyous, fun celebration. By popular demand, father, son and daughter performed their acts. They'd come prepared. A large loaf of freshly baked whole wheat bread to be served later with dinner also served as Annie's prop in *Das Brot ist Gut.*

After dinner we sat around singing traditional Christmas carols, our mood quiet and serene. It reminded me of early childhood Christmas holiday seasons in Centennial Heights when we were at peace in our home despite the war raging in Europe and the Pacific. Father Aldo and George said prayers for everyone present and asked for God's blessings in their lives in the coming New Year. My friends expressed optimism the coming year would bring peace of mind and purpose to our lives, and despite strong reservations, I began to believe my own prospects held promise. This idyllic holiday season portended a promising future as had past periods in my life when everything went well. I'd forged new friendships in St. Louis as I had in the logging camp at Weaverville. Once again the future looked bright. I only had to stay sober.

I said a final goodbye to my friends. I would be leaving for Chicago in two days. Aldo left for Racine the following morning. Father Aldo Vella proved to be a good friend to have in time of difficulty.

Except for the junket to skid row with Boats Finerty I'd been to Chicago only once as a six-year-old. My mom and I travelled from Heights with my Uncle Kyle along with his wife, Dotty, and their daughter, Carolyn. We would be visiting two elderly aunts, Allie and Edla. One memory of that visit remains permanently locked in my mind: While sitting on a stoop in front of their northside apartment one warm afternoon two black teenagers passed by on the sidewalk. I'd never seen a black person before, not in real life.

"Have you ever seen a hippopotamus?" I asked.

They laughed good-naturedly. "Only in the zoo," one of them replied.

Being familiar with a pictorial geography primer for children, and assuming the young men were citizens of an African nation on a visit, I thought perhaps they'd seen the animal in the shallows of the Nile or the Limpopo.

"What are they doing in Chicago?" I wondered. I'll never forget the young black men and the hippopotamus.

It would be a fresh start; I knew no one in the city. My great-aunts Allie and Edla died years ago.

I did not go to skid row as planned. I did not say "I'm going to go to skid row anyway," despite being bailed out of an awaiting thirty-day stint in a stinking jail by Abby. After the rejuvenating Christmas holiday season with my friends in St. Louis, living on skid row as a bum would be utterly mindless. I'd been granted another chance. Instead I found comfortable room in a private home in a quiet neighborhood near South Halsted Street, not far from The Great Western Casket Company. My landlady, Mrs. Harding, an elderly widow provided board at a reasonable cost in addition to the room she'd furnished with a lounge chair, a desk and a reading lamp. An elderly gentleman nearing retirement by the name of Fritz Halder also boarded at her home. Fritz Halder worked as a bricklayer. Prince, Mrs. Harding's dog of a mixed breed, kept us company. A spacious back yard with several shade trees provided ample space for tossing sticks to Prince to retrieve and for outdoor relaxation in warm weather. We always looked ahead to outdoor grilled barbeques prepared by Fritz.

I promised Abby I would stay in contact with her. I wrote her a letter. In view of how matters stood when I left Three Oaks, I refrained from words intended to inspire a renewal of our relationship, which would, of course, resurrect an engagement to be married. We each had too much to sort out. I had no good reason to believe otherwise.

I sent her the money I owed her for paying my fine just as I would payment for a utility bill. I resisted an urge to be facetious: "Do you want me to come to be a guest lecturer at Ames Hall?"

She wrote few words in reply. She advised me to take care of myself and reminded me to keep her apprised of my whereabouts should she have need of contacting me. Other than that Abby told me she still cared for me very much.

I did not have a phone in my room. Instead I sent her my work phone number and the number of Great Western's main office.

She did not call me.

"Mahogany, these are our most expensive coffins," Donald Boltz said. "Some of the bulkheads are four inches thick, really could use eight pallbearers to lift these things at a funeral. We use oak and cherry for mid-priced caskets and for a more economical product we use pine."

I'd just started to work at Great Western. During my first day on the job Donald Boltz guided me on a tour through the entire facility. Although I would be employed at the subsidiary product line in the manufacture of shipping containers Boltz thought it best to show me the entire operation.

"We make several brands of caskets using various materials—metals, wood or a combination of both. At some time in the future we hope to be making caskets made of fiberglass."

We paused at a work area where caskets were being fabricated of wood having no metal parts, including screws, handles or pins.

"These wood coffins are built for Jewish burial," Boltz informed me. "Except for the upholstery everything must be made of wood including dowel pins and handles. Further, the adhesive must either be a resin-based glue or a flour or wheat derivative. The use of an animal glue is prohibited."

From there we proceeded to another plant where the coffins were of a bronze or a steel manufacture. We watched as welders fabricated the enclosures and then moved downstream to watch upholsterers pad the coffins with luxurious thick quilted linings before we moved on to the facility where I'd be engaged as the quality control engineer on the fiber shipping containers. The entire process of casket manufacture I found to be quite instructive.

"I'm going to be buried in a pine coffin when my time comes," I quipped. "A pine box. To save money for survivors I'm going to make sure that's stipulated in my last will and testament."

Donald Boltz responded with a loud horsey laugh, a laugh one would expect from a farmer.

"You might be wondering why Great Western got into shipping

containers," he said. "What with more and more people opting for cremation I guess you can judge for yourself how that'll eventually impact casket manufacture.

"Best to start with the raw materials," Boltz said as we stood outside the plant where the fiber shipping drums were being made. Metal containers were fabricated in a separate facility. "Basically the same wood processed into making paper," he added as we stood near piles of debarked logs.

"What is this wood? Looks like you've got a lot of spruce and balsam from the smell."

"We use a lot of balsam along with some other soft wood such as poplar and some pine and hemlock. Plenty of spruce too. This wood goes through a shredder and it's got to come out as thin shavings or flat strings if you prefer. The shavings can't be too coarse or too fine and neither too short nor too long. They are what give tensile and shear strength to the final laminates. If it's of a "dusty" texture it's no good. We keep a good backlog of this stuff to keep things moving. The shredder you're looking at is quite reliable but like any other machine it breaks down from time to time. We might get another one and hopefully we can keep the bugs out of the one we got, maybe eventually run both shredders at the same time if the demand increases. At least have some redundancy."

A loud whirring sound coming from the shredder, almost deafening, practically drowned out conversation. No surprise there considering the job it had to do—a nine-foot-long balsam trunk fed on a track into a hopper literally disappeared as it was chewed up by what appeared to be a large number of sharp blades mounted on a complex of rotors.

"Larger logs got be cut to shorter lengths and then split for a smooth operation. What you see coming out of the shredder is ready to be blended in a slurry consisting mostly of binders, or adhesives if you will, that are mixed in water along with stabilizers. The excess pulp shreddings are stored to maintain a backlog.

"Once the slurry is blended in vats it is heated and churned for at least six hours to cook off the water to become a viscous sludge. Then after it's cooled close to room temperature it's spread over a table before it hardens completely, and as you can see, guided through rollers forming sheets of prescribed thicknesses depending on the size of the drum we're making. Our standard drum is of a fifty-five-gallon capacity. The rolling process also adds a modest curvature after which the cooled sheets are cut to size and then baked to rid residual moisture.

This is a slow process, and as with concrete, a slow chemical process follows that ensures durable laminates.

"We'll take a quick look at several more operations to see how the drums are assembled. There's a lot of ground to cover for what may be considered a mundane product. You'll have time to familiarize yourself with the entire process. For now while there's a few hours left I'll introduce to our staff and the people you'll be working with and then get you situated."

I had a lot to learn. The plant operation, the paperwork and the formulas or recipes were indeed formidable, and not simply a matter of mixing a batch of ingredients to pass through a shredding and forming process. The abstruse chemistry itself required not only a substantial review of what I'd learned at Michigan Tech but demanded much more learning. At Hick's behest I'd taken courses in physical and organic chemistry as electives, which fortuitously, would help me now. What I'd considered to be a straight-forward procedure, a process no more difficult perhaps than cobbling orange crates, demanded all my ingenuity where I first arrived in a state of ignorance. Ironically, here I stood with no direct experience, responsible for the quality assurance of an entire product line. I contrasted this with my aerospace experience where at least I had an applicable educational background but functioned as only one of very many players involved on a very large project. But after all, I thought, a fifty-five-gallon fiber drum is not exactly a marvel of scientific and engineering achievement. "How could I have been so mistaken," I would soon discover.

I devoted most of my waking time to the project and worked many gratis hours during evenings and on weekends. While on the floor, I asked a lot of dumb questions if there is any such a thing as a dumb question. One of the more experienced hands, obviously testing me, asked me one afternoon how much of an adhesive blend needed to be added to the slurry to obtain the correct proportion of the constituent ingredients prior to heating the batch. Knowing the ingredients already in the vat I correctly determined the required addition by means of a simple algebraic expression. Reasonably impressed, he gave me a sidelong glance of approval.

Weeks and months sped by. The dry rot problem became obvious when swellings resembling large pustules appeared on the drums. A swelling resulted in a weakened drum and an eventual crumbling of the synthesized material, and it made no difference whether the drums were stowed in a low or high humidity environment. Perhaps locked-in pockets of moisture hadn't been expunged but this ultimately proved not to be the case. This seemingly simple problem, which eventuated into numerous complaints by customers, had the entire staff baffled as to how to go about implementing a fix. The circular drums, ideal for compact shipping of soft items such as clothing and blankets had to remain moisture proof, and as matters stood, the containers were not impervious to moisture. Long term storage resulted in mold even though desiccants or moisture absorbing substances were utilized as a preventative measure.

Life at The Great Western Casket Company challenged all my mental faculties. Slight modifications to the design of the clamping rings fixed the problem with loose lids. The dry rot problem remained unsolved. But long hours of hard work began to pay dividends.

"The problem with the fiber drums might be caused by a fungus," I told Donald Boltz. "I don't think there's anything wrong with the glue."

I'd accepted a dinner invitation to Boltz's residence where I met his wife Jane and their two children. Afterward we'd lit cigars and sat over coffee in a ventilated room Boltz referred to as his sanctuary. The room provided a comfortable space furnished with commodious lounge chairs. Shelves on the walls were lined with books and a pleasant warm glow cast from a small fireplace made for a relaxed setting.

"A fungus? How can this be possible after the heat treatment and the baking process the laminates have to go through? Are you sure? You'd think after the heat and baking, the wood would be immunized from fungus. We've done a lot already varying the processing times and temperatures during the cooking and baking. Quality control of the pulp has been rigorous—you've seen that once the bark is removed we discard the pulp showing any sign of wood rot or mold. Hell, we use the best sealant we can buy to waterproof the exterior surfaces of the drums. Still we see deterioration appearing like big ugly fat pimples."

"At this stage I'm really not too sure of anything but let me tell you what I've discovered. I at first dismissed the possibility of fungus. Perhaps others dismissed this possibility as well. But wood is wood and after some research I found out certain fungi can survive a wide temperature excursion, surviving even well outside the range of temperatures we impose to regulate our processes. I believe the baking process retards fungus growth to a large degree but does not stop the decay altogether. When wood rot occurs due to fungi, I discovered the pH does not stay constant but can vary quite a bit. What may start with an alkaline or high pH can turn acidic. During the past couple of months I've done some pH tests indicating fungal rot may be wiping out our containers. Had to be real patient since the changes are slow. Our fiber drums do not deteriorate overnight. And when you look at the failed sites on the containers through the naked eye the material color-wise doesn't look any different from the healthy stuff."

"What are you suggesting as a fix?"

"Here's what we ought to try. None of the pulp is treated before it goes into the shredder. It's only debarked and as you say the boles are inspected for wood rot or mold. We may want to try saturating the wood in a copper solution after it's shredded. I've done some research and there are some promising candidate solutions we may try to immunize the pulp against fungus. At first I thought let the boles soak in a solution and then let them dry; it's the same process applied for treating outdoor wood used for decks, railings or any structure exposed to the weather. But better yet treating the wood after it's shredded will be much faster and far more effective. A short soak to expedite the saturation of the shavings followed by a drying process will save a lot of time and money. What have we got to lose? It's what I believe will be one extra but low-cost step in the overall process."

"That's not a bad idea. We'll give it a shot. Keep me abreast on what's happening; I suspect it'll take some time to see if it works. It usually takes at least two months before the swelling begins to show and then the dry rot," Boltz replied.

Three months had elapsed since we treated the wood with a copper acetate solution. We were seated in a diner for soup and sandwiches after a long shift at Great Western.

"So far so good," I said to Donald Boltz. "It's been well over two months and so far there are no signs of swelling or dry rot on any drums. And that's from a batch of two hundred treated drums. Previously at least ten percent of the batch would be rejects or would be found defective by our customers. We'll have to wait some more and see if the treatment is really working."

"That's good news. I'd hate to lose good customers because of dry rot. Let's keep our fingers crossed until we have definitive results. In the meantime I'll reassure our customers we may have a fix. They've been quite happy with the unaffected containers. Good work, Paul."

Completely relaxed, optimistic, we made small talk.

"I thought you'd be a farmer," I said.

"That's what I wanted to be but my dad had other plans for me.

"You're going to college, son," he said. "If things don't work out for you in the business world you can always come back to the farm. Your older brother will handle the livestock and manage the farm operations. Right now we've got some good hired hands helping out. But for you it's going to be college.

"My father has a fairly large farm a few miles from Bloomer. We've got a large herd of Holsteins and a fair number of pigs. We've also got a couple forty-acre plots for growing corn. Two hundred forty acres altogether. Things have gone well enough without my presence."

I remembered the swampers he wore as we were leaving bible camp when I humbly looked down at his feet; I could easily envision him slopping pigs. And after the drubbing I got from him "manly and tough" Donald Boltz thoroughly vindicated Bloomer, Wisconsin as being a town of "tough guys." Certainly not a town of sissies I'd so rashly assumed as an adolescent.

"After four years at the University of Minnesota I picked up a degree in business administration. I may have already mentioned to you I took some math and engineering courses as electives. I got married while still in college. My wife and I were both members of a church we attended in Bloomer. We were both barely twenty-one at the time and it's been a good marriage. I can't complain. I got started at Great Western right out of school and have been here ever since."

We got on to the bible camp days.

"You remember the kid who used to splash around in the water, barking like a seal? Axel Gustafsson, or what did we call him, 'Widdle Weenie Wen Ben?'"

"I sure do," I said, "he kept everyone entertained on the piano."

"Well now he's a concert pianist. He gives recitals in Minneapolis and Milwaukee. Jane and I have gone to see him perform a couple times."

"Those were some fun times; I missed not being able to attend camp the following summer."

"By the way, what ever became of that pretty dark-haired girl from

Marquette, Marie something, I believe she had an Indian name. I kind of had my eye on her then but as I recall she favored you. I seem to remember another girl, an Abby I believe, who liked you too.

"None of them liked me," he added with a chuckle.

I did not reply at once. Noticing my downcast features Boltz asked, "What's wrong, Paul, indigestion perhaps?"

"Marie Loonsfoot was murdered."

I related the circumstances how I'd met her years later, omitting none of the details of the party at Humboldt and how Marie Loonsfoot and I had become intimately involved. Boltz listened intensely as I told of the trouble caused by Luke Garber and how he'd later murdered Marie in fit of rage.

We sat in silence for several long minutes. What could we say? I did not mention the guilt I still experienced might have been somehow responsible for her death. I'd tried long without much success to put the matter to rest.

Relieving the silence Boltz remembered Rolfe Ellefson. "You guys were mixed up in this Zoroaster business. I did some study on him in college and now you can ask me anything you want to about him.

"Another thing, I phoned Ellefson concerning your reference. Needless to say he backed up everything you told me about your work ethic and why Alameda had to let you go."

Donald Boltz, a man slow to lavish praise on anyone, did not expect praise himself from anyone for anything he'd done well. Something troubled his mind. He shuffled about humbly before we left the diner.

"Paul, I appreciate the work you've been doing for us," he simply told me.

A bar on almost every corner, a mecca of taverns clustered nearby to where I roomed on the south side of Chicago. For those seeking a neighborhood tavern ambiance one would have to search far to find an atmosphere as inviting as that which prevailed in any of the close-by taverns. One of the more popular places was Stosh's Old Times Tavern. Just like the place where I'd drank with the farmers outside of Three Oaks the patrons were fun-loving and sensible hardworking people. A haven for polka music, Stosh's of course, featured Frankie Yankovic along with many lesser known artists from the greater Chicago and Milwaukee area. Customers sometimes accompanied the jukebox by thumping a contraption on the floor. It stood handy in a corner for anyone wanting to give it a try. A rubber cap fitted a sturdy wooden rod, at least three feet long, on its business end. A couple of springs stretched between the rod and a large metal can attached to the rod, halfway up its length, made for a lively jingle as customers pounded the makeshift instrument on the floor to the rhythm of the music, while tapping the can with a drum stick. Giving the instrument a try I discovered with practically zero practice I easily kept time with a polka. I pictured Riisto Salmi alongside me rattling his bones in accompaniment. Good conversation could always be had with the hardworking patrons; there were housewives to be danced with and a jovial camaraderie always prevailed. Skulkers preying on the wives for sex were not welcomed at Stosh's Old Times Tavern. They were promptly given the heave-ho.

There we sat, Fritz Halder and I, at a table enjoying a pitcher of beer one Saturday afternoon. Stosh's, only two short blocks from where we roomed and boarded, had long become Fritz's favorite tavern and for a while it would also be mine. After almost a year of not touching a drop of anything with alcohol in it I joined Fritz at his invitation for a few mugs of beer at Stosh's. I did not hesitate to go along.

For I deserved to celebrate. I'd been given a hefty raise. Treating the shredded wood appeared to be a successful remedy to the swelling and decay problem based on early observations. Four months had elapsed without any sign of swelling or dry rot on any of the drums from a large batch, which had been fabricated with the treated shreddings.

"All we have to do now is wait to hear from our customers. I believe they'll be happy with the treated drums we delivered," Donald Boltz said.

"It's time to go home," Fritz said after our fourth mug of sparkling fresh beer off the tap. "Mrs. Harding will have dinner ready for us."

Fritz Halder maintained a limit of four beers regardless of the occasion. During subsequent visits to Stosh's Old Time Tavern I made it my limit as well. At least to start with.

I expanded my horizons. I sought new adventure. Fritz Halder showed no interest in touring the bars on West Madison Street so I went alone.

"That's not a good place to be. You've got nicer taverns here," he said. "Besides you can't beat the prices here and you're close to home."

I discovered the Foxhead Tavern where Boats Finerty and I spent a boot camp liberty still in business. As I entered I noted a freshly painted facade and that the windows had been recently washed. Due for a surprise, I began to believe I lived as a character in a Dickens novel—where informants or busybodies from the past would appear under improbable or inopportune circumstances—such as Trabb's boy in *Great Expectations,* for instance, popping up like a pest to harass Pip, the central character of the novel, but whose annoying actions ultimately conduced to Pip's betterment. In my case, in likewise protracted but more opportune situations, there were Rolfe Ellefson and Donald Boltz from the bible camp days appearing once again in my life. Seemingly by mere happenstance Patricia now emerged, one of the ladies who'd shared in the activities with her friend Marcy, Boats Finerty and me on our short one-day liberty from the Great Lakes Naval Training Center over twelve years ago. Though aged considerably she appeared to be still quite hale for a fiftyish woman. Instead of sitting at the bar Patricia stood behind it serving customers. I ordered a Pabst Blue Ribbon.

Patricia did not notice me and I pretended not to know her as she served my beer.

"What happened to Marcy?" I finally asked. "Your school teacher friend from Southern Illinois."

She stared at me long and hard. A faint glow of recognition came over her features.

"OK, sailor boy. I get it now even though it's been a long time. You've got a good memory and maybe I do too. As I recall you and your buddy were low on funds."

"Low on money is part of being in boot camp, Patricia," I pontificated. "On eighty bucks a month money is always scarce.

"I'm Paul," I added, extending an arm for a handshake.

"Thanks, Paul, for remembering my name after such a long time. Marcy had enough of Chicago. She went back to southern Illinois and is teaching school which she said she should have done in the first place when she got out of college. But Marcy's a very independent girl. Now she says teaching is an easier way of making a living than what she'd done earlier. She's probably right. She got her belly full of the profession she adopted up here on West Madison Street—said what she did for ten years caused her nothing but trouble. What brings you here after these many long years?"

"Curiosity. Nothing more than curiosity. The Foxhead brought back some good memories. Maybe just a bit of nostalgia."

Other than mentioning I had a new job in Chicago I spared her details of where I'd been and what I'd done in the intervening years.

"Well it's good to see you again. On the house," she added as she served me a Pabst Blue Ribbon after I'd already bought three bottles of the zesty beer. She ordered someone in a back room to roll in a fresh keg to tap.

"I'm now the owner of the Foxhead Tavern in case you're wondering. I've had it for seven years; bought it for a bargain. Like Marcy, have gone respectable."

"Thanks for the beer and congratulations on owning a business."

"Mostly blue-collar workers and there are still some old hillbilly friends of mine who come in occasionally. I'm getting along well enough."

The unpretentious but clean interior of the Foxhead Tavern signaled hospitality, enhanced by light-hearted conversation heard from a couple guys seated at a table A few patrons sat at the bar imbibing contentedly in silence. There were no loudmouths present. The old juke box I noticed occupied a convenient spot near the rear wall. I checked its selections—the recording Boats Finerty and I heard over and over nostalgically aroused my interest—the Foxhead must have had to replace that 45 RPM more than once—Sparkling Brown Eyes still remained popular with the Foxhead customers over the course of many years.

"There are a few transients who stop in. Most of these guys make just enough to get by on working as temps unloading trucks or hauling furniture to office buildings from warehouses. They live from hand to mouth and spend most of their money in joints up the street where prices are even lower than mine but enough of them come here. If they're hungry I keep a kettle of soup going in the kitchen. Sometimes we have a fish fry. Just for the regulars."

"Nice seeing you and it's great you're doing OK," I said as I rose to leave.

"Stop in again, Paul, and don't wait twelve years until you do," she replied.

"Listen, Paul, you're not going to be fired. The new fiber drums have shown no sign of dry rot after five months and Great Western's customers are pleased. You've saved us a product line and a lot of money," Donald Boltz told me in his office.

I'd got back into my old habit of missing work. At first I missed an occasional day as I'd done in the past and then didn't show up for two or three days or even a week due to excessive drinking, no longer content with four mugs of beer at one of the friendly neighborhood taverns with Fritz or a few brews at the Foxhead Tavern where I'd become a regular customer. I began to suffer bloating from beer as I had on previous occasions. I went back to liquor. Forsaking beer during forays to the numerous watering holes on West Madison Street, rum and cokes or straight up bourbon with water chasers became my potables of choice. I kept a bottle of bourbon at the side of my bed within easy reach for a quick night time snort.

"Come what may you're not going to be fired. If you need help working out your problem I'm here for you for what it's worth. Remember that," Boltz added.

My stay at Mrs. Harding's came to an end. Night after night I came home drunk in the early hours of the morning after spending the entire evening in the bars. I tried not disturb my elderly friends as I tiptoed cautiously to my room but nevertheless managed to stumble audibly in the hallway. One night I tripped over an expensive floor lamp, knocking it over. Luckily for me the lamp sustained little damage and I made good the repair. Once again the frequent bouts required lengthier time to overcome the effects of nerve-jangling hangovers. Sleep came about slowly until I finally dozed off into a tortuous stupor. I began having terrifying dreams. In one of the nightmares I started bawling loudly in my sleep like a mad bull, waking Mrs. Harding and Fritz Halder. When I kept it up Fritz rushed to my door. He solicitously asked if I needed help as I sat up dazed in a cold sweat. A nearly empty fifth of bourbon lay in the middle of the floor.

Mrs. Harding and Fritz Halder invited me to join them the next evening in the parlor. Both were concerned for my well-being. Both knew the cause of my problem. They said nothing about my missing work and coming home in the early hours of the morning after hitting the bars. I heard no words of remonstrance from either of them. Instead these kindly people only asked what they could do in the way of help. I'd roomed and boarded at Mrs. Harding's home for almost a year and she treated me like a son. The three of us had spent many quiet evenings together engaged in pleasant conversation or playing word games. Fritz was the champion at the scrabble board. Now they appeared awkward, at a loss for words. Even Prince always eager to chase a ball or a stick sensed our pensive mood and began to whine softly. I'd knocked over a lamp and I'd kept these good people awake by screaming in my sleep and probably worrying them sick due to the long hours I spent in the dives. Fritz told me the next morning I'd kept it up for a good ten minutes before he came in to see me. Moreover, I couldn't remember a thing about the nightmare.

"Paul, if you'd like, I can arrange for you to meet with Father Scalise. He's a very understanding man who's helped a lot of people with drinking problems. I can ask him to come here if that's alright with you," Mrs. Harding humbly ventured.

What would it hurt? While not enthusiastic, I nonetheless agreed to meet with Father Scalise, the parish priest of the church Mrs. Harding attended. At the invitation of Mrs. Harding, I'd attended services with her several times and had met him personally at a social hour following the Mass. A highly intelligent man, I found him to be a warm and engaging person; his easygoing mannerisms put everyone at ease as he related that as a son of Italian immigrants, he'd foregone an opportunity to become a member of his father's business to instead enter divinity school. I had no doubt Father Tullio Scalise would be an understanding person.

"There's no good reason why you and Fritz can't sit in with us," I told Mrs. Harding.

We met the following evening. Father Scalise made no attempt to probe the reasons for my excessive drinking. At ease, completely relaxed, I heard no discourse on theology or moral admonitions from Father Tullio; rather, he only offered words of encouragement to me. "Both Mrs. Harding and Fritz tell me you're a good person and I believe them. There's nothing wrong with you, you've got good health and from what I've come to know of you, intelligence. You've got too many brains to let liquor get the best of you. Please know I will help you in any way I can. You can come to see me anytime you wish. We're pulling for you."

The next morning I gave Mrs. Harding notice I would be leaving. I had no desire to inflict any more disturbance on these fine elderly people. Despite the well-meaning efforts of those trying to help me to kick my habit I'd had too many false starts and invariably wound up getting drunk again. The sprees were getting progressively worse; I had little reason to believe matters would improve. This time I had neither the desire nor the will to embark on what I believed would only be another failed attempt. Mrs. Harding and Fritz deserved a quiet peaceful life and should not have to play the role of nursemaid to a thirty-three-year-old drunk.

"I'll have to solve this problem on my own. I thank you for everything you've done for me and I'm going to miss both of you and Prince as well. Please tell Father Scalise I appreciate his words of encouragement very much."

"Paul, you'll be in my prayers. You can call here or stop for a visit anytime you wish," she told me before I retired to my room.

I relocated soon after I gave my notice to Mrs. Harding. I still had a week left on my room and board. Further she offered me a stay until I found a suitable arrangement elsewhere. This proved to be no problem. Patricia had a friend who owned a low-rent apartment building a short block away from Halsted and Madison, near to the heart of skid row. Patricia acted as her friend's agent for handling the rentals. Some of the tenants were patrons of the Foxhead Tavern.

I still had money, even more than what I had after my dismissal from Phoenix Aeronautical Systems. I'd skimped and saved my earnings. Besides I still had a job thanks to Donald Boltz. My new accommodation wasn't fancy but it had more than enough space for my needs. I had a phone put in and sent a short letter to Abby. The tenants weren't by any means exclusively skid row types; most units were occupied by blue collar workers trying to stretch a dollar. A couple of college students, a Wasserzieher and a Johnson, occupied a ground floor unit adjacent to my apartment. Both men were enrolled at a business school in the Loop. They were seniors and I'd come to know them casually at the Foxhead Tavern where they attended an occasional fish fry. Wasserzieher and Johnson seemed like decent fellows. Patricia had also intervened on their behalf when they rented their apartment.

I continued to miss more work. It got to the point where I showed up at Great Western only one or two days a week at the very most. Boltz faced a lot of pressure from his superiors to fire me.

"There's no way I'm going to fire a good man who saved us an entire product line," he firmly told the president of Great Western. "Unless you can defeat me at arm wrestling," he jested.

"I've got faith in Maki. He's proven to be an effective worker wherever he's been employed and I'm positive he can work out his drinking problem," he added.

The Great Western Casket Company settled the issue by giving me an indefinite leave of absence without pay.

"Play football, football player, play football."

This came from a man before me on the floor in a four-point stance. I'd just arrived at a skid row dive not far from the intersection of Halsted and West Madison Street. The man appeared to be of medium height. Judging from his loose-fitting trousers he'd lost weight. His rather strong-boned frame suggested at some time he'd been of a heftier physique. The arms I noticed were large but spare of muscle. He appeared to be an Oriental, perhaps of Japanese extraction, and as it transpired, I'd guessed correctly. A prominent jutting chin accentuated an almost flat face, slightly concave when seen in a profile view. A glimmer of intelligence showing in his eyes manifested itself in a wide smile revealing a perfect array of teeth. I wondered about this—most teeth I'd seen on skid row were either missing or badly in need of repair. He reminded me of a Japanese fighter pilot I'd recently read about in a book concerning Japanese aces of World War II. Lieutenant Commander Junichi Sasai flew a Zero and lost his life in aerial combat, shot down during the battle of Guadalcanal. Fresh in my mind from pictures of Sasai I'd seen in the book, the guy in the four-point stance looked just like him.

The man now went through motions of charging at opponents. "Play defense, play defense," he barked. He must have done this before, no doubt many times, as the other patrons in the dive drearily minding their own business paid but scant attention to his antics.

I easily imagined this man in the cockpit of a Zero smiling his wide smile as he looked out the paneled window. When he finished going through his motions I invited him to my table and bought him a beer.

A man of Japanese extraction who played football? He impressed me as someone trying put on a show, playacting to impress me, in a hope I'd buy him a drink. Highly unlikely this guy played football. He had to have *me* sized up as a football player. I'd never heard of an Oriental playing football. Yet that's exactly what he'd done; Keiichi Genda had starred as a running back for a high school squad in Beloit, Wisconsin. He had pictures and newspaper clippings showing a robust young teenager hoisted high on the shoulders of victorious teammates after winning their league championship—Keiichi Genda ran for three touchdowns in their climactic game and claimed he played both offense and defense during the contest.

"Keiichi," I ventured hesitantly, "how do you say a name that's got three vowels running with two "i's" in the middle?" I'd been tentative in addressing him after reading the clippings.

"Easy, it's pronounced 'Kī-**eech'**-ee.' There's no good American shortcut for this one. Everyone calls me Keiichi."

Keiichi Genda did not have to pretend simulating the four-point stance. Now like me he'd reconciled himself to bumming on skid row. An ex-football player and at present a bum? I'd never met an Oriental cast in either of these roles, but here I sat with one in a dive, both of us thoroughly at home in the gloomy premises. Despite the fact we'd both had quite a few brews we chatted for hours. I believed I found a good skid row companion to do some bumming with.

"What brought you to skid row?" I asked Keiichi Genda, whom I'd met a couple times afterward.

We crossed paths at an inexpensive restaurant on West Madison Street frequented by down-and-outers where one could get toast and eggs for forty cents and a cup of coffee for a dime. We were both sober and except for mild hangovers were in relatively good condition. I'd obviously seen him in prime spirits when he demonstrated his football maneuvers. As we began to talk I found him to be an articulate person and discovered he'd practiced dentistry.

"Gambling. Addictive gambling. I had a flourishing dental practice in Beloit for nine years. I have a wife and a son or I should say I did have as we've been separated now for four years. Never got divorced, though. Once I started gambling it got into my veins; I couldn't stop. I took some big losses and the gang of guys I played with were real pros of suspect occupation. I got suckered in and they let me win at first—they let me win comfortably for several sessions. Then slowly but surely I began to lose. Just when I thought I should quit altogether I found myself winning again. Went back and forth like this a few times until finally the roof fell in—on a winning streak and the stakes were high. We doubled and tripled the ante. In a fit of elation I bet everything I had—lock stock and barrel if you will—and lost it all.

"So here I am, a bum on skid row. I lost the house, and would you believe, my practice as well. Needless to say things deteriorated rapidly with my wife until we finally separated. She and my son are living with her parents today. I haven't seen or talked to my wife and son for over two years. I took up drinking to forget everything. I went on binges lasting for a month. As much as I hate to admit it now it's addictive drinking.

"That's my story, how about yours?"

Keiichi did not mention his upbringing. I found out later that along with his parents and a sister the family had been interned in a relocation camp for Japanese Americans during World War II. And at the very least the teeth were explained; a dentist had to have associates who knew what they were doing when it came to getting the best treatment. His admission to addictive drinking impressed me most of all. Very few I knew having a problem with alcohol would admit to it.

"Me? I belong here. My story is long. What do you say we go to the Foxhead just up the street? I could use a beer about now."

"I could use one too but let me warn you I'm a little low on cash."

Genda lived from hand to mouth as did many others on skid row loading and unloading trucks for a day or so at a time. I'd told him I had a job but had taken a leave of absence.

"Here's some money so it won't look like you're bumming," I told him, slipping him a five-dollar bill.

"Thanks, I'll make it up to you after my next job. But I've got no problem with the bumming. I've learned to gladly accept generosity," he laughed, "something unthinkable for me in the past."

After we'd walked several blocks from the restaurant to the Foxhead Tavern, Patricia served us each a Pabst Blue Ribbon.

"I've had a lot of good times and some bad in my drinking career. I've often thought I simply manufactured problems out of thin air. I've been called a big phony and a real bum by some who've claimed I only tried to prove to the world I could drink more than anyone else. There's a lot of truth to that, or at least I so thought during the early days of my drinking. And maybe I've read too many books glamorizing the careers of down-and-outers who'd reclaimed their lives after going through a purgatory on skid row. Would I find a superior wisdom on skid row not known elsewhere? Would skid row become a sanctuary where I would stay and live happily ever after? A college-boy engineer who becomes a big drunkard and goes to skid row to realize his fantasy? You don't hear about these. Most engineers I know lead stable family lives and have nice homes in the suburbs. They manicure lawns or fool around with bicycles in their spare time. That's not for me. At times I thought I'd let myself be one big experiment; you know, I can quit anytime I want to stop drinking. I'd even made plans to come here to be a bum before I wound up on skid row almost by default. Skid row is where a bum belongs."

I spared Genda the confession of unworthiness I'd made to Abby. I wasn't about to tell him I started bawling after I gave that no-good lout a drubbing at the Laurium dump. I think he would've disavowed our very brief albeit prospering friendship or maybe even given me a swift kick in the prat if I whined about the ROTC. About to relate my experiences at Alameda and Phoenix and how I'd come to Chicago, he cut me off.

"One big experiment—making plans to come to skid row and be a bum—cut out the bullshit," Genda interrupted. "That sounds hollow. Come up for some air. You've still got a job, haven't you; you can go back there anytime. Your coming to skid row doesn't make any sense at all—you're not going to find any wisdom here. You're an enigma."

Perhaps I'd been handed the wisdom I sought on skid row although I didn't realize it then.

"There's a lot more to my story if you care to listen. Not everything is cut and dried."

"Go ahead, I've got lots of time to spare. I've listened to a lot of stories from guys on this street pretty much along the same lines as my own. But yours sounds different. I don't quite understand you. What you're doing is suicidal."

Patricia kept the beer coming as I related how I'd come to be fired from two lucrative engineering positions. I would wait until the afternoon before I started on rum and cokes. I had no worries of being arrested for drunk driving as I'd taken the precaution of putting my car in a storage facility for safekeeping. Living near the heart of skid row the bars were within easy walking distance. Public transportation sufficed for other needs.

"Well here's something I understand quite well. I love to drink. The euphoria makes it worth the many defeats I've suffered. Sounds crazy doesn't it?"

I went on to relate an incident in my life I hadn't told anyone previously. In my early childhood years my dad occasionally reminded me of the incident though I don't know why, and although only three years old when it happened, I still remember it quite well this very day.

"Both my parents enjoyed their beer for several years after they were married. They quit drinking because of their faith in God, believing what they were doing displeased Him. Getting drunk made their married life difficult trying to make ends meet. They were playing cards—four of them—both my parents and my dad's cousin and her husband. They'd tapped a small keg of beer, a pony keg almost eight gallons. If you can imagine a three-year-old chap barely out of his diapers stumbling happily about the kitchen table after drinking three small glasses of beer, you've got me pegged. I loved its tangy bitterness—that beer tasted much better than any soda pop or cocoa I'd ever had. And I cannot recall a having a hangover the next morning. And me just a three-year-old kid."

Genda remained silent for a long moment, deep in thought, after which his mood lightened appreciably.

"Show off your German and discuss chemistry? You mentioned something when we met in that dive that's all you and your college buddies ever did on your outings. Talk college? Discuss the valence of metals? If that's all I had to do I'd have become a big drunk myself. It wouldn't have taken huge gambling losses," he chuckled. "What kind of college did you attend anyway?"

"Twenty guys to every girl limited our choices. There's something else I haven't told you." I'd not mentioned to him my broken engagement with Abby and my brief but torrid affair with Marie Loonsfoot and her subsequent murder. I omitted none of the details.

"It would weigh heavily if that happened to me," he finally said. "I don't really know how I'd handle it and I can't speak for you. But if you want my opinion her murder wasn't your fault. And I can appreciate the fact it's still bothering you a lot.

"As far as I'm concerned her murder makes the most sense to me why you drink so much," he added.

"You've got to remember I'd already become a big drunk before I even met Marie."

"Are you sure you've settled everything with Abby? And I see no reason why you can't go back into aerospace engineering."

I let the matter drop. Keiichi Genda had nothing more to offer in the way of reproach or advice. We continued to imbibe well into the afternoon.

In addition to being a good drinking buddy I found Genda an interesting man. We enjoyed many stimulating conversations, in one of which he related his experience in the relocation camp. Not happy, he bitterly explained to me how interred Japanese Americans were mistreated by the government after evincing a demonstrable proof of loyalty by most to the USA. Until I met Keiichi, as many Americans, I'd been poorly informed of the unquestionable loyalty of the "Nisei" who'd volunteered for service and fought bravely as US soldiers in Europe.

"The Japanese soldiers of the 442nd Division are the most decorated infantry regiment in the history of the US army," he flatly proclaimed.

We continued making the rounds of skid row bars on an almost daily basis. One day we got on a bus to check out the dives on South State Street. Most of the patrons appeared to be complete down-and-outers with no place to go except the soup line. Many of them appeared to have totally given up on getting out of their ruts. A lot of good men, however, reclaimed their lives through the outreach of the Pacific Garden Mission or "The Old Lighthouse," purposed to win conversions for the homeless they sheltered on their premises to become born again Christians. Bums showing up the first time for a meal were afterward obliged to listen to a sermon.

Keiichi and I took in a service at the mission after making a round of several bars on South State Street. I noticed a picture on a wall of Billy Sunday, a professional baseball player turned evangelist, who attributed his conversion as a Christian to the Pacific Garden Mission. Approached by staff members following an evening service we politely listened to their exhortations to us to make things right with God.

"I'm already alright with God," Keiichi told them, "I'm just not right with myself."

Before we left, I happily surprised the staff members by putting a ten-dollar bill in the collection plate. I've always believed contributing to a worthy cause is most pleasing to God. Money is ofttimes better than admonitions to be good.

"How about it, Keiichi, have you given any thought of getting out of this rut?" I asked him one day at the Foxhead Tavern.

"Every day," he replied, "but I don't see how I can do it."

"Listen, pal, you dug a deep hole for yourself but the cause of your being here is at least easy to pinpoint. So you lost everything to addictive gambling and then you became a drunkard. You can go back to your profession just as you said I can go back to engineering. Here's what. There's a clinic further west on Madison Street advertising a need for professional help including doctors, dentists and nurses. It's on a volunteer basis."

Keiichi remained silent except to say, "I'm not ready for anything like that."

"At least think about it. Maybe set up a five-year plan, alternate your schedule between the clinic and unloading trucks. Just a thought, Keiichi. If nothing else I owe you some advice after you told me to come up for some air. I'm not ready to go back to engineering either. Life on skid row for me isn't by any means bad."

I've always feared being broke. Although I still had eight thousand dollars in my possession I could see my savings rapidly eroding. I finally took precaution of transferring five thousand dollars to a bank in the Keweenaw where it would remain untouched, except I made provision to allow my parents access to the money should they ever have need, a slim possibility since they'd managed their savings well. Further I took an additional measure of not opening a checking account. The five thousand dollars would remain safe.

I began to see less of Keiichi. After initial reservations he gave the clinic a try. He did not need to be certified as a dentist in Illinois largely due to his status as a volunteer dentist receiving no payment for his services. His credentials in Beloit were verified, however, and although he'd lost his practice there, he'd not been disbarred from a future practice.

He initially found it a tough go; he resumed his binging after several false starts at sobriety. But eventually he quit his drinking altogether and he became a valued practitioner at the clinic.

"I'm making my agenda a four-year plan," he told me one morning at breakfast. "If I can hold things together I might once again be practicing as a fulltime dentist. I've also started going to Alcoholics Anonymous meetings. Those attending have helped me a lot to stay sober. You might try AA yourself."

"Alcoholics Anonymous meetings? I don't need AA meetings."

I managed to avoid trouble as my life on skid row matured. To avoid being conspicuous I dressed shabbily, and except for the Foxhead Tavern where most of the clientele had steady jobs, I didn't spend too much money in any one place. I very grudgingly dispensed charity to panhandlers and most of the time turned them down. To the denizens on skid row I was just another down-and-outer broke most of the time like them. I even took an occasional job unloading trucks to fit in better.

Donald Boltz called me periodically. "Do whatever you have to do to lick your problem," he'd advise. "Just remember your job is still here for you when the time comes. Want to let you know everything is fine at the shipping container plant. We've increased fiber drum sales thirty percent in the last quarter alone. Pulling for you, old bible camp buddy."

Operations may have been proceeding well at The Great Western Casket Company but matters were going rapidly downhill for me. "You'd better slow down, Paul," Keiichi told me, "or you'll wind up needing one of those caskets yourself."

I began drinking more and more and eating less and less. I'd lost weight. "Paul, you'd better eat more," Patricia said. "Help yourself to some soup at least. You're starting to look skinny."

So what. My trousers, no longer fitting trimly, hung apologetically down from my diminished waist and bloatless belly. The seat bagged low forming a big pouch that blossomed into a classic Chicago Drape. I thus had no problems identifying with the spare denizens of skid row. I wisely spent most of my time, however, at the Foxhead Tavern where I'd come to know some of the customers instead of barhopping the numerous dives on West Madison Street. I missed Keiichi's presence as a drinking buddy to roam some more on skid row; he'd become seriously involved in the AA program.

I felt safe at the Foxhead. If I had too much to drink Patricia had a room in back with a cot where I could sleep it off. Sometimes I spent an entire night there and awoke to imbibe afresh after hearing the hubbub at the bar opened for morning business. Life on skid row could not have been better.

Almost a whole case of whiskey—all bourbon—I kept it simple. That's what I had; the bottles were neatly arrayed on a shelf in my pantry. Just one bottle short of a whole case is nothing to look down on, and remaining true to my philosophy of never being caught short, I made sure I kept my larder well provisioned. Just like the St. John's Day celebrants at the Otter Lake Dance Hall whose apprehensions were put to rest only when wholesalers hauled in a truckload of Bosch and Stroh's beer—not just enough for one night of drinking but an excess to last for days. Each evening as I returned home from the Foxhead I stopped at a liquor store to buy a fifth or two just for good measure. My hoard accumulated. My detractors used to criticize me for being a hoarder but they always rejoiced when I produced a flask just when everyone thought we'd run dry.

Now there were eleven fifths of bourbon in the pantry with no rotgut blemishing the shelf. I complacently viewed my stash of some top shelf potables and a bulk of decent-grade bar whiskey. A bottle would always be kept open for present needs whether at midday or midnight.

Perfectly content, I swilled a couple belts followed by some pickled herring or Slim Jims before I left to join the hubbub at the Foxhead Tavern for a few hours of gabbing. Maybe grab a sandwich there before going back to my apartment to work some more on my whiskey. I had no apprehension of running dry with such a substantial larder. I tried some beer. The beer didn't do me any good. I had a case on hand and after drinking a few bottles one morning, I got an uncomfortable bloat and a lot of gas. I should have known better—I let the beer sit. Undiluted whiskey sustained my inebriated euphoria much more effectively. One day of heavy imbibing followed another.

"Why go to the Foxhead today?" I asked myself late one morning upon arising from a good night's sleep. "I'll stay home for a change and mull things over. I'll finally get matters organized and straightened out for the last time. I've still got a job; I'll give Donald Boltz a call soon and I've got plenty of money—should last me for a quite a long while if I play it safe. How long should I stay on skid row now that my chum Keiichi had joined the AA? But hadn't I found skid row a home, the place I always wanted to be? Major decisions could wait. First I'll have a drink."

A gourmand about to sample some truffles could not have experienced greater pleasure than I as I poured a liberal double shot into a water glass. I sniffed the heady contents glowing warmly in the late morning filtered sunlight—I'd drawn the curtains. No ice cubes, straight up with a little water chaser— liquid amber to be sure—the usual sting in the gullet as I tossed down the first drink of the day. I sat back and groaned contentedly as the high-voltage liquor pervaded my head. One quaff followed another, absent the sting.

There's no need to go anywhere, solitude is just what I need. Just me by myself in my apartment. What could be more sensible than spending a day or two in salubrious reverie with ample potables on hand? There's nothing to worry about. I should be a new man after some well-deserved relaxation. Then I'll call Donald Boltz.

However no major decisions were made. Bottle after bottle disappeared as my days idyllically passed in a drunken reverie. Quitting my daily junkets to the Foxhead altogether I continued to drink entirely at home. Day and night, it made no difference; time came to be nothing.

I ventured outside my apartment only to gawk around for a bit and to check on my car in the parking lot until I remembered I had it in storage. I picked up a copy of *The Kalevala* I'd had in my possession for some time. The life of a mystical society evolving in Finland during an early millennial age evoked waves of nostalgia as I turned its pages during half-lucid intervals. I read prosaic tales of butter churns, hand-turned stones for milling flour, fields of grain and saunas. Butter churns and especially saunas are still widely extant in the Keweenaw farm country.

Except for assignments in a college literature course I'd taken as an elective I'd read from *The Kalevala* only with passing interest. Now in my drunken euphoria I found the classic fascinating. I thought of Abby and how she would thrive as my wife in a log cabin existence in early Finland. Had we lived then would Abby, a hen under my arm, be obedient unto her husband?

The Kalevala provides clear instructions to husbands for disciplining froward helpmeets. Men in the land of the ancient Fenni did not tolerate dereliction of wifely duty. I'd learned this region includes the Karelia, much of present-day Finland and parts of the Baltic States. The Fenni are described as a savage, primitive lot. While the men did mostly as they pleased the women had a lot to do. Floors had to be swept, sauna wood split, the yard kept clean and a cauldron of hearty stew always kept heated on the stove. A list of chores seemed endless. There were buns to be sliced, loaves to be kneaded, hens' eggs to be looked for and cows to be milked and fed. However, measures of discipline were lenient; usually a word or two of reprimand or even a wink proved sufficient for a stubbornly errant wife to correct her ways and properly assume her wifely responsibilities. But if a wife persisted in her insubordination she swiftly found it unprofitable as more drastic means of chastening were then applied. Shoulders had to be warmed and buttocks softened without creating a neighborhood disturbance. The log cabin—well chinked with moss—provided for an ideal acoustical scheme preventing noises emanating within from being heard by gossipy neighbor women snooping about outside the dwelling. Men were warned, however, against putting a lump on an eyebrow. A blueberry over the eye would cause untold gossip amongst the women in the village.

The Kalevala became a boon companion as I read on with a bottle always at my side. Exploits of fabulous characters performing feats of magic in the land of my forbears fit right in with my euphoric mood. There were fish, magpies and trees that talked. Boats were "sung" into existence. There were conniving old hags. And how about the Farmind, the roistering Lemminkainen, the envy of Finnish school boys? The wanton Lemminkainen not only reveled with just one or two or even a dozen but with hundreds of braided-head lasses and potbellied frumps, Old Harry's waddlers, on a remote island for three refreshing summers. "Old Harry" is another name for the devil. Beer and honeyed mead flowed copiously.

Very late one night while thoroughly drunk I phoned Erma Jamison. It had to be well past midnight her time. Happily she answered and did not hang up. In my drunken ebullience I hazily remembered enough of our conversation. Still employed at the same company she'd received a promotion as the leader of a larger group of technicians. Still unmarried, she mentioned the supervisor who'd interrupted our proceedings in her apartment over two years ago had become a close friend but would only remain as a friend. She had no plans of marrying a second time.

During the course of our conversation I felt an urge to sing. People always said I sounded like Ernest Tubb. I must have awakened everyone in the building, at least my immediate neighbors, as I bawled "Waltz Across Texas" to Erma in a loud drunken voice over the phone. I heard the college boys in the adjacent unit stirring about and muttering to themselves.

Although in a drunken fog my days passed contentedly. I continued to drink without restraint. Food had practically become nonessential: the few Slim Jims and some pickled fish were enough to sustain my needs. After a week I took an inventory. My larder had diminished appreciably; now there were only two fifths of bourbon left. Still enough for another day or two.

In the daylight hours of my drunken reverie important matters occupied my mind when not reading from *The Kalevala*. Heady thoughts of rotting wood in fifty-five-gallon barrels and a baboosha thumping on the floor rummaged through my mind. "The noods of nump," Walt Kelly of *Pogo* fame would call rambling thoughts. Throughout the drunken siege in my books the bourbon seemed a help and not a hindrance.

I took notes on weighty matters as I went along. A *baboosha*—that's what Stosh called his contraption. I planned to make a baboosha and for sure would join Riisto Salmi someday at the North Country Tavern in providing extra rhythm to lively polkas. I'd made some crude sketches and jotted dimensions of how I would construct the instrument, what kind of wood I would use for the pole and whether the can would be of a cylindrical or of a box shape. Mine would be the Stradivarius of babooshas.

"There's no reason why I can't help the Great Western Company from home," I thought smugly as I scribbled voluminous notes on the pH of rotting wood. "Free of charge."

"Well, might as well finish these and see what happens next," I grumbled early one morning. There would be no gratis scribblings on rotting wood today. Tossing and turning throughout the night I had not sleep well and awoke in a shaky and an uneasy mood. Drinking without restraint during previous days I'd slept soundly each night. What happened? I poured a stiff drink from one of the remaining bottles. The whiskey tasted like water—no kick at all. The alcohol lacked its desired effect—no longer did I experience the complacency, the euphoria I'd come to expect after a quick bracer or two. "Maybe if I have a few more shots I'll feel better." But nothing seemed to work; the bourbon still failed to produce its desired effect. By mid-afternoon I polished off the first fifth and had progressed well into the second, the last remaining bottle of my stash. By late evening I'd nearly drained the second fifth. Almost two fifths of whiskey and I still didn't feel any better. Two fifths of ninety proof whiskey in one day? Any other time I would have been passed out, stone-cold drunk. Maybe even dead. Not this time. I felt more sober than I'd ever been as the day wore on. The whiskey did nothing to make me feel better, but only enhanced a profoundly sober frame of mind, as though I'd nothing to drink and were occupied in morbid contemplation over some abstruse matter.

The accustomed euphoric mood—gone. Toward evening I began

to feel fearfully apprehensive. I found the right word —mokus, that's it—the bourbon produced no intoxicating effect whatsoever. It seemed practically tasteless as I took a few last swills. This had never happened to me before. Had a malevolent imp crept into my pantry and somehow watered down my whiskey? Spiked my whiskey with water?

My restiveness worsened as the evening progressed. My pleasant dream world had become ordinary and the surroundings inside my already drab apartment became even more depressing in consonance with an increasingly morose mood. An inner voice kept telling me something had gone wrong. Very wrong. I tried to keep my mind off things, of how I'd permitted this foolishness to happen, but to no avail.

Another night of fitful sleep followed. Never to be caught short? What should I do? Caught short, dismayed, I surveyed the empty shelf. Almost a whole case of whiskey gone, the entire stock depleted except for some minor dregs in the last fifth of bourbon. Forget the beer. Too apprehensive just now to shuffle out to the liquor store and buy some more whiskey, I'll first wait a while and hope my high-wired nerves will settle. Then I'll go out and buy some more whiskey—I had plenty of money to spare. Most drunks I knew wouldn't quit until they spent every dime they had regardless of consequences. With the money I've got I could drink to my heart's content and still be solvent. Some more bourbon, then, should cure my apprehensiveness and I could push my luck a bit further with The Great Western Casket Company.

But the nerves did not settle and I'd only become more nervous and apprehensive. Like a child reluctant to venture outside his home during darkness, I'd become fearful. I jumped at the slightest noise, whether it was the creaking of floor timbers or a neighbor slamming shut a door. At any other time replenishing my supply of liquor would be the sensible thing to do to cure this suffering. But now with my strength depleted and nerves shot I decided in my misery to wait a bit longer and see if I felt any better. To pass time I attempted to read some more from *The Kalevala.* Tuonela, the land of the dead, meant death for anyone happening to venture there. First defeat and then death. The gloomy passages added to my bleakness as I rummaged through the classic.

Things just weren't right; this became a worsening realization. Mokus. Ninety proof whiskey tasting like water. No taste at all. Morbidly sober, profoundly depressed and experiencing a growing sense of gnawing fear, my inner voice kept telling me I had to quit this bender without any more liquor. I had to recover from this one cold turkey. I stayed holed up in my apartment the entire day not eating anything at all without a drop to drink. No trip to the liquor store, no more whiskey, the inner voice won.

I endured still another sleepless night. Going on two days without a drink and without a bite to eat I arose from my bed where I'd tossed and turned the whole night, shakier than ever, my nerves strained and taut and my body thoroughly defeated. I had no appetite for food at all. I milled about the apartment aimlessly unable to focus on anything except my misery. "Why did this have to happen," I mewled. I reviewed the notes I'd taken in an attempt of further clarifying data obtained from the pH tests of the fungus but I could not concentrate. I put the notes aside (a subsequent look at the notes I'd taken of the fungus while inebriated showed my appraisals to be quite accurate). I could not focus while trying to read some more from *The Kalevala.* In gloom and in squalor—I'd neither bathed nor cleaned my premises in two weeks—I felt like a rat trapped in a cage. Vague fears worsened as the day wore on. Time dragged on—something had to be done. Maybe a long walk would help to get rid of the shakes.

Well into the afternoon I walked for many long blocks away from West Madison Street through a respectable neighborhood. I began to experience a keen paranoia; faces I encountered in the neighborhood yards and on the sidewalks appeared as grotesque leering masks. A basketball escaped its court and bounced on the sidewalk directly in front of me. My tightly jangled nerves wired to react instantly to the slightest threat, I jumped nearly three feet in the air much to the glee of children frolicking on a nearby playground.

In a sweat I continued back to the Foxhead Tavern.

"Paul, what's wrong?" Patricia solicitously asked. "You look like you've seen a ghost."

"Patricia, may I please have a seven-up?" I whimpered in a quavering voice.

"Is there anything I can do for you? I've never seen you like this before."

"No, I must be leaving. I'll be alright after some rest."

"At least have some soup before you go."

I declined her offer and left for my apartment.

I avoided the curious looks of my college-boy neighbors standing outside the apartment building. They must have just got home from school. They appeared to be grinning at me as though reading my innermost thoughts as I slunk furtively like a thief into the building. Apprehensions worsened as I tried to settle into my drab apartment. Time dragged by painfully, almost it seemed coming to a halt. "*Schicksal, nehmen deinen Lauf*," I ruminated morbidly, or "Fate, take thy course." Defeated, at a total loss what to do, my nerves strained tautly, and though early in the evening I went to bed.

I tossed about fitfully. Rest would not come.

CHAPTER 17

Hell

"**Oddball!** Waltz across Texas. **Oddball!** Look at me with the stars in your eyes," I heard a voice mimicking Ernest Tubb's song. "**Rowr-rowr-rowr, ba-a-a-a-h-h-bah,"** a second voice bawled loudly. "**Oddball!** My world's in disguise," the first voice continued. The sound came through a bulkhead common to my neighbors' bathroom and my own.

On and on it went. Here I was, seated on the toilet in a morbid state of mind. The walk did nothing to alleviate the shakes and my paranoia only worsened. The college boys on the other side of the bulkhead surely had something sinister up their sleeves. What could this possibly be about? The two voices boomed unabatedly through the wall into my privacy as though some devils had come to haunt me. "Oddball! Waltz across Texas, **ba-a-a-a-h-h-bah.**"

It finally came to me. Hadn't I sung Waltz Across Texas to Erma Jamison in a loud voice maybe two evenings ago? Hadn't I heard my neighbors moving about then, muttering to themselves but not complaining loudly? I lost count of days during my bender but I'd without doubt sung to Erma. So now my college-boy neighbors were getting even. They'd waited for an opportune moment. They must have sensed my disquiet in the parking lot as I sneaked into my apartment. Their knowing grins, paranoia or not, told me as much. The leering expressions I'd imagined were real after all. Get this guy when he knows he's utterly embarrassed himself.

They'd timed their mocking hullabaloo perfectly. I bumped about restively once inside. Rest would not come—my frazzled nerves were totally shot. These guys must have heard me fumbling in my medicine cabinet for some toothpaste before they boomed through the bulkhead. I had just roosted my taut-wired body on the commode. Somehow I managed to refrain from jumping off the seat. After enduring their torment for long minutes, and to avoid being heard anymore, I tiptoed furtively to my bedroom. I did not bother to flush. "We know you're in there," one of them yelled.

The voices eventually stopped after one last "Oddball." What a relief.

To hell with those college boy neighbors of mine. Crap on them for putting the final touches in ruining an otherwise miserable day. Yet I had to persevere. A night's sleep if even for a few hours should cure my extreme tension. Hopefully by morning my nerves will be settled and I should be good as new. I would give Donald Boltz a call. "I am ready to return to The Great Western Casket Company," I would tell him. "I've had enough boozing and I'm going to quit for the last time. I'm going to work harder than ever." Having made this firm resolve I waited for sleep to come.

"I should be OK by now; it's been at least two days since I had a drink," I thought. The hours slipped by, but still no sleep. Tossing turning rest would not come. I could not focus on anything. Weird jumbled thoughts coursed through my mind from one crazy business to another. The thoughts of those leering faces and the college boys making a big ruckus would not go away. What a humiliation; I wouldn't be able to face those guys again. I'd lost control—extremely tense, a bundle of nerves, I jumped at the slightest noise.

"Nothing but the 'heebie-jeebies,'" as Jolly Jazz, an old chum from Saginaw, used to put it. "Jolly Jazz" as cronies called my chum vacationed in the Keweenaw every summer to do some fishing and drinking. Mostly he came to do some serious drinking. He always kept a pint stuffed under his belt. He'd earned his nickname due to the fact he at all times maintained an amiable mood, always cheerful and optimistic and never once cross. Knocking off a case of beer in one day, not an unusual occurrence for him, gained him renown as the beer drinking champion.

Musing on some of his experiences brought a modicum of comfort as I lay tossing about.

Even when he came down with the D.T.'s he remained jolly and cheerful. They kept him in a hospital in Saginaw for three whole days ridding his delirium tremens. In his case no demons and snakes appeared to him but only vocalists, horns blowing and pretty girls.

"What happened to Bing Crosby?" he asked the nurse as he began to recover. "And where's Benny Goodman and his band? Bring them back," he insisted of the solicitous medical staff. "And where's Betty Grable?"

Jolly Jazz probably owns the most remarkably pleasant case of the D.T.'s on record: three days spent in a world of fantasy experiencing hallucinations of the finest quality with few adverse physical symptoms. He continued to drink heartily afterward but finally quit altogether when his doctor informed him of a deteriorating liver. He heeded his doctor's advice and never touched a drop after that.

Three o'clock in the morning and still no sleep. Jolly Jazz had come and gone. A clear night and a half moon admitted a dim light through a thinly curtained window. Acclimated to the dimness I had no problem seeing objects in the room. "When am I going to get some sleep?" I wondered morosely. My heebie-jeebies were getting worse. Shadows began to grow in the room. Objects appeared to move about though imperceptibly. Overwhelmed, I struggled to be rational for clarity of mind. I stoically managed to convince myself that sleep deprivation solely caused my disquiet, my extreme restiveness. After all, in almost three days I'd had maybe three hours of sleep total.

Still sleepless, dawn finally broke. An early morning chill had set in and I raised my blanket higher. Startled, I perceived on its underside the mottled skin of a huge anaconda and not the fabric of a blanket. No blanket? I shook this off as being due to extreme fatigue and lay in bed for more long hours waiting for sleep to come. Even though the shadowy shapes disappeared with daylight I became even more highly strung and nervous. What should I do? I resigned myself to another day of restive fatigue but determined I would fight this out with my entire strength and will power. In my present muddled condition, however, I wisely decided against calling Donald Boltz.

It would be a glorious, sunny warm day but one thoroughly inconsonant with my depressed mood. Trying to sleep I tossed and turned unproductively. Well into the morning I got out of bed and stirred about restlessly in my untidy apartment. With no appetite whatsoever I couldn't even manage to eat half of a Slim Jim, and neither in the mood for coffee, which for long had addictively become my staff of life. The coffee pot stood half full on the stove, the coffee old and stale.

"What should I do?" I asked myself again. Although my frayed nerves had somewhat settled, but still too apprehensive to go outside for a walk or even call anyone I knew, I resigned myself to another day of misery. What could I tell them? Coming off a major drunk, the biggest and most unbridled binge I'd ever been on and now thoroughly unraveled, would I ask them to please feel sorry for me? Time will take care of everything I grimly surmised.

I tried reading. Trying to focus on *The Kalevala* proved to be futile—the verses failed to make any sense when I opened the book to favorite passages. The words jumped out from the pages mockingly—the mystic passages are challenging enough even for one clear of mind. I put the classic aside. I'd nothing better to do than go back to my bed and lie down some more. This proved to be an excellent decision.

Reclined on my bed I relaxed and began to experience a strange new euphoria. In harmony the early afternoon sun shining brightly through the windows heated my dank apartment. Basking in its pleasant warmth my apprehensions and my vague fears vanished completely. At peace, I rejoiced inwardly, convinced I would be exposed to a marvelous new reality. I did not have to wait.

"What is that on the windowsill? I've never seen such a strange sight there before."

There in plain view on the sill roosted Howland Owl with his bosom companion, Captain Churchill LaFemme, the turtle, right from the pages of Walt Kelly's *Pogo*, which I'd urged my friends to read. With them were Albert the Alligator, Beauregard Hound, and Pogo himself in his cane-striped vest along with a raft of other characters from the strip. Now here they were in real life doing wonderful things on my windowsill. Snavely the Snake appeared to be having a big discussion with the Flea, no doubt involving profundities too abstruse for the common jay on the street to apprehend. I could not hear what everyone said but from the way they were capering about they certainly appeared to be having a good time. As usual they must have been getting in some clever digs against each other. "How come I'd never witnessed this before?" I wondered as I chuckled delightedly at their antics. My eyes now opened to a brand-new world I speculated on the causes which had prevented me from ever beholding such a scene before. I must have been blind—I'd become elevated to a higher level of consciousness— bravo for the whiskey. Most certainly this could not be the D.T.'s or even the onset thereof; I'd always heard delirium tremens were an affliction of the night.

Intruders appeared on the scene, rudely interrupting my lively entertainment. Figures began to appear in a glass panel or shade above me. Directly above my bed a translucent glass shade in the shape of a shallow pyramid shielded the light bulb to soften its glare. This most ordinary panel possessed rank as perhaps being the finest fixture of anything to be found in my drab apartment I'd equipped with old and well-used secondhand furniture and appliances. As though in a photograph I saw it revealed a car with four shady-looking characters parked in an alley outside of the parking lot, and I heard a muttering of menacing threats directed at me. These yeggs were up to no good. Irritated, emboldened, I strode out of my apartment to investigate this disturbance.

Sure enough, I beheld the car and its shady passengers, all wearing sunglasses. One of them appeared to be a woman. These unwelcomed intruders were rather hazy in appearance such that I could not get a good read on their features. As I approached the car it scorched loudly down the alley but not before its occupants gave me sinister looks. Satisfied I'd scared them away I returned to the bedroom to see what Howland, Churchy, Albert and the rest of the characters were doing on the windowsill.

What rotten luck. Pogo and his friends had vanished. What had happened? My high spirits ebbed precipitously and I began to experience a strange eeriness. Those thugs still had to be watching me. Lying on my bed I tried to get some rest but once again rest would not come. Too afraid to look around in fear of more trouble my anxiety crept back to weirdly haunt me.

I apprehensively looked up at the glass panel. Sure enough, the car and its unsavory occupants returned. Again, I stepped outside only to see the car speeding off before I got too close, the same way as it did before. I got no rest at all. The car came back several more times and each time as I approached it, it sped off after its occupants gave me some more sinister looks. Oddly enough there were no complaints of the disturbance from any tenants in the other units. No other occupants came outside to investigate this nuisance. Were my neighbors sleeping?

Eventually the car stopped coming and going. Had I at last triumphed over these unwelcome intruders? I believed I had. As the afternoon transitioned into early evening my euphoria returned, this time in even greater measure than earlier. I'd become ebulliently confident. I heard my neighbors, the two college students, stirring about in their apartment. What could they be up to now? Strangely I had no apprehensions they might cause further mischief—I instead experienced an epiphany. A great awakening occurred; a tremendous sense of gratitude suffused my entire being. Had these young men been providentially sent to direct me onto a path leading toward salvation? Was their falsetto rendition of Waltz Across Texas naught but a mild reproach, their message to me to shape up and sail a straight course? I realized now I'd been entirely mistaken in believing they'd mocked my heartfelt sentiments when I sang to Erma Jamison. Their clarion call intended for me to be good resounded loud and clear in my mind, purged of doubt and confusion. Something had to be done. I would not be remiss in expressing my gratitude to them for the message they'd so opportunely and magnanimously sent me through the wall of my bathroom.

I took swift action.

Without bothering to wash and tidy my disheveled appearance I confidently stepped outside my apartment and knocked loudly on their door. One of the students opened the door and without waiting to be invited I stepped boldly inside. I noticed there were no knowing smiles or leering expressions as they withdrew a bit toward the opposite side of the room. They appeared exactly as aspiring college students thirsting for knowledge ought to look: earnest of expression, fiercely determined of mien and unintimidated. "We intend to succeed in life through higher education and hard work," their faces read. Neither spoke; each student undoubtedly anticipated what their distinguished visitor had to say.

"I received your message, young men," I addressed them sonorously, "and I'm here to thank you. Words fail to express the gratitude I owe you. Mr. Wasserzieher and Mr. Johnson, I'm truly indebted to you for what you've done trying to help me."

Still neither of them spoke; no doubt both men were overwhelmed by my profuse acknowledgement of what they'd done on my behalf. Suddenly a voice popped into my head.

"Something's going to happen pretty soon," the voice said.

I had a vision of beautiful women, all of them desirous of me. With such promise surely this would be my reward for bearing tidings of gratitude to my well-deserving neighbors. I became exhilarated as the voice began a rhythmic chant. Capering about like a faun in their living room, I began to dance. Muttering the words resounding in my head I felt as light as a feather as my feet tapped faultlessly on the floor in a lively double-time cadence to the chant. Prior to this I'd only danced to polkas. The young men I noticed granted me a wide berth:

"Here's the one, here's the pretty belle
she's the one for you, only you can tell
There's another yet, yet I'm not through
these thirty flirty girls are all for you
Century present, centuries past
timeless march, the die long cast
Fact or fiction e'er the same
passion swelling sparks the flame
Grim daughter of mystic Fenni land
Lord Väinä grasps with gnarled hand
Captive wench no longer free
no pity, no hope—eternity
We're together now, we're one, we're all
in great Valhalla there is no pall
Valkyries coursing over northern fell
take one, take two, take them all to hell"

The chanting stopped and I stopped dancing. A long countdown began: *thirty, twenty-nine, twenty-eight, ... three, two, one, zero.*

"And it's going to go on for a long, long time," the voice said.

I stood sanctified. The epiphany had most assuredly borne fruit. My young neighbors sat staring at me in amazement. "Who is this great man," they had to be thinking in awe. "He certainly possesses a superior wisdom."

"Again, I thank you for your message and for your kindness and patience," I told them before I strode victoriously back to my own apartment. I thought I perceived tears of joy welling in both their eyes as I walked out their door.

I felt invincible, manifestly superior. There in my living room rested a set of barbells I'd purchased shortly after I arrived in Chicago. It consisted of a three-hundred-pound set altogether including the plates and some dumbbells. Also included were assortments of straps, hand grips and a bench. A longtime believer in physical conditioning, I'd managed workouts at gyms in Southern California, St. Louis and while on board the USS *Holgate*. I did not need a gym working the conifers in Weaverville. During my stay at Mrs. Harding's I put the weights to good use in a spare space she provided me in her garage. The weights had sat idle since I relocated to skid row.

On the bench rack sat the barbell loaded to one hundred and sixty pounds waiting to be used. While at Mrs. Harding's I discovered the weight to be just about right for doing sets of bench presses, during which time I'd aptly conditioned my physique after many strenuous workouts. Occasionally I would do the entire stack of barbells totaling over two hundred pounds with relative ease. I'd done a lot more in the gyms.

I not only felt sanctified; I felt powerful. While being suffused with gratitude only short minutes ago I now realized an untapped strength. I'd never in my life felt this strong. Who needs food? Who needs coffee? Who needs sleep? Except for the few Slim Jims, a sandwich or two at the Foxhead Tavern and some pickled fish I'd had nothing to eat in over a week. And sleep? Flexing my muscles demanding to be put to test I felt more invigorated than if I'd awakened refreshed from ten hours of undisturbed slumber.

I removed the weight from its rack and set it on the floor. The barbell felt light, and in one clean, jerk-less steady motion, I picked the weight off the floor and raised it effortlessly above my head as easily as one would hoist an empty cardboard box. What happened to gravity? Neither a clean and jerk nor a snatch and not even close to a military press I'd accomplished the lift with a slow, smooth and steady motion. Rejoicing in my new found strength, I held the weight over my head steadily for a long minute. So now I possessed not only a greater awareness; I'd discovered physical power.

"*Zis little veight iss farry light, eet iss nut-tink*," I muttered in a strange tongue as I set it back on its rack.

"Two events of significant import realized within the past half hour—no mean accomplishments," I reveled inwardly. Everything had proceeded well beyond expectation with Mr. Wasserzieher and Mr. Johnson. My strength and confidence had returned in multiples.

Gloating over his accomplishments, Paul Maki remained blissfully unaware of the conversation taking place in his neighbors' apartment. The muted conversation coming through the wall of the toilet obliviously escaped his notice. His newly acquired super-sharp senses failed to respond to what his benefactors who'd so magnanimously sent him their message were saying.

"What do you make of that, Bill?" Artie Johnson asked his roommate Bill Wasserzieher. "Maybe we should have kept our mouths shut when we heard him creeping around."

"We had to get even with him," Bill Wasserzieher replied. "What the hell is wrong with him? Did you see him in when he crept by us in the parking lot yesterday afternoon? Criminy Pete, he looked like a scared rabbit then, just a matter of waiting once he got inside. I wonder what that goofball thought he was doing the other night singing to himself."

"He seemed like an OK guy when we talked to him at the Foxhead. Patricia seems to think he's alright too. She acts like a mother to him the same way she does to us, always making sure we're doing fine in school."

The students were perplexed. They had mid-term exams coming up at the Chicago Institute of Business Administration and Accounting less than a week away. As seniors both were running top grades in accounting and would soon be entering the job market. Slippages in grade point averages at this critical juncture would be unacceptable.

"That guy belongs in a nuthouse. I don't know about you, Artie, but I nearly shit my pants when he barged in."

"Same here. One thing I got to admit is that guy sure knows how to dance. Fred Astaire hasn't got anything on him. And it's a good thing we kept our mouths shut. Who knows what would have happened if we'd just told him to leave?"

"That stuff he carried on with and muttering about the Valkyries? He must have read a few books along the way. Maybe the Valhalla is part of his Finnish culture he told us about at the Foxhead."

"Perhaps the Finnish people claim Norse heritage as the Swedes and Norwegians do."

"Anyway, Artie, let's hope he stays quiet. We ought to talk to him later once he gets control of himself."

"That's a good idea. I'm going to try and hit the books for a while. I'm sure glad he didn't start any serious trouble. Maybe we should have called the police."

"Hard to feel sorry for a guy like him. Do you think he put us on with what he told us of being an aerospace engineer?"

"That's a tough one to swallow. Said something about working on shipping containers but I've never seen him going to work."

"Well let's just hope for the best. If he carries on anymore maybe we ought to call Patricia. This guy's crazy but seems harmless. But just in case we shouldn't take any more chances."

"Just one last thing, Bill. No more singing Waltz Across Texas. We've had our go at that one."

"Not so fast. You might be wrong there," Bill laughed. "At least he thanked us for sending him a message. He seemed grateful for that."

Nothing more happened until after sunset. After my weight lifting feat I spent a perfectly tranquil hour idly daydreaming on my future. Although I'd neither eaten anything nor slept throughout the day I felt at peace and did nothing but smugly contemplate on what a fortunate man I'd become. My jangled nerves were once more at rest. Tomorrow I would call my good friend Donald Boltz.

But even greater discoveries awaited. They were short in coming.

The sun had gone down. Now dark outdoors I began to have visions, not mere mental pictures in my mind, but grand scenes appeared on the opposite wall from where I sat on my couch. This time Pogo and his friends did not show. There on the wall appeared vivid images in hues of scarlet and gold. Wondrous beings, godlike men and women seated in repose about a festive board, imbibed from goblets filled with wine. Green bottles stood before them on the table, the labeling in a foreign language. No words were spoken. Aware of my presence they gestured for me to participate with them. The images were distinct, the men benevolent old sages and the women invested of beauteous perfection. The wine flowed copiously; goblets were raised and arms extended toward me. I sat riveted to the scene of royal splendor unfolding before my eyes. I wanted desperately to join in the festivities yet I could not move; I could not move whether due to an actual or perceived infirmity. It made no difference—the happening before my very eyes truly astounded me—I'd really achieved a higher state of consciousness. I regarded myself as blessed.

The silence broken, my august visitors began to speak. "Young man, please join us," golden resonant voices implored, "come and partake with us this blood of the vine." Uttered in a foreign tongue, their invitation spoken in a strange language I'd never heard before, I yet implicitly understood what they were saying. Inscriptions appeared on the wall. Were the inscriptions in a runic tongue? I could not tell—my guests did not resemble Norsemen. Then the divine figures left the wall and became insubstantial beings of vaporous substance, hazily floating about me in the room. Still unafraid, the events unfolding before me in my heightened state of consciousness seemed perfectly natural. The women hovered close, close enough I could see directly into their eyes.

I received a jolt, plummeted from a state of heightened blissful awareness and shocked into a terrifying new reality. The eyes were not the eyes of seductresses seeking amorous adventure but eyes empty and devoid of soul. In my immobile state, in dread, I tried to ward them off but I could not move, my body paralyzed from head to foot.

My godlike visitors vanished. The sages and the seductresses departed. The roseate hues, the vivid gold on the wall disappeared, only to be replaced with drab images in shades of ochre and brown. A sole wraithlike woman appeared on the wall. "Where had I seen this woman before?" It seemed long, long ago Knute Haugland and I stood in an impoverished apartment in a Hong Kong tenement on a hot steamy summer day, both of us befogged from having too much to drink. It came to me…the same haggard prostitute appeared on the wall, the one with whom we'd bickered over price and at the last minute declined her services when everything appeared to be settled.

Her eyes were cold and foreboding. "You would not take me then while you had the chance but you will take me now," she cackled in a metallic voice.

Materializing into a shadowy body she left the drab scene on the wall. She drew near, her visage deformed and her body skeletal, her entire being transmuted into a persona of death. What would happen to me now? Suffused with fear, I panicked.

I no longer remained immobile. I jumped from the couch and staggered weakly across the floor. My mind ravaged with fear, the woman and the scene on the wall vanished, leaving only the drabness of my surroundings. Everything had become eerily vague, bizarre. What should I do? A bit of rationality remained. My strength depleted, I desperately needed help but who should I call? I thought of Keiichi Genda but he did not have a telephone. I lacked courage to walk to his shabby room eight blocks away facing terrors of the night and in my weakened condition deemed it not wise to attempt—my wobbly knees barely held me up as I lurched about in the room. And who knows what other demons lurked in the shadowy darkness of skid row?

I could not call Mrs. Harding or Fritz Halder. I'd already caused these good people enough trouble stumbling in at late hours of the night and bawling loudly during a ghoulish nightmare, waking them from their sleep. And my neighbors—these college-boy frauds—what kind of a message had they sent me? I had not bargained for the woes besetting me now. Forget them. I had to do something quick for the car with its inhospitable occupants had returned. This time I did not need the glass panel to realize they were back in the alley.

"Did you think we would neglect you?" sibilant voices hissed in my ear. "You are being watched," the voices said as I heard the engine revving loudly. This time I did not go outside to flush them off. The engine revved even louder; the noise became unbearable.

The noise finally stopped as I fished Donald Boltz' phone number from my wallet. Before I called I wrote it down on a tablet in large numbers. I dialed the number and waited—the phone rang at least ten times without a response. Who to call next? There remained but one person. Didn't Abby say to always let her know where I could be found? Now I would ask her for her help even though she were miles away. I likewise wrote her number on the tablet before I placed a long-distance call with the operator. I counted the rings—all the way up to twelve without a response. With names and numbers I kept the tablet handy on a chair near the phone.

What happened to time? I had my last drink only three days ago but it seemed much longer than that. When had I taken the long walk through the respectable neighborhood? Only yesterday but it seemed as though it could have been a week ago. And just last evening I got my neighbors message in my bathroom. I'd lost my sense of time. And how about today's bizarre events? Everything that happened seemed so remote. When had I stopped to thank my neighbors for their message? Only four hours ago? It could have been a whole day. I began doubt reality—Pogo and his friends coming to visit and then the car full of hoodlums seemed just as real as going to the Foxhead for a few drinks. Everything had become surreal.

At a loss, totally weakened, my body drained of strength, I began to stiffen. This time my immobility became far more palpable than when the royal figures appeared on the wall, and I felt as though I were being stretched as taut as a high-strung wire. My knees failed to bend properly and my arms stiffened. I experienced even worse symptoms; I became convinced I'd begun to shrink. My genitals seemed to be retracting inside my body and only after I staggered to the bathroom to check my privates in the mirror I realized otherwise. Stiff as a board I could barely walk any longer. Desperate for relief, I rejected the limiting comfort of the couch for the hard surface of the floor where I could lie fully extended.

I mercifully blacked out and did not remember any more.

"He's at it again," Artie.

"What time is it?" Artie Johnson asked groggily. "I must have just fallen asleep."

"It's almost two in the morning. You better get up and take a listen. You won't be getting much sleep the way Maki is carrying on. Hell, just when I thought he'd settled down he's at it again."

"Well let's just hope he doesn't come here again. That guy sure is weird."

The students did not have to listen closely to the din coming from their neighbor's apartment. No other tenants apparently were disturbed as Maki had an end unit and the second-floor units directly above his and his neighbor's apartment were presently vacant. At first they thought a wrestling match was in progress, as sounds of tumbling about on the floor could be heard, but it soon became evident their neighbor was alone. Talking volubly to himself, his talk interspersed with periods of prolonged laughter, every so often they heard loud thumping sounds on the floor.

"At least I got some studying done," Artie said. "Another midnight-oil session or two and I should be in good shape for the midterms."

"Me too," his roommate replied, "I just hope he cuts out the nonsense pretty soon. His visit, barging in like he owned the place sure had me frazzled."

"I could use a beer. How about you, Bill?"

"That sounds great. Might as well have some refreshment after what we went through today. He should be tired out pretty soon."

"Hey Bill, get a load of what he's saying now. He's ranting something about Väinämöinen and the Sampo. What the hell is that all about?"

"That's some stuff from *The Kalevala.* That's an epic poem or saga of Finland, quite famous. Read the book in a literature class."

"First it's the Valkyries and listen to him now, he's carrying on about some Juokahainen singing Väinämöinen's trousers into wood. Bill, do you know anything about this 'singing' stuff? Singing trousers into wood? What's this all about?"

"In *The Kalevala* it means incantations are uttered to produce magic. Instead of using words just to win arguments they are 'sung' magically to produce desired physical changes. Look at it this way, Artie, you're getting a free education on Finland's greatest epic poem. Our friend Maki must be versed in the classics but what an eccentric fellow."

The sounds from their neighbor's apartment grew stranger. They heard no more passages from *The Kalevala.* Wasserzieher and Johnson continued to listen for more noises, and after a minute of silence a long plaintive bellow coming from Maki reverberated eerily through the wall. The bellowing started again following another minute of silence, this time even louder and more plaintive than before. The bellow had a forlorn otherworld quality as though a bull, bawling its way in desperation through the night, had lost its way on a desolate moor. Maki's loud bellowing continued followed by a series of convulsive kicks thumping loudly on the floor. Then their neighbor began to scream loudly for help. Bill Wasserzieher and Artie Johnson were no longer annoyed or amused. Both men had become dead serious.

"Something's very wrong with Maki," Wasserzieher said. "This guy needs help and he needs it right away. We'd better check on him."

"His door is locked and he's not responding," Artie Johnson said after they'd pounded on the door several times. The loud thumping noises in the apartment continued.

"Can't see anything," Bill said standing at a window. "He's got his shades drawn."

"Here, I've got Patricia's number," his roommate replied. "I'll give her a call right now. She's got keys to the apartments so we can take a look."

"That's probably best, Artie. We can drive him to a hospital right away if needs be. That'll probably be faster than calling an ambulance. Who knows how long it would take for them to get here?"

"I'll be there right away boys," Patricia said. "I've been worried about him. He did not look well when he stopped in at the Foxhead yesterday."

Most of my recollections of my stay in the hospital are vague. Some remain startling clear to this very day.

I came to and found myself strapped to a gurney. An intravenous tube had been tapped into my left arm. I noticed the medical staff standing about the gurney appeared apprehensive. There were three visitors as well.

A mass of large white caterpillars, naked except for some sparse bristly spines, populated the ceiling directly above my gurney. I watched them with an intense loathing as they crawled on the ceiling, their corrugated bodies inching slowly as they maneuvered for space. Orange globular heads probed tentatively as they wriggled about on the ceiling. I prayed none would fall; many of them were directly above my face.

"Get rid of those caterpillars, don't let them fall on me," I implored the staff.

"There's nothing to be afraid of. There's nothing on the ceiling," one of the aides assured.

Some of them fell only to vanish within inches of my face. I groaned hysterically.

The visitors came into focus. Patricia, Bill Wasserzieher and Artie Johnson stood off to the side talking to someone. He had to be the doctor in charge. In my muddled state I somehow managed to remember snatches of their conversation.

"He should be alright in three or four days at the most," I overhead the doctor telling Patricia and the students. "Right now we've got him sedated. The sedative should be kicking in soon. Tomorrow we'll begin intravenous feeding.

"He's got a severe case of delirium tremens, one of the worst I've seen," I heard the doctor say. "It's a good thing he's young and has a robust constitution. Otherwise I don't know."

"Criminy Pete, he knocked off a case of whiskey," Artie Johnson related to the doctor.

"At first he didn't recognize us. He thrashed about on the floor of his apartment, totally incoherent. He finally recognized me and we were able to get him in my car and drive him here to the emergency room," Patricia told the doctor.

I blacked out and heard no more.

I awoke the following morning or maybe the morning after that. I didn't know for sure. Served a breakfast, the coffee went great with scrambled eggs and toast, the first solid meal I'd had in how many days? Still in a fog, I became aware of a roommate, an emaciated and gaunt fortyish man.

"You've had a rough time of it boy. You kept the staff busy for two nights with those wild dreams of yours. Didn't make much sense to me—what's the pH of rotting wood? And something about an adventurer. Wasn't quite as bad last night."

So I'd been in the hospital for two nights. I noticed the IV in my arm. My roommate's arm had likewise been tapped.

"D.T.'s, the same as you," he said. "The second time for me but hopefully the last," he said resolutely.

The delirium tremens. The delirium tremens, the rock bottom physical experience a drunk can have except for death. By no means a Jolly Jazz experience for me despite the euphoric highs, just plain hell. The fears, the apprehensions were still there although my nervousness had ebbed. In my mind I tried to recollect events of the last few days. Nothing made any sense.

The white caterpillars on the ceiling; how about them? They had to be real. What were Patricia and my neighbors doing in the emergency room? Or had I simply imagined their presence? How did I get to the hospital in the first place? Then I hazily remembered dancing for my neighbors in their living room. Had this really happened, or maybe I just had another crazy dream. How could I have done such a thing—the dancing had to be a wild dream. But if it were real? How would I ever again be able to look Wasserzieher and Johnson in the face? Cripes, I practically lived with these guys—that flimsy bulkhead between our toilets did not contain secrets. Drowning in a flood of embarrassment I nearly wept.

Too troubled to fathom any more complications I dozed off into periods of fitful dreams. Aldo and Rolfe Ellefson came to deliver long sermons. When they were finally done preaching my dreams became even more bizarre.

Abby appeared as a young child. She'd come to sit on my face. Absent of her Gold Medal dress she instead wore the drapes which had adorned the big bay window in Grandma Maki's parlor. The drapes, hiked above her waist, billowed voluminously above my face as she prepared to perform her squat. She had an assistant. This time instead of Football, Marie Loonsfoot popped into the nightmare, not as a spritely Pocahontas, but as a malevolent imp as she pinned me firmly to the ground. They gleefully took turns.

Then Marie appeared as a child splashing water in my face at the Moose Lake Bible Camp and again as a young woman at the Beef-A-Roo. When she appeared at the rock battleship in Centennial Heights she seemed so alive. Then both Maries appeared together, as a grownup and as a child. I could not tell them apart before the crashing reality of her death struck forcefully home.

I awoke drenched in a cold sweat.

There were more meals followed by periods of restive sleep. At least I no longer had the shakes. Still heavily sedated I took my first shower in days. On what must have been the fourth day of my stay in the hospital I awoke to discover I had visitors. In my sleep I'd heard familiar voices in subdued conversation. I first saw Donald Boltz standing near the foot of my bed.

"I'm glad to see you, Paul. Jane and I and Great Western are pulling for you. You can come back with us any time you're ready," that good man said.

"But enough of that. There's someone else you might be interested in seeing," he added.

I turned on my side to see my second visitor. Abby stepped out from a spot behind me where she'd remained concealed from my view

Words were unnecessary. We looked at each other intently for a long minute. She took both my hands and clasped them in hers. She finally spoke.

"I love you, Paul," she said softly.

"I love you too, Abby."

The clasp unbroken, I fell into a deep untroubled sleep. I would see brighter days.

The End

EPILOGUE

We sat watching a rerun of a Lawrence Welk show during a Saturday evening. Lawrence Welk, old Pat Boone recordings, some hillbilly songs and even some occasional opera—that's our repertoire. We keep everything simple. We got married thirty years ago.

"How's that lemon pie coming? Are you sure you put enough lemon in it? You know I like it tart," I demanded.

"Coming right up, boss. It better be sour enough for you; I doubled up on the lemon juice so there you are," Abby replied.

"One other thing, Abby, how does it feel calling a man six months your junior 'Boss'?"

"Just be grateful I don't call you 'Junior' in public."

I'd goaded her many times with this "Boss" business and she didn't mind it at all—she rather looked ahead to my teasing: "Boss and Junior."

"Do you have your Sunday school lessons prepared," I asked.

For several years Abby has taught a Sunday school class at a small church we joined in Carnegie, Pennsylvania. The beliefs are basically the same as those espoused at the Emmaus Hall. As for me I grudgingly let myself be co-opted into performing janitorial chores. But the thought of John D. Rockefeller pushing a broom following his Sunday school session brightens my day as I exercise a mop.

We are still non-retired.

"Good to have you back," Donald Boltz said.

A week after my release from the hospital, and still somewhat apprehensive, I returned to work at The Great Western Casket Company.

I did not recovery easily from the delirium tremens. Following Abby's and Donald Boltz's visit to the hospital I slept for long peaceful hours after my release, the first such rest I'd experienced in many months. My stay in the hospital lasted for four days. I got a stern warning before I left.

"You're a lucky man, Maki," Dr. James Holt, my attending physician advised. "You're lucky to be alive. You've had a severe case of delirium tremens, one of the worst I've ever seen. And if it happens again your chances of surviving are remote."

Even after I returned to my apartment some of the hallucinations I'd experienced during the D.T.'s returned. The second day after I got home, I distinctively heard and saw the same car and its unsavory occupants outside in the alley, and sure enough, when I stepped outside to check on this the car roared off the same way as it did before. Again no one else appeared to take notice. But this did not concern me too much; Dr. Holt advised me upon my release that residual symptoms of D.T.'s could last up to a week or even longer. He told me not to be too concerned if hallucinations occurred even after I'd taken the medication he'd prescribed for short term relief. After a few more instances of this illusory disturbance the car vanished altogether. No more trailing chimerical disturbances occurred.

Abby remained to see me released from the hospital. She spent an afternoon at my apartment to make sure I'd be OK. It did not take long for us to make my messy apartment presentable.

We made no hasty commitments; a commitment to share a life together would come later. Our profession of love for each other at the hospital bedside tacitly sealed our bond. Seeing me settled, I made her but one unsolicited promise before she returned to Three Oaks: my drinking days were over. Not one more drop would pass my lips. We would be seeing each other shortly afterward.

All alone, I had plenty of time for introspection. I thought of Willard Janke. One never heard a cussword from him while he remained sober. His unholy imprecations in supplication of Satan heard by the three Heights boys when he floundered in Karhu's ditch were most likely an aberration. By no means did he intend advocacy for Satan; he lived his life just the opposite. When sober Willard was a soft-spoken, mild-mannered man and well-liked by his neighbors. Could I claim this distinction? Fortunate to be alive I would try.

I visited my neighbors, Bill Wasserzieher and Artie Johnson. This time I didn't thank them for sending me a message to be good, a message transmitted through the bulkhead in the toilet, or to dance for them in their living room, but to thank them for their timely intervention on my behalf. Dr. Holt had assured both men without their quick action I might have suffered permanent mental impairment if not death. Patricia joined the three of us for a dinner outing a few days later during which time she related how we'd met at the Foxhead Tavern years ago. She omitted some of the details. Wasserzieher and Johnson magnanimously refused my apologies for the disturbance I'd caused them. They offered to help me in any way they could, however small, during the shaky period of my recovery. They even apologized for mimicking my rendition of Waltz Across Texas. Both men went on to successful careers as accountants.

Abby and I sat on the old stone battleship where I'd asked her to marry me so many years ago. Several months had elapsed since I recovered from delirium tremens. There for a second time I asked her to marry me. Without hesitation she said yes. Again, Rita and Hicks were the first to hear of the good news. Rita wept tears of joy as she embraced Abby and me. The scholarly, pancake-faced Hicks seldom at a loss for words merely offered his congratulations in a few short words while looking steadily at me through his clear blue eyes. Two pancakes: one happily married for years and the other about to claim his bride.

We were married on a clear summer day. Pastor Henry Bylkas, now well advanced in years but still hale, officiated our ceremony at the Emmaus Hall. Our childhood friend and Abby's lifelong friend, Shirley Binoniemi, flew in from Oregon to attend Abby while my lifelong friends, Hicks and Aldo, stood by to give me support.

Many of our old friends and neighbors were present. Uncle George showed up from the strawberry farm with hampers of his choicest crop. More than a few of Abby's friends from Three Oaks had come. Rolfe and Muriel Ellefson, Wally and Karen Grimes and their son Henry drove in together from California. August and Elise Palosaari made it from the logging crew. George Carpenter and Abel Cooper among others from Brickhouse Logging unable to attend including Gary Brickhouse sent their best wishes along with gifts.

Three couples drove in from St. Louis. First to arrive were George and Dolly Haagejndas along with George Jr. and Annie followed shortly by Mr. and Mrs. Fred Mercer and Mr. and Mrs. Frank Ralls who'd come together. Adrian Parks and Juliette Campeau could not have found finer husbands.

Donald and Jane Boltz arrived from Chicago. A sobered Keiichi Genda arrived on a Greyhound bus. I'd extended invitations to Mrs. Harding and Fritz Halder but the onset of health problems for both kept these good elderly people from attending. They instead sent us some fine chinaware in addition to extending their best wishes and letting us know their problems were not too serious.

Abby "reintroduced" me to her friends from Three Oaks. This time names were mentioned. I somewhat awkwardly exchanged greetings with Abby's guests, as more than one jaundiced eye were cast warily at me, mainly from some who'd met the prospective groom under less than auspicious circumstances. Among them were the receptionist who'd given me directions to the Ames Hall, the hall monitor and the justice of the peace about to lock me up during my visit to Three Oaks. "I've got to see it before I believe it," the hall monitor told her companions before departing Three Oaks. Once in Heights, the hall monitor and the receptionist warmed to my presence after some initial reservations. I could hardly blame them for being a bit leery. "Take good care of Abby," the justice admonished me.

"See, I was right all along," Rita told Hicks. "I always knew Abby and Paul were meant for each other." Major Maurice St. Cloud slapped me on the back after congratulating me on making such a wise choice in taking Abby as my bride. The only blemish on the reception occurred, when once again, my dad ignominiously defeated me in a bout of arm wrestling in full view of everyone present.

"I wonder if he's got it in him," I heard Matt Roces say to Jake Bloomdahl, loud enough for me to hear, while feigning a suspect look.

"You've vindicated the claims of Lieutenant Pence. He always said you could do it," Wally Grimes told me. "Quite a journey from the Moose Lake Bible Camp," Rolfe Ellefson said. "OK you guys, tell me everything you can about Zoroaster and his ideas," Donald Boltz said. He addressed his remark to Rolfe and me. Frank Ralls and Fred Mercer, mingling easily with everyone, had brought along a surplus of excellent Nicaraguan cigars. They passed them around and we'd lit up at the stone battleship located just a short hundred yards from the Emmaus Hall.

"You've chosen well," Juliette said to me, "and I'm truly happy with Frank. I could not have met a gentler, more loving man."

All the Heights Bunch were present. Mabel Lahti, seldom seen without her army fatigues and now tastefully attired in a dress, regaled an assemblage of men with outrageously funny stories after she'd had a few brews near the battleship. The group included the justice of the peace. Seizing an opportunity she maneuvered alongside an unaware justice and planted a big slobbery kiss on his cheek. For once Mabel herself was surprised—the justice returned her kiss with fervor. This did not escape the notice of the hall monitor standing off to one side.

August Palosaari pulled me aside.

"Here's what Elise and I would like to do for you and Abby. Remember our family reunion in Finland I mentioned? It's scheduled for next summer in Pudasjarvi about the time of the St. John's Day festival and we're planning on a week's stay. We are inviting you to be our guests. I've already made the travel arrangements for us and we can stay with relatives when we get there. Think of it as our wedding present to you and Abby."

August continued to prosper well on Brickhouse's logging enterprise and his family life flourished. Nearing retirement, Gary Brickhouse offered him a buy-out opportunity once he'd fully retired. As I'd done, August had made a commitment to quit drinking altogether.

Keiichi Genda and I kept in close touch once I recovered from the D.T.'s, and shortly after I'd returned to The Great Western Casket Company, I began to attend Alcoholics Anonymous meetings with him. The scare I got from the D.T.'s convinced me to quit drinking altogether, minus factors often attributed to an alcohol addiction, such as extreme anxiety or depression. I'd experienced neither. Still I needed time to better understand how a harmful addiction can progress to ultimately destroy one's life.

After the D.T.'s I finally had to admit I'd become alcoholic and had become much more than just a big drunkard. For too long I'd ingenuously believed I'd been born with a proclivity to drink intemperately. "It's in the genes," I'd heard some claim. I'd naively believed an alcoholic had to keep a bottle handy every single day and night. I discovered otherwise. Many attendees at the meetings were a lot like me—binge drinkers following lengthy periods of productive sobriety. Some had experienced the delirium tremens more than once. For whatever reason, be it a cause to celebrate, carousing with buddies, spending hours and days alone in either euphoric or morbid introspection, or imbibing without restraint for no good reason at all, a habit becoming increasingly addictive ultimately led to a total bondage to alcohol. One failure after another interspersed with intervals of success invariably progressed to bleak outcomes. I'd come to accept the fact, after rejecting unavailing rationalizations for my habit, drinking for me had become a total addiction to alcohol. Finding most people at the AA meetings to be sincere and intelligent I continued to attend meetings in various places for a couple of years after I'd attended my first meeting. The people I met helped me a lot and I did my best to reciprocate what they'd done for me by standing at the side of a newcomer to the program. Sometimes this meant answering a phone call in the middle of the night from a "baby" struggling with alcohol.

"What do you make of 'coming to accept a higher power?' From the way the guys talked this sounds rather subjective. What's it supposed to mean?" I asked Keiichi after the first meeting I'd attended with him, where I'd heard a lot of talk of coming to believe in a "higher power."

"I try to keep it as simple as possible. For me the important thing is to first stay sober. Remember what I told that staff member at the Pacific Garden Mission? I'm OK with God but not with myself? I've got no problems with God. He's the ultimate higher power. I'm further convinced our meeting on skid row had to be more than fortuitous. I believe that's at least one occasion where my higher power intervened."

"What do you think of a higher power?" Keiichi asked me after a later meeting.

"For me it's a firm belief in the death and resurrection of Jesus Christ and his promise of eternal life for those repentant of their sins. In my hometown church I attended with my parents, the Emmaus Hall, we call it getting saved, or as some put it, converted. If it wasn't for Him I don't think I'd be here now."

I felt very awkward saying this to skeptical listeners or even friends. My knowledge and understanding of spiritual matters were and are still limited. My views are simplistic: I had no weighty theological issues to resolve or demons to be wrestled with as there had been for Rolfe Ellefson, or in Aldo's case, an assured certainty held steadfastly from early in life to his ultimate priesthood. I would continue to be awkward in professing my beliefs. Professing to be saved has never been easy for me as it appears to be for some. (Is there anyone that's good at this?) Most of the time I mumbled as one thus saved an eternity in heaven would be my reward. Even when drunk and out harming myself I believed this implicitly. Further, I avoided complications by not heeding too closely gratuitous prescriptions from others on what it means to be saved or by trying to read the mind of God.

"So you got saved. When did that happen?"

“I can’t remember any specific time or place when I got saved. I’ve always believed I’ve been saved right from the time as young kid in Sunday school. I can’t recall a specific event where I made a public declaration whereby I’d confessed my sins before God and man. But I’ve done this in private prayer and that’s worked OK for me.”

“Getting saved sounds like a tough sell but I’m going to look into it anyway.”

“I’ll help you in any way I can, Keiichi, but it sure can be a tough sell.

“Once when quite drunk I tried to impress my beliefs on some guy minding his own business at the bar. He’d just stopped in for a beer. I’d reached one of those maudlin, drunken moods of feeling sorry for everyone, ready to air my simplistic views on salvation to anyone within earshot. ‘Are you saved?’ I humbly asked this guy. ‘Cut out the crap and shove off,’ he told me. ‘Maybe we can talk when you sober up’.”

“You picked the wrong venue at the wrong time however you say it, buddy. Anyway, good luck, Paul. For me it’s been a teetotaler’s life as well and it’s going to stay this way,” Keiichi asserted.

“Abby is an angel. Take good care of her,” Keiichi told me after our wedding ceremony.

After a careful study of church history, Keiichi Genda later became a Roman Catholic. At my behest, he’d also met with Aldo on one occasion who patiently answered questions concerning the faith and provided him with guidance.

“I’m going back into aerospace engineering. I believe I’ve helped you as much as I can at Great Western,” I told Donald Boltz, a year after my return to work.

“You’ve got to do what’s best for you but you’ll always have a job here if you ever change your mind. We’re finally going into fiberglass products for a new line of burial vaults and maybe caskets. This should be happening soon. You’d be a good fit and we can always use your help,” Donald Boltz replied. “We can’t thank you enough for your contributions on the shipping containers. You’ve proven yourself here and I wish you the best in aerospace engineering.”

After several years of contractual engineering service or job shopping, Abby and I realized an aim of forming a small home-based consulting service. I would provide the engineering expertise while

Abby would take care of the business affairs. As such she handles the paperwork, makes travel arrangements to prospective clients, and with the help of a financial advisor, set up a pension plan. At peak work periods we find it necessary to hire additional help. We are seldom without work.

We located in in Carnegie, a suburb west of Pittsburgh, which allows convenient access to companies not only in Pittsburgh but in places such as the Washington DC area and with firms further west in Ohio and Indiana. In addition to aerospace I eventually transitioned into doing structural analysis on nuclear reactors. Pittsburgh being a major hub for the nuclear industry means a lot of work for us there.

Situating in Carnegie permitted Abby to accept a teaching position at a nearby community college. She started on a substitute basis and eventually accepted a fulltime position, notwithstanding other activities and the time committed to our consulting firm. She'd earned a reputation as an able teacher.

Our family reunion visit to Finland with August and Elise Palosaari remains among our most memorable events occurring after our marriage. Their children, Helen and Carl, now both in their teens accompanied us on the trip. Twenty other relatives from the states joined us in Finland where we were greeted by over two hundred Finnish cousins who traced roots going back to our great-great grandfather Hannu Palosaari. Many including ourselves met in Finland for the very first time to celebrate a common heritage.

Once settled, we were introduced to some old country humor in which August and I played a major role:

"Pull up those pants," Abby commanded me. August and I had both "dropped trou" to half mast, our pants bungeed and held in place just above our knees by our bow-legged stances.

Elise stood in rigid silence, her mouth agape. "Shame on you, August," she finally said, her face reddening. Abby appeared similarly mortified.

"Where do we undress," Elise had asked our Finnish hosts as we were about to take a sauna. She'd blithely assumed couples would take their steam separately and not communally.

"Right here, right here on this front porch," Mikko Salminen, one of our Finnish cousins replied with a straight face. His wife Selma standing to the rear tried her best to suppress laughter at this farce.

We'd heard stories of old country Finns bathing communally, everyone of course completely nude. August and I had set this up with Mikko to see what liberal SISU our wives had. Judging from their reactions Abby and Elise were found to be totally lacking of SISU. With the help from our hosts, we'd successfully spoofed our wives.

Apart from numerous festivities and sightseeing visits to historical sites and museums, the trip to Pudasjarvi would be a telling experience for the American relatives. Long accustomed to living in peace, long absent of war on our own soil, we would discover what it meant to live in a country ravaged by war—brutal war experienced by many of our relatives still alive in Finland.

Solemnities were observed. Retired Colonel Timo Hukkari impressed upon his American cousins the determination and the true SISU with which the Finns fought invading Russians in the one hundred and five-day Winter War in late 1939 and early 1940, and during the Continuation War from 1941 until 1944. They fought with extreme valor, but up against overwhelming forces in terms of numbers and firepower, Finland finally surrendered and signed a peace treaty with its huge neighbor.

During a visit to Raatteen Portti on Finland's eastern border with Russia we were shown trenches where the doughty Finns had dug in to fortify themselves against large infantry and armored Russian divisions attempting to advance into Finnish territory. Attacking in long columns with their flanks exposed, Russians sustained a ruinous cost. At the *Talvisodan Monumentti* or the Winter War Monument some twenty-three thousand large stones placed on a parcel of land commemorate soldiers from both sides who'd fallen in combat near Raatteen Portti. The vast majority of the stones are for Russian soldiers. A thought of young Finn blustering into thin air at the Houghton County Memorial Airport came to mind. Strung across the tops of four inward facing arches in the center of the field are one hundred and five bells, one for each day of the Winter War, which toll continuously in the breeze for visitors as a solemn reminder of the conflict.

A final grim reminder of both the Winter and Continuation Wars came when Hukkari accompanied us on a visit to a cemetery in Pudasjarvi where several of our relatives killed in these conflicts are buried.

Here we are thirty years later, both of us still in the prime of middle-age life. Our life together is harmonious with but a few minor squabbles every now and then. No admonitions to Abby commanded unto obedience are necessary as they might have been had we lived in early millennial Finland—we thrive on a level playing field with the balance tipped slightly in her favor. It is not necessary to warm shoulders or to soften buttocks as demanded by strict husbands during the days of the ancient Fenni.

Thoughts of enduring friendships crossed my mind as we sat enjoying Abby's peerless lemon pie. She'd added the right amount of lemon, the pie brisk, slightly tart and mouth-wateringly delicious. "Where would I be without the friendships I formed along the way," I ruminated. Even small kindnesses such as those shown me many years ago by Eugene Seppala at the Hubbell Hall beer bash will never be forgotten.

Friendships formed early in life and new friendships made throughout my career continue to prosper. Hicks made major breakthroughs in his biomedical research at Michigan Tech and gained wide recognition for his contributions in the field. After raising a brood of eleven healthy children Rita continued her practice as a physical therapist. Her children went on to promising careers, some of her sons like their father flourishing in engineering or science. There would be no children for Abby and me.

Father Aldo Vella, his magnificent dark mane now turned gray, refused early retirement. Loved by his parishioners, the man continued to support those in need of help regardless of their circumstances. He visited with us in Carnegie as his schedule permitted.

For a number of years we've been the owners of a cottage on Lac La Belle. Both Abby's and my own work schedules permitted lengthy stays there during long twilight summer months, and if I couldn't make it to the camp at times, Abby accommodated our guests during her breaks from teaching. The Ellefsons and the Grimeses drove in together from California on two occasions. Frank and Juliette Ralls along with Fred and Adrian Mercer came to spend a week. We had ample room to spare; both their marriages were blessed with children. George Haagejndas and his family visited with us twice to join in taking hot saunas and fishing trips. George Jr. to his immense excitement caught a near record-size fourteen-inch yellow perch along the weed beds. A record for our cottage.

Early on we both decided our cottage should have a name and not an ordinary name. I suggested "The Chicago Drape Roadhouse."

"The Chicago Drape Roadhouse? You've got to be kidding," Abby said. "You must have a fetish for garments fitting loosely below the waist."

"If I've got a fetish then you've got to share some of the blame for it. How can I ever forget that Gold Medal dress?"

I'd expatiated on the Gold Medal dress she'd worn during the face sittings and on Hick's low-bagging trousers. I did not mention the loose fit I sported during my stay on skid row nor did I mention the nightmare I had of Grandma Maki's drapes descending on my stricken features when coming out of the D.T.'s.

"And the weird dream you had coming home from bible camp. Something about the drapes in grandma's parlor. How could I ever forget that?" she added. She had to be reading my mind.

With some misgivings Abby came to accept "The Chicago Drape Roadhouse" as a suitable name for our cottage. For obvious reasons, we did not post a sign at the entrance. Our Roadhouse is located on a two-hundred-foot stretch of waterfront not far from the weed bed where Abby spotted the frog sitting on the lily pad when we were trolling Lac La Belle for northern pike years ago. That's on the weedy south side of the lake. In the years to come, The Chicago Drape Roadhouse would become synonymous with lasting friendships. The Palosaari's and the Boltz's were among our most recent visitors.

I continued lengthy correspondence with my friends on the Brickhouse logging crew. Abel Cooper, as hale as ever, finally retired in his early seventies. George Carpenter continued in his logging career and received even wider recognition as a musical talent on the West Coast along with his partner. "Dirty George" and "Little Ukiah" flourished in the roadhouses. Having scaled down his activities with Brickhouse Logging Gary Brickhouse turned over major responsibilities to August Palosaari who ably continued to run a prospering enterprise. Gary Brickhouse's generous buyout offer to August remained in effect. Should he opt to accept the offer, the buyout would occur after Brickhouse's full retirement.

In less than three years Keiichi Genda, still a recovering alcoholic like myself, got his family back together and resumed his practice of dentistry in Beloit. Recovering alcoholic did I say? An alcoholic, it is claimed in AA, is always in a recovering stage, whether or not he's had a drink, even if he's been dry for ten years. I've no problem with that. The Genda's also spent time with us at the Chicago Drape Roadhouse.

Erma Jamison did not remain single as she'd told me she would. She'd become Erma Grimm. The Ellefsons wrote to say Erma, whom they'd long befriended, married her nosy strait-laced supervisor by the name of Charles Grimm after a prolonged friendship of ten years. Muriel noted they were getting along well. "Her husband still has a hard time believing you've turned things around," she wrote. I replied to her letter, adding that as a prospering and happily married man, I wished both Erma and her husband well. No more singing about caca in the toilet.

Many of our elderly friends are gone. Of the old-timers only brittle Old Lady Mattila nearing the century mark is still going strong, as feisty and clear-minded as ever. The old stalwarts of Centennial Heights, Niilo Kaipio and Jacob Binoniemi, both passed away in their nineties. Pastor Henry and Sylvia Bylkas have both passed on as have Gladys and Jake Bloomdahl. Close to my heart and home my dear hockey-playing mom passed on a few short years ago after a short but vigorous fight against cancer. She lived long enough to see her son find happiness with one he truly loved. For my stalwart and still hale dad, Oscar, his beloved Elsa would remain his only love.

Maybe the junket Boats Finerty and I took to skid row wasn't such a bad venture after all, maybe even fated, at least for me. Where would I be hadn't I met Patricia at the Foxhead Tavern while on our liberty from Great Lakes? Where would I be hadn't it been for her timely intervention on my behalf years later when I had the D.T.'s? Then of course there were my neighbors, Artie Johnson and Bill Wasserzieher....

Cause and effect? It's got to be more than that, more than mere happenstance or even making choices, whether good or bad. I'm convinced a divine providence remained at my side throughout the many dangerous situations in which I'd put myself while drunk. But isn't this nothing more than a fanciful notion embellished by a once hopeless alcoholic? Perhaps Paul Maki had too many whiskies over the course of his drunken excesses, causing permanent impairment to his mental faculties, which at the end of the day became too severe to repair. Or at the very least, maybe he's in his dotage. I nevertheless stand by a belief in an omnipotent God who guided me safely through the danger. And my belief in His merciful Son, Jesus Christ, has been reinforced.

How about Patricia? She's now comfortably retired from the bar business and she still lives in Chicago. We exchange letters from time to time and Abby and I once paid her a visit. During our visit to the city we made certain to see Mrs. Harding and Fritz Halder. Unable to attend our wedding, they were glad to finally meet Abby. Both these good people were enjoying reasonably good health in retirement. Prince, at thirteen years of age and still lively, joyfully retrieved sticks I tossed him after Fritz served us a backyard barbeque.

On a grim note, Luke Garber died in prison after serving more than twenty years of time.

For long I remained conflicted over the cause of Marie's untimely death. I would always remember her in a bright light.

"That lemon pie hit the spot. I realize my lips are like leather, but once again I beg you, I implore you my love, may I please impart my unworthy lips upon thy ruby own."

"What do I get for this?" Abby replied. She drew closer to me on the sofa where we'd sat to examine a pictorial book on the Civil War. During the last ten years she'd read at least eighty books on the Civil War and the leading figures involved in the conflict, especially Abraham Lincoln. She'd even been invited to give lectures at meetings of various civic groups such as the Kiwanis and the Rotarians.

"The man of romance has great things in store for you. It'll be a surprise."

"It better be good," she replied without hesitation.

Abby, my dear Abby, my greatest love and my dearest friend of all. My childhood friend and now my wife. I could not imagine a life without her.

As we lazed on the sofa thoughts came to mind I'd entertained when deciding my drunken trip to Three Oaks College. Why hadn't Abby married? Why hadn't some well-respected administrator proposed to this most attractive woman? With spinsterhood looming she certainly must have entertained thoughts of acquiring a husband. Why hadn't I thought of this since then? Thirty years is a long time to let a good poke lie fallow. I couldn't resist teasing her about this.

"You mean to tell me you couldn't find anyone after all those years at Three Oaks."

"No more lemon pie for you," she said, giving me a gentle nudge in the ribs. "There were no serious relationships from the time we first parted and the thought of a spinster life never once crossed my mind. If it wasn't going to be you, I would do it alone. Now don't get a big head and go thinking you're some big hero. What you are is a sixty-eight-year-old man and my loving husband."

A big hero? Who's a hero? Perhaps Abby, and how about the undefeated Rita? Heroines to be exact.

"But come to think of it take a look at Aldo and Hicks," I said. "They're more than ordinary guys the way they handled problems and achieved what they set out to do in life. Maybe they're not heroes but I find it quite easy to look up to them. I doubt if I'll ever be a hero. If I were, you'd be constantly swooning and I don't think I could handle that."

"You're right about Aldo and Hicks and you truly are my hero. You big hero, you can even count on more swooning. What do you think I've been doing for the past thirty years?"

Rita was right. We were meant for each other. In times of difficulty Abby always stood by for me when I needed her most. After the many reversals, after the numerous disappointments and misfortunes I'd caused, suffice it to say all's well that ends well.

"At the Emmaus Hall I took a wife, she's the darling of my life. Abby, dear Abby, is her name, of Palosaari, Maki, Tulppo fame," I chatted to her merrily.

Abby moved closer, nestling her head on my shoulder just like the way she did driving back from the Moose Lake Bible Camp.

We clasped hands warmly.